Marriage For One

Marriage For One

Ella Maise

**SIMON &
SCHUSTER**

London · New York · Sydney · Toronto · New Delhi

First published by Ella Maise 2019

This paperback edition published by Simon and Schuster 2022

Copyright © Ella Maise, 2019

The right of Ella Maise to be identified as author of
this work has been asserted in accordance with the
Copyright, Designs and Patents Act, 1988.

5 7 9 10 8 6

Simon & Schuster UK Ltd
1st Floor
222 Gray's Inn Road
London WC1X 8HB

Simon & Schuster Australia, Sydney
Simon & Schuster India, New Delhi

www.simonandschuster.co.uk
www.simonandschuster.com.au
www.simonandschuster.co.in

A CIP catalogue record for this book
is available from the British Library

Paperback ISBN: 978-1-3985-2162-9
eBook ISBN: 978-1-3985-2163-6

Printed and bound in Great Britain by
CPI Group (UK) Ltd, Croydon, CR0 4YY

For anyone who has ever felt like they didn't belong.

CHAPTER ONE

ROSE

Note to my past self: Do NOT, I repeat, do not say yes to marrying the handsome stranger you happen to know absolutely nothing about.

"Do you, Rose Coleson, solemnly declare to take..."

No. Nope.

"Jack Hawthorne to be your lawfully wedded husband?"

Hmmm. Let me think about that. I don't. Nope.

"Do you promise to love, honor, cherish, and keep him for as long as you both shall live?"

Keep him?

Wide-eyed and a little shaky, I stared straight ahead as the officiant said the words I was dreading. Was I really doing this? When the silence in the mostly empty and sort of depressing room stretched on and it was my turn to speak up, I was on the verge of hyperventilating. I tried my best to swallow the lump in my throat so I could speak, but I was afraid the words that desperately wanted to break free weren't *Yes, I do.*

I wasn't getting married in a lush green garden while the few friends I had cheered us on as I had always imagined I would. I wasn't laughing or crying from extreme happiness as every bride did at one point during the ceremony. I had no beautiful wedding bouquet, only one single pink rose which Jack Hawthorne had thrust into my hands without a word right after we met in front of city hall. I wasn't even wearing a white dress, let alone my dream wedding gown. Jack Hawthorne was wearing a tailored black suit that was quite possibly worth a year of my rent, if not more. It wasn't a tux, but it was just as good. Next to him, I looked pretty cheap. Instead of a beautiful wedding dress, I had on a simple blue dress—it was the only thing I owned that was expensive and appropriate enough for the occasion, yet somehow it was still... cheap—and I was standing next to the wrong man, one who did nothing but frown and glower.

Also, there was the handholding, his grip surprisingly tight around mine, especially compared to my loose hold. Such a simple act, but holding a stranger's hand while you're getting married? Not fun. Hell, forget about handholding—I was about to be the wife of a man I knew nothing more about than what a quick Google search had provided.

Yet I had willingly and knowingly agreed to this, hadn't I?

"Miss Coleson?"

As my breaths started to come faster and panic began to take hold of me, I tried to pull my hand out of Jack Hawthorne's grip only to feel his fingers tighten around mine even more. I didn't know what I was thinking or what *he* thought I was going to do, but I couldn't lie and say running away hadn't crossed my mind.

His tight hold was a small warning, and then it was gone. My gaze jumped to his face, but he was staring straight ahead, eyes on the officiant, his sharp features set in stone. Cold. So cold. I thought I saw a muscle in his jaw ticking, but then I blinked, and it was gone.

The man showed his emotions about as much as a cement block did, so I tried to do what he was doing: focus on the present.

"Miss Coleson?"

Clearing my throat, I did my best to put steel into my voice so I wouldn't cry. *Not here. Not now.* Not every marriage is about love. What had love offered me anyway other than heartbreak and late-night emotional eating?

My heart was beating loud and fast in my chest. "I do," I finally replied with a smile I was sure made me look deranged.

I don't. I think I really, really don't.

As the smiling man repeated the same words for my non-smiling almost husband, I tuned everything and everyone out up until it was time for the rings.

God, to think I had been planning my wedding to a different guy only a few months earlier, and more than that, to think I'd thought weddings were always romantic... This wedding felt more like I was about to skydive from 13,000 feet, something I would much rather die than try, and yet there I was. Not only was I *not* in a garden surrounded by greenery and flowers, the only piece of furniture in the room was a couch that was a rather ugly shade of orange, and for some reason, that single piece of furniture and the color of it annoyed and offended me the most. Go figure.

"Please face each other," the officiant said, and I followed his instructions like a robot. Feeling numb, I let Jack reach for my other hand, and when his fingers gave mine a tiny squeeze, this time I met his questioning eyes. I swallowed, tried to ignore the little jump my heart gave and offered him a small smile. He was truly striking in a cold, calculating sort of way. I'd be lying if I said my heart hadn't given a small jump the first time I'd laid eyes on him. Completely involuntarily. He had the strong-and-silent thing down pat. His equally striking blue eyes dipped to my lips and then came back to my eyes. When I felt him slowly push a ring onto my finger, I looked down and saw a beautiful wedding band with a half-circle of round diamonds staring back at me.

Surprised, I looked up to meet his eyes, but his attention was on my finger as he gently rolled the ring back and forth with his thumb and index finger. The sensation was as alien as it could get.

"It's okay," I whispered when he didn't stop playing with it. "It's a little big, but it's okay."

He let go of my hand and the ring then looked at me. "I'll take care of it."

"There is no need to do that. This is fine."

I didn't know if Jack Hawthorne ever smiled. So far—the three whole times I'd seen him—I hadn't been a witness to it, at least not a genuine smile, but I would have assumed if he was marrying someone he was in love with instead of me, there would at least be a small playful grin on his lips. He didn't look like the grinning type, but surely there would be a hint of it. Unfortunately, neither one of us was the picture of a happy newlywed couple.

I reached for his hand to put on *his* wedding band, but call it nerves, clumsiness, or a sign, if you will—before I could even touch his hand, the cheap, thin ring slipped from my shaky fingers and I watched it fly away from me in slow motion. After the surprisingly loud clinking sound it made when it hit the floor, I ran after it, apologizing to no one in particular, and had to drop to my knees so I could save it before it rolled under the ugly orange couch. Although the light blue dress I had chosen to wear was by no means short, I still had to put one of my hands on my butt to cover myself so I wouldn't flash everyone as I caught the damn thing before I had to crawl on my knees.

"I got it! I got it!" I yelled a little too enthusiastically over my shoulder, holding the ring up as if I had won a trophy. When I saw the unimpressed expressions around me, I felt my cheeks turn a bright shade of red. I dropped my arm, closed my eyes, and released a very long sigh. When I turned around on my knees, I noticed that my ringless, almost husband had made it to my side, already offering his hand to pull me up. After I got back on my feet with his help, I dusted off my dress. Looking up to his face, I belatedly noticed how stiffly he was holding himself—jaw clenched, the muscle tick definitely back.

Had I done something wrong?

"I'm sorry," I whispered, thoroughly embarrassed, and got a curt nod in response.

The officiant cleared his throat and gave us a small smile. "Shall we continue?"

Before he could drag me back, I discreetly leaned toward my soon-to-be-maybe husband and whispered, "Look, I'm not sure about...you look..." I paused and released another long breath before gathering enough courage to look straight into his eyes. "We don't have to do this if you've changed your mind. Are you sure? And I mean really, really sure you want to go through with this?"

His eyes searched mine as we ignored the other people in the room, and my heart rate picked up as I waited for his answer. As much as I was reluctant to do this, if he'd changed his mind, I'd be screwed six ways to Sunday and we both knew that.

"Let's get this over with," he said eventually.

That was all I got.

Lovely.

What an encouraging start to a new marriage—a fake one, yes, but still.

We walked back to stand in front of the officiant and I quickly and successfully managed to push the ring onto his finger on my second try. It fit him perfectly. Next to the beauty he had gotten me, the flat wedding band I had picked up for him just the day before looked just as cheap as my dress did, but it was the only thing I could afford. It didn't look like he cared anyway. I watched with curious eyes as he stared down at the ring and then made a fist of the hand I'd just put the ring on, his knuckles whitening with the force of it before he took my hand again.

My attention shifted as I caught the end of the officiant's words: "...I now pronounce you husband and wife. You may kiss your bride."

That was it? I was married? Just like that?

I looked at my now official husband and didn't know how to react for a second. His eyes caught mine. What was a simple kiss after saying I do to a stranger, right? Thinking he was waiting to see what my move would be and wanting to get it over with so we could get the hell out of there, I was the one who took the first step. Our hands still clasped together, I avoided his eyes, rose up on my toes, and brushed a small kiss on his cheek. Just as I let go of him and was about to back up, his now free hand grabbed my wrist in a gentle hold and our eyes met.

For the sake of the few people around us, I forced another smile on my face and watched him slowly lean down to press a kiss to the edge of my mouth.

My heartbeat quickened because I thought he had lingered for a second too long, and that was a little too close and too long for comfort, but considering we were playing a part, I supposed an innocent kiss didn't mean too much. It didn't for me, and I was sure it definitely didn't for him.

"Congratulations. I wish you two a happy life together." The officiant's voice broke us apart, and I reached for the man's waiting hand.

As our only witness, who I knew for a fact was Jack Hawthorne's driver, shuffled around to congratulate the man who was now my husband, I closed my eyes and willed my heart to take it easy and look on the bright side of things. This whole charade benefitted me more than it did Jack Hawthorne. It didn't matter that I had been engaged to another man, Joshua, just weeks ago. This particular marriage to this particular man had nothing to do with love.

"Are you ready to leave?" my very real and official yet still fake husband asked, and I opened my eyes.

I wasn't. Suddenly I was feeling all hot and cold, which wasn't a good sign, but I met his gaze and nodded. "Yes."

Up until we exited the building, the driver following us from a safe distance, we didn't utter a single word to each other. Then the driver disappeared to get the car and we just stood there, watching the people around us in an awkward silence as if neither one of us knew how we'd ended up out on the street exactly. After a few moments, we both started to speak at the same time.

"We should—"

"I think—"

"We should get back," he said firmly. "I need to be at the airport in an hour if I'm gonna make my flight."

"Okay. I don't want to hold you up. I'm gonna need to change first before I get back to the coffee shop, and I can easily take the subway back to my apartment. I don't want you to get stuck in traffic just because I—"

"It's fine," he answered distractedly. His eyes were not on me but on the black car that had just pulled up to the curb. "Please," he murmured, and I felt his palm briefly touch the small of my back before it was gone then he moved to open the door to the car.

Shoot!

I didn't know him enough to argue about how I'd get home, not to mention arguing was the last thing I had in me to do. In the time it had taken us to walk outside, I had started to feel sick to my stomach with each step. As he stared at me expectantly, I tried not to drag my feet too much as I took his unspoken offer and got in the car.

When he got in after me and closed the door, I shut my eyes with the finality of everything.

Fuck me, I'm married. Didn't matter how many times I repeated it to myself, I still couldn't believe I'd agreed to this.

"Everything okay?"

The hard, rough tone of his voice broke me out of my jumbled thoughts, and I turned my head to look at him with a small smile. "Of course. I should really say thank yo—"

"You don't need to." He gave me a curt nod before I could even finish then focused on his driver. "Raymond, change of plans. We need to drop by the apartment first, and then we will head to the airport."

"Yes, sir."

I swallowed and fisted my hands on my lap. *Now what?* I thought. *Now do we talk? Do we not talk at all? How does this work?* Surprisingly, he was the first one to break the bleak silence.

"I might be out of reach for a few hours each day, depending on my meetings, but I'll get back to you as soon as I can." Was he talking to his driver or me? I couldn't tell. "If something comes up with Bryan or even *Jodi*, if they give you any trouble about our marriage, leave me a message. Don't talk to either one of them until you hear back from me." Me then. He was staring straight ahead, but he was talking to me because Jodi and Bryan were my cousins. "If everything goes as planned, I'll be back in a week at most." He paused. "If you wish...you can accompany me."

Nope.

"Oh, thank you, but I can't. I need to work on the coffee shop, and as much—"

"You're right," he interrupted before I could finish. "I'd rather go myself as well."

Well, then...

I nodded and looked out the window. I wasn't sure if I'd managed to hide my relief well enough. Him being away for a week meant seven more days I could take to come to terms with my decision. I'd take every extra minute I could get.

"Where are you going again?" I asked, realizing I had no idea.

"London."

"Oh, I've always wanted to visit London—anywhere in Europe, really. You're lucky that you get to travel. I don't know if lawyers do a lot of traveling, of course, but..."

I paused and waited for him to say something, if nothing else just to help me make pointless conversation, but I had a feeling it wasn't happening. I wasn't wrong.

"Do you have a client in London?" I tried again, but I knew it was hopeless.

Jack lifted his arm and checked his watch while shaking his head as an answer to my question.

"Raymond, take the next turn. Get us out of here."

When there was nothing but silence in the back of the car, I closed my eyes and pressed my temple against the cold glass of the window.

Ever since I'd said okay to this crazy plan, I had done my best not to think about it too hard. Now it was too late to do any kind of thinking. We hadn't even had time to discuss where I would live. With him? Without him? Would we even get along if we lived together? *Joshua*... Would he hear that I had gotten married? And so soon after our breakup, too. Suddenly, every single question I had and ones I hadn't even known I had all rushed into my mind all at once.

Ten minutes had passed where no one in the car had uttered a single word. For some reason, that was causing me to panic more than anything. What had I gotten myself into, really? If I couldn't even manage to have a simple conversation with the guy, what the hell were we gonna do for the next twelve or twenty-four months? Stare at each other? Feeling sick, I pressed my palm against my stomach as if I could hold it all in—all the emotions, disappointments, forgotten dreams—but it was too late for that. I felt the first tear slide down my cheek, and even though I quickly tried to brush it away with the back of my hand because there was no reason for me to cry, I couldn't stop all the others that followed. In just a few minutes, I was full-on silently crying, the tears a quiet stream I didn't know how to stop.

Very aware that my mascara had probably made a mess of my face, I cried without making even a peep until the car came to a stop. When I opened my eyes and realized we were heading toward the wrong side of Central Park, I forgot about my tears and looked at Jack.

"I think..." I started, but the words died in my throat when I saw the expression on his face.

Oh shit! If I thought he had been angry when I dropped the ring, I was sorely mistaken. His brows snapped together as his eyes roamed my face and the tension in the car tripled.

I tried my best to wipe the evidence of my tears away without looking into a mirror. "This is the wrong side—"

"Take her to the apartment, please. I'll get to the airport on my own," Jack said to the driver. Then his expression closed up, his face blanking as he addressed me. "This was a mistake. We shouldn't have done this."

I was still staring at him in shock when he got out of the car, leaving his bride—AKA me—behind.

This was a mistake.

Words any girl who had gotten married only thirty minutes earlier would want to hear, right? No? Yeah, I didn't think so either.

After all, I was Rose, and he was Jack. We were doomed from the very beginning with those names. You know... the *Titanic* and all that.

The number of times Jack Hawthorne smiled: zero.

CHAPTER TWO

JACK

After spending days trying to ignore what I had done, I was finally back in New York and still nowhere near ready to face the clusterfuck I had created. Exiting the car the moment Raymond pulled up in front of my building, I walked past the doorman and stepped into the elevator. As I was checking my voicemails, I tried not to think about who and exactly what kind of situation would be waiting for me in my apartment.

Would I have to carry on a conversation with her? Answer more questions?

I certainly hoped not because talking to her was the last thing I wanted to do. Not if I was planning on sticking with my plan of keeping her at arm's length.

The moment I stepped through the threshold, I knew she wasn't there. Feeling both relieved and annoyed at the same time —relieved because I was alone just as I liked, annoyed because she wasn't where she was supposed to be—I dumped my luggage in my bedroom and slowly walked through the apartment, just to make sure. Turning lights on and off, I checked every room, inspecting everything, looking for anything that was out of place, looking to see if *someone* had even been there after I left. When I reached the last room—the room she was supposed to be staying in—and found it just as it had been when I'd left for London, I rubbed my neck, hoping it would help with the headache I could feel coming on. Walking through the room, I stepped out onto the terrace to stare down at the busy city, wondering what I was supposed to do next.

What have I done?

A FEW WEEKS earlier

As soon as I got the call from the lobby, I walked out of my office to wait for her in front of the elevators. My main goal was to intercept her before she could get to the meeting room where her remaining family members would join her in another thirty minutes. A few minutes later, the elevator doors slid open with a ping and Rose Coleson stepped out. Her brown hair was down in waves, her bangs long enough to almost cover her eyes. She had minimal makeup on, and she was wearing simple black jeans and an even a simpler white blouse. I waited as she walked over to the reception desk.

"Hello. How can I help you?" Deb, our receptionist, asked with a practiced smile on her face.

I heard Rose clear her throat and saw her fingers grip the edge of the front desk. "Hi. I'm here for the Coleson mee—"

Before she could finish her sentence, Deb noticed me waiting and, ignoring Rose completely, turned her gaze to me. "Mr. Hawthorne? Is there anything I can do for you? Your two-thirty appoint—"

"No, there isn't." Ignoring Deb's surprised look, I focused on Rose Coleson. "Miss Coleson." When she heard her name, she glanced at me over her shoulder and let go of the desk to face me.

"Your meeting is with me," I continued. "If you could follow me."

Deb cut in as Rose took a step to follow me. "Mr. Hawthorne, I think you are mistaken. The Colesons' meeti—"

"*Thank you*, Deb," I interjected, not caring whether she took offense at my tone or not. "Miss Coleson," I repeated, maybe a bit harsher than I'd intended. I needed to get this meeting done and move on with my day. "This way, please."

After a quick glance at Deb, Rose moved closer. "Mr. Hawthorne? I think there might be a mistake here. I'm supposed to meet with Mr. Reeves—"

"I can assure you there are no mistakes. If you wouldn't mind stepping into my office for some privacy, there are some things I'd like to go over with you." I watched, impatiently, as she thought it over.

"I was told I was needed to sign something and then I could leave. I have another appointment in Brooklyn, so I can't stay for too long."

I gave her a curt nod.

After a brief hesitation and another look at our receptionist, she followed me toward my office in silence.

After a long walk, I opened the glass door for her to step in. I reminded Cynthia, my assistant, not to forward any calls, and then I waited until Rose was settled in her seat. Holding her bulky brown handbag on her lap, she gave me an expectant look as I took my own seat behind my desk.

"I thought the Colesons' lawyer was Tim Reeves, at least the estate lawyer. Has there been a change?" she asked before I could utter a word.

"No, Miss Coleson. Tim is the one who drafted the will, and he is the one handling everything at the moment."

"Then I'm still not sure—"

"I'm not an estate lawyer, but I did help the team who was

handling your late father's corporate cases on a few occasions last year. Can I get you anything to drink? Coffee, maybe? Or tea?"

"No, thank you. Like I said, I have another app—"

"Appointment you need to get to," I finished for her. "I understand. That's—"

"He was my uncle, by the way."

"Excuse me?"

"You said father. Gary Coleson was my uncle, not father."

I raised an eyebrow. This was something I already knew about, but apparently I was too distracted to remember every detail. "That's right. I apologize."

"That's okay... I just wanted to mention it in case you weren't already aware. I'm afraid it's also the reason why I wasn't mentioned in the will, which brings us back full circle, Mr. Hawthorne. I'm not sure what you could possibly want to talk to me about."

This wasn't going like I had planned. Granted, I hadn't given how I wanted to do this much thought, but it was still not going smoothly enough.

"I read the will," I admitted after taking in the stiff way she was holding herself: sitting on the very edge of her seat, impatient and ready to bolt. Maybe she'd appreciate a more straightforward approach, which was something I excelled at.

"Okay," she prompted, raising an eyebrow.

"I'd like to talk to you about the property on Madison Avenue that was owned by your uncle."

Her shoulders stiffened. "What about it?"

"I'd like to know what your plan is going forward regarding the property. I believe you and Gary had signed a contract a little while before his death indicating that you would have use of the property for a short time period, something like two years, and would only pay him a small amount of rent instead of the actual worth of the place. At the end of the two years, you would relocate. Correct?"

She frowned at me but nodded.

Satisfied that she was following me, I continued, "The contract was entered into the will, but Gary chose to add a stipulation I believe you only recently learned about. In the case of something happening to him during those two years, he wanted ownership of the property to transfer to your husband—"

"If I were married," Rose finished, her chin held high.

"Yes." I pointedly looked at her left hand and she followed my gaze. "If you were married, that is."

Her eyes lifted back to mine in the next second and I watched a frown form between her brows.

"I already know about all of this," she explained slowly. "Gary was excited about me marrying Joshua, my fiancé. They got along well, and he liked him—we both had a business degree, but evidently it looked like he trusted Joshua more—"

"Your *ex*-fiancé, you mean," I reminded her.

She paused at my words, but her fingers finally let go of the death grip she had on her handbag as she tried to follow my meaning. "Yes. Right. Of course, ex-fiancé. It's still a habit. We only broke up a few weeks ago. I'm sorry, but how do you know he's my *ex*-fiancé?"

I paused, trying to be careful with my words. "I do my due diligence, Miss Coleson. Please continue."

She studied me for a long moment as I waited patiently. "I wasn't even aware that he would enter our contract into his will. I was also never supposed to have ownership of the property, that wasn't in the contract. He was letting me have use of the property for two years only, after the time limit, I was to leave. Then my uncle and his wife, Angela, died in the car crash and I learned that in the will he was planning on leaving the property to my husband."

"Maybe that was his way of giving you something. A surprise maybe. A wedding gift of some kind."

"Yes. Maybe. Maybe that was his way of leaving us the place, but I'm not married to Joshua at the moment, am I? So I get nothing." She shrugged. "I only knew that Gary thought Joshua's presence would be necessary if I was serious about opening my own coffee shop. I disagreed with him. It didn't matter that we'd started discussing the possibility of me using the space a year prior to Joshua even coming into my life. He didn't think I could handle the work on my own, and Joshua was in between jobs so he thought it made sense. I didn't. I believe he trusted Joshua more than he trusted me because he went to a better school. Also, can't forget about the fact that I'm a woman and Joshua is a man. He was old-fashioned and didn't believe women could handle themselves in the business world. However, when we talked about it again and I told him about my plans for the place, he agreed to let me use his property. Joshua wasn't a part of the conversation then—or the contract, for that matter. He never made stipulations other than the fact that I'd only be able to use the space for two years and then I'd have to find myself a different location. That was all the help he was willing to give me. Nothing more, nothing less. I was thankful either way. I have no idea why he felt it was necessary to add Joshua in his will regarding something concerning me. And why am I telling you all this?"

I leaned back in my seat, getting comfortable. Now we were getting somewhere. "He still isn't part of the conversation."

"I... Excuse me?"

"Gary never used your ex-fiancé's name. He never specified who would be the owner of the property in case he passed away. There is only the mention of a 'husband.'"

"I don't see how that matters. I was supposed to get married to Joshua sometime this year and he knew that, but in the end, I didn't. Joshua broke up with me two days after their death. So, because I'm not married, Mr. Hawthorne, and I'm not planning on marrying anyone any time soon, I don't get to use the space let alone own it. I talked to my cousins, Bryan and Jodi, but they aren't interested in honoring the contract I'd signed with their dad, which means I'm not going to be able to open my coffee shop. At this point, I'm just trying to accept the fact that I threw away fifty thousand dollars—fifty thousand dollars that I managed to save by working for I don't even know how many years at this point—on a space that was never going to be mine anyway. All that aside, I lost two people who were important to me in the same car crash that day. Even though I was Gary's niece, they never saw me as their own flesh and blood, but they were all I had after my dad passed away when I was nine. Whatever the case may be, instead of letting me get lost in the system Gary agreed to take me in and that's all that matters. So, to answer your previous question, I have no plans regarding the property because I'm not allowed to use it anymore."

A little out of breath and, from what I could tell, a lot pissed off, she stood up and hooked her bag over her shoulder.

"Okay, I really don't want to be rude, but I believe this was a waste of both our time. I was a little curious when I was following you here, I'll admit that much, but I don't have time to go over things I already know for no reason at all. I have a job interview I need to get to, and I can't afford to be late. I think we're done here, right? It was nice meeting you, Mr. Hawthorne."

Thinking our conversation was done, she extended her hand over my desk, and I stared at it for a second. Before she could decide to walk away, I let out a breath, rose from my seat, and looked into her eyes as I took her hand.

This was it. This was the part where I should've said *It was nice meeting you* and gone on with my day. I didn't.

In a calm and collected voice, I said what I'd been waiting to say. "You're not being rude, Miss Coleson, but before you go, I'd like you to marry me." Breaking our connection, I pushed my hands into my pockets, watching for her reaction.

After a short moment of hesitation, she replied, "Sure, how about we do that after my job interview, but before dinner. Because, you know, I already made plans with Tom Hardy and I don't think I can postpone—"

"Are you mocking me?" I stood absolutely still.

Her narrowed eyes moved across my face, searching for an answer, I presumed. When she couldn't find what she was looking for, the fight went out of her, and right in front of my eyes, her entire demeanor—which had hardened the second I'd started asking questions about her ex-fiancé—softened and she puffed out a breath.

"You weren't making a bad joke?"

"Do I look like someone who jokes?"

Making a noncommittal sound, she shifted in place. "At first glance...I can't say that you do, but I don't know you enough to be sure."

"I'll save you the trouble—I don't make jokes."

She gave me a baffled look like I had said something astonishing. "O-kay. I think I'm still going to leave now."

Just like that, she surprised me and turned away to leave. Before she could open the door, I spoke up.

"You're not interested in hearing more about my offer then?"

Her hand was already on the glass knob when she stopped. With stiff shoulders, she let go of the door and turned to face me.

After opening and closing her mouth, she looked straight into my eyes from across the room. "Your offer? Just so we're on the same page and I can make sure I didn't hear you wrong, could you repeat said offer?"

"I'm offering to marry you."

Hiking her bag higher on her shoulder, she cleared her throat. "Mr. Hawthorne, I think...I think I'm flattered that you'd—"

"Miss Coleson," I cut her off bluntly before she could finish her sentence. "I assure you, my marriage offer is strictly a *business* deal. I'm sure you're not thinking I'm expressing an interest in you. I was under the impression that you could use my help—was I wrong?"

"Your help? I don't even know you, and I definitely don't remember asking for any—"

"If you accept my offer, you'll have enough time to get to know me."

"If I accept your offer...which is a business deal disguised as a marriage. I don't think I'm following you here."

"Maybe if you explained what you're having trouble under-standing, I could help you."

"How about everything? From where I'm standing, that sounds like a good place to start."

"Right, of course. If you'll take your seat, I'd be *thrilled* to go into more details. For example, I can make sure your life savings, which you already spent on a coffee shop that's not happening, won't go to waste." I was guessing she could see from my expres-sion that I wasn't thrilled about any part of our conversation.

"How do you know that was my life s—"

"Like I said before, I do my—"

"Due diligence, right. I heard you the first time." She looked out, her eyes scanning the busy hallway outside my office. It took her a few seconds to make a choice between walking out and stay-ing. Then, reluctantly, she moved back toward my desk and me, and equally as reluctantly sat down on the edge of the seat again. Her untrusting eyes had all my attention.

"Good." When I was sure she wasn't going to jump up and run away, I took my seat as well. "Now that you're staying, I'd like you to consider my offer."

Briefly closing her eyes, she took a deep breath and let it all out. "See, that's not really explaining anything to me. You keep asking the same thing, and I keep experiencing the same urge to get up and leave."

"I'd like us to get married for a number of reasons, but the one that would interest you most is the fact that you'd get to open your coffee shop on Madison Avenue."

When she didn't make any comments, we remained silent.

"Is that it?" she finally asked, her tone impatient. "You want to marry me—sorry, make a *business* deal with me by marrying me so I can open my coffee shop?"

"Sounds like you understood me well enough."

After another baffled look, she leaned back in her seat then got up, dumped her handbag on the chair, and walked over to the floor-to-ceiling windows to gaze at the skyline. A whole minute passed in silence, and my patience started to wear thin.

"You're insane then," she said. "Are you insane, Mr. Hawthorne?"

"I'm not going to answer that question," I replied tersely.

"That's nothing new. You're not answering my questions, you're not explaining things."

"I want to help you. It's that simple."

She glanced at me with her big brown eyes, staring as if I had lost my mind, and when I didn't go on, she raised her arms and dropped them. "That simple? Could you be helpful right now and explain further, please? You want to help me, for some insane reason—me, someone who incidentally doesn't even know your first name."

"My first name is Jack."

She studied me for a long moment, our gazes holding.

"You're serious, aren't you? Is this a service you offer to all your clients, Jack Hawthorne? Offering to help them by marrying them?"

"You're the first, Miss Coleson."

"So, I'm the special snowflake."

"In a way, yes."

Turning back to the view, she dropped her head and rubbed her temples. "Why?"

"Are you asking me why you're a special snowflake?"

Snorting, she glanced at me over her shoulder. "No, I'm not asking you... Can you give me more information, please? Like actual sentences that explain things and actually makes sense? I'm pretty sure you're not asking me to marry you just to help me out. What's in it for you? What are all those reasons you mentioned?" She looked around my office, taking everything in, me included—all the expensive furniture, my clothes, the view, the clients and lawyers walking by. "I'm gonna go out on a limb and say it isn't about money, because I don't think I have anything to offer you on that front."

"You're right, I don't need money. Like I said before, this is strictly a business deal. It means nothing else to me. When we go ahead with the marriage—"

"You're awfully sure of yourself while I'm still trying to figure out if *you're* the one who is mocking *me*."

I ignored her assessment and continued. "It'll be nothing more than a business transaction between two people." I got up and walked toward her. "I made partner this year, Miss Coleson. I'm thirty-one years old, the youngest partner in the firm, and to properly deal with some of my current and future clients, I need to make a good impression. There are formal and informal dinners, events I need to attend. Although it's not a requirement to be in a serious relationship or to be a 'family man', as they put it, I believe I can use the illusion a marriage will provide to my advantage. I don't want to lose any of my clients or any potential clients to other partners."

Crossing her arms against her chest, she faced me, and we looked at each other. I couldn't even begin to guess what was going through her mind. My own damn mind, however, was at war with my conscience.

"Why not marry someone you love? Someone you're dating? Someone you actually *know*? Why would you even consider asking *me*? You know nothing about me. We're nothing but two strangers." Seemingly trying to hold back her emotions, she took a deep breath. "Call me old-fashioned, Mr. Hawthorne, but I'm a romantic. I believe in marrying someone for love and only for love. Marriage is... Marriage *means* something completely different to me than what I think it means to you. I don't want to be insulting, I don't know you, but you don't strike me as someone who necessarily puts much meaning..."

"You can finish your sentence, Miss Coleson." I jammed my hands back into the pockets of my pants.

"I think you get where I'm coming from."

I nodded because I did get it. "I don't have time for personal relationships at the moment, and I'm not going to marry someone who'll end up expecting more than what I'm offering. I'm not offering you something I'm not ready to give, and you can't be *that* naïve, can you? You can't think I only want to marry you to have someone hang on my arm on appropriate occasions and pay me a small amount of rent."

Her spine straightened, her eyes shooting daggers at me. "Naïve? Trust me, Mr. Hawthorne, I'm not *that* naïve. If I was married my husband would own the property, that's what the will says. So if you're my husband..." She paused and then shrugged. "I get that you're after the property as well, but I'm still waiting to hear about the part where you'd help me. So far all I've heard is you getting everything you want out of this. I'm failing to see how marrying you will help me save the—to you, very meager, I'm sure—life savings I've already spent to buy everything for the coffee shop. Where does me opening the coffee shop fit? In this scenario, you get the fake wife and the property, a property I'm assuming you can buy from my cousins if they're considering selling it, if that's what you want."

"I don't think they're interested in selling. Even if they were, why would I spend so much money on something I can get for free? And to give you more context on the subject, I wasn't actively searching for someone to marry, but when I was asked to read the will to advise on a few subjects, I found out about your situation and thought we could help each other out. To expand on another thing you mentioned, we're not complete strangers. We did meet before—once, a year ago. It was just a brief encounter at one of your uncle's parties, but it still helped me put a face to your name. As vague as it was, I had an idea of who you are, and as for the rest...I had enough time to learn what I needed to learn about you, and I'm sure you'll have the same opportunity regarding me."

"We met? Where? I don't remember."

Uncomfortable, I shifted in place and, not wanting to go into too much detail, waved her question off. "If you don't remember, there is no point in repeating it. Like I said, it was nothing more than a brief introduction anyway. Anything else you'd like to know?"

"You're genuinely being serious about this? Really?"

I glanced at the clock on the wall. Time was wasting. "I'm not going to keep repeating myself, Miss Coleson. If you accept, we'll get married and the property will be transferred to me. After that, I'll honor the initial contract terms and you can go ahead with your plans."

She sighed and seemed to mull my words over. "That's it? That's *all*? The property, attending events, and acting like we're married in front of other people? Nothing more?"

"That's exactly it, and only for two years. Nothing more, nothing less."

Glancing away from me, she worried her lips between her

teeth. "Two years—right, because that's nothing. Isn't this illegal? Wouldn't it *be* illegal?"

"Why would it be?"

She gave me an exasperated look. "Fine. What about Jodi and Bryan? There is no way they'll believe it was a real marriage. Can't he dispute, challenge, or whatever it is people would do in this situation to stop me from opening the coffee shop and you having ownership?" With a frown on her face, she shook her head. "I'm not saying I'd do this, but if for some insane reason I accepted your offer... I can't even believe I'm thinking this, let alone saying it out loud."

It wasn't hard to see the hopeful look on her face. Knowing it was the right time, I gave her another small push.

"It's not a hard decision, Miss Coleson. If I suspected there would be blowback, for me or for you, I wouldn't make this offer. I'm the best at what I do, and no one will be disputing anything. If you accept, I'll handle your cousins. They won't be an issue, I can assure you of that." I lifted my shoulder in a careless shrug. "It's no one's business but ours, and you don't owe anyone any explanations."

Her eyes focused on the ground, she kept shaking her head. I already knew what her answer would be—she was asking questions, which meant she was considering it. It was already a done deal. If I hadn't already been sure of the outcome, I wouldn't have come to her with the offer. She had spent all her savings on her dream, and I didn't see her passing on my offer, which would benefit us both. I also knew it didn't mean I'd get her answer with no resistance.

Startled, we both looked at my assistant, Cynthia, when she knocked on the glass door and stepped inside. "Your next appointment is here, Mr. Hawthorne, and you wanted me to inform you when the other meeting had started."

"Thank you, Cynthia. I'm going to need a few more minutes here."

As Cynthia nodded and closed the door, Rose Coleson headed back to her chair and picked up her bag. "I'm going to leave...and I'll think about—"

"I'm afraid you'll have to give me your answer now." I didn't move from my spot.

She stopped messing with her bag and met my gaze. "What? Why?"

"Because as Cynthia just let us know, your cousins are in the meeting room at the moment, discussing how to handle the properties. If you accept my offer, we'll go join them and announce our situation. If you don't, you'll lose your last chance."

"You can't really expect me to decide right now. Do you think they're just going to believe we fell in love at first sight? And then decided to get married in a week?"

"And how would they know that? How would they know when or how we met?" I took my hands out of my pockets and shrugged, moving back toward my desk. "It's not our problem if they assume we met weeks or months ago."

"My fiancé just left me a few weeks ago, Mr. Hawthorne. Out of the blue. For no reason whatsoever. They know me enough to know I wouldn't marry someone else that quickly."

"Your point being?"

"My point being?" Frustrated, she shook her head. "I can't believe this is happening right now."

Overwhelmed and looking confused, she dropped down on the chair. I felt like a bastard for forcing an answer from her, but I had a million things to do and not enough time to do them. If we were going to go forward with this, I needed to know immediately because I wouldn't put myself in this situation again. "I'm going to need that answer from you, Miss Coleson."

"And I need to know more details, Mr. Hawthorne. Also, could you please stop calling me *Miss Coleson*?"

"The details aren't important at the moment. It's either a yes or a no."

"You're pressuring me. I don't like it. I don't like this."

"I'm doing nothing of the sort. You can walk out of my office at any time—after you give me a definitive answer, that is. You don't have to say yes, but when you do answer, don't forget that this is completely your own decision. I have nothing to lose in this. If I don't end up with that property, I'll find something else on Madison Avenue. Can you say the same?"

Her hands resting on her lap, palms down on her jeans, she lifted her head and looked up at me. "This is insane. If I do this, I'm insane. You're insane."

"I think I'm quite clear on what you think of me." Half sitting on my desk, I crossed my arms. "This will benefit us both, Miss Coleson. If we sign that simple piece of paper that states we're married, you'll get to open up your coffee shop, and nothing else will change for two years. If we don't, you'll lose all your money on furniture and equipment you've bought that you can't use at the moment. From where I'm standing, there is no decision to make. I'm offering you a lifeline. If you're okay with losing all that, we have nothing more to discuss."

"We're not a good fit, Mr. Hawthorne. Surely you can see that."

"No, I guess we're not. I completely agree with you, but then again, I believe it's good enough for what we have in mind. If your answer is no, please let me know so I can get on with my next meeting."

Seconds ticked by as I waited for her answer, and I could see the exact moment her dream of opening her own coffee shop swayed her decision, just as I'd suspected it would. "I can't believe I'm saying this. I can't even believe this is happening right now, but if we're going to make them believe we're getting married, I think you should start calling me Rose."

"Good. We'll discuss the details at another date. In the meantime, I'll draw up a marriage contract that covers everything." Straightening from the desk, I crossed to the door and opened it for her.

"Six months," she blurted out.

I arched an eyebrow as she got up and turned around to meet my gaze.

"Six months?"

"Yes. I want you to give me six months before I start paying you the amount of rent that was discussed in the original contract." She nodded with a frown, as if she wasn't so sure what she was asking. "I know that was not in the initial contract I made with my uncle, but since you're going to end up with the property anyway, I want those first six months to be rent free so I can at least try to make some profit." She paused, thinking. "I think you can afford it. And truth be told, I can't. Sure, the rent I'll be paying you is nothing for a place on Madison Avenue, but with everything going on, I won't be able to afford it. But those rent-free six months will help me get a good start."

I studied her more closely. "You're right, I can afford not getting rent from you. Deal. Is that all?"

"I... Yes, that's it."

"You could ask me for the half of the property. If you had gotten married to Joshua, you'd get the half."

"Would you give it to me?"

"I'm afraid the answer would be no."

"I thought so. Not paying rent for six months will help me."

"Good. Then we have no problem. Let's join the meeting."

"Just like that?"

"Do you have any more questions?"

"Only about a hundred." She stopped next to me and met my eyes.

I arched an eyebrow. "I'm afraid we can't go through them all at the moment. Maybe next time. You'll have plenty of time to ask me anything you want after we're married. Let me do the talking in the meeting and we'll be fine."

Paler than she'd been when she had first entered my office and maybe a little shell-shocked, she nodded and followed behind me as we headed toward the meeting room.

I cursed myself for the bastard I was with every step I took.

When we were only a few steps away from the meeting room and I could see Bryan and Jodi Coleson sitting next to each other, their backs to us, I glanced at Rose and saw her breathing was a little out of control, her eyes huge and unsure.

"Ready?" I asked, already guessing what her answer would be.

"Can't really say that I am."

I nodded. That was good enough.

"When was the last time you talked to your cousins?"

She rubbed her temples before looking up at me. "Last week, maybe? Maybe more? Why?"

"Leave it to me."

We stepped in the room. Standing side by side. She had that particular death grip on her handbag that was hanging on her shoulder again.

"Tim," I interrupted and everyone in the room, including Jodi Coleson and Bryan Coleson, turned to look at us. "I'm sorry for being late to the meeting."

Tim shuffled the pages he held in his hand, stood up and took off his glasses, his eyes on Rose. "Hello Jack. Miss Rose, I'm glad you could join us. I won't hold you for too long, we just need you to—"

"Tim," I said again and waited until his gaze met mine. "I

thought you'd like to be informed so you can make the necessary changes. Rose Coleson is my fiancée and we're getting married in a few days."

"You're...you're getting married to Miss Rose? What?" While Tim stood there staring at me and Rose with a stupefied expression, Bryan slowly pushed himself up and faced Rose.

"What's going on here?" he asked, his already hard gaze jumping from Rose to me. "Explain."

"Bryan, Jack and I are getting married." She forced out a laugh and shifted on her feet. "I know that sounds a little—"

"It sounds like you're fucking with me, cuz."

I took a step forward and left, putting myself in front of Bryan and forcing Rose to take a step back.

"I know this is a surprise to your family, Mr. Coleson, so I'll let that one go, but I'd suggest you watch your words when you're speaking to my fiancé." I looked away from him and addressed the room. "I proposed to Rose last week, and we thought this would be a good time to share the news with you. We couldn't do it before because we wanted some privacy to celebrate. Tim, I believe this will change the situation regarding the property on Madison Avenue."

"This is complete bullshit," Bryan burst out as his sister, Jodi, sat there and watched it all unfold with a bored expression. "This situation, whatever the hell this act is, changes nothing. She still isn't getting the property. How stupid do you think I am?"

"Oh, I couldn't say, Mr. Coleson. We'll be family shortly and I wouldn't want to insult you." I watched as the color on his face darkened. "Also, in the will, Gary Coleson clearly states that, in the event that he passes away, the ownership of the property on Madison Avenue will transfer to Rose's husband. The time limit was until 2020, I believe, but we can always check. I'm only explaining this for your sake, Mr. Coleson, because I'm not marrying your cousin for a property. My feelings for her has nothing to do with what's going on here."

"Jack, maybe we should—" Tim started.

"If it has nothing to do with what's going on here, you'll lay no claim on the property," Bryan forced out through clenched teeth, his eyes sliding to Rose.

"The property, I believe is Gary Coleson's last gift to his niece. I'm sure you're not trying to ignore your father's wishes."

Bryan's hands slowly balled into fists and he took one more step forward.

Tim cleared his throat and rubbed his eyes with his thumb and index finger. "Jack maybe this wasn't the best time to...uh, share the good news. Maybe we can schedule another meeting for—"

"Yes, I think that would be better. Rose and I will expect to hear from you soon."

"I will contest the will," Bryan said, his eyes glittering with anger before I could get us out of there. He was talking to Rose, his eyes on her. "I won't let you have this. You're doing this because I wouldn't let you use the place and told you I had other plans."

"If you contest, you'll have to wait a long time to get your own share. I fight back Mr. Coleson," I warned.

"Bryan," Rose said from behind me. "I'm not marrying Jack for the property. I know the timing is...awkward, but it isn't what you think. We met when..." She stepped up next to me and pushed her arm through mine.

I forced myself to relax.

"You don't have to explain anything to him," I said, glancing at her.

Her mouth pressed into a thin line when her eyes met mine. "Yes, I do, Jack. Of course, I do."

"I'm not listening to one more word from you," Bryan cut in. "This is not happening. If you force my hand, I will fight this."

With that, he strode out, making sure to bump his shoulder against mine.

Finally, Jodi got on her feet. "Well. Well. Our pretty little Rose finally does something interesting." Her eyes took me in from head to toe as Rose let go of my arm. "Not bad, little cousin," she said. "Not an upgrade from Joshua, but since you've lost him, I guess this one will do."

When I arched my brow, she smiled as if she had a secret and shrugged. "Not my type. Too serious, too stiff, but oh, well who am I to talk about your fiancé?"

Stopping in front of Rose, she leaned in to kiss her cheek and I felt Rose stiffen next to me, pulling a little back.

"You know I don't care about the property stuff, I got my millions and the home from the will, but you knew Bryan had his eyes set on this. I don't think this little marriage scheme will change anything." She lifted her hand and studied her pink fingernails. "May the best one win, I guess. It'll be fun for me either way."

CHAPTER THREE

ROSE

Present

I was trying to paint the wall behind the counter and doing my best not to fall asleep midsentence as I was talking to Sally, my very own employee. It'd been a long day, just like it had been a long day every day for the last week and a half, but I wasn't complaining—how could I when it had been my dream to open my own coffee shop for so long? Not even attempting to stifle my yawn, I dipped the paint roller in more dark-ish green paint and ignored the humming ache in my shoulder as I kept painting.

"You sure you don't want me to stay longer?" Sally asked, going through her backpack as she looked for her phone.

"You've already been here longer than you were supposed to, and I'm almost done for the day anyway. I only need another fifteen minutes or so just to add a last coat. Somehow I can still see a hint of red underneath it." I sighed and it turned into a groan. "As soon as this is done, I'll head home too."

Glancing over my shoulder, I gave her my most stern *You better listen to me* look and watched her burst out laughing.

"What?" I asked when she looked at me with a wobbly smile.

"You have green dots all over your face, and I'm not even gonna point out the state your t-shirt is in—or your hair, for that matter. I'll only say this: you're officially a work of art now."

I could imagine the mess I'd made on my t-shirt, but my face was news to me. "Oddly, I'm gonna take that as a compliment, and...well, paint splatters," I mumbled with a sigh as I wiped my forehead with my arm. "Even my face muscles are tired—how the hell did that happen?"

"Beats me. My face is fine, but my ass is pretty sore."

"Well," I started, making a face. "I'm not sure what you've been doing when my back is turned, but..." Before I could finish, I saw Sally's expression and couldn't hold back my laughter.

"God, that came out wrong!" she groaned, looking at the ceiling. "We sat on the floor for almost two straight hours, it was inevitable—"

"I know, I know. My ass is hurting, too, and it's not just my ass—every inch of my body hurts. I'm just heading toward delirious, so I'm gonna laugh like a lunatic regardless of whether what you're saying is funny or not. Get out of here so I can finish and get to my beloved shower and bed."

Sally was a dark-haired, dark-eyed, always smiling twenty-one-year-old and had been the fifteenth applicant for the barista/everything-else-I'll-need-you-to-do job. It had been a love-at-first-sight kind of thing. To save myself from the headache, I'd opted not to post about the job online, or anywhere, really. I'd only mentioned it to a few friends so they could ask around to see if someone they knew needed a job, and I'd also asked a few other people I'd worked with at my last job as the manager at Black Dots Coffee House before I had quit when I thought Gary was going to let me use the place. Word had gotten out, and I'd ended up talking to a lot more people than I'd anticipated I would. None of them had felt like the right person, though.

Sally, however, was a complete stranger who had just been walking to her apartment after a dreadful blind date and had seen me struggling to carry boxes from the curb into the shop. She had offered to help, and in return, at the end of the day I'd offered her the job. It didn't hurt that we had bonded over our mutual love of and obsession with coffee mugs, puppies, and New York in winter. If those things didn't prove we were a perfect fit, I didn't know what else would.

If there was one thing I wanted the most for Around the Corner—my coffee shop!—it was for it to be inviting, warm, and happy. Popular wouldn't hurt anyone either. Even though I was well aware I was going to be the boss, I didn't want to work with people I couldn't get along with just because their resumés were impressive. If we were happy and friendly, I believed it'd have a different kind of pull for the customers, and Sally's personality and cheerfulness checked all the boxes for me.

"You got it, boss." She wiggled her newly found phone at me in goodbye and backed away toward the door. "Oh, when do you want me to come in again?"

I put the paint roller down and groaned as I straightened back up with my hand on my waist and gazed at my almost finished work. "I think I'll be fine on my own this week, but I'll text you for next week if I have a lot of stuff going on. Would that work for you?"

"Are you sure you don't need help with the painting this week?"

"Yeah, I can handle it." I just waved her off without turning because I didn't think my body was capable of doing anything that complex at the moment. "I'll call you if anything changes."

"Got it. You be sure to go home before you drop dead." With her lovely parting words, she unlocked the door and opened it. Before I heard it click shut, she called my name and I glanced at her over my shoulder, which took some serious effort on my part.

"Only two weeks or so now," Sally said, grinning. "I'm so excited," she squeaked, bouncing up and down.

I gave her a tired but genuinely happy smile and managed to pump my hand halfway into the air. We only had five years of age difference between us, but I was feeling every single one of the years I had on her. "Yes, definitely yay! You probably can't tell from my face right now because I can't move it much, but I'm excited too. Can't wait. Woohoo."

Her body disappeared behind the door, and all I could see was her head. "It's gonna be great!"

"I'm crossing my fingers in my mind because I don't think I can do it in real life."

After she gave me an even bigger grin, her head disappeared too and the door slid shut. Since we'd boarded the windows up, I couldn't see outside, but I knew it was already dark. Reaching for my phone in my back pocket proved to be harder than I'd expected, but I was able to check the time. I was pretty much moving in slow motion, but who needed speed on a Monday night?

Eight o'clock.

I knew I shouldn't take a break, but my legs, feet, back, neck, arms, and everything in between were killing me. Left with no other choice, I slid down behind the counter, right where the cash register would be in just a few days, groaning and whimpering the entire time it took my ass to reach the ground. Then I dropped my head back with a loud thud and closed my eyes with a heavy sigh. Now, if I could only manage to get up, finish the last coat on the wall, and make sure I couldn't see any damn red anymore, I could lock up then move my feet enough times to get to the subway so I could get home and step straight into the shower. If I didn't drown myself in the shower, getting into my bed would be nice, too—and food. At some point, I'd need food.

Then it hit me again. If you ignored that I was dying a slow death from all kinds of aches, Sally was right—I was getting really close to the opening day. Ever since I had taken a job at a local coffee shop when I was eighteen, I knew I wanted to open my own place. Something that belonged just to me. Not only that, but it would also be where *I* belonged. And that would be a first as well. As cheesy as it sounded, there was something about the idea of my own place that had always lifted my heart when I daydreamed about it.

Just as I felt myself drifting off, the front door opening and closing with a soft click jolted me awake. I had completely forgotten that I hadn't locked it after Sally left. Thinking she had left something behind, I tried to get up. When my legs didn't want to cooperate, I had to get on my hands and knees with much effort and then held on to the counter to pull myself up.

"What did you forget?" I asked, and it came out half as a groan and half as a whimper.

Finding my cousin, Bryan, just on the other side of the counter was not the best surprise I could've wished for. At his unexpected appearance, I tried to come up with something to say, but I was completely tongue-tied. He tapped the counter with his knuckles and took a good look around. So far, I had ignored every single one of his calls and had even turned off my phone when his threatening texts had started to get a little out of hand.

"Bryan."

His eyes only moved to me when he was done with his perusal and you could easily see that he wasn't happy.

"I see you already got comfortable," he said, the anger obvious in his voice.

"Bryan, I don't think—"

"Yes," he interrupted, taking a step forward. "Yes, you don't think. You didn't think. I'm not going to let this go, Rose. Surely, that's obvious. You don't deserve this place. You're not family, not really, you know that. You've always known that. And having that lawyer behind you will change nothing." His gaze fell to my hands. "I see you're not even wearing a wedding ring. Who do you think you're fooling?"

I gritted my teeth and balled my fists behind the counter. If I could just hit him once. Just once. Oh, the pleasure it would give me.

"I'm working. I'm not gonna wear something so precious to me while I'm painting. This is pointless, I think you should leave, Bryan."

"I will when I'm ready."

"I don't want to argue with you. You don't see me as family so that makes us strangers. I don't have to explain myself to a stranger."

He shrugged. "Who is arguing? I only wanted to drop by to let you know that you shouldn't get comfortable here. We'll be seeing each other more. Your lawyer might have managed to stop me from taking this place from you, for now, but I don't give up that easily. Since I already know that your marriage is nothing but a lie, all I have to do is wait and prove it."

"I know you think—"

"Good luck with that," someone said and with a jolt, I turned my head and locked eyes with Jack. The one that was my husband.

Oh, jeez.

It was not my night, that was for sure. If Jodi had walked in with bouquets of roses in her hands to congratulate me on the coffee shop, I didn't think I'd have been as surprised as I was. I had successfully continued to ignore the memory of the day I'd gotten married to *this* specific stranger, and since he hadn't been in the city for eight or nine days, it'd worked well—up until now. To be fair, it shouldn't have come as a surprise. We were, in fact, married so I knew I'd eventually have to see him again, but his timing was the absolute worst. If I'd had the option to choose, I'd have much preferred a phone call where I could make my case much more easily before we had to face each other.

Before I could say anything, he focused on Bryan. "Since I don't think you're here to congratulate us, I'm asking you to leave my wife alone."

Bryan had to take a step away from the counter when Jack almost got in his face.

"So you do know you have a wife then. From what I heard you weren't even in the country."

"Excuse me, Mr. Coleson, my apologies. I didn't know by marrying your cousin I'd have to share my schedule with you as well. I'll remedy that as soon as possible."

I really wanted to snort, but managed to hold it in.

Jack continued. "Since you're already here I like to take this opportunity to repeat what I told you before. I noticed that every time you're around my wife you're making her uncomfortable and unhappy. I really don't think I like it, Bryan. I'm not sure how many times you need me to repeat myself. But I'll say it again: I don't want to see you around her."

Since I couldn't see Jack's expression with his back to me, I watched the muscle in Bryan's jaw twitch and then he forced a smile onto his face.

"I was just on my way out anyway. I said what I came here to say, right, Rose?"

I said nothing.

Jack said nothing.

Bryan let out an insincere chuckle. "I'll leave you two love birds alone. And later you and I will have a chat, Jack."

Jack followed Bryan all the way up to the door and made sure to lock it after him.

Groaning, I closed my eyes.

"This was a good lesson on why I should never forget to lock the door."

I opened my eyes and he was standing right there. Right in front of me where Bryan had stood only a few minutes ago. I wasn't sure if he was the better option.

"Rose," Jack said as a greeting. Just Rose.

For a brief moment, I didn't know what to say. I was fairly sure it was the first time he had called me by just my name and not Miss Coleson when we were alone. When we had attended that meeting with Jodi and Bryan, I was just Rose, but the second he'd walked me to the elevators after we were done there, I was back to being Miss Coleson. I supposed since I wasn't technically a Coleson anymore, using my first name was the appropriate choice.

Also, dammit, what a sight he was for my sore eyes. Despite the late hour, he was wearing a suit: dark grey slacks and jacket, white button-down, and a black tie. It was simple, but it still packed an expensive punch. Considering what I looked like in that moment, it was a pretty hard punch, too.

In that first glance, he was nowhere near being my type. I wasn't into the broody and aloof who didn't like using their words all that much, as if you weren't worthy of a conversation in their eyes. Definitely wasn't a fan of the fancy, rich types who came from money and grew up assuming they owned everything and everyone in their vicinity; I'd met my fair share of them living with the Colesons, and we just didn't mesh well. Other than that, I had nothing personal against them. So, yes, Jack Hawthorne wasn't my type. However, that didn't mean I couldn't appreciate how good he looked with stubble, that sharp jawline, his unique and captivating blue eyes, or the fact that he had a body that wore suits extremely well. No, my issue with my new husband wasn't his looks—it was his personality.

That's how the universe works: it gives you *the* one thing you said you'd never want.

"Jack...you came back." Given my half-dead state, that was

the best answer I could come up with, pointing out the obvious. Considering I hadn't seen or talked to him since the day he left me in that car, I felt like I had every right to be surprised.

With the look he gave me, like I was so beneath him, a knot of dread formed in my stomach. I had plenty of self-confidence, but guys like him always excelled at making me feel less than. Dealing with Bryan hadn't made things easier either.

"Did you think I would disappear? Was this the first time he showed up here? Your cousin."

I nodded.

"Good. He won't come back."

That didn't sound ominous at all.

"We need to talk," he continued, completely unaware of my nerves.

Hands gripping the counter for support, I nodded again and tried my best to stand straight.

The guy didn't beat around the bush, that was for sure. He wasn't exactly a conversationalist, either, from what I'd learned so far. Thankfully, that would work in my favor this time around, because even though I had not been looking forward to seeing him, I'd been getting myself ready for this conversation ever since his parting words to me after the ceremony. A lot of mirror practice sessions had taken place. I was sure, he was there to tell me he wanted a divorce, and I was dead set on changing his mind.

"Yes, we do need to talk," I agreed once I was sure my knees wouldn't give out on me.

I didn't know if it was because he wasn't expecting me to agree so quickly or because of something else, but he looked taken aback. I ignored it and started my speech.

"I know why you're here. I know what you came to say, and I'm gonna ask you not to say it, at least not before I finish what I need to say. Okay, here goes nothing. You're the one who came to me with this offer. Well, *I* came to your office, but technically you were the one who lured me to your office."

His eyebrows slowly rose. "Lured?"

"Let me say this. You started this thing. I was making peace with the situation, was even looking for a new job, but you changed things. Your offer changed things. I've come here every day since we made our deal. I've been working nonstop and now it's too real to let go. So, I can't do it. I'm sorry, but I can't sign the papers. Instead, I have a different offer for you, and I really want you to consider it."

With every word out of my mouth, his brows furrowed deeper, his expression turning murderous. I still pushed through before he could get a word in, call me on my bullshit, and mess up my thought process.

"I'll go to as many events as you want me to go to, no limits—as long as it's after I close the coffee shop, of course. I'll also cook for you. I don't know if you cook or not, but I can cook for you and save you the trouble. Free coffee," I added excitedly when the thought randomly crossed my mind. How had I not thought of that? "Free coffee for two years. Whenever you come in, whatever you want, however many times a day. Pastries would be free, too. And, I know this is going to sound a little silly, but hear me out. It doesn't seem like you're the most...sociable person—"

"Excuse me?" he said in a low voice, cutting me off.

"I don't know, maybe that's the wrong word to use, but I can help with that, too. I can be a good friend, if that's something you need or want. I can do—"

"Stop talking."

The harsh tone he used was unexpected and shut me up pretty quickly.

"What the hell are you talking about?" he asked, putting his hands on the counter and leaning in.

I leaned back. "I'm not divorcing you, Jack." I dropped my

head and let out a long breath. "I'm sorry, I can't. I hate myself for saying this, but I'll make trouble for you." God, as threats went, it sounded pretty weak even to my own ears.

He blinked at me a few times, and I thought maybe my threat was working. "You'll make trouble for me," he repeated in a detached tone, and I closed my eyes in defeat. He wasn't buying it. If one of us was going to make trouble for the other, it would be him making my life miserable. He had all the power. "Just out of curiosity, what kind of trouble would you make for me, Rose? What did you have in mind?"

I looked up to see if he was making fun of me, but it was impossible to tell anything from his stony face. When I couldn't give him an answer, he straightened up and pushed his hands into his pockets.

"If I was planning on divorcing you why would I say the things I said to Bryan? I came here to ask why your things aren't at my place, why you haven't moved in."

Oh.

"I...what?"

"You were supposed to move in when I was gone. You didn't. Even though this isn't going to be a real marriage, we're the only ones who know that, and I'd like to keep it that way. From everything you've said, it sounds like you don't want a divorce. If that's true, we need to live together. Surely you could've guessed that, especially with your cousin coming around."

That was not what I had been expecting to hear from him at all. Had I spent almost two weeks worrying about nothing? "You said, before you got out of the car...you said we shouldn't have done this and didn't call or contact me in any way for the entire time you were gone."

"And?"

I found the strength to get a little pissed. "And what was I supposed to think after that remark? *Surely* you knew I would think you regretted your decision."

"And you wanted to get married that day?" he retorted.

"No, but—"

"It doesn't matter. Didn't Cynthia call you about moving into my place?"

Momentarily rendered speechless by his audacity, I closed my eyes and barely managed to lift my hand high enough to rub the bridge of my nose. "I didn't get any phone calls."

"It doesn't matter anymore. I have work to do, so we need to leave now."

Meeting his eyes, I frowned at him. "What do you mean we need to leave now?"

"I'll help you pack a few things from your apartment and then we're going back to my place. You can get everything else later."

My frown deepened and I shook my head. "You can leave if you want to, but I *also* have work to do, as you can see, and I'm not going anywhere before it's done."

If he thought he could order me around just because we were married, he had another thing coming. Before he could come up with something else and piss me off further, I turned my back to him and gently bent down to pick up the paint roller, quietly wincing as I tried not to whimper or make any other sound though my back was actually killing me. Just as I started on the first wet roll, I heard some rustling behind me. Not thinking anything of it—because, in my humble opinion, if he wanted to leave, he was more than welcome to do so—I kept painting. It was at a much slower pace than before, but I was getting the work done, and more importantly, I wasn't backing down.

Only a few seconds later, his palm circled my wrist and stopped my movements. I only felt the heat of his skin for a quick second, and then it was gone.

Taking the roller from me, he put it back down and then started to roll up his stark white—and extremely expensive—sleeves. I'd always thought there was something irresistible about watching a man roll up his sleeves, and Jack Hawthorne was just so meticulous and thorough about it that it was impossible for me to take my eyes away.

"What do you think you're doing?" I asked when he was finally done and in the process of picking up the paint roller.

He gave me a brief glance and started painting. "Obviously I'm helping you finish what you were doing so we can get out of here faster."

"Maybe I have other things I need to get done here."

"Then I'll help with them too." I thought that was uncharacteristically sweet of him—annoying, but in a sweet sort of way.

"I don't need—" Another quick glance from him had the words dying on my lips.

"You look awful." He gave me his back while I was still staring at him in shock. "Didn't you like how the professionals painted it?" he asked.

Maybe he wasn't so sweet after all, just plain old rude. To be honest, that comment hurt a little. "Thank you. I tried my best to look awful today—glad to hear it worked. Although, if I had known you were coming, I would've tried harder. Also, what professionals are you talking about? I'm painting the place myself."

That confession earned me another indecipherable look, this one longer.

"Why?"

"Because I have a budget and I can't blow it on things I can easily do myself. Does it look bad or something?" I narrowed my eyes and looked at the wall more carefully. "Do you still see that damn red underneath?"

The roller stopped moving for two seconds, but then he

continued painting. "No. Considering you painted it on your own, it looks fine. Is this the only wall you'll be painting?" he asked, his voice tighter.

"No. Tomorrow I'm starting on the rest of the place. I was only going to do one more coat for the green then call it a day."

I moved forward, grabbed the small paintbrush, and dipped it in the paint bucket that was sitting at the end of the counter. "I'll do the edges—it'll go quicker."

"No," he replied in a clipped tone, blocking me. "You look like you're about to keel over. I said I'll get it done." Without touching me, he pried the brush out of my hand.

"You don't know how I want it done," I protested, trying to take the brush back.

"I think it's a pretty straightforward process, wouldn't you agree? Sit down before you—"

"Keel over. I got it."

It was tempting to stand upright the whole time as he painted my wall, but he was right—if I didn't sit my ass down, I was about ready to pass out. Since the chairs hadn't arrived yet, the only thing I could sit on was an old stool I had found in the back room and had cleaned just that morning.

After a few minutes of quiet where the only sounds you could hear were the traffic outside and the wet sounds of the paint roller, I couldn't take it. "Thank you for helping, but Mr. Hawth—"

He stopped and turned around. Even with a paint roller in his hand, he looked attractive, not that it was any of my business. An attractive jerk didn't hold much appeal.

"Jack," he said quietly. "You need to call me Jack."

I sighed. "You're right. I'm sorry. It...it still feels weird. I just wanted to say that I can't stay in your apartment, not tonight," I added quickly. "I'm really tired and I need to go home, shower, and...it really isn't the best time for me to pack and move my clothes. Give me a week and I'll—"

"Do you want to stay married?" Nonchalantly, he leaned down and dipped the roller into more paint. I didn't reply; it wasn't necessary—he knew the answer. He got back to painting and spoke toward the wall. "Good. We'll go to your apartment and I'll wait for you to grab a bag. If you don't want your cousin to create problems down the road, you need to get rid of the apartment as soon as you can."

I gritted my teeth. I knew he was right, but that didn't mean I liked what he was saying. I still thought letting him know my thought on the matter was a good idea. "I don't like this."

That got him to look at me. "Really? I'm so surprised to hear that. And here I was having the time of my life."

My lips twitched, but his face was unreadable—as always. I shook my head. "I'm glad I was able to provide that for you, and I know you're right. It's just that...I have a million things to do here in the upcoming days, and packing my stuff on top of all those things...I'm not sure I'll have the energy. So, since I'd be more comfortable in my own space, how about I'll keep paying my rent at least for another month or so and go back and forth while I'm working on the coffee shop and move slowly—"

"That's not gonna work. You can pack whatever you'll need for a few days, and I'll send some people back to your apartment to pack your furniture."

Send some people? What the hell was he talking about?

"I... The furniture isn't mine. It's a one-room studio apartment, a very small one. All it has is a Murphy bed, a small couch, and a coffee table, basically, and none of it is mine. Also, I don't need someone else to pack my stuff. I'll do it myself."

"Good. Then after we drop by your place, we'll head back to my apartment. In the next few days, you'll bring the rest of your stuff."

Just like that, I was out of excuses, so I closed my mouth and gave myself permission to sulk in silence for a few minutes. It lasted until he picked up the small paintbrush and started on the edges.

"I don't know how to do this," Jack stated quietly with a slight touch of anger tinging his voice.

My elbow was on the counter and I was resting my head on my palm when he spoke up. I opened my eyes to check his progress.

"It looks good from here. Again, you don't have to do it, but thank you."

His movements with the brush faltered for a second, but he didn't stop. "I'm not talking about the painting. I'm saying I don't know how to do this with *you*. I don't know how to be married."

I stared at the back of his head, blinking and trying to make sure I'd heard him right. I took my time trying to figure out how to answer. "I've never married a stranger before either, so I think we're on the same level here. I'm hoping we can figure it out together along the way. Can I suggest one thing, though? I think it would make our lives easier."

"Can I stop you?" he asked, glancing at me over his shoulder.

Did he mean I talked too much? "You'd have to try and see for yourself, but I'm pretty sure you can't, so I'll just go right ahead and share. You're not very talkative, and that's okay. If I tried, I could talk enough for both of us, but even though we won't be in each other's faces all the time, we're gonna have to figure out a way to...communicate, I think. I don't think I'd be too off the mark if I said you seem like a guy of very few words."

He turned to look at me with an arched eyebrow, and I gave him a small smile and a shrug before continuing.

"It's gonna be difficult to get used to each other. This whole situation is awkward and new. Plus, living with you is going to be...to be honest, a little weird for me, not to mention the fact that you're gonna have to live with a stranger in your apartment, too. I'll try to stay out of your way as much as I can. I'll be spending most of my time here, anyway, so I think you'll barely notice my presence. And we're helping each other out, right? You get the property and the every-now-and-then fake wife, and I get two years in this amazing location. I promise, I'll do my part."

His eyes holding mine, he gave me a small nod.

"Despite what you saw tonight, I'm pretty easy to get along with," I continued as he focused on dipping the brush into more paint. "You won't even know I'm in your home. I'll be wherever you need me to be when you need me, but other than that, I'll stay out of your hair."

"That's not what I'm worried about."

I was having a really hard time keeping my eyes open. "What are you worried about then?"

Instead of explaining further, he shook his head and turned back to the almost finished wall. "This is almost done. If there is nothing else to do, we should leave."

"There are a million things to do, but I don't think I have the strength to lift my finger, let alone do anything. I'll get my things from the back then we can go."

"Your ring," he said as I pushed myself up, his back to me. "You're not wearing it."

"I..." I touched my finger where the ring was supposed to be. "I left it at home because I'm working here. I didn't want to lose it or damage it with all the work I need to do."

"I'd prefer you to wear it from now on."

He didn't turn back and look at me, but I did notice the band I'd bought him was on his finger.

"Of course," I mumbled quietly before going to the kitchen to get my things.

The number of times Jack Hawthorne smiled: none.

CHAPTER FOUR

JACK

The car ride to her apartment was silent. After she said a quiet hello to Raymond after entering the car, neither of us said a word to each other. I didn't have anything else to say, and she didn't look like she had any strength left in her to string two words together. That saved us from trying to make small talk, which was something I didn't do willingly anyway.

Sooner than I expected, we came to a stop in front of her old apartment building in the East Village. I offered my help, but she politely declined. After promising she wouldn't take long, she quickly—as quickly as she could drag herself away, that is—exited the car. Thinking she'd take her time to pack no matter what she said, as every single female I'd known to that day would have done, I focused on answering some emails while I waited in the car with Raymond.

Twenty minutes later, just as I was about to send out my sixth email, I looked up from my phone and saw Rose coming out with just one small duffel bag. She'd also changed out of her paint-splattered clothes into blue jeans and a white t-shirt, and she looked freshly showered with her damp hair framing her face. If I wasn't mistaken, she was favoring her right leg.

Before I could do anything, Raymond opened his door and rushed to help her. Following a brief push and pull between them, which I watched in confusion and unexpected amusement, Rose gave up and let Raymond carry her bag.

"Thank you," she said quietly when he opened the door for her after putting it in the trunk.

"You're welcome, Mrs. Hawthorne."

I froze. With her hand on top of the open door, Rose froze as well.

"Uh, that's really not necessary. Please call me Rose."

As she finally got in and Raymond closed the door, I locked my phone and put it back into my pocket.

"Will that be enough?" I asked.

She glanced at me with a small frown. "Excuse me?"

I gestured to the back with my head.

She followed my gaze. "Oh, yes. I can't do much tonight. I'll pack everything tomorrow. I'm sorry if I took too long, but I had to jump in the shower because of all the paint."

"It's fine. I took care of some emails."

She nodded and we fell silent for a few minutes until she spoke up again.

"That was a little weird for you too, right? It wasn't just me."

I quirked an eyebrow and waited for her to explain.

"Mrs. Hawthorne," she whispered after a quick glance at Raymond. She put her right hand on the leather seat between us, leaning her upper body toward me as if she was sharing a secret. "That's the first time I've been called that. It's gonna take some getting used to. I'm Mrs. Hawthorne now."

"Yes, you are," I agreed curtly then looked out my window as she leaned away. In the reflection on the glass, I saw her lose the small smile that was playing on her lips and straighten up in her seat. I closed my eyes and took a deep breath. This whole fake marriage thing was going to be harder than I'd initially thought, especially since I seemed to be doing a bad job of it already.

I only looked at her again when Raymond stopped the car in front of my place on Central Park West. She glanced out the window and I watched her release a long breath.

"This is it?" she asked, peering back at me.

"Yes."

I got out of the car. Rubbing my temple, I made it to Raymond's side just as he opened her door and then walked to the back to get her bag. It seemed like the little fight she'd had in her back at the coffee shop had deflated during our car ride, and she just stared up at the building.

After smiling at my driver softly and thanking him when he held out her bag, she walked a few steps away from us.

"The usual time tomorrow, Mr. Hawthorne?" Raymond asked quietly, both our eyes on the woman standing just a few feet away from us.

Sighing, I pushed my hands into my pockets and shook my head. "I'll call you in the morning."

Giving me a quick nod, he got back in the car and drove away, leaving me alone on the sidewalk. Taking the few steps to close the gap that separated me from my newly acquired wife, I stood beside her.

"This is it then," she repeated, but this time it wasn't posed as a question.

"This is it," I agreed, and we stood side by side like that for a few agonizingly slow seconds.

"It's really close to the coffee shop. I was afraid you lived around Bryant Park, closer to your office." She gave me a quick look then faced forward again. "I take the subway from my apartment so I could've still done that, but this is better, of course."

"I did live close to the firm at one point. I moved here two years ago. Shall we go up?"

She nodded. I opened the door for her, and we finally entered the building we'd been staring at. I ignored the doorman's greeting and walked straight toward the elevators.

With each second it took us to reach the top floor, I could almost feel her drawing away from me more even though we were physically only inches apart. So far every interaction I'd had with her was turning out to be a disaster—not that I was expecting anything different. This was the bed I'd made for us, and now the time had come to lie in it.

Eventually, the elevator doors opened, and I stepped out ahead of her. After unlocking the apartment door, I pushed it open and turned back to look at Rose, really look at her. The quick shower she'd taken had helped with the paint splatters on her face—most of them—but not the fatigue. Her pale skin only accentuated her big and dark eyes and her long lashes. Despite looking like she had been done with the day some hours ago, somehow she still looked strong. She was a determined one and I respected that. Quite. She was clutching the handle of her bag with one hand and gripping her own elbow with the other. She met my eyes and offered me a small and unsure, but pretty smile.

Pretty.

Christ, Jack.

"Please," I murmured, gesturing to the inside of the apartment with my hand and taking a step aside so she could enter. Just as she was passing me, I reached for her bag, and I supposed I managed to surprise her because she let it go without a struggle.

"Thank you," she muttered quietly, looking around the space.

I closed the door after her, locked it, and took a deep breath before I faced her again. I was starting to feel like, somehow, the quiet had gotten louder behind the locked doors now that we were there and alone.

"Would you like to look around or would you prefer to see your room first?"

I wasn't sure if she was feeling up to a tour—I was actually confident she'd want to pass on anything I would offer that would force her to spend more time with me—but I wanted her to feel comfortable since we had two years of this, of *us* in our future.

"Thank you, but you don't have to do that. If you could show me where I'll be staying, that'll be enough."

"I wouldn't offer if I didn't want to, Rose. For the foreseeable future, this will be your home too. You should feel comfortable."

"I appreciate you saying that, I really do, but still, can I take a rain check on the tour for tonight? I have to be back at the coffee shop tomorrow morning and I'm really tired, so..."

"Of course." Walking through the foyer, I gestured toward the staircase to our right and followed her silently as she took the lead. Her hand held on to the black steel railing as she slowly and very carefully climbed up to the second floor. As soon as she was up on the landing, she stepped to the side and waited for me.

"This way," I offered, taking her to the left. The penthouse I had bought only two years earlier had four bedrooms, three of them being on the second floor. One of the rooms was set up as a home gym. The second, which was my bedroom, was on the other end of the hallway, and the third would now be Rose's. Just hours earlier it had been way too much space for only one person, but with Rose in the apartment, it seemed to shrink in size.

At the end of the short hall, I opened the door to the spacious room that would be hers and placed her overnight bag just inside before backing out again. Giving me a quick look, she stepped inside and took everything in. I had asked the interior decorator to keep it simple and functional, so there were only a few pieces of furniture in the room: a king bed, a neutral-colored headboard, nightstands, a small sitting area with one soft nude velvet chair, and another chocolate brown one next to a simple white and gold floor lamp.

"You have your own en suite through the right door," I explained when she didn't say anything. "The left door is the walk-in closet. If there is anything you don't like, let me know and I'll take care of it."

After looking around for a few seconds, she finally faced me and tucked her damp hair behind one ear. "This is... I think it's bigger than my entire apartment." When my expression didn't change, she cleared her throat and continued. "Everything looks great, Jack. I hope you didn't go to too much trouble for this."

"I believe every guest room has a bed and a chair. I didn't do anything special."

"Of course they do, but considering your guest room is so massive..." She trailed off. I waited for her to keep going, but she just shook her head. "Thank you. That's what I'm trying to say. This is beautiful, so thank you."

"You're welcome. Is there anything else I can do for you, or would you like to be alone?"

"I think I'll just try to get some sleep. I..." Pausing, she lifted her wrist to check the time. "I need to get up really early."

"Everything going okay so far? I don't want to keep you for long, but did you hear anything from your other cousin?"

Shaking her head, she moved closer to me, holding on to the door between us as if she didn't have enough strength to keep herself upright.

"A few days ago, she called, but I think she was just curious if I had gone through with it or not."

I frowned, not following. "Gone through with what? The coffee shop?"

She offered me a tired smile.

"No, she doesn't really care about that. She was trying to learn more about...us, I guess—you and me and the marriage. She isn't like Bryan, she rarely cares about things that doesn't concern her. And so far, so good with the coffee shop. There is a lot of work to be done as I'm sure you saw yourself, but I'm not complaining."

Satisfied with her answer, I reached for my tie and loosened it, noticing the way her eyes followed my movements. "Good. And you don't have to worry about Bryan either, there is nothing he can do at this point and if he does, I'll take care of it. Good night, Rose. If you need anything, my room is at the end of the hall, across from you."

Straightening, she nodded. "Thank you, and good night...Jack."

It took me a second to move. I wasn't sure why I was reluctant to leave, it couldn't possibly be because I wanted to talk to her more, but there I was just standing there like an idiot. I took a deep breath, trying to think of a parting word so I could leave, but all I managed to do was notice her smell and drown in it. Coconut and some other mysterious fruit I couldn't quite figure out. It must've been her shampoo since I'd noticed it in the car first. I gave up on trying to think of something else to say, gave her a quick nod and walked away from her before I did something stupid. Midway down the stairs, I heard Rose's door gently click shut.

FOR THE HUNDREDTH TIME, I checked the clock on my nightstand, and finally when I saw it was four AM and I still hadn't managed to fall asleep, I sat up. Rubbing my face, I sighed and got up. Not wanting to get dressed and go down yet, I stayed in my pajama pants and put on the grey t-shirt that was already hanging on the back of the chair in the corner of the room then headed toward the black steel doors that opened up to the terrace. I breathed in the cold air as soon as I stepped outside and took in the city.

It didn't take a genius to understand why I couldn't sleep, yet I'd still tried my best to ignore the fact that I wasn't alone in my apartment, that everything was just as it should be. The only issue was that my mind was determined not to let me forget about it, to forget about my wife's presence in my home. Ever since I'd left her crying in the car, it had been all I could see when I closed my eyes at night—*she* was all I could see, the look in her eyes. So lost and confused. The fact that I'd practically pushed her—us—into this wasn't helping at all. Hell, I didn't even know what to feel anymore, other than guilt that is. I was drowning in guilt. And living under the same roof with Rose...it was helping nothing at all.

Looking down at Central Park as I leaned on the railing, I tried to clear my mind so I could get back to bed and get at least a few hours of sleep in order to actually face and survive the next day and the upcoming days. But, after standing out there for God knows how long, I decided it was a futile endeavor. Just as I was turning around, I saw Rose turn the corner at the end of the terrace and let out a loud gasp when she spotted me.

One hand against her heart, the other on her knee, she bent down. Letting the blanket she was bundled in hang from her shoulders, she started to cough as if she was choking on something. Without comment, I moved toward her, and before I could decide whether I should try to help her or not, she straightened up. Her face was completely flushed, her chest falling and rising rapidly.

A second later the cause of her reaction became more clear when she opened her fist and showed me a half-eaten Snickers bar. "You almost killed me," she wheezed out, her words barely making any sense.

"Excuse me?"

"I was dying," she mumbled after attempting to clear her throat again. Finally regaining her composure, she released a long breath and pulled the blanket around herself.

"I saw that." Thinking it'd make her feel more comfortable, I turned away from her and faced the city in front of us.

After another deep breath and a cough, she took the last few steps to stand next to me. "It's getting chilly," she commented quietly, and I automatically glanced down at her feet. She was wearing socks, but she was resting one of her feet on top of the other.

"You might want to wear thicker socks," I commented, and her gaze followed mine down to her feet and she shifted in place. "But, yes, the weather is changing. You couldn't sleep?"

Out of the corner of my eye, I saw her look up at me and shake her head. I kept my eyes on the city.

"Nope. You couldn't either?" she asked, filling the silence between us.

"I tend to wake up early." That was what I was telling myself, and I certainly didn't want her to think I was struggling with having her in my space.

She hugged the blanket tighter.

"I hope your bed was comfortable."

Another quick glance at me. "It was. It's really comfortable and big. It's my first night here and it's a strange place, you know. I thought I heard something when I woke up and couldn't go back to sleep."

"I understand." I didn't prod for more details, but she kept going.

"I'll get used to it. I did manage to pass out for two hours—I was too tired not to—but then I woke up and my stomach decided it was a good time to remind me that I hadn't eaten anything in twelve hours, so..." Lifting her hand from under the blanket, she showed me the remaining few bites of her candy bar.

"Here I am with the Snickers I found in my bag. I'd give you a piece, but..."

"I think I'll live. You should've told me you were hungry when we first came in. We do have a kitchen downstairs."

I glanced at her then and she looked up at me with a smile. "A kitchen? What a novelty. As tempting as that sounds, if I eat anything more than this, I'll stay up all night and I won't be able to do anything tomorrow. I need to start getting ready in a few hours anyway, so this will hold me over. Plus, nothing beats chocolate."

"You should go back to bed then."

"I will," she murmured, agreeing easily. "I'll go back inside in a few minutes."

I nodded, but I knew she couldn't see me; she was watching the night sky. We fell into another long stretch of silence and, not sure what I should do, I crossed my arms against my chest and leaned back against the wall at the same time she moved forward and propped her forearms on the railing.

"The lake looks beautiful from up here," she whispered. Glancing at me over her shoulder, she waited for an answer. "You must love the view." I nodded in agreement, and a small sigh fell from her lips as she faced forward again. "The leaves will start changing color in a few weeks. I love Central Park in fall, and the lake is one of my favorite spots. It's so cool that you can see it from here. Do you have a favorite spot, Jack?"

"In Central Park?"

"Yes."

As the loud sound of sirens filled the night, I took a few seconds to answer so I wouldn't have to raise my voice. All bundled up in her blanket, she faced me, ready to hear my answer. She was definitely an insistent one, my wife.

"I never thought about it. I guess the lake is all right."

She arched an eyebrow and just stared at me.

I returned her stare. "Is there anything I can help you with at the coffee shop?"

She cocked her head and studied me as if she could figure me out if she only looked hard enough. I had no idea what she was thinking. Not only that, I had no idea what I was doing out there, pulling her into more conversation when I'd decided the moment after we'd said I do that I didn't want to get too close to her. The only thing I had to do was keep reminding myself that this was going to be a business deal and nothing more.

"You already helped. If it wasn't for you, it would've never happened. When I got Gary's permission to use the space and we signed that contract, I started ordering the furniture, the machines, and all the other bits and pieces I'll need. I knew it would take time for everything to get here, so I thought I was being smart. When...Gary and Angela passed away, I completely forgot about the whole thing. Then things started to arrive, but I no longer had a coffee shop to put them in, so I had to rent a storage place for the items from the companies that couldn't hold my orders for the foreseeable future, like the chairs. Some things I bought were from sales and other deals, so they wouldn't cancel my orders, either. When I came to your office that day, I had no hope of things going my way. I was on my way to another job interview."

Uncomfortable with her admission, I shifted in place and cleared my throat. Before I could stop her, she kept going. Not only was she insistent, she was turning out to be quite the talker.

"So, as weird and awkward as this marriage is and probably will be for quite some time as we get used to having each other around, I'm really thankful for it. I know we made a deal and obviously it's not gonna be a one-sided thing, but I'm still very thankful that you decided not to get a divorce."

"You don't have to keep thanking me. It's a business deal. I'm getting a free property out of this. We're both benefiting."

Her eyes steady on me, she nodded and rearranged the blanket on her shoulders. "I know. I just wanted you to know the details, too."

I already knew the details surrounding her situation, but I didn't think it would be wise to let her know that.

"Why do *you* want it then? What are you planning on doing with it once our deal runs its course?"

I didn't know how to answer that question, so I took the easy out.

"I rather not share."

"Oh. Okay."

When I didn't comment further, she took a deep breath and looked toward the corner where she had appeared from. After giving Central Park another quick look, she sighed. "You probably want to be alone, so I'll just go back to my room. Tomorrow is gonna be a long day of painting anyway. Good night, Jack."

I watched her in silence up until she turned her back to me and took a few steps away. Sighing, I straightened up from the wall and took her spot at the rail. Turns out I didn't like putting that hurt look on her face. Raising my voice, I asked, "You think you'll be able to go back to sleep?"

"I don't think so, but I'll rest a bit."

I'd thought as much. I didn't think I was gonna get any sleep either. How are you handling their death?" The question rolled off my tongue before I even thought about what I was going to say to keep her out on the terrace for longer. So much for not wanting to talk to her.

The amount of time it took for her to reappear at my side was unmistakably shorter than the time it had taken her to walk away.

"Can I be honest?" she asked into the night as I studied her profile.

"Usually, I prefer people lying to me, but if you insist..."

That earned me a side-eye look.

"I'm not sure exactly how I feel," she responded finally. I thought I heard a small smile in her voice when she started to speak, but I didn't know her enough to be sure. "Obviously, I'm sad about it. That's not what I mean, but it just doesn't feel real. We didn't talk every day, or even every week, after I turned eighteen, I moved out of their house and after that barely even saw Angela. That's how she wanted it anyway. But, I talked to my uncle about once every two weeks or so, and sometimes he even had enough time to have lunch with me. He always seemed to tolerate having me around a bit more. Since you worked with them before, you probably already know this story, but they took me in when I was nine. My dad had just passed away. Cancer. And even though Gary and my dad were only half-siblings and they hadn't been in contact for more than fifteen years, Gary agreed to become my guardian."

"What about your mom?"

"I don't remember her. She left us when I was two. I believe they looked for her, but from what my uncle told me she had disappeared. Maybe changed her name, who knows. So they took me in. I can't say they were always nice to me, I remember too many nights I'd cried myself to sleep, but at least I didn't go into the system. I didn't have anyone, not really."

"Your cousins?"

"Bryan and Jodi. Ah. I think they just took their cues from Angela and stayed clear. They're just a few years older than me, yet they barely talked to me. I was the very unwanted and bothersome niece."

I was watching the park when she started her story, but my eyes went back to her when I felt her gaze on me.

"That was probably a little more personal information than you were looking for."

"It's okay," I replied simply, not giving her anything else. "I think for the marriage to look believable to everyone around us, we need to know personal details like these."

"Okay then. To give a more definite answer to your question: I'm doing better—not great, but better. There are days I wake up and completely forget it happened because they haven't really been super involved in my life for a long time, but I think it's okay to admit that I have days where I miss hearing my uncle's voice." I heard a small chuckle and genuine happiness in her next words. "He used to read me bedtime stories for a few years in the beginning, once or twice a week. If you know him at all, you also know how unlike him that is, but he worked pretty hard and it was the only time I'd get to see him. He was always a little gruff about it and tried to read super quick as if he was racing against time, but then he'd get into the story and read longer than he had promised. I used to really look forward to that when I was little. '*I only have ten minutes for you tonight, Rose.*' He'd always start with that." She paused, but before I could even comment, she turned the tables back onto me. "What about your parents? Are they alive?"

"Yes."

"How is your relationship with them?"

"We're not close."

"Oh? You had a falling out?"

"You could say that. I haven't seen them in years."

"Do they know you got married?" she asked.

"I didn't inform them, no, but I'm sure they'll hear it from someone soon enough." I glanced at her and our eyes met for a brief moment before I looked away. "I'm afraid they wouldn't approve of my choices, so I didn't feel the need to let them know."

"I understand." There was an awkward pause. "Wow. I really needed that confidence boost, so thanks for that."

I didn't think she understood at all, but I didn't correct her.

"And can I say two peas in a pod? Look at us, we don't really have any family."

"Looks like that."

She huffed out a breath and leaned on the railing, mirroring my stance. After a peaceful stretch of silence between us, an ambulance passed with the sirens blaring and screeched to a halt somewhere down below us, interrupting my thoughts. Having a heart-to-heart conversation with my wife under the night sky was absolutely not the best way to keep my distance.

"When do you think you'll be opening the coffee shop?" I asked, shifting the subject to something safer.

"I'm mostly ready, mostly being the operative word. When I finish painting, I'll have all the big things out of the way. The chairs and the sign that will go outside are coming soon, and I need to buy a few more kitchen things." She sighed and rested her chin on her propped-up hand. "I think three weeks? It depends on a lot of things. All the paperwork is ready, so there is no reason not to jump right in. Thank you for that, too—you know, for handling the paperwork stuff."

I noticed her trying to cover a yawn.

"Don't mention it. You can't paint to save your life. You know that, right?"

"Excuse me? I paint beautifully," she shot back with a frown on her face.

"From what I saw today, it was patchy. I could still see the red of the old paint underneath. That's not an indication of beautiful painting."

She snorted. "Again, excuse me, but that was a very bright red—it would show no matter what I did with only one coat of new paint over it. Everyone knows that. First coat is always patchy. I did the hard part then you came at the end and stole my work."

"Everyone knows that?" I asked with an arched eyebrow.

"Yes! Ask any professional painter."

"How many professional painters do you know exactly?"

"How many do you know?"

I met her eyes and shrugged. "A few." Relaxing a little further, I waited for her comeback.

"Fine. You win that one. I don't know any, but it still doesn't change the fact that I paint beautifully."

"If you say so."

"I do say so. You did one wall, but I'm gonna paint the whole place. Say I don't paint beautifully after you see that."

"Actually, since you'll be painting my property, I'd like to make sure you're not ruining my walls. I'll be there tomorrow to keep an eye on things."

"You're kidding."

"No."

"Fine. Keep an eye on things then. The property might be yours now, but those will be my walls for the next two years. I'm not letting you mess anything up."

Trying to cover my unexpected smile, I cleared my throat. "Thank you for the permission. If you're planning on doing more of your 'beautiful' painting, as you put it, you need to get some more rest."

"Are you provoking me?"

"Why would I want to do that?" And wasn't that the truth? Why the hell would I want to do that? Too bad I didn't have an answer to my own question.

She faced me, and I was forced to return her gaze.

"You really think you can do a better job than me?" she asked.

I arched an eyebrow. "I did do a better job than you."

"Right. Instead of just keeping an eye on things, pick up a paint roller then."

Apparently, I was canceling my meetings for the next day or so. "We'll see how it goes."

She paused.

"I know it looks pretty bare right now, but wait until you see everything together. More importantly, I'm really good with coffee, and the pastries will be to die for. If I can manage to do everything that's in my mind, it'll look great in about a week or two."

"What else is on your mind?" I asked, genuinely curious, her enthusiasm catching.

She smiled up at me. "I think I'm gonna keep the rest to myself, just in case I screw it up or can't get it done in time."

"Sounds like you have everything planned and under control."

"There are so many more things I need to deal with though, a million little things. Are you going to be there on opening day?"

"Do you need me to be there?" It didn't matter what her answer was—I knew I was going to be there anyway.

"I wouldn't say need—"

When the wind kicked up, pushing at her hair, she lifted her hands to get it out of her eyes and the blanket started to slip down from her shoulders. I straightened and caught it midway to her waist. Suddenly we were standing too close and she was trapped between me and the damn blanket. My eyes met her surprised big, brown ones, and I halted, not so sure what to do with the blanket and *her*.

I cleared my throat. She dropped her hands after having pulled all her hair to one side, and I let her grab the edges of the blanket from me.

"Thanks," she murmured as I took a step back.

Goddammit!

After a brief pause, she went back to answering my question. "It's not so much a need, but it would be good just in case Jodi or Bryan show up. I don't think they will, but after tonight who knows."

"I'll try to free up my schedule if you think I need to be

there." A quick glance at my watch, and I noticed the time: almost five. After not wanting to talk to her, I had spent an hour doing the exact opposite. I straightened up. "I'm heading back inside."

"Oh, okay," she mumbled, still holding on to the blanket I had almost reluctantly let go of just a few seconds earlier.

"If I'm going to paint an entire coffee shop, I need to get some sleep," I added at her puzzled expression regarding my abrupt exit.

"Wait a minute—you were serious about that?"

"I'm not sure how many times I'll need to repeat this, but if I say something, I always mean it."

"I thought you were just..."

I raised my brows. "You thought I was what?"

"Never mind. You won't be painting an entire coffee shop, though—I'll be painting too."

"We'll see how you do first before I let you do that."

Her eyes narrowed. "Fine. I'll show you how it's done tomorrow then."

"Meet you downstairs at seven? Or would that be too early for you?"

"Seven is perfect."

"Right. Good night then, Rose."

"Good night, Jack."

CHAPTER FIVE

ROSE

T*wo weeks later*

I HAD OFFICIALLY MOVED in with Jack Hawthorne, AKA my beloved fake husband, the night he had returned from his London trip, which could also count as the beginning of my sleepless nights. The next day, just as we had discussed, he accompanied me back to the coffee shop because he didn't trust me with the walls of his newly acquired free property. While I did get him to agree—after a very convincing and long talk—that I could, in fact, do a beautiful paint job, he ended up painting most of the place himself, souring my victory.

He exasperated me to no end the entire time and I had no clue what to do with him.

He also wanted me to clear out my apartment in the East Village right away, but I ignored his wishes and slowly packed everything during the painting business. The hell with Bryan's threats.

Sitting alone in the middle of the coffee shop, munching on a sandwich I had put together in the back, I was waiting for the IKEA delivery guys to bring me my bookcase. Soon after, they arrived, but before I could tackle that project, the chairs were delivered.

When everything was said and done—the bookcase assembled, the chairs where I thought they should be—hours had passed, and I'd only just then sat my ass down for the first time. I groaned and leaned my head back against the wall. I thought closing my eyes just for a few seconds wasn't a bad idea because my eyesight was starting to get alarmingly blurry.

Of course doing that only reminded me of how much I needed more sleep. Every morning, I quietly got dressed and, as if I were an intruder, tiptoed out of Jack Hawthorne's little mansion to get to the shop. At night, I chose to disappear into my room the moment I stepped into his apartment.

All my attempts at talking with my husband had failed, one after another, so I had stopped after attempt number four. The more questions I asked, the more I tried to talk to him, either the quicker he annoyed me or the quicker he walked away from me. The short conversation we'd had on the terrace that first night had been our longest one.

Yet...*yet*, even after the painting was done, he had shown up every single night to pick me up on his way to the apartment. Was it to check on the property?

To say I was confused about my husband would've been an understatement. I had no idea what to think about the man.

He had been the one to make the marriage offer, but with the way he was acting, so cool and distant at all times, you'd think I'd held an invisible gun to his head to make him say I *do*.

I didn't see things changing any time soon if I didn't do anything about it.

I also had no idea how we were going to keep this charade up if we actually had to stand next to each other and talk to people as a married couple. If anyone had seen us working together at the coffee shop, or even on the terrace that first night, they would've thought we were out on a never-ending blind date, forced to endure every minute instead of making a quick escape.

I must've been on the verge of falling asleep because when I heard a loud knock, I leaped up and somehow managed to hit the side of my thigh on the edge of the table in front of me. "Jesus Christ!" Pressing my hand to my leg to ease the pain, I hopped over to the door just as another loud knock filled the coffee shop.

Feeling a little drowsy and maybe a little jumpy too, I lifted the side of the newspaper that was protecting everything going on inside from wandering eyes. My heart rate *somewhat* slowed down when I saw it was just Jack Hawthorne standing on the other side of the glass. Lifting my finger to indicate it'd be a minute, I taped the newspaper back in place and let out a long breath before I started unlocking the door.

Here we go, I thought.

When he stepped inside, I closed and locked the door behind him. "Jack?" Massaging my leg with my left palm, I let my eyes wander his body from head to toe. If someone had forced me to say one positive thing about my husband, it would be that he was born to wear suits. I would have been lying if I'd said I minded that. The black suit, white button-down, and black tie he was wearing at that moment somehow managed to make his ocean blue eyes stand out even more, and I stared at him a little longer than necessary or acceptable. "What are you doing here?"

"That's a great question. I wondered the same thing, because it's not like I come here every night or anything. I called you an hour ago. You didn't answer."

"What?" I asked, confused. Rubbing the bridge of my nose, I tried to snap out of my still half-asleep state. If I was checking him out and noticing how his suit accentuated his intense eyes, how his stubble looked so amazingly good on him, I must have still been in dreamland. Instead of giving an answer, he went with another question, looking all kinds of exasperated with me.

"Where is your phone, Rose?"

Taking care not to bump into him, I walked around his perfectly muscled body and perfectly stubbled face back to the counter and leaned over to get to my phone, which I had left on one of the lower shelves a few hours earlier. "I haven't touched it since the chairs got here, and I must have put it on silent by mistake. Is something wrong?" I looked down at the screen and saw two missed calls from Jack Hawthorne and one from Sally. Sally was gonna have to wait while I dealt with my husband.

"Are you okay?" he asked with a frown on his face.

Glancing up at him, I was finally starting to get it together—only I still didn't have it together *enough* to realize he'd asked a question, so I didn't answer. I just kept staring. For several long seconds, I was thinking he'd somehow managed to look better at the end of the day, *every day*, while I looked worse as the day went on. Not one single light brown hair was out of place on his head. The longer I looked, the deeper his brows dipped, which added this weird appeal to him that I shouldn't have noticed. He looked amazing when he frowned—which happened often, as I could attest to—and I was starting to like that expression on him more and more. He didn't need the frown to make him look all intense and broody, but it definitely worked in his favor.

"Rose?"

"Hmm?"

"What's wrong with you?"

Accepting the fact that I had long ago lost my mind since I couldn't stop thinking about how truly attractive he was, I chose to act like nothing was wrong and nodded. Then I realized that was the wrong direction for my head to move and quickly shook my head instead. Flustered at being caught, I moved to stand behind the counter to put some space between us. I wasn't planning on throwing myself at him, but still.

"I fell asleep for a few minutes so I'm a little out of it, that's all. Why did you say you called again?"

"I was heading out for dinner and was going to ask you if you'd like to join me. I ate already."

I yawned. "Oh, no. Was it a work thing? Did I miss the first work thing? I'm sorry if—"

"No, it was just me. I thought we could go over a few things and have dinner."

That was a first—him voluntarily offering to talk and have dinner. "Go over things...like?"

"We'll do it another time. I'm assuming you're done here since you were sleeping?"

The guy didn't budge. He didn't smile. He certainly didn't laugh or look happy or look...anything other than broody and serious, really.

"I didn't mean to fall asleep. I was just taking a break, resting my eyes and I guess I dozed off for a little while."

Looking around the shop with disapproval, he shook his head. "It's not safe for you to be here alone at night, let alone fall asleep. What if you hadn't locked the door, which you forgot to do before? It could've been anyone walking through that door and finding you sleeping."

"But I didn't forget to lock the door. It was just that one time. I've been making sure it's locked no matter what time it is," I countered. I wouldn't admit that for a brief moment when I'd heard his hard knock, I'd been just a bit scared.

My reply earned me another disapproving look. "I see you finally got your chairs," he commented, his gaze taking everything in.

"Yes. The delivery was delayed, but I finally got them a few hours ago. What do you think?" I asked. Even I could hear the hopeful tone in my voice. He was the first one to see the place filled with the furniture and so close to what it would look like on opening day. I was desperate to hear from someone that it wasn't just my imagination and it actually did look good.

Our eyes met as I held my breath, waiting.

"About?" he asked.

I tamped down the urge to groan.

He couldn't find any fault in them—there was no way. They looked perfect with the color scheme. Elegant, chic, comfy, inviting—all the good stuff. So, I smiled instead and tried again. "Everything. The chairs, tables, everything."

He followed my gaze, but his hard features stayed exactly the same, not a single smile in sight.

"Is it done?"

"Not yet," I said slowly, my smile dimming. "I'm working on it, but it's pretty close now."

All eleven—I hated that it was an odd number—of my wooden round tables were exactly where I wanted them, and I'd placed the brownish nude cotton-velvet chairs that looked gorgeous with the flooring and the freshly painted walls in their places. I'd also taken out the black steel bar stools and the dark green cushions from the kitchen where I'd kept them stacked. They were the same material as the chairs, and I had put them all in front of the coffee bar I had running along the front windows. It already looked amazing, but apparently only to my eyes.

"Never mind," I said, breaking the silence in an effort to avoid hearing Jack's negative thoughts. His rigid body language and disapproving gaze were telling me everything I didn't want to hear anyway. "I'm sorry, you don't have to deal with this. If you need to be somewhere else, I wouldn't want to keep you. I'm gonna be here for another hour I think, to put some stuff up."

He opened his mouth to speak, but I got there before he could.

"I know—I'll go to your place when I'm done here. You don't have to keep coming back here every day. I know the way."

His hands in his pockets, he walked toward the big archway that connected the two sections of the coffee shop and turned toward the back, out of my sight. I'd have bet money he was shaking his head after noticing my bookcase sprawled on the floor, or if not that, he was probably scalding the bookcase with a disapproving look. I'd assembled it just fine on my own, but I hadn't dared to actually lift it and move it. That would be the next day's job, or the next. It all depended on how my back was feeling.

"How are you planning to get in exactly?" he asked, his voice just barely rising so I could hear him.

"Get in where?"

"Into my apartment—*our* apartment."

Our apartment. *Dear God.* Exactly when would I get used to the fact that I was living with *this* man now, and how, for two entire weeks, had it not even crossed my mind how I'd get back into his little mansion? Then again, since he came to the coffee shop every night to pick me up, I had no reason to think of keys.

To be fair, he had never acted as if I wasn't welcome in his home. Sure, he was curt and exasperating sometimes, but still, every night, he offered to give the tour he had mentioned that first night and asked if I'd had anything to eat. You'd think that was sweet of him, but that was all he would say. Still sweet though.

"I tried to leave a set of keys with you this morning, but when I knocked on your door, you were already gone and I had to leave for work," he explained. Surprised, I couldn't think of anything to say. Then he reappeared in the archway and came back to stand in front of me, patiently waiting for an explanation.

It hit me, and I winced. "Ah, is that why you come here to pick me up every night?" I blew out a breath and sighed. "I was just thinking I shouldn't keep apologizing to you, but for the last time, I'm sorry. I hope you haven't been cutting your plans short and coming here just because I don't have a key."

"No need to apologize. I only thought about the key last night, and no, I'm not coming here every night just because you don't have a key. Today, I was already on the east side, and when I couldn't get in touch with you, I thought I'd come here and give you a ride back."

What about all the other nights? I wanted to ask but kept my mouth shut.

"I'm still having trouble sleeping. I'm not exactly sure why, but I always wake up at four or five. I wait until six and then leave. Instead of tossing and turning in bed, I try to do something useful around here." I met his gaze, out of words, out of explanations.

"I know what time you leave, Rose."

As soon as he finished his sentence, he started to take off his suit jacket, and my attention shifted again.

"Uh, what are you doing?"

"I'm assuming the bookcase won't be living on the floor and you want it up, correct?" He looked around and then pointed to the exact spot I'd planned to put it, right next to where my humongous espresso machine was going to happily take up residence in just a few days. "There?"

"Yes, that's wha..."

He unbuttoned his cuffs and my gaze dropped to follow his movements. This again? Then he started to roll his sleeves up, and I couldn't remember what I had been about to say—which was becoming annoying, if nothing else—but also his fingers looked really long. Apart from having strong features, insanely beautiful eyes, a very enjoyable-to-look-at face, and a jawline that worked *extremely* well with that broody personality he had going on, he also had very manly hands. That must've been nice for him. They were easily twice the size of mine. They looked strong.

The kind that made you look twice, if you were into that sort of thing. Apparently I was. Very.

Jeez, Rose.

I mentally shook myself out of it, looked away, cleared my throat, and spoke up. "I was planning on doing that tomorrow. You don't have to get your clothes dirty, Jack. I can handle it myself."

I wasn't one of those people who would reject help at all times, but getting help from Jack...I didn't want to be indebted to him more than I already was.

Ignoring me, he moved toward the bookcase while still working on those sleeves, for Christ's sake. I followed him in quick steps, my eyes—the traitors—stealing glances at his hands rolling those sleeves up. He was still wearing his ring, he never took it off.

"Jack, I can take care of it. You really don't have to—"

"You don't have to handle it all on your own. I'm here. I'm capable of moving a bookcase."

"I know that. Of course you are, but I'm saying you don't have to do it. I'm used to handling things on my own, and that's what I'm comfortable wi—"

The sleeves had been rolled meticulously, so he lifted his head to give me a long look. I shut up.

Fine.

If he wanted to get his expensive suit dirty, he was welcome to do so. After scolding me with a simple stare, he started to walk around the bookcase.

"It might scratch the flooring," he said as he glanced up at me and then back down.

"No, it won't. I put four of those soft thingies under the legs, so it won't scratch."

That got him to look at me. "Thingies," he deadpanned.

I couldn't help it—my lips slowly curved up and I smiled,

with my teeth showing and all. "Sure, it sounds ridiculous when *you* say it." If one of us didn't relax around the other, I was surely going to commit murder before the twenty-four months ended. Since I didn't think Jack ever relaxed or *had* ever relaxed before, it looked like I was going to be the lucky winner in this marriage.

I was going to try my best to loosen up around him and ignore the fact that he was the type of guy I always stayed away from.

Because we were complete opposites.

Because we had very different outlooks on life.

Because, because, because...

He was standoffish, prickly, arrogant at times, aloof.

He gave me a quick unimpressed look and turned his back to me. "That's because it *is* a ridiculous word."

When he wasn't looking at me anymore, I took a deep breath and glanced up to the heavens, though I couldn't actually see them. "Your suit is gonna get dirty," I said for the last time. When those hard eyes met mine, I lifted my hands up. "Fine. Don't say I didn't warn you. Oh, wait!" Before he could give me a sarcastic answer, I rushed out of the alcove, all the while yelling over my shoulder, "Give me a second and I'll wipe it down first."

He didn't say anything so I assumed he was waiting for me to come back. As soon as I had a wet dish towel, I hurried back only to see he already had the bookcase up and standing.

"It's not a big thing, but I want you to meet some of the partners in my firm," he started as I stepped aside with the towel in my hand and he started to push the bookcase toward its new home. "There is a dinner tomorrow with two of the partners and a potential client, nothing formal, just a simple meal. They know we got married and asked me to bring you with me. I know you're working day and night to open this place so if you can't spare the time, you don't have to join us for this one. I'll explain it to them."

I put the towel down on one of the tables and pulled the two chairs and another table that were in his way to the side. "No, I'll come."

He stopped pushing and tilted his head to look at me from the other side of the bookcase. "Are you sure? Like I said, you don't have to."

"We made a business deal, right? And you keep helping me when you come here. I have to do something in return," I answered as I gripped the other end of the bookcase and started helping him turn it around so we could push it the rest of the way with the back facing toward the wall. A dinner wasn't such a bad thing as long as we didn't freeze up and he didn't go all cold on me in front of other people—which wasn't my problem.

"Right," he said in a clipped tone, and we both started pushing.

The *only* problem about going out to dinner with Jack and his partners was that I could only imagine what kind of restaurant partners at a high-profile law firm would go to, and unfortunately, I didn't have anything nice enough to wear to a place like that. Every cent I had earned up till that day, I'd put aside for the dream coffee shop I would open in New York. Now that dream was actually coming true, and when you were working as hard as humanly possible to do that, other things usually suffered, like my fashion choices.

"So, I'll come. Okay, stop. Just give me a sec and I'll move the tables so we can push through."

While I moved the table on the right, he took care of the one on the left. Then we pushed the chairs aside, opening up enough space for the big bookcase to go through.

"You want it to touch the wall? The dinner is at seven."

"Yes, flush against the wall. I'll be ready before that. Sally will drop by for a few hours tomorrow to help so it shouldn't be a very long day like today was."

With a small grunt from me, we started pushing again until it was in place. After putting the tables and chairs back where they'd originally been, we stopped.

I stepped all the way back to the archway so I could make sure it was centered on the wall. Jack followed and silently stood beside me.

"Thank you. That looks perfect right there." I glanced at him and caught his small nod.

"Sally?" he asked, his eyes still assessing the bookcase.

"My employee, the second and last one. I hired her while you were in London. She's been here a few times to talk about what we're going to do here, and she officially starts on opening day."

"Who is the first?"

"Oh, that would be Owen. We briefly worked together at a café before, that's where I know him from. His pastries are amazing. He'll be here part-time, come in around four-thirty in the morning and start on the baking before I join him. Sally will help me in the front."

"What else needs to get done today?" he asked.

Even though the bookcase was perfectly placed, the two tables in front of it just didn't look right where they were, I retraced my steps to move them so they'd be on the sides of the bookcase instead of in front of it.

When I looked up, Jack was already standing across from me, grabbing the edge of the table and helping me lift it. "What do you mean what else?" I asked as we put the table down where I wanted and then moved the chairs.

"What else needs to be done?"

We went to the other table and repeated our actions. "You don—"

"If you say I don't have to help one more time—"

"As a matter of fact, I was *not* going to say that." I actually was. "You should listen first before accusing someone. You'd think, as a lawyer, you'd know that." When he looked at me, I gave him a sweet smile without teeth. He didn't return it, of course. He wasn't a fan of sarcastic comments; I had discovered that much on my own, which was probably why I enjoyed making them in the first place.

"I want to get this up." I walked behind the counter and stood directly in front of where I wanted the floating shelf to be. "I drilled the holes, and the brackets are secured and everything, but it's a pretty damn big wooden shelf, almost two feet I think, so I couldn't lift it on my own."

He joined me, and I moved to the side to give him space. It was a big enough area for four people to work comfortably, but still. After looking at his hands that much, I couldn't trust myself.

"You drilled these?" he asked, inspecting the brackets.

My feet were starting to kill me again, so I leaned against the counter and waited for his disapproving comments to start. I had some comebacks still. "Yeah. I borrowed a drill from the chair guy and got them done quickly. Go ahead, tell me how bad of a job I did. I'm ready for it."

He sighed and glanced at me over his shoulder. "Where is the shelf, Rose?"

I straightened and squatted. There was a lot of pain involved in that process. "Here." I pulled just one side of the wood from under the counter so he could see it. He held on to the other side and we lifted it up with a small grunt from me then placed it on the counter. The damn thing was extremely heavy, not to mention expensive, but it was going to look perfect with the dark green walls.

There were a few seconds of inspection on his side then he grabbed his end again. "Ready?"

I released a long breath, nodded, and gripped the edge tighter.

He paused and gave me a new look I couldn't interpret.

"On three. You ready?"

My exhaustion was coming back in full force so I simply nodded again, heaving it up when he said three. I was pretty sure he was taking most of the weight because my arms didn't hurt as much as I expected them to, and in a few seconds, he'd slid the shelf onto the brackets and we were done.

Facing me, he studied my face. "Can we leave now?"

Again, I just nodded.

He strolled out into the open area in front of the counter.

I went into the kitchen and grabbed my things from the big island. Coming out of the kitchen with one arm in my jacket, I struggled to get the other one in.

Jack was rolling down his sleeves. "You don't have anything else heavy that needs to be moved, do you?"

Frowning and trying to think as I watched him, I shook my head. "No. That was the last one, I believe."

Then he put his suit jacket back on, and he looked just as he had when he'd showed up earlier, minus the tie.

"You look like you're about to crash."

He wasn't even looking at me—how did he know?

"I think I can make that happen." Feeling a little silly after his comment and about the fact that I was still struggling with the other jacket arm, I cleared my throat. "The crashing, I mean." He came forward and, with a long-suffering sigh, pulled the jacket off, freeing my arm. Then he held it up for me and I felt myself blush as I successfully got both arms in.

"Thank you," I muttered quietly.

"I'll call Raymond so he can park out front." He was looking down at his phone, but then his eyes met mine for a brief second. "You look worse than you did last week."

I opened my mouth then decided to close it. I looked down and noticed that my knees were covered in dust. *Nice touch, Rose. Really nice touch.* I gently dusted myself off, all the while thinking who knew what other substances I had on my face or what said face actually looked like. Jack apparently did know, and it so happened to look worse than it had the week before. No biggie. Every husband made comments like that to their wives...I thought. Essentially, we were settling into married life. I thought he was broody male perfection, and he thought I was...well, to be honest, I was too scared to ask and hear his answer.

I sighed and looked up so I could meet his gaze. "I can't believe I'm saying this, but I think I'm actually starting to consider keeping you around as my husband, permanently, Jack. I'm really liking these compliments so far, but I'm warning you, you can't blame me when all these pretty words start to go to my head."

I thought I imagined his lips pressing together in an effort to hold back a smile, though maybe it was a lip twitch. I would never know, but I squinted to make sure I was seeing right. Then again, my eyesight was still kind of blurry, so I was almost certain it had been just a trick of my eye.

When he commented in his businesslike tone, I knew for sure there were no smiles involved. "Would you like me to lie to you instead? I'm not sure I can be that guy for you."

"Oh, no. I know you're not that guy. Like I said, I'm content with my choice of husband right now. We're settling into married life. When I ask you if I look fat in my jeans one day, I will always count on you to give me your honest answer. I'm sure it'll come in handy."

"If you have everything you need, we can leave. Raymond is waiting out front." After pocketing his phone, he met my eyes. "You're not fat."

And right when I thought he wasn't even listening to a word I was saying.

I grabbed my handbag from the counter where I had left it while I was struggling to get into my jacket then I followed Jack outside.

"I could lose a few pounds, actually—ten, maybe fifteen. Chocolates are great for your soul and happiness, but they don't tend to be good for the hips. You know how the saying goes, right? A moment on the lips, forever on the hips."

He stepped out onto the sidewalk as I turned off the lights and set the alarm.

"If you can't give up chocolate maybe you can work out more."

After locking everything up, I turned to him and caught him looking at my ass. My face heated, but thankfully, the chilly air prevented it from being obvious. Trying to ignore where he had been looking when he'd said his last words, I tried to play it cool by placing my hand on my heart and saying, "See, now you're just trying to spoil me. If you keep this up, I'll never want to leave you when the time comes."

His eyes focused on my hand and I knew, I *knew* what he was going to say before he even parted his lips.

"You're not wearing your ring."

"It's in my bag. It's a very expensive ring, Jack. I don't want anything to happen to it while I'm working."

He gave me an unimpressed look then turned around and left me standing on the sidewalk. His ring was on.

We were settling into married life just fine.

At least I thought so.

The number of times Jack Hawthorne smiled: nil.

CHAPTER SIX

ROSE

"Rose! Your phone is ringing!" Sally shouted from the main area where she was unloading some old books I had bought from the cutest bookstore earlier that day.

"Coming!" I yelled back from the kitchen where *I* was unloading a huge amount of baking and sandwich-making staples. Putting down the half-empty sugar bag I was getting ready to pour into a huge glass jar, I came out of the kitchen.

"It just stopped ringing," Sally commented, her eyes still on the book in her hand. Then she resumed her humming to the soft music coming through the speakers.

Even though she wasn't looking at me from her spot on the floor in front of the bookcase, I nodded and scrounged in my bag to find my phone. Just as my hand connected with it, it started to go off again. Pulling it out, I saw his name flashing on the screen.

Jack Hawthorne.

I thought maybe I should change it to *Ball and Chain* sometime.

I checked the clock on the wall and hesitated. I was sure he was calling about the dinner with the partners.

My finger hovering over the green button, I made an unintelligible sound in my throat. I wasn't sure if I really wanted to answer a call from Jack at that moment. I clicked on the side button to silence it and put it on the counter, just staring at it as if he would magically appear on the screen and give me a scowling look.

It stopped ringing and I sighed. I was being stupid.

After we'd headed home the night before, he had given me the keys for the apartment, and I had gone straight up to my room again. Since I was up at five AM again, I'd pulled the same disappearing act I had all the days before. It wasn't that he wouldn't guess where I'd gone if he came looking for me again, but I was starting to think maybe I was being impolite by not hanging around.

With Jack being proper and polite at all times, every one of my actions was...well, I was sticking out like a sore thumb. The guy had moved my bookcase, helped me with the wooden shelf, *and* painted my walls, for crying out loud. Men like Jack had people to do stuff like that for them. He had a driver. His house was perfect. He always wore expensive suits, day in and day out. He was distant with everyone. Again, men like that had other people do their dirty work. Living with the Colesons I had seen people like him plenty of times.

When I was a teenager, I would go out with *the* family when they wanted to show me off to their friends—not because they loved me like their own or anything remotely close to that, but because they wanted their rich friends to think they were generous and big-hearted people.

Look at us, we saved this girl.

I remembered going to fancy restaurants and dinner parties 'as a family' but ending up being completely ignored by everyone, including Gary, who was the only one who cared about me even a little. All I did was wear what Angela wanted me to wear, show up, eat what was put in front of me, be quiet and look happy.

However, my happiest memories were not born in those places with those people. They were born in the kitchen of their home where I spent most of my time when I wasn't in my room, and they were made with the housekeeper, Susan O'Donnell, who I had breakfast and dinner with every day. Some days, Gary wanted me to join them in the dining room, but they weren't like Susie, who made me laugh with her stories. They didn't have easy conversations even when it was just the four of them. They didn't laugh from the heart, didn't love from the heart.

Still, there was one fact we'd all agreed on: Gary had saved me. Reluctantly or not. I was thankful, just like they wanted me to be, and I would be for the rest of my life.

However—and that is a loaded *however*—I couldn't say I'd forgotten about those dinners, the house parties, the get-togethers, and tonight's dinner with the partners was one of the last things I wanted to do, but I had made a deal. Playing pretend was something I wasn't so bad at. Didn't mean I enjoyed it, but I wasn't bad at it.

When the screen lit up with a new text message, I picked it up.

Jack: Answer your phone.

For some reason, that simple text had me smiling harder than a text that short should have. It definitely drew Sally's attention.

"What's going on? Good news?" she asked, her neck stretched so she could see what I was doing.

I waved her off. "Nothing. Just a text." A text that was pure Jack Hawthorne.

"Oh! Share with the class, please. Love stories are my favorite kind of stories."

"Unfortunately, no love story here." I still hadn't told her I was married, not because I was trying to hide it but because I didn't know how to explain my husband. "Maybe you've spent enough time with the stories there. Wanna switch out books for sugar and flour?"

"Sure." In one quick move, she was up and sauntering toward me, her ponytail swishing from side to side. "You mind if I turn on the music back there, too?"

"Not at all. Go for it."

I grabbed my phone and headed toward the books that were scattered on the floor. I lowered myself onto the cushion she had been sitting on, crossed my legs, and took a deep breath. As Sally started another playlist on Spotify, I called Jack back instead of waiting for him to call me once again.

He answered on the third ring. "Rose."

"Jack."

I kept waiting for him to say more since he was the one who had called first, but he said nothing. "If you're busy, I can call later."

"No. I wouldn't answer if I was busy."

"Okay then. Why were you calling?"

I was hoping maybe dinner had been canceled.

"It's almost five. We need to be at the restaurant at seven. I'm heading out of the office in a minute—would you like me to pick you up?"

"Oh, yes please. Around six, maybe?" My eye caught on a book that was still in one of the cardboard boxes, so I grabbed it and checked the back cover.

"That won't work. With the traffic, it will take us at least forty-five minutes to get to the restaurant. Add to that the drive from your coffee shop to the apartment, and we wouldn't make it in time."

"No, you can just pick me up on your way to the restaurant."

He said nothing.

"I'll get dressed here. I bought the dress today, so I don't need to go to the apartment. I'll be ready when you get here."

A few seconds passed where neither one of us spoke. I placed the book in my hand on the third shelf and picked another one up from the floor. "Jack?"

"Why didn't you tell me you didn't have a—never mind. I'll be there at six."

"Okay. I'll be ready." I hesitated for a moment, not sure if it was my place to ask. "Is everything okay?"

"Of course. I'll see you at six. Goodbye, Rose."

"Okay. Go—"

And the line went dead.

It was going to be a long night for sure.

———————————

WHEN SALLY LEFT around five-thirty after sitting around and chatting with me, I went straight back to the kitchen to get ready. Since my wardrobe didn't include a dress fancy enough to go with one of Jack's expensive suits, I had gone out and looked for something I could wear that wouldn't look too cheap while I was standing next to him. I didn't want a painful repeat of the day we got married. Thankfully, I'd found something in the second store I rushed into when I headed out on my lunch break.

It was as simple as a black dress could get. It was made of a thin material, the name of which I had no idea whatsoever, and had short sleeves. It hugged my hourglass body lightly from what I could see after craning my neck to the left and right in the dressing room, and it ended about six or seven inches above my knee. The front V was a bit deeper than I was accustomed to, but it wasn't bad enough to look for something else. More importantly, since it wasn't exactly a winter dress, it was on sale. I didn't have the time to search every store in the city for just the right thing. I tried it, it fit, so I bought it. It was also a bit pricier than I would normally pay for a dress, not a luxury brand or anything like that, but again, I was going for a look that wouldn't make me feel *extremely* cheap next to Jack. So, I accepted that this specific look came with a price tag.

I was able to get ready in twenty minutes and had even managed to turn my light makeup into something more suitable for evening. In other words, a whole lot of concealer was covering the dark circles under my eyes, and my cheeks were touched with a little blush—quite a bit, actually. Checking the time, I rushed through my eyes by applying a little black pencil along my lash line and smudging it with my finger until it resembled something smoky and acceptable instead of a complete mess. Just as I was done applying mascara, my phone pinged with a new message.

Jack: Open the door.

I snorted; my husband had such a way with words. I looked at myself in the mirror we had on the inside of the little bathroom in the back. Smoothing my dress and trying to tame my boobs, which looked bigger because of the deep V, I inspected my makeup closer. I didn't look like a complete hot mess, which meant I looked okay. "Shit!" I exclaimed, noticing I'd completely forgotten about my hair. I had braided it two hours earlier so I could have something that resembled a wavy look, so I tore off the hair tie at the end and started to unwind the strands in a hurry. Before I could finish, my phone started to go off.

I ran back to the counter, and after confirming it was Jack, I ran to the door, my hands in my hair, trying to tame it down and mess it up at the same time. It was a very special look.

Stopping next to the door, I ran my hands through my bangs

for the last time, unlocked the door, threw it wide open and ran away before he could get a good look at me.

"We've been waiting for you outside. You're late," Jack said as soon as he stepped inside.

"You're five minutes early," I countered over my shoulder without looking back as I kept running straight back to the kitchen to put my jacket on. After tying the thin belt around my waist, I grabbed my handbag and rushed back to Jack. "I'm ready," I mumbled, a little out of breath. My eyes were down as I was struggling to open the front zipper on my bag so I could throw my phone in. When it was done and I finally looked up, all the white noise coming from the city outside my door seemed to disappear. I couldn't think of anything intelligible to say.

Fuck. Fuck. Fuck.

My favorite curse word was the only thing that came to my mind, and I didn't think it would be appropriate to say out loud in this situation.

Jack was wearing black slacks, which wasn't anything surprising, but it was definitely the first time I was seeing him without a button-up shirt on. Instead, he was wearing a thin grey sweater with the arms slightly pushed up, giving me a view of the watch on his wrist.

A simple grey sweater and a watch had rendered me completely speechless. Like the jackass I was, I let my eyes wander from his fitted sweater to his belt and down to his black shoes. His face was just as it always was: same sharp jawline, same deep blue eyes, same rough stubble, a no-nonsense look in his eyes and the usual frown between his eyebrows. His hair looked like it had been roughly raked back with his hands with some sort of matte product.

Overall, he looked...okay. Fine, maybe a bit more than okay.

Staring into his eyes, wanting to play it safe, I waited for him to say something. I didn't want to give it away too much that I might actually be attracted to him.

"Something wrong?" he asked.

I shook my head.

He studied me some more. "Ready then?"

I nodded, not saying a word.

"What's wrong with you?"

I released a long sigh. "Nothing is wrong with me. What's wrong with *you?*"

His stare intensified, so before I could get myself in trouble, I reached past him and opened the door, lightly bowing like an idiot who didn't know what to do with herself and gesturing for him to leave. He stood there for another moment then, shaking his head at me, walked out. Taking care of the lights and pushing in the code to the alarm, I locked everything up and closed the door. Resting my forehead against it, I quietly murmured to myself and faced Jack, who was waiting for me with his hands in the pockets of his pants just a few steps ahead. I looked down the street a short ways and saw his car waiting for us.

As soon as I was next to Jack, he walked ahead and opened the door for me. I got in and scooted to the other end. "Hi, Raymond. I'm sorry for making you wait."

Jack got in after me and closed the door. I was fairly sure Raymond was the only person who knew about our fake marriage. He had been our only witness at city hall, and even if he hadn't been there, there was no reality where he would believe we were a newly married couple who were crazy in love after seeing us together for the last two weeks.

Since I was looking at the rearview mirror, I saw his small but genuine smile. "It's all good. We didn't wait for too long."

I smiled back.

See, I thought as I gave Jack side eye. *Why can't you be like Raymond and smile at me just once or twice?*

He started talking to Raymond and then we were on the way to our destination. I closed my eyes and breathed in, only to be assaulted by Jack's cologne.

Dear God.

Dear God! That was all I could think of as I slowly let it all out and tried not to breathe much. His other cologne, the one I'd smelled on him every day for the last two weeks, was not as deep and musky as this one. This one would pretty much knock anyone off their ass and make them start salivating, fake wife or not. I pushed the button on the armrest to roll the window down a bit and let a little fresh air snap me out of my idiocy.

"How far away is it, Raymond?" I asked when I found my voice again. "The restaurant, I mean."

"Half an hour, maybe a little more, Mrs. Hawthorne."

I groaned on the inside and looked at Jack. "Did you change your cologne?"

"Why?"

"I'm not sure if I like it." I loved it. I loved it too much.

He rolled his watch around his wrist and looked away from me. "Too bad for you."

How had I known he would say something along those lines? I faced the window and smiled. He was starting to grow on me. If I had learned one thing about Jack Hawthorne, it was how unwilling he was to make small talk, and since I wasn't eager to spend almost an hour in silence, I decided I'd have to be the one to start talking. Yet, when I glanced at Jack and saw him sitting so relaxed and looking out his window, I couldn't come up with any interesting topics. I thought I was really good at pushing his buttons, but for some reason, I decided the cologne comment was enough for our car ride.

Giving up on every idea of small talk that came after that, I rested my temple on the cold glass window and closed my eyes. I didn't know how many minutes passed in silence, but when I heard Jack's soft voice, I forced my eyes to open with some difficulty, not having even realized I'd fallen asleep.

"Rose?"

I glanced to my right only to find him watching me carefully. The car wasn't moving, so apparently I'd dozed off for longer than I'd thought. "Are we there?" I covered my mouth with the back of my hand and yawned.

His frown smoothed out and he shook his head. "We're at a stoplight, almost there. You're tired."

At least that was better than *You look awful. You're tired* was just a fact and I could live with that. "The makeup didn't hide it enough, then," I muttered. I was a whole lot of things, not just tired. I dropped my head back and took a deep breath. "Sorry for dozing off."

The light turned green.

"I take it you didn't get any sleep last night either?"

"I did, actually—five hours this time. I'm hoping tonight is the night I'll sleep my usual amount."

Two police cars with their sirens blaring passed us and my eyes followed them.

"Are you sure you're up for this dinner?" Jack asked when it was quieter—as quiet as New York got.

Sitting up straighter, I turned to him. "Of course. I won't disappoint you, Jack." At least I wouldn't make things worse, I was sure of that much. If all else failed, I'd just be silent and moody like Jack, and they'd think we were a good fit.

The frown came back in full force. "That's not what I asked."

"No, I know, but I'm up for it. I got ready, and I'm here. I just wanted you to know...that I wouldn't disappoint you."

After we shared an awkwardly long look as the passing city lights illuminated his face, we both fell silent.

Too soon, Raymond stopped the car and I looked out the

window. We were parked in front of the restaurant where we would meet with Jack's partners.

"Try to look half alive at least," Jack said.

It was going to be a complete disaster. They were never going to believe we were in love. There was no way.

"Such pretty words. If you want half alive, that's what you'll get. If you had asked me to look fully alive, I would've definitely disappointed you. Half alive, though? You're in luck."

The butterflies in my stomach instantly started a riot. I didn't even notice Jack had gotten out of the car until he opened my door. Snapping out of my private panic, I scooted forward to exit. Noticing the bulky handbag clutched in my fingers, I paused and met Raymond's gaze. "Would it be okay if I left my bag in the car?"

"Of course, Mrs. Hawthorne."

I met his eyes in the rearview mirror again and gave him a pleading look. "I'd really feel so much better if you would just call me Rose. Please."

He gave me a small nod and a barely there smile. "I'll do my best."

I forced my lips to curve up and got out of the car without my purse. Brushing my hands on the fabric of my jacket, I waited for Jack to close the door. Then Raymond pulled away and it was just the two of us, standing on the edge of the sidewalk right in front of the double doors of the very brightly lit and full restaurant.

"No handbag?" he asked, noticing my empty, nervous hands.

I stopped the fidgeting and shook my head, my eyes still on those big double doors—the gateway to my hell. "I didn't have one that was elegant enough. This is better." I caught Jack's tight expression right before he took a step forward. Before I knew it, my hand was clutching his arm. I gave him a desperate look. "Jack, we forgot!"

His eyebrows drew together. "We forgot what?

"We don't have a story. I was going to ask you, but your cologne confused me and then I dozed off."

"My cologne did what?"

"Forget about the cologne!"

He sighed. "What story are you talking about?"

For someone who was about to lie to a bunch of his work friends, he looked oddly relaxed, which only made me more nervous and slightly angry. "A story about how we met! How you asked me to marry you!" I burst out and then lowered my voice. "They will ask something, if not those questions, something about us—you know they will. Everyone asks those questions."

He shrugged, and this time it was me who looked confused. "We'll come up with something if they do. Just act natural," he said. "Are you nervous about this?"

Just act natural?

I gave him an exasperated look. "Of course I'm nervous about this. How can you not be? They're your work friends. And what do you mean *act natural*?"

"They're not my friends, Rose. We're partners. And act natural means act natural. What else is it supposed to mean?"

He was driving me into madness with his cold demeanor. "What difference does that make? You're partners, so you must at least be *friendly*, and if we're acting natural, does that mean you're gonna frown and be silent the entire evening? What am I supposed to do then?"

"I don't frown." He frowned as he said it.

Surprise, surprise.

I tilted my head. "Really? You're gonna go with that? Why don't we walk a few steps so you can stare into the nice, shiny glass windows and see for yourself."

He sighed. "I'll keep my frowning to a minimum, if it'll please you. It'll be fine. Come on. They're not going to ask questions.

Stop worrying. Remember, I told you, a potential client is joining us, too. They'll be too busy with him."

"So this is a schmoozing dinner. All the attention will be on him."

"Schmoozing..."

"What?" I asked. "What?!"

He shook his head and sighed. "Your choice of words fascinate me. Are you sure you're up for this?"

Maybe I was worrying over nothing. Either way, I was going to go into that restaurant and try to look like a happily married couple with a man who never smiled. And eat. I'd also eat. If my mouth was full or I was fixated on my dinner, they couldn't ask questions. It wouldn't be too hard to achieve either because I could already hear my stomach growling. Taking in a deep breath and letting it out, I thought I might as well get it over with as soon as possible. Only the first one was going to be this painful. After this one was over, I'd be a pro.

"Okay. Okay, you know them. I trust you." I smoothed down my subtle waves and my bangs as Jack followed the movement of my hands.

When I met his eyes, he turned and walked away, leaving me behind. I looked up at the skies.

God, please help me.

I rushed to catch up until we were side by side. When someone opened the door for us to step in, Jack gestured for me to walk in ahead of him. I was trying my hardest to look like I fit in with the crowd, so I didn't notice when Jack stopped in the entryway just before the hostess. Backtracking, I stood next to him again and tried not to fidget.

After he let the girl know about our party, someone helped me take off my jacket, and I started on the smoothing down process all over again.

"Rose?"

I looked up and got caught in Jack's deep blue gaze.

"What?" I asked, leaning toward him.

"I..." His eyes moved all over me. *All over*. He'd already seen my tired face, yet he lingered the longest there. My lips, my eyes. My gaze caught in his and we stood still.

Stop looking, Rose. Stop staring.

Blinking, I broke the weird connection and felt my face heat up.

I cleared my throat. "Yes?"

He took a step closer. Standing too close for my comfort.

"You look beautiful," he said out of nowhere, softly, but loud enough that even though there was laughter and soft music spilling out from the dining area, there was no way I could've misheard that compliment. I ran my hand up and down my arm to get rid of the goose bumps his gaze and rough voice had caused. The way he'd just blurted it out, I wasn't sure if he had been waiting for a good moment to say it where other people could hear him or if it was an actual compliment.

"I...Thank you," I whispered.

There was this weird feeling in my chest, this unreasonable excitement. Before I could process the unexpected shift between us and come up with an answer, his gaze dropped low. I followed his eyes and my heart started to beat faster—a whole lot faster when I saw his raised hand between us.

Tilting my head back up, I met his gaze and slowly, uncertainly placed my hand in his open palm for the first time since the ceremony. His hand was warm as he gently closed his fingers around mine. And my heart...my heart was having some issues.

The number of times Jack Hawthorne smiled: zilch.

CHAPTER SEVEN

JACK

Closing my hand around Rose's much smaller one, I followed the hostess and had to pull a bit when Rose didn't move with me. As the woman guided us through the front tables and deeper into the restaurant, I quickly glanced down at Rose. She looked a little flushed and unsettled with that small frown plastered on her face. I was unsettled too. Hell, maybe even more than her. The only difference was that I was better at hiding my emotions. You could read everything from just looking into her face, her eyes.

Her dress, and the way she looked in the dress had blindsided me, that much was apparent. And I hadn't been able to keep my mouth shut. But that red flush on her cheeks, the widening of her eyes, the goose bumps she had tried to hide. Those little facts were really interesting.

"Are you okay?" I asked, leaning down close to her ear and giving her hand an involuntary squeeze as we took a turn to the right that led to the private area of the restaurant.

Jumping a little at my words, she looked at our clasped hands then up at me and nodded.

"It's just dinner, Rose. Relax."

Before she could even respond, we reached the round table where George and Fred were already sitting, but there was no sign of Wes Doyle, the potential client. As soon as they saw us, they stood up.

"There you are, Jack," Fred said, pushing his chair back and walking around the table to get to us. "There's a first time for everything. I never thought I'd see the day you were late anywhere."

"We're right on time," I commented, and watched as Fred's eyes dropped to Rose's hand in mine. Instinctively, I gave her hand a little pull until she was plastered to my side. Rose gave me a quick surprised look then turned back to Fred.

Fred shifted his focus to her and his smile got bigger. At forty-five years old, Fred was the only one of the partners I could stand to spend more than an hour with. "Usually, he is the first one through the door whenever there is a meeting or work dinner," he said to Rose. "And you must be the very unexpected but beautiful bride. Fred Witfield, pleased to meet you." He extended his hand to Rose, and I had to let go of her.

I looked down at my hand. Still feeling the warmth and shape of her hand on my skin, I flexed my fingers.

"I'm pleased to meet you, too, Mr. Witfield. Jack has said lovely things about you," Rose lied.

Fred laughed and *finally* let go of her hand. "Oh, I highly doubt that."

I stood where I was, just a step behind her, and greeted George with a short nod while still listening in on their conversation.

"We're really sorry for being late—it is completely on me," Rose was saying.

"We weren't late. We're right on time," I repeated as I pulled out her chair. "The client isn't even here yet."

Ignoring me, Fred pulled out the chair next to the one I had just grabbed, thinking she'd sit to my left, with me between her and Fred. Since she had her back to me, she couldn't have seen that I was waiting for her, so she accepted his offer and took a step forward. Before I could comment, Fred was introducing her to George. When everyone was done with their introductions and niceties, we all sat down. I waited until Rose was settled and then took the seat I had originally pulled out for her. Fred sat down to her right, all his attention still on her. George, being the oldest partner, wasn't as curious about my new marriage as some others in the firm.

"So, Rose, you have to tell us how you convinced Jack to marry you," George started as soon as everyone was settled. Maybe I was wrong. Maybe every damn person on the firm was curious about my marriage.

A waiter leaned down between Fred and Rose and filled their glasses with water, causing the table to fall silent.

I couldn't see her face, but I could imagine she was smiling and trying to come up with a lie. Done filling her glass, the waiter came to my left. I put my hand on the small of Rose's back and spoke up before she could. Her spine straightened, but she didn't move away from my impromptu touch. "Actually, it was the other way around, George. I was the one who had to convince her to marry me. Where is Wes Doyle?"

"Oh, I didn't miss the big proposal story, did I?"

I pulled my hand back from Rose and turned my head to look at the owner of the unexpected voice: Samantha Dennis, the only female partner in the firm and someone who'd had no plans to attend this dinner.

"I didn't know you'd be joining us, Samantha," I said lightly.

"They only arrived a minute ago. You're just in time," Fred jumped in.

George's phone started ringing and he excused himself from the table. "I'll be right back."

"You know how Wes Doyle is," Samantha replied to me. "He always has more questions and wants everyone to cater to his needs. We want to get him on board. The more partners he sees, the more likely he is to sign the contract. Plus, my dinner plans fell through, so I didn't want to miss the chance to meet your wife." Samantha put her hand on the back of my chair and looked between me and Rose. "You don't have a problem with me being here, do you, Jack?"

"Why would I have a problem with it?"

"All right then." Her red lips curved up in a smile as she leaned down and pressed a kiss on my cheek. I stiffened, and it didn't escape her notice. "Relax, Jack." Rolling her eyes, she laughed at herself. "Old habits, sorry." Putting down her black clutch on the table, she leaned forward and, in the process, her breast pressed against my shoulder. As she shook hands with Rose, I pushed my chair back and moved a few inches to my right, closer to Rose to leave more space for Samantha.

"Samantha Dennis," she said. "The fourth partner in the firm."

Surprising me, Rose didn't even hesitate before responding. "Rose Hawthorne. I would be the wife, as you already know."

"Yes, I do know. I actually didn't believe it when I first heard he had tied the knot, but here you are."

Rose's smile turned up a notch, matching Samantha's. "Here I am."

Dismissing Rose, Samantha pulled her chair out and looked at Fred, giving him a more genuine smile. "Fred, Evelyn isn't joining us tonight?"

"The kid caught some stomach virus from one of his friends, so she stayed home with him."

I was still annoyed with Samantha's kiss so I didn't even think what I was doing. "Samantha has been dating the district attorney for the last year and a half," I blurted out to Rose quietly then frowned at the table and picked up my water glass. This wasn't a real marriage, I didn't have to tell her about my old relationships. If sleeping with someone a few times four years ago would count as a relationship that is.

What the hell is wrong with you?

"That's good. I guess. Good for her?" Rose whispered in confusion.

I put my arm around Rose's chair. She stiffened even further, so I leaned down to speak into her ear. "This is not acting natural." She was reaching for her glass, and as soon as the first word was out of my mouth, she almost knocked it down. Maybe I was too much in her face.

"Oh, sh...oot," she exclaimed quietly. A little color touched her cheeks and she apologized to Fred, who had reached forward to catch her glass.

"Wes is pulling up—he was stuck in traffic," George explained as he returned and took his seat again. "Samantha, glad you decided to join us."

"Are you kidding me? I wouldn't miss this for the world."

As the three of them started to talk among themselves, Rose scooted back in her chair, met my eyes for a quick second, and leaned sideways toward me. I leaned down until her mouth was closer to my ear to make it easier for her and so no one else could hear what we were saying.

"I *am* acting natural," she whispered.

"You haven't looked at me once since we sat down. At least try to act as if you don't mind my company."

Her head was bowed as I was whispering into her ear, but as soon as I finished speaking, she pulled back a little and looked up into my eyes with surprise.

"Got caught up in New York traffic. There was a small accident a few blocks away—a guy rammed into a cab. Please forgive me," Wes Doyle said as he rounded the table. "Good evening everyone."

Rose and I had to pull away from each other to start another round of handshaking, and as soon as the introductions were done, everyone finally settled down.

The waiter showed up again, and the next few minutes passed with everyone ordering their drinks.

"No menu?" Rose asked discreetly when everyone was distracted.

"This restaurant is known for the prix fixe menus. The chef changes it every few nights. He is supposed to be very good. It's seafood night, I believe."

She nodded and pulled away from me. Before I could catch her attention and ask what was wrong this time, the first course arrived: seared scallops with an almond vinaigrette served on a half shell.

Because Wes Doyle was someone who would be considered a big fish, everyone around the table started with their promises and assurances that he'd be on the list of people who were number one priority to the firm, but I was occupied with something else. I was watching Rose's movements as she placed her napkin in her lap and stared at the scallops on her plate. Taking up her knife and fork, she cautiously cut a small piece and slowly brought it up to her lips. Oddly fascinated, I watched her chew it longer than was necessary and then force herself to swallow it down. Softly coughing, she reached for her glass and took a sip of water. For anyone looking at her, she'd look elegant as she enjoyed her dinner, but to me, she looked like she was being forced to eat garbage.

"Jack?" George called, and I had to shift my attention as they all stared at me—everyone except Rose. "Don't you want to add something?"

It took me a second to shift gears. "I think Wes knows my opinions on this subject." I glanced at Wes and he gave me a small nod. He had built an incredibly successful tech company from nothing in the last few years and had recently decided to change his law firm when his previous lawyers lost him a case that was being splashed all over the media and tarnishing his company's reputation. It should've been an easy win, but they had made massive mistakes along the way, mistakes I had pointed out to him. "I can assure you, just as I did yesterday, if you decide to go with any other firm, you'll be making a big mistake. I think after what happened with the last one, you're done taking chances with the company you worked so hard to get to where it is today."

I'd explained everything I would do for Wes and his company when he had dropped into my office the day before. He had taken his time to ask every little question he had, and I had answered every one of them with full honesty. If he decided to go with us, he knew what he'd be getting from me. I didn't find it necessary to add anything else—he'd either make the right decision or he wouldn't. He had all the facts, and the rest of it was up to him.

Everyone at the table focused on me, though my wife still didn't. She stopped with the fork halfway to her lips for just a second, a slight hesitation, then resumed eating.

Samantha cleared her throat. "I think what Jack is trying to—"

Wes cut her off with a wave. "Oh, no. You don't have to cover for him, Samantha. I like that he doesn't hold back his thoughts. I *need* that honesty. And yes, we talked more about this yesterday in his office, and he is right. I can't afford to make bad decisions about the people who are supposed to protect me and what I've built all on my own."

Fred joined in and they kept the pointless discussion going. If I wasn't mistaken, Wes had already come to a decision, but it seemed he wanted to hear more assurances. However pointless it was, I understood his reservations. Everyone loved getting pampered, and he was someone who seemed to enjoy being the focus of attention.

I took a few bites of my dinner and discreetly kept watching Rose even though I knew what a bad idea that was considering our situation. This was a work dinner, not the time to ogle my fake wife as if she was the most interesting thing in the world. But the more I couldn't take my eyes off of her, the more I realized that she was doing her best to act like I wasn't sitting right next to her. Then her quietness started to get to me as well. By helping her at the coffee shop I'd realized how much she loved to talk. About anything and everything. As much as she gave it her best shot she hadn't quite managed to pull me into her conversations, not yet. The more she failed the harder she tried, as much as I admired her for it, I hadn't lost my damn mind that much.

I didn't want to get used to her. Didn't want to get close. Not anymore than I already was. That was *not* the plan. Not at all.

When I couldn't keep quiet anymore, I stopped thinking and placed my hand on her leg, my thumb and first finger making contact with her bare skin. She jumped in her seat, her knee bumping the underside of the table, rattling the dishes. I forced myself to relax and tried to keep still. After apologizing to everyone profusely, she put down her knife and fork and finally looked back at me with murder in her eyes. If she'd had any idea how much I enjoyed her reactions, she would have acted differently just to annoy me. I was sure of it. I leaned toward her, and our shoulders and forearms lined up on the table as she met me in the middle.

"What are you doing?" she whispered harshly.

"Why are you avoiding me? What's wrong?" I asked, pulling my hand away.

She pulled back a little, but we were still huddled together as we looked into each other's eyes as if in a challenge. Her brows drew together before she whispered back, "What are you talking about? How can I be avoiding you when I'm sitting right next to you? What's wrong with *you*?"

She straightened up, took another small bite from her plate, and started the slow chewing process again. I leaned closer and my lips got dangerously close to her neck, so much so that I got more intimate with her smell. A fresh flowery scent mixed with a fruit, maybe citrus. "I..." It took me a moment to remember what I was going to say and I faltered. "Just relax a little. Don't you like your appetizer?"

I pulled back, and this time she leaned toward me.

"I'm not a big fan of seafood. Is it too obvious?"

After a quick glance at everyone else around the table to make sure we didn't have their attention, I turned my body completely toward Rose and put my arm around her chair again. My chest rubbed against her shoulder. I thought she would flinch or even pull away, but this time she stayed put. We were supposed to be newlyweds. As much as I was trying my best to stay away from her when it was just the two of us, while around other people, I knew we needed to act more intimate if we wanted to seem believable as a couple. "Yes, Rose. The whole menu is seafood—why didn't you say something?"

"It's a prix fixe menu—I didn't think we could change anything."

"Doesn't mean you have to eat something you don't like." Still keeping my arm on her chair, I looked around the restaurant. "Stop forcing yourself to eat." Not finding who I was looking for, I drew back from Rose, even managing to push my chair back a bit before she put her palm on my thigh. I paused and we both looked down to her hand on my slacks with surprise. She immediately pulled it back. That was a good decision. That was a really good decision.

In the spur of the moment, surprising myself and her, I believe, I leaned forward and pressed a quick kiss on her cheek. It was something a husband would do before leaving the table. Her eyes widened slightly, just like it did when I'd complimented her, but she managed to keep it together.

I rose.

"Something wrong, Jack?" Fred asked, looking up at me.

"Please continue," I said to the table. "I'll be right back."

It only took me a minute to track down someone who could change our order. Even though the restaurant only offered set menus the elite of New York couldn't stop talking about, with just the right amount of persuasion, they agreed to make a slight change just this once. When I got back to our table and sat down, Samantha and George were deep into their conversation with Wes while Rose was chatting with Fred, her cheeks flushed.

"Everything okay?" I asked, curious to hear what they were talking about.

"You didn't tell me she was related to the Colesons', Jack. Gary had been with us for what five years? I didn't even know about her."

Rose gave me an apologetic look.

"I only lived with them till I was eighteen. After that we didn't see each other as much. Holidays and a random lunch or dinner every month or so. Gary was very busy with his firm and well, his own kids."

"It didn't come up," I explained briefly, wanting to end the conversation.

"Is that how you two met?"

Rose gave me a look I couldn't understand, but looked a lot like *told you so*, then turned back to Fred. "Yes. Well, kind of."

When the waiter came and started to collect the mostly empty dishes, Samantha piped up, taking advantage of the lull in their conversation with Wes. "When are we going to hear the proposal story? That's what I'm waiting for."

"Proposal?" Wes asked.

"Jack and Rose just got married," George explained. "Only a few weeks ago, I believe, right? It was a surprise to everyone in the firm."

Wes looked from me to Rose. "Congratulations! I had no idea. We should've ordered champagne to celebrate."

"Thank you. We're just getting used to it ourselves. It happened so fast. I mean we fell for each other so fast," Rose said.

"Give us all the details," Fred chimed in. "So we can overlook the fact that none of us were invited to the wedding."

Rose laughed then turned to look at me. "See, Jack, how nice —everyone wants to hear the proposal story." When I just stared into her sparkling eyes, her smile tightened and she turned back to Fred. "Oh, I couldn't. If I started, I'm afraid I wouldn't stop. I have no brakes when it comes to talking about Jack." She turned to me and patted my arm, a little too hard if you asked me. Trying to hide my smile, I licked my lips and reached for my whiskey as she said, "And this is a work dinner so I wouldn't want to take over."

"Nonsense," Samantha pushed. "We have plenty of time to talk about work. Jack, however, is a complete mystery when it comes to his private life. We're dying to hear anything you're willing to share."

Leaning back, I kept silent and waited to see how she would get herself out of this.

Rose sent another pleading yet angry look my way. "His proposal was actually very special to me, so if it's okay, I'd like to keep that between us. That said, I'm sure Jack wouldn't mind telling you how we met." My hand was resting on the table when Rose covered it with her own and patted it twice. "Right, honey?"

The waiter returned with the second course—more seafood.

Her hand seemed a little cold, or maybe it was just her nerves, but her ring bit into my skin. She had finally worn it without me having to prompt her. Turning my hand over, my palm against hers, I linked our fingers together and our eyes met again. I didn't realize it wouldn't escape everyone's notice and they would look at me in shock.

"It's not as exciting as you're all thinking," I warned. "I made a complete fool of myself and it somehow worked on her."

"Oh, now you *have* to give us more than that." Samantha placed her hand on my forearm. "Especially after saying the cold and calculated Jack Hawthorne made a fool of himself."

I reached for my whiskey with my left hand, getting rid of Samantha's touch in the process. "If Wes doesn't mind taking a little break from talking about work—"

Wes cut in before focusing on the plate in front of him. "Of course. Please go on."

After everyone's seafood dishes were served, another waiter came over and leaned between Fred and Rose to place a different one in front of her. It was larger and fuller than the other plates he had just delivered. "Creamy steak fettucine with shiitake mushrooms," he explained quietly, only for Rose's ears.

Her surprised gaze flew to mine. I wasn't sure if she was aware of it, but her fingers tightened around mine and she softly said, "Jack, you didn't have to say anything. I'm the only one who—"

When I was served the same pasta dish as her, she didn't finish her sentence, instead giving me a big smile that reached her tired eyes for the first time since we'd walked into the restaurant. She mouthed a silent thank you.

My eyes dropped to her smile and I had to let go of her hand or otherwise... "A better option than seafood, I hope."

"This is perfect, really. Thank you."

Fred broke into our little conversation. "Come on, you've

been whispering all night with each other. You'll have plenty of time to flirt with each other once you leave here. Tell the story, Jack."

"I already told you it's not that exciting, certainly not exciting as your story with Evelyn."

Fred turned to Wes. "He's probably right. The first time we met, my wife, who is also a lawyer, threatened to put me in jail, and she almost managed it, too."

"Oh, I'd love to hear about that," Rose cut in, most likely trying to get them to stop talking about us so we wouldn't have to come up with a lie. I had no intentions of lying, at least not about the entire thing. Also, I was curious about what her reaction would be.

"I saw her at last year's Christmas party the Colesons were throwing at their place. If I'm not mistaken, you were also there, right George?" I asked.

George paused with his fork in the air and frowned, trying to recall the night. "Wasn't that when Gary called us to talk about one of the startups he was considering buying? It was after Christmas, though, wasn't it?"

"Yes, right after."

"I remember the night. I thought you left before me, right after the meeting."

I nodded. "I was about to." I met Fred's eyes since he was the one who was the most curious about how Rose and I had met, and Rose looked just as interested in hearing it. "I was at their place before you, and I think Rose arrived seconds before me. Gary briefly introduced us before we went up to his office to wait for you. At the end of the meeting, I left George with Gary and went downstairs. It was pretty crowded, actually, so I was trying to get out as quickly as possible. Then my eye caught something in the kitchen and I stopped."

Rose's eyebrows crept up, waiting for the rest. Did she remember the night?

I looked away from her. "I couldn't walk away. Of all the things she could have been doing at a Christmas party, she was playing with a puppy, and I couldn't take my eyes off of her. I watched for a minute or two, trying to decide if I should talk to her again or not. Introduce myself again or not. Then a little boy came and took the puppy from her, and she finally came out of the kitchen." That was where I had to change my story.

"And *did* you talk to her?" Samantha asked, clearly into it.

"Yes, I did. I told her I wanted us to get married." Everyone at the table started laughing. My eyes slid to Rose. "She didn't say yes, of course. I tried everything I could think of, but it didn't look like she was going to budge."

Rose's confusion disappeared and her smile grew. "He really did try, maybe a little too hard, and the entire time he was so serious, so confident, not even a hint of a smile on his face," she added, joining in telling our made-up story.

I placed my hand on her back and then changed my mind, pulled it back. "She thought I was insane, kept saying it over and over."

Rose looked around the table. "Who wouldn't? But I couldn't walk away, either. As much as I wasn't taking him seriously, I think anyone would be insane to just walk away from Jack." She paused. "My husband."

I took a long sip of the whiskey in front of me. "I wasn't planning on letting you." I cleared my throat and avoided her gaze. "I was sure if I came up with the right offer, she'd at least say she'd consider it, but she turned me down each time. Eventually, she agreed to give me her number, but I'm afraid it was just so I would leave her alone. I took out my phone while standing right next to her and called to make sure she wasn't giving me a fake one. The next day, I called her, and we started talking."

"He grew on me." Rose looked at me while she spoke. "He was so different than what I thought he would be. I didn't know how to act around him."

"And?" Samantha prompted. "That's it?"

I turned to Samantha. "If you think I'm going to tell you what happened every day after that—"

"There's the Jack we know and love." Samantha shook her head. "God, you got married! I still can't wrap my mind around it."

"Be ready to tell this story from the very beginning to Evelyn, too. I'm not going to ruin it for her. You have to finish your sentences as you look into each other's eyes, too, just like you did now. She lives for this stuff, and she'll be very pleased to hear that you're happy, Jack."

After that, the table slid back into easy conversation as Rose and I mostly stayed silent. Once she had finished her plate, I leaned down to ask if it had been okay just so everyone would think we were having our own private conversation apart from them, like a newly married couple who were very much in love would do, but that was only once. Toward the end of the dinner, after dessert was served and the evening was finally winding down, Samantha spoke up.

"Rose, I'm sorry we ignored you all night. So, tell us more about yourself. Are you working?"

I sent Samantha a warning look, which she completely ignored.

"I'm getting ready to open my own coffee shop," Rose answered.

"Oh, really? A coffee shop—how cute. Where is it?"

"Madison Avenue."

"When is the opening?"

"Monday, hopefully. Everything is mostly done, thanks to Jack, of course."

Surprised, I glanced at Rose, and she gave me a small smile.

"Jack?" Samantha marveled. "What did he do?"

"Apart from handling all the official stuff, he'd been dropping by after work and helping with the things I couldn't do by myself."

Giving me a curious look, Samantha propped her head on her hand and leaned forward. "What has he done so far?"

As I turned the whiskey glass on the table, Rose's eyes slid to me and then back to Samantha. "He painted the walls and helped me move some heavy things around."

"Wow. Jack painted?"

"Samantha," I said flatly, giving her a second warning.

"What?" she returned. "I'm making conversation. You can't have her all to yourself. So, Rose, why didn't you hire professionals to deal with that stuff?"

"I have a budget, so I'm taking on the things I can do on my own."

"Jack, why are you not helping your wife with the money rather than offering her actual labor?"

I got as far as opening my mouth to cover for Rose, but she beat me to it. "Because his wife wants to do this on her own. Jack is respecting that, and him offering his help with the manual labor stuff means more to me than if he would have just thrown money at it to get things done. I'm a little old-fashioned like that, I think. It also means we get to spend more time together while working."

I hid my brief smile by taking a sip of my drink. So she wasn't afraid to show her claws when she was pushed. That was one of the things I liked about her. Only one of the things. I'd provoked her too many times and had been on the receiving end of her fierceness.

"Jack Hawthorne, the brilliant lawyer painting a coffee shop."

Samantha laughed. "I wish I could've seen that. I'm afraid marriage is already not agreeing with you, Jack."

Surprising me for the second time, Rose looped her arm around mine and rested her chin on my shoulder. This time it was my turn to stiffen, but Rose ignored it and kept her eyes on Samantha. I downed my whiskey.

"You really think so? Please don't take this the wrong way, Samantha. I'm sure you two had a great time while you were together—I mean, how could you not? Just look at him—but I'm very glad you actually don't know Jack the way I do. I know he is a private person—that wouldn't be a surprise to anyone, I don't think—but boy am I relieved he is only like this with me. You're gorgeous, but I guess I'm the lucky one who got the big prize."

I started coughing and reached for some water.

George cleared his throat across the table.

"Rose, I hope you'll join us again another night, when Evelyn will be there, too," Fred interrupted, trying to cut the tension.

Rose turned to him, her face softening. "I'd love to. I'm looking forward to meeting her."

While she fell into an easy conversation with Fred, I took the opportunity to focus on Samantha. I didn't care who could hear us. "Ease off."

With a smile on her face, she leaned closer. "What are you talking about? I'm just getting to know your wife."

My lips tightened. "You're pissing me off, Samantha. That's all you're accomplishing here, and I think you already know I'm the last person you want to anger. Don't play games with me."

"Oh come on, Jack. Don't be so touchy. She is adorable, the complete opposite of what I'd expect you would go for, but then again, I wouldn't expect you to ever get married in the first place. At least it seems like she loves you."

I leaned my elbows on the table, but Wes' voice stopped me before I could say anything else.

"I think I'm ready to call it a night. If you'll have the contract ready on Monday, we'll make it official."

When he stood up, everyone else followed his lead. George was the first to shake his hand. Rose stood up as well but chose to wait on the sidelines. As I was talking to Wes, telling him he wouldn't regret his decision, I saw Rose discreetly run her hands over her bare arms. I looked at Samantha and noticed she was wearing a long-sleeved dress. As warm as it was inside the restaurant, Rose's dress was still not appropriate for the temperature, inside or outside.

Separating myself from the group, I walked back to Rose's side and took off my jacket, gently draping it over her shoulders.

She looked over her shoulder in surprise. "Jack, you don't have to—"

"You're cold. I'm not," I said, trying to keep it simple. After a brief hesitation I put my hand on the small of her back and guided her out of the private area and into the brightly lit main dining room as the others followed us. Rose pulled my suit jacket tighter around herself and didn't make any other comments. As we were all waiting for our cars in the entryway, I took Rose's thin coat and draped it over my arm.

"It's cold outside," she muttered quietly as she leaned her shoulder against mine so the others wouldn't hear. She started to shrug my jacket off, but I put it back over her shoulders. My hand covering hers in the process.

Our gazes held for a moment as I had to search for the right words. "I'm fine, Rose."

As Raymond was the first to pull up at the front of the restaurant, we said our last goodbyes and headed out into the cold then got into the car.

"Mr. Hawthorne, Mrs. Hawthorne."

Rose sighed. "Hello, Raymond."

We all fell silent.

I was going through my schedule for the next day in my mind when Rose's voice interrupted me only a few minutes into our ride.

"Well?" she asked quietly, giving me an expectant look.

"Well," I repeated, not understanding what she was asking.

She took a deep breath with closed eyes, let it out softly, and then opened them. "You kill me sometimes, Jack Hawthorne. How did it go? I didn't mess anything up, did I? At least not too badly? I sorta don't want to apologize for the...thing I had with Samantha. She was pushing me, and I had to say something. I don't like people like her, all the fake smiling when they're actually insulting you and believing they're the sharpest tool in the shed while you're just few fries short of a Happy Meal. I'm a little bit sorry if I went too far with the *I know him better than you* stuff and *He is only like this with me* crap, though."

"Are you sorry or not?"

Another deep breath. "Fine, not really."

"If you're not sorry, you don't need to apologize. I didn't mind it. She deserved more."

"How old is she anyway?"

"Thirty-seven."

"Well, she acted like a teenager," she mumbled as she stared out the window.

I couldn't argue with that so I didn't. I awakened my phone and started scrolling down, double-checking my schedule. "You need to relax more. Next time, try to look more interested in me."

"I—what do you mean?"

I sighed and put my phone down. "Every time I touched you, you either jumped up or flinched."

"I know, but you didn't warn me."

I quirked an eyebrow. "I was supposed to warn my wife before I touched her?"

"Not in there, of course, but before, when we were in the car.

We should've talked more, gone over a few things. We were unprepared, and I don't want to say I told you so, but I did tell you. They asked all the questions."

"If I remember correctly, you fell asleep in the car, and what's the big deal? We answered them." I carefully considered my next words. "You were warmer to Fred."

I looked at her when only silence followed my words. Her eyes were slightly widened. "I was...trying to be nice to your friends. You didn't think that I...that I would—that I was flirting with him or anything—"

I frowned at her. "What are you talking about? Of course not. Why would I think that?"

"You just said—"

"I said you were warmer to him. You smiled and talked to him more than you talked or smiled to me. That's all I meant. Also, again, they're not my friends—"

"Just partners, I know. I got it." She released a longer sigh and massaged her temple. "If we want to keep up this charade, we desperately need to communicate more, Jack. You have to talk to me."

I looked out the window and stayed quiet for the rest of the way back to the apartment. How was I supposed to explain that I was actually trying my best to talk to her as little as possible? That I *had* to do so?

Once we were in the building, the doorman stood up. "Mr. Hawthorne, Mrs. Hawthorne. Welcome."

"Good evening, Steve," Rose said, smiling at the older man. To my surprise, she stopped next to his station as I called down the elevator. "How are you feeling today? Your migraine is gone, I hope?"

"Much better. Thank you for asking, Mrs. Hawthorne."

"I told you before, you can just call me Rose. Has it been a busy night?"

The doorman's eyes darted my way. "Erm, just the usual."

With my hands in my pockets, I watched their interaction with interest.

Steve's eyes cut to me then back to Rose again before he quickly added, "Mrs. Hawthorne."

The elevator doors pinged open and she looked toward me. "Looks like our ride is here. Have a good night, Steve. I'll see you in the morning?"

"Yes, Mrs. Hawthorne. I'll be here."

I held the doors open as she quickened her steps and got in the elevator. I stepped in after her. We only managed to go up two floors in silence before my curiosity got the better of me. "You know the doorman?"

"Yes. I met him the first morning I was leaving for work. We chat a bit in the mornings. Why?"

"You've only been here for two weeks."

"So?"

"I didn't know his name," I admitted uncomfortably.

She hugged my jacket tighter around herself. "You never asked?"

"I—no." I didn't want to admit that I hadn't deemed it necessary, because I didn't like how that made me sound.

A moment later, I couldn't stop myself from asking what had been on my mind for days now. "Do you still talk to Joshua, your ex-fiancé?" I blurted out at the same time the elevator doors opened, surprising both of us.

Rose froze and gave me a startled look. I cursed myself for bringing it up, but after the dinner, I was too curious to ignore the idea completely.

"No, I don't talk to him. Haven't talked to him or seen him since we broke up and I'm not planning to do it in the future either. Why would you ask that?" she finally asked, walking out of the elevator before I could answer. I followed her to our door.

"I thought maybe you weren't over him yet and that was why tonight was more difficult."

"Trust me, I'm over him. I got over him pretty quickly, considering. Tonight wasn't difficult, Jack. I'm not a stranger to awkward dinners. Tonight was...just a first. That's all. It was our first dinner, too, and I actually think we did a pretty good job, don't you agree? Still, I think we should work on getting to know each other a little bit, just talk about random stuff. The next one should go down better. Also, I thought you'd be distant when we were around other people—that's why I was surprised when you touched me...so much." She peered at the door. "Aren't you gonna open it?"

She still had my jacket on. "The key is in your right pocket," I replied, reaching for it before she could do it herself. She froze when my hand slid into the pocket and inadvertently touched her body through the lining. I stopped when my fingers touched the keys and met her startled eyes. We stood exactly like that as I slowly pulled the keys out. Her throat moved as she swallowed, and she looked away first, laughing awkwardly.

Unlocking the door, I stood back so she could enter. Inside, after taking off her shoes, she slid my jacket from her shoulders and handed it back to me. "Thank you." She avoided my eyes, and I realized I didn't like it.

"You're welcome." I took it off her hands and neither one of us walked away from each other.

I thought she looked beautiful with her hair down and a little messy, her lips bare and her eyes still sparkling. I was heading straight for trouble if I was noticing the details.

She smiled a little. "Well, do you think we should—"

My phone started ringing in my hand and she paused mid-sentence. Dragging my eyes away from her lips as her smile slowly faded, I looked down at the screen and my entire body tightened. Ignoring the call, I looked up at Rose. "I need to take this. It's about work and I might need to drop by the office for a bit."

"Now? At this hour?"

I clenched my jaw. "I'm afraid so."

"Okay then. I hope it's not something too important."

"We'll see. If I don't see you around when I come back... Goodnight, Rose."

Riding the elevator down, I put my jacket back on and tried not to lose it. When I was back in the lobby, the doorman rose again.

"Good evening," I said, trying my best not to sound angry.

He looked startled for a second, making me feel even worse, but then gave me a quick smile and nodded. "Good evening, sir."

Before I could step out of the building, my phone started to go off again. Anger surged through my body and my fingers tightened around the phone. I had known I would eventually hear from him, but hadn't thought it would happen so soon.

Finding the cold bite of the air refreshing, I took a deep breath and caught a whiff of Rose's scent from my jacket. With her smell surrounding me, cursing myself, I answered the call.

"What the hell do you want?"

"How nice of you to ask. I think we need to have a talk, Jack. I imagine we have a lot of things to say to each other."

I gritted my teeth. "When?"

"How about now? Do you think you can get away from your beautiful bride for a late-night drink?"

"Tell me where."

He was just a few blocks away from us, the son of a bitch also known as Joshua Landon. Rose's ex-fiancé. Had he watched Rose and I as we returned from dinner? Livid, as soon as I ended the call, I headed toward the bar where he was waiting.

CHAPTER EIGHT

ROSE

I had known the last few days leading up to Monday, my opening day, would be hectic and maybe not so easy, and I wasn't wrong. If Jack hadn't been dropping by to pick me up, I would've probably ended up sleeping on the floor inside the coffee shop just so I could make sure everything was ready. But, Jack...he had been...Jack was...a whole other subject.

I had deemed Friday the second biggest day next to the opening day. It was the day the coffee shop's sign was going to go up and all the people of New York would be able to see it.

The black and white striped awnings had been installed around noon, and the sign was up only a few hours after that. I might have shed a few happy tears looking up at that thing.

Around the Corner Coffee Shop.

I knew I was officially freaking out about the opening when I started making lists for everything I could think of: what kind of freshly made sandwiches I would prepare, the first week's pastry menu, the first *day's* pastry menu...the lists just went on and on. While I was happily busy with all of that, a slow drizzle of rain had started, a pretty soundtrack in the background. As much as some people hated winter in New York, I loved it.

Jack showed up earlier than his usual time. I wasn't surprised to see him when he showed up anymore, and it felt normal to have him in the space. I was looking forward to it even. It was the first time I'd realized I was starting to enjoy his grumpy company. It'd been three weeks since he had returned from London and started to come around every night. That was a lot of help I hadn't expected to have, and I thought somewhere along the way something had changed between us.

This time, before he could ask me, I asked for his help as soon as he stepped over the threshold.

"Good, you're here. Can you help me put the custom decals up on the windows?"

He hesitated only for a moment, as if he was surprised. "Sure. Why not? I'm here anyway," he said at last, as if he wasn't there specifically to help me. As he took off his coat and then suit jacket, I settled in for my daily show: the sleeve roll-up. And what a show it was, every single night. You'd think it would get repetitive, but no. Just no.

"Slow day at work?" I asked after wiping the invisible drool from the side of my mouth. He took the word *Around* from my waiting hands and climbed up the ladder until he could reach the top left corner of the window facing north.

"What do you mean?"

"You're here early."

"I was in the neighborhood, had a quick meeting with an old client, so I thought I'd drop by."

I smiled up at him, but he wasn't looking at me. "You seem to have so many meetings around here. There was another one the other day, right?" He frowned down at me, but before he could say anything, I pushed forward. "Anyway, as I keep saying every time you're here, I appreciate the help."

"I can see that." He opened his palm, waiting for me to give him the next decal.

I sighed. "I marked where that's gonna go."

He didn't reply or even acknowledge that I'd spoken, but placed *the* exactly where I'd marked for it to go.

I took a deep breath. "So, how are you, Rose?" I started. "I've been pretty busy with work these last few days, and so have you. How are you? Did you manage to get a good night's sleep last night? Are you excited about the opening?"

Then I answered myself. "Aww, thank you so much for asking, Jack. I have a killer headache right now, but I can't complain too much. I did manage to sleep the entire night last night, thank you very much for asking. It was one of the very few good sleeps I've had since moving in with you. I guess you went back to your office again last night—how late did you get in? I think I was fast asleep. Also, did you have a good day at work today?"

Finished with the second decal, he glanced down at me with that look of superiority featuring the arched eyebrow he had probably perfected in a meeting room or wherever. It wasn't helping that he was literally standing over me.

"What are you doing?" he asked, his hand open, waiting for the last one.

I placed *Corner* in his palm.

"Just having a conversation," I answered, shrugging.

"With yourself?"

"With you. Since you don't find me interesting enough to talk to, I'm making it easier for both of us and just doing it by myself. This way you won't have to trouble yourself with asking random questions and making small talk. Plus, you're up there, which means you can't run away from me. So...win-win."

For a long time, we stared at each other, and I did my best to look innocent. Then he just sighed and shook his head as if I'd lost my mind and he was astonished with himself because he'd married this weird person willingly. He turned back to the window.

"It's not about not finding you interesting to talk to, Rose. You are probably the most interesting person I've ever met. I just don't think we should get—nevermind I've had a long day, too—a long week, actually. That's all."

And didn't that made me feel like a jerk.

"Oh," I mumbled, shifting in place. "I'm sorry. I didn't mean anything by it. Anything you want to share?"

"No need to apologize. It's nothing specific, just lots of meetings and phone calls."

"I baked some brownies to test out a recipe for opening day. Would you like some? Brownies always make me happy."

"Maybe after we finish this. Why Around the Corner?"

I tried my best to keep my grin to a minimum but wasn't sure if I quite managed it. "As Tom Hanks would say, the entrance is Around the Corner."

"Tom Hanks?"

"I'm a big fan of the movie *You've Got Mail*. I love Meg Ryan's character and her bookshop was called Around the Corner in the movie. It's also simple, elegant, and sweet, not just because of the movie, but on its own. I like it. You've seen that movie, right? It's a classic."

"Can't say I have."

"No, Jack. Just no. No husband of mine can answer that question with a no. You have to watch it. Maybe we can watch it together one day when you're free."

"Maybe." He paused, and I thought that would be the extent of our conversation. "It's good," he muttered.

"What?" I asked absently, looking out the window as people passed by with their umbrellas. The rain was starting to pick up.

"The name—it's good for a coffee shop."

That had my eyebrows rising and my attention going back to Jack. "Really? You think so?"

"Yes, it suits you for some reason, and it sounds like it has a good memory attached to it. You did a really good job around here, Rose. You should be proud." He looked down. "This is it?" I nodded and he got down. "Good enough?" he asked, looking up at the decals.

I backed up and stood next to him. "It's more than good enough. It's perfect. Thank you. Can we do the same for the window at the front?"

Instead of making up an excuse like any other guy would have and leaving when I kept coming up with stuff I could use his help with, like arranging some of the tables and chairs—multiple times—he stayed put, *and* he complimented my brownies. When we were ready to leave, it had gotten dark out and the rain had started to fall harder. I still had the biggest smile on my face. Partly because of Jack, partly because of everything else. Like magic, Raymond was already waiting at the curb when we locked everything up, and we headed to Jack's apartment.

On Saturday, I met up with Owen. Sally wasn't coming in so I couldn't introduce them, but it was Owen's first time at the coffee shop with all the furniture set up nicely. I basically held my breath the entire time he was looking around and let out the longest sigh when he finally said he thought it looked amazing. We spent hours talking about what we wanted to do for the first month and created our menu together.

After Owen left, I sat down in the middle of the coffee shop and started working on the shopfront flower installation, which I hoped would be rather striking. I'd seen it in several shops in New York and in cities like Paris—thanks to Pinterest—and I'd fallen completely in love with the look and the way it transformed a space. Since we were living in a social media age, I wanted to do everything in my power and budget to make my coffee shop eye-catching, comfy, cozy, and beautiful.

Of course, this was all rooted in the hope that I would get actual living customers on opening day, and every day after that.

When Jack knocked on the door, I'd been waiting for him to show up for at least an hour. I had a big smile on my face when I opened the door for him, and he had a bewildered expression on his own.

"Hi. Hey. You're late. Where were you?"

Those thick and prominent eyebrows drew together, but it still didn't dampen my enthusiasm. This was Jack—frowning was like his version of saying hello.

"I'm late?"

"You always come around earlier. So...you're late."

"You were waiting for me?"

"Jack, I wait for you every day. It's been almost three weeks." I shrugged, not even realizing what I had just blurted out. "Come in, come in, it's cold outside." I opened the door wider and grabbed his arm, pulling him in since he was too busy staring at me.

"What do you mea—what is this?"

I came up behind him and bounced on my feet. He gave me another look, one that said he thought I was being weird. I ignored it completely. "It's the flower installation that's going to go outside. It'll start on the ground and arch over the door. I'll also add the group of flowers that's over there to the back of the door so from the inside, it will look as if the flowers kinda went through the glass and bloomed on the wall inside."

He nodded and I smiled again. I couldn't contain it for some reason. "That's a really great idea," he said.

I was still bouncing, smaller bounces, but still...I was bouncy.

His forehead creased and his eyes looked me up and down.

"What's wrong with you?" he asked, and I burst out laughing, unable to contain myself.

"Nothing, Jack." I shook my head, keeping the smile. "Absolutely nothing. Too much coffee, maybe?" I walked around the fake flowers that were covering almost every available surface. "Come help me?"

"I'm not so sure about that."

I got on my knees and grabbed a bunch of roses from the ground. "You always help me."

His jaw clenched. "Yes. Yes, I do, don't I?"

"So? You're not gonna help because helping with flowers isn't manly enough? I won't tell anyone, promise."

He looked around the shop, around the floor, taking in all the shades of pink. Then he sighed and took off his black coat, followed by the black suit jacket.

"You can sit on the chair," I said when he looked around as if he wasn't sure where he should go. After a moment of hesitation, he pulled up the closest one and sat down to my left, his back to the door. "Why are you on the floor?"

"I started on the chair, but it goes quicker from here. You can hand me a wire with every flower." I grabbed the wires from my right and handed them to him. "Different shades, though, okay? Don't give me the same shade or shape back to back."

He looked so lost with a small frown on his face, I couldn't help but feel something in my chest. He wasn't uttering any objections so I didn't feel the need to let him off the hook, not to mention I really needed his help if I wanted to get out of there before the sun rose. When he took out a wire from the package and bent down to reach for a fake—but beautiful—rose from the pile, I cleared my throat.

"Ah, aren't you gonna..."

He met my eyes. "Am I gonna...what?"

I was an idiot. "Your sleeves...you always roll them up." I was a gigantic idiot, but...it was always one of the highlights of my day, so why should I have to suffer just because he forgot about it? It was my daily forearm porn, and I had started to look forward to it.

His frown got a tiny bit deeper as he looked down to his wrists and then—*thank you God!*—he put down the rose and the wire in his hand and started the process. I watched him the entire time without him even noticing it. When he grabbed the rose and the wire again, holding them straight up in his hands, I couldn't hold back my grin.

"Something funny I should know about?"

"Nope." I shook my head. "You're all dressed up. Did you go to your office today?"

"Yes."

"Do you work every weekend?"

"Usually." He paused. "I don't have to go in on the weekends. I only do if I don't have any other plans."

I reached for the rose he was holding and secured it to the fake branch with the wire, making sure it wasn't at the same level as the others. I wanted some of them to stick out and some to be farther back so it gave the illusion of a big explosion of roses blooming.

"Do you make plans with your friends?" I asked, not looking at him because I had to pick up my pace.

"My best friend moved to London. Work keeps me busy as it is."

"You?"

"Me?"

"I haven't seen any of your friends around."

"Oh, I'm usually busy with work, too. To save money, I had to spend a lot of time at home and that doesn't help you have a social life."

After our admissions, we worked along in a comfortable

silence, and with his help, it started to go a lot faster. I'd done a lot of it before he showed up, but it looked like we'd be out of there in an hour at most.

"Isn't this something a florist would do?" he asked after quite some time.

I gave him a quick look then focused on the flowers again. "Yeah, but the budget thing, remember? I scrolled through Pinterest, watched a few YouTube videos, and read some blog posts, and I think it's turning out just fine. I know the florists do it with fresh flowers sometimes, but that would be extremely expensive. *Extremely*. These look all right, don't they? I mean, it'll look better once it's up and arched over the door, but..."

"It's beautiful," Jack said softly. It was soft enough that it got my attention, and I noticed his eyes were on me, not the flowers. "What are those for?" he continued, gesturing toward the yellow roses I had on the side farther from us.

"Oh, I'll distribute them on the tables on Monday. Again, I can't buy fresh flowers every week, so I'm gonna go with fake on those too. Hopefully, if things go well, I'll upgrade to fresh roses on the tables in a few months and I'll buy more plants to put around the place."

His fingers grazed mine and I had the oddest feeling. Ignoring it, I kept working and secretly enjoyed every little touch, every little graze.

"You know I could lend you money, right? The place is mine, so it would be an investment, and since you're going to pay me rent after the six month period has passed, I wouldn't want you to close it down before that."

I gave him an incredulous look. "Come on, Jack. Let's be honest with each other—if I can't make this place work, it'd work in your favor because you'll get your hands on it faster. What did you say you were planning on doing with it? A restaurant?"

"I didn't say anything."

I was so curious, but he wasn't giving it up. "Either way, thank you, but I couldn't accept your money."

An hour later, my fingers aching and a little scraped, I finally spoke up. "I think we're done. This is it." Groaning, I pushed myself up.

"Would you like to have dinner with me, Rose?" he blurted out.

"What?" I asked, looking at him with a puzzled expression as he stood up as well.

"Have you had dinner?" he asked instead of giving an answer.

"No. I think the last thing I ate was a small sandwich. I snacked on a few things, but not a full meal. But..." I looked down at myself and cringed. "I'm not really dressed for going out, and my hands..." Holding my arms out in front of me, I opened and closed my hands, looking at my red fingers. I hid them behind my back and tucked them into my back pockets, hoping they would warm up. "Would it be okay if we ordered in? If you don't mind. If you have other plans, you don't have to stay in with me."

"I wouldn't ask you to have dinner with me if I had other plans."

"That's true." My mind was getting a little fuzzy.

Keeping an eye on me, he rolled down his sleeves, I really appreciated the view in silence. Then he grabbed his suit jacket from the back of the chair and put it on.

I just stood there in front of the flower arrangement, not sure what I should do next. It was dark outside so there was no way I could put it out and secure it before morning.

"Rose." Jack interrupted my thoughts and I glanced at him. "Come on, let's go home."

"No, I should probably do...first I should..."

"Rose." I looked at him again, meeting his eyes. "You're going to crash soon. You've done enough. Let's go."

With perfect timing, my stomach grumbled, as if agreeing with him. I looked around again. "That sounds like a plan," I mumbled, but I still didn't move. "But maybe first I should clean the place up a bit."

He ignored me completely. "Where is your coat?"

"In the kitchen. It must be in the kitchen."

Wordlessly, he headed toward the back, walking around the huge rose explosion in the middle of the shop. I thought I heard him talk to someone on the phone, Raymond I think, but then he was back, and he was ordering me to put my arms into the sleeves. He pushed me all the way out, got the lights, even put in the code for the alarm, and locked everything up. With his warm hand on my back, he guided me down the road to where Raymond was parked.

Why did I always feel so safe when he was near me?

"I think I leaned down a little too much for too long. I'm just feeling dizzy, but I'm fine." As soon as the words left my mouth, I stumbled on something and Jack caught my arm before my face could hit the ground. "Whoa. Really dizzy."

I remembered getting in the car and maybe saying hi to Raymond, but I didn't remember how I got up to the apartment and onto the couch. When Jack woke me up with a hand on my shoulder, I was feeling extremely disoriented. He helped me up and gave me two slices of pizza. It was cheese, pepperoni, and black olives, and he ordered me to eat up, and eat up quick. I finished in two minutes flat and even asked for another slice.

I had no recollection of what we talked about, but I did remember mumbling my answers and then wishing him a good night before stumbling to my bed.

The number of times Jack Hawthorne smiled: zero. (BUT...it's coming soon. I can feel it.)

CHAPTER NINE

ROSE

It was finally Monday, *the opening* day I'd been waiting such a long time for, and now that it had arrived, I didn't know how to contain my happiness or my anxiousness. One minute I was on the verge of hyperventilating just thinking about opening the doors enough that Owen and Sally had to force me to sit down, and the next minute I couldn't stay still and felt like I was about to burst from happiness. Mostly, though, I was feeling sick to my stomach, worrying everything was going to go wrong and everyone was going to hate everything.

What if no one showed up? That had been the first thing I'd thought the moment I had opened my eyes that morning. What if no one walked in? My goal was to at least serve fifty coffees on the first day. That sounded like a fairly doable number.

"I feel like I'm about to lose my virginity," I blurted out as Sally pushed a glass of water into my hands.

"Was it a good experience? Mine was pretty cool."

"I mean, it was okay. No orgasms in sight, but at least it didn't hurt much." Owen grumbled something I couldn't make out. "What did you say?"

"This place looks legit," Sally said, ignoring him. "What you did with the flower thing is still blowing my mind. It looks so beautiful with the black exterior. The furniture, the colors—everything came together so nicely. You put out the flyers too. We'll easily reach fifty coffees."

When Sally left me and went to the kitchen, I got up from one of the chairs they had basically pushed me into, walked to the door to flip the closed sign to open, and just rested my forehead on the cool glass for a few seconds. Flipping that sign felt like I'd welcomed an elephant to come sit on my chest. People passed by. I even saw some of them stare at the roses as they walked by, but no one pushed each other out of the way to get in.

"Okay." I sighed. "Now all we have to do is wait." When I turned around, both Sally and Owen were standing in the doorway to the kitchen, Owen wiping his hands on a kitchen towel and Sally smiling and munching on a lemon bar. Taking the last bite, she walked up to the espresso machine.

"Would you like to have the very first latte of the day? I've been polishing my latte art skills."

I let out a deep breath and smiled. "You know what, that's a great idea. In fact, lattes all around, on me. We might need to drink forty-seven more today, but that's not all that much, right? Death by caffeine is a real issue, but I'm sure we'll be safe."

We clinked our mugs together, at least Sally and I did and hoped for the best for the rest of the day. The first customer came thirty minutes after I'd flipped the sign from closed to open. Owen was in the back, but Sally and I were ready with our overly excited smiles plastered on our faces.

An hour or so had passed and we had a few more customers. Sally was preparing a second cup of cappuccino for the customer who'd come in earlier as she was looking through the food selection on the counter. She'd already had her free blueberry muffin, so she decided on a sandwich this time.

I grabbed a plate, lifted the glass dome, and picked up a turkey & swiss that was wrapped with parchment paper and secured with red twine. The bell on the top of the door rang, but I was busy taking payment so I couldn't look away. After giving her the change and thanking her, I finally looked to my left, excited to greet a new customer.

And right there...right there standing with the most uncomfortable look on his face was Jack Hawthorne. I didn't think I'd ever been that happy to see him before, but him being there so early, him just being there... The smile that broke out on my face was embarrassing.

"Jack, you came," I managed to say softly, and even though he couldn't hear me, his gaze dropped to my lips.

Before he could walk in farther, Raymond came in with an armful of roses and handed them to an unhappy Jack. My breath hitched and my smile brightened up a bit, taking it from embarrassing to a touch closer to manic. Jack's expression, however, didn't change.

Were they for me?

I begged my heart to stay calm as he walked toward me.

"There was a mix-up at the flower shop, and they couldn't bring these themselves," he said, and my smile faltered.

"I don't understand. They're from a flower shop?" I asked, my eyes going from the roses to Jack's face in confusion.

His lips tightened and his brows drew together. "No."

I waited. I could feel Sally standing just behind me, on my right, too.

Jack released a frustrated sigh. "They're from me. You don't have to use the fake stuff on the tables. It's so the property looks good. That's all." He leaned forward and thrust the bouquet into my hands.

Feeling something weird and very much unexpected in my chest, I took them. There were maybe fifty or sixty long stemmed roses in every color—pink, white, yellow, peach—and they were all wrapped up in slightly shimmery brown paper. They were gorgeous, way more than what I would need for the tables, way more than anyone had ever bought me. Flowers would add no value to the property; that was plain and simple bullshit. These were for me.

I was still looking at the roses, taking them all in one by one, not sure what to say or how to say it, when I saw Owen put another plate of freshly baked blueberry muffins to my left. He whistled next to me, his shoulder barely touching mine.

"These are just for me," I mumbled, almost to myself. "And they're so beautiful, Jack. Thank you." For some reason, I felt myself choke up, and my chest constricted. Hugging the bouquet with one arm, I pressed my palm against my chest where my heart was truly losing it. Sally cleared her throat, and I briefly glanced at her to see her raised brows and the expectant look on her face. "Oh, I'm sorry. I should introduce you guys. Sally, Owen, this is Jack. Jack, Sally and Owen." My attention was still on the roses when I heard Jack's gravelly voice as he introduced himself.

"Rose's husband," he said, extending his hand first to Sally and then to Owen. Goose bumps covered my arms, both because of the tone of his voice and the word itself. *Husband.* My husband.

"Yes, sorry. Jack is my husband."

"Husband?" Sally blurted out in a slightly raised voice. "You're married? You never said anything!" She grabbed my hand and inspected my naked ring finger. "No ring?"

I inwardly winced and sent an apologetic look Jack's way, but he had his hands in his pockets and his eyes were on the food, his expression completely unreadable as always.

Sally was looking between Jack and me in bafflement.

"I took it off before I started baking. It's in my bag. With everything going on, I forgot to put it back on."

I was explaining it to Sally, but my eyes stayed on Jack the entire time. He looked up, and I offered him a small smile.

"It's so beautiful," I said, turning my gaze to Sally. "I keep taking it off when I'm working here because I don't want to lose it. That's why you didn't see it before."

"I need to get back. Congratulations on the marriage, Rose. Nice to meet you, Jack," Owen said before giving my shoulder a quick soft squeeze and disappearing into the kitchen. Sally just stood there.

I looked up at Jack, he was staring at Owen's back with a clenched jaw, but he averted his eyes before I could try to tell what he was thinking. Forcing myself out of this weird guilty feeling, I asked, "Would you like something to drink? Or eat?"

"Yes. I want fifteen...I don't know, espressos, lattes, or just black coffee—whatever you recommend."

"Fifteen?"

Finally, he looked at me. "I'll take it to the office."

"Do you have a big meeting or something?"

"No."

Just one word, that one word... He was putting in a coffee order that big because he wanted to help me—again.

"Oh, Jack, you don't have to do that." This time I could feel the tears blurring my eyesight. It was going to happen. The edges of my lips started to tilt down, and I knew I wasn't going to be able to stop it. "I'm going to hug you," I blurted out.

A line etched between his brows and his eyes finally came back to me. "What?"

Gently, I put the flowers down on the counter and walked toward the end so I could make it to the other side through the small opening. Before he could process it and quite possibly stop me, I closed my eyes and threw my arms around his neck, rising up on my tippy toes. To be fair, my movements had been slow. I'd given him time—enough time to stop me if he really wanted to.

But he didn't.

After the initial second or two, his arms came around me and he returned the embrace. I rested my temple on his shoulder, drew in his wonderful and dizzying smell and whispered, "Thank you, Jack, for everything. For the coffee shop, all the help, the flowers, the coffee order—everything. Thank you so much." The tears made their way down my cheeks, and I slid my hands down from his neck and stopped when my palms met the lapels of his charcoal grey suit jacket. His arms dropped so he could push my hair away from my face and tuck it behind my ear. A shiver worked its way through my spine and I couldn't move away from him.

When his eyes landed on my face, his jaw was clenched, and I had no idea what was going through his mind. I just looked at his face, taking in his features, my favorite blue eyes and straight full lips. Still not a smile in sight. I dropped back to my soles and wiped my tears with the back of my hand. I looked around the coffee shop to the three tables that were occupied. No one was looking at us, and even Sally had her back turned our way.

I smiled at him, a big happy smile. "Okay. If you're sure you want that many, we'll get started on them for you."

His eyes stayed on me. "I wouldn't be here if I wasn't sure, Rose."

My smile widened. "Of course you are. Okay." Walking around the counter, I asked, "Do you know what anyone drinks or are we just making a mix of everything?"

He shook his head. "I don't know what they drink."

"Right. Okay, we'll do a few different things. How do you want yours?"

"Just...black with a splash of milk, if you can."

I picked up my flowers, smiling. "Of course I can. I'll collect all the vases and change out the artificial flowers with these after you leave. I love them. Thank you, Jack. You have no idea what this means to me."

He cleared his throat but didn't say anything. I helped Sally and we did a mix of everything: a few macchiatos, a few lattes, four black coffees, and two matcha lattes, just in case someone preferred that. When Sally started on the extra black coffee, I gently took over. It wasn't that it required any extra attention, but I wanted to be the one who prepared Jack's coffee. When the whole order was ready, I started packing the free muffins and lemon bars. "These are free," I explained without looking at Jack. "For the first day, I'm giving everyone a lemon bar or a muffin, whatever they prefer."

"You don't have to—" he started, but I was already closing the box.

"They're free, and you will take them. Otherwise I'm not giving you your coffee. Don't argue with me."

"The roses look great on the door," he said after a moment, and I looked at him.

"Really?"

"How did you put it up?"

"I did it this morning, with Owen's help."

His face hardened a little for some reason. "I woke up early to see if there was anything I could help you with, but I guess I missed you. When did you leave?"

"Around five, I think."

"How did you get here that early?"

Confused, I gave him a brief look over my shoulder and started on making another quick coffee. "Like I always do—I walked through Central Park."

"On your own."

"Well, yeah. That's how I get here. I won't come in that early every day, but it was the first day, so..."

We fell silent as I finished the second cup I was preparing.

"Everything is ready to go, Rose," Sally said, sliding four bags toward me on the counter.

"Okay. Thank you, Sally. Just one more second, Jack. I hope I'm not making you late."

"It's fine," he muttered as a new customer walked in and started to look at the food and ask Sally questions. I welcomed the newcomer and put the lids on the two coffee cups I had prepared myself, grabbed two small paper bags that had our logo on the front, and quickly put two lemon bars inside each one along with an extra chocolate muffin in one of them. "Okay. We can go," I announced, smiling at Jack.

He held out a credit card to me between two fingers. "I hope you don't forget to ask for payment from all your customers."

"My husband gets a free pass," I pointed out softly as we stared at each other and I ignored the credit card. Sally walked behind me toward the espresso machine. "Ready to go?" I asked Jack.

"Rose, I'm not taking anything if I'm not paying for it."

My smile started to melt off my face as he spoke.

"It's your first day—if you start giving away free coffee to everyone you know on the first day, you won't have this coffee shop for very long." There went the rest of my smile. "I wouldn't have ordered so many if I'd thought you weren't going to accept payment for it."

He extended the credit card farther forward and I reluctantly took it.

Before pushing in the amount, I glanced up at him. "I'm not taking payment for your coffee, Jack. I'm...just not."

We had a short-lived but intense staring match where I came out as the winner. "Okay. Okay, that's fine," he agreed. "I didn't mean to make you upset, Rose."

"It's okay."

I handed him the four bags and the card. Then I took the two coffee cups and the extra small bag myself. "Be careful not to tip the cups," I warned as Jack glanced inside the bags. "I'll be right back, Sally!"

I followed him out to the curb where Raymond was waiting. He rushed out as soon as he saw us coming with our hands full. He opened the door for Jack and waited.

"You should put the bags on the floor, Jack, keep them between your feet so they don't make a mess in the car." Jack leaned down and arranged everything carefully as I turned to Raymond. "I'm sorry, I don't know how you take your coffee, but I made you what I made for Jack, black with a splash of milk, and if you want, there are sugar packets in the bag too." I handed him the cup and the small paper bag. "And there is a lemon bar in this. I made it myself. It's good."

"Thank you, Rose, and congratulations on your new place. It looks amazing."

It was the first time he'd called me Rose. "Thank you so much, Raymond, and you're welcome." I beamed after him as he walked back to the driver's side.

"And these are yours," I said as I handed my husband the other coffee cup and paper bag, feeling a little shy all of a sudden. "I put a lemon bar and a chocolate muffin in yours because I wasn't sure what you liked, but if you don't like —"

"You made the muffin, too?" he asked, peeking into the bag.

"No, Owen baked the muffins. I made the lemon bars and the sandwiches. He is..." Did I need to give him an explanation? He hadn't asked, but I felt like I wanted to. "Owen, I mean, he's my friend. Barely even a friend. We worked at this café two years ago and talked every now and then after that. So, I just wanted you to know. He is just a friend."

"I don't need an explanation about your friends, Rose."

Despite his harsh answer, I thought I saw his shoulders relax a fraction. I could live with that.

"Okay." Not sure what to do with my hands, I just stood there.

"Did anyone unwanted show up today?"

I arched a brow. "Anyone unwanted? You mean like Bryan? No, he didn't. Neither did Jodi."

"Good. I had a quick talk with him. He won't bother you again."

"What? When?"

"After he showed up here. It doesn't matter now."

He had a coffee cup in one hand and the bag in the other. With his tailored suit and that *I'm not exactly sure what I'm doing here* look on his face, he looked so...so grumpy and adorable that I couldn't stop myself from giving him another hug.

Since his hands were full, he couldn't do anything but stiffen this time. Before I realized what I was doing, I found myself pressing a hand on his cheek and kissing him on the other side, surprised by my sudden act, I lingered. When I let go of him and backed up, he was looking straight into my eyes. I flushed but managed a smile. "Thank you, for the flowers and the coffee order. That you'd even think of buying coffee for your work friends—and they're not even your friends—and only because it's my first day...it means so much to me."

"I'm not doing it for you."

"You keep telling yourself that. You're hating it all the way, but you're starting to get used to me." When his steady gaze became too unsettling to return, I gave him a weird wave, mumbled something like, "Have a good day at work," then rushed back into the coffee shop.

My cheeks slightly flushed—maybe from the cold outside, or maybe because of Jack's gaze on me—I made it back to Sally's side. When the thing that was fluttering wildly inside my chest became too much to ignore, I looked back outside to see Jack standing on the curb and looking inside.

Had I really just kissed him *and* lingered? And then run away like a school girl?

I thought my cheeks flushed even more, so to forget all about it, I started to collect all the little vases on the tables, took my roses into the kitchen, and started on making my coffee shop even more lively and beautiful with a big, permanent smile on my face.

WHEN THE CLOCK hit seven PM, I was drained. I was happy, but the excitement had gotten to me. Owen had left right after lunch when he was done with his work, and Sally had left just half an hour ago. We had sold well over fifty cups of coffee, crushing my goals. It'd been just a bit over the one hundred mark, actually.

A knock on the door made me stop what I was doing, which was getting the last few bits of baked goods into containers and then in the fridge. I'd dimmed the lights in the coffee shop right after Sally left and had flipped the open sign to closed, as well as locking up. Holding the doorframe, I peeked toward the door. When I saw Jack standing in the rain, I put the brownie plate down and ran to the front of the coffee shop.

"Jack, what are you doing here?" I asked as soon as I opened the door. "It's raining."

"Really? I hadn't noticed."

I took a deep breath to keep myself from rolling my eyes at him. "You should've called from the car so I could open the door for you."

"I did, actually, but you didn't answer."

I winced and just stood in front of him, not sure what to do now that he was standing right in front of me and we were alone. "I'm sorry, it's in my bag. I haven't checked it the entire day. But, still, I didn't expect to see you here." I watched him as he ran his hand through his wet hair, somehow making it look like the rain had styled it for him—whereas the minute *I* stepped out into that rain, I knew I was going to look like a drowned rat.

"Right, because it's not like I'm here every night," he said before looking around the shop. Apparently that was all the explanation he was ready to give. "Are you going to let me in, or do you want me to stay out in the cold?"

"Oh, shoot, come in. Sorry." I opened the door wider and he stepped in. "Since you came in this morning, I thought maybe you'd skip the pickup today." I smiled as he brushed off the rain from the arms of his coat.

"Looks like I didn't." I just stared at him. "Ready to leave?" he asked, eyes coming back to me.

"You're really gonna make me ask?"

Distractedly, he kept brushing rain off of his coat as his forehead creased. "Ask me what?"

I raised my brows. "The coffee, the lemon bar? Did everyone like it? More importantly, did *you* even eat it? Did you like it?"

I waited with bated breath, which was stupid. Almost all the customers had commented on how much they'd loved everything —the space, the coffee, the food, the roses outside. Even so, hearing what Jack thought felt important. I cared.

He finally stopped messing with his coat and took a good look at me. "Everyone loved it."

"That's all you're going to give me? Are you being serious?"

The creases on his forehead got deeper. "I'm always being serious."

I laughed. "Yes, yes you are. I think you loved it, but you're just too proud to say it out loud." I didn't give him an opportunity to answer. "Do you mind sitting and waiting for a few minutes? I need to do a few more things in the kitchen, but after that we can leave. I can make you a coffee for while you wait?" My eyes still on him, I started backing away toward the kitchen.

With his coat still on, he pulled up the closest chair and sat down, his eyes on me. "I'm good. You go take care of whatever you need to take care of."

I gave him another overly bright smile and disappeared through the doorway. Grabbing the brownie plate from the counter, I raised my voice so he could hear me.

"Did you have a good day?"

I stopped transferring the brownies and waited for his answer.

"It was fine," he said finally. "Busy and long, as usual. Fred wanted me to congratulate you on his behalf."

"Oh? That's so nice of him."

I waited another few seconds and when the follow-up question didn't come, I answered it for myself. "Mine was good. Thank you so much for asking. It was just like yours, actually— busy and long." I paused for a second. "Ah, thank you so much, Jack. I hope it becomes a usual thing, too. You're so right."

Another quiet few seconds, and then his delicious voice came from very close.

"What do you think you're doing?"

No, not delicious—it wasn't delicious as in *delicious*, but it felt like it was delicious as it touched my skin. It was just a normal male voice, nothing to get excited about, just a little thick and rumbly and smooth at the same time.

I knew exactly where he was, but I still looked to where he was leaning against the doorframe. His coat was off, but he was wearing his suit jacket, hands in the pockets of his pants. Maybe it was for the better that there would be no forearm porn today, because if that had happened, I wasn't sure how I would react anymore.

"Just talking to you."

"You mean to yourself."

"No, I mean to you. I really enjoy talking to you."

He stared at me boldly and I fell into the blue trap.

"Can I help you in here?" he asked.

For some reason, I flushed. It was a pretty small space for two people. Sure, I worked with Owen just fine, but we baked across from each other and I wasn't attracted to him at all. I couldn't exactly keep Jack at arm's length when we were carrying pastries to the fridge.

"Nope. I'm good." I mean, it wasn't the first time he had offered his help, and if he did help, he would actually...but...no. No, skipping the forearm porn was the smart choice here. Definitely. "Just a few more things I need to...ah...do, then I'm ready. If you have somewhere else to be, I don't want to make you wait. I'll be done in—"

He crossed his arms, his shoulder still holding him up against the doorframe. "No. I'm good right here, too."

I didn't even attempt to stop the smile growing on my face, and to be honest, that weird sense of pleasure his words had caused was completely uncalled for. I bit my lower lip just to stop my mouth from curving up. Considering I hadn't even stolen one genuine smile from him, I was giving mine away too easily for my liking. When the brownies were done, I grabbed my cheeks and pushed them in. "I've been smiling so much today, my cheeks are hurting."

"How good was it?"

"Hmm?" I mumbled distractedly, keeping my eyes on the last few brownies.

"How good was your day? Still happy?"

He was making small talk. Granted, I'd already answered the question, but he was making small talk without me having to prompt him. The itch to grin and lose my cool was growing with every freely offered word out of his mouth.

On my way to the fridge, my eyes cut to him and I brushed my bangs away from my forehead with the back of my arm. "I'm exhausted, as you can probably tell from how I look, but it's the good kind of exhaustion. I'm still over the moon, still a little high on it." I reached for the remaining two chocolate chip cookies and put them in another container.

"I was going to ask if you would like to go out for dinner tonight, but I don't think you'd make it through, especially if you still feel like you're high on it."

"That actually would've been nice, but I agree with you." I held my arms out and looked down at myself. "Probably not the best night to be out in public anyway."

"What are you talking about? You still look just as you did this morning."

I tried to hide my wince, but I wasn't sure how successful I was. "Welllll, that's not saying much."

"Actually, it is," he muttered, but before I could ask what he meant, he straightened from the doorway and started walking toward me. I focused on my hands, which were reaching for the last two lemon bars with the tongs. I grabbed one of them, put it in a small container, and was in the process of grabbing the other one when Jack's chest brushed my shoulder.

I stopped breathing. My body pretty much stayed still, but my eyes were moving. He wasn't so much pushing me, but he was leaning on me enough that his chest was brushing my shoulder—his broad and warm and inviting chest.

"Can I have that?" he murmured in the vicinity of my ear, not too close, but closer than I expected him to stand.

I cleared my throat so I would be able to sound serious and normal like him. "Can you have what?"

"The last lemon bar."

That had me looking over my shoulder and...what a bad, bad idea. Our eyes met and I kinda got stuck on his steady and expectant ocean blues. Then I looked at his lips because they were *right* there, so full. In my defense, I was looking so I could catch his next words, but they didn't come.

"Hmm? Oh? You liked it then?" I forced my eyes back to his and extended the tongs toward him. He took it. "Would you like a plate?" He met my eyes again and just shook his head. I faced forward. *What is happening?* "I didn't think they would almost completely disappear by the end of the day, even though they were free."

"They are good enough to come back for every day, Rose." Before I could process those words and at the same time try not to analyze them to bits too much, he continued, "Will you bake more tomorrow?"

"I can make you a batch at the apartment, if you want," I offered as I started to just push things around randomly, hoping to keep the conversation going.

"I don't mind coming here."

Finally, I turned to face him, leaning my hip against the counter. If I just leaned a little forward, I could fall into him, so easily.

"Just for the flowers you brought this morning, you earned free lemon bars for an entire week."

He bit into his treat, already halfway done with it, and nodded.

Forcing myself to look away from him because I had no idea what was wrong with me that suddenly I was having trouble just looking away, I started to put everything in the fridge.

I came back for the last container. "We can leave in a minute."

My right hand was gripping the edge of the island when his fingertip touched my ring finger. I froze.

"You're finally wearing your ring," he murmured, and my eyes closed on their own.

Is he getting closer?

I focused on my breathing as he picked up my hand and played with the ring, moving it right to left, right to left, just as he had done on our wedding day. I might have swayed, I might have bit my lip, I might have shivered. I have no recollection of what I did, but I knew I was teetering on the edge of *something*.

"I put it on after you left," I whispered, my hand still in his. Then he gently put it down on the island again.

"Good."

I forced my eyes open but didn't look up at him. I was still feeling the ghost of his touch on my skin.

"Ready to leave?"

I nodded. "Mhmm." I put the last container away and quietly got ready, my eyes safely away from him.

However, it didn't escape my notice that my movements were getting more sluggish by the minute. The adrenaline was leaving my body, and pretty quickly, too.

As I took one last look at the coffee shop before I locked it down for the night, I felt immense pleasure knowing I'd get to come back the next day and do it all over again.

Thinking about Jack and the business deal between us, I went down the other road, too, the ex-fiancé road: Joshua Landon. I was a little surprised with myself that I wasn't thinking of him more. We'd had good days. In the beginning. He had swept me off my feet. He'd been perfect; said everything I didn't even know I needed him to say, acted as if I was his world and slowly won me over when I wasn't interested in something serious. After I'd said yes to his proposal things had started to change. He had started to change. If we'd married, if he hadn't disappeared on me after breaking the engagement over a stupid text, would I have had this? Would he have dropped by every day after work to help me? I didn't think so. I'd been with Joshua for a whole year and I couldn't remember a time he'd gone out of his way to help me with something—unless, that is, he wanted something in return. I hadn't needed his help; I didn't even remember ever asking for his help. That wasn't the issue, though. I hadn't needed Jack's help either. I hadn't asked for his help, yet he'd been there anyway, day after day.

For the first time, I didn't say a word in the car, didn't try to engage Jack in small talk as Raymond drove us back to the apartment. He ordered Chinese and I went up to take a quick shower before it was delivered. When the doorbell rang, I was coming down the stairs. By the time he paid and closed the door, I was standing next to him. I took one of the bags and we headed toward the kitchen.

"You're quiet tonight. You barely even said anything in the car." I only realized how hungry I was when the delicious smells coming from the containers had my stomach growling. A little embarrassed, I stepped away from him to put some distance between us and opened the fridge to take out two water bottles.

"I have a little headache," I mumbled. The fact that I had a headache wasn't a lie in itself, but something else was wrong. I had no idea what had happened, but I was feeling even more awkward next to him than I had before that day. Maybe it was the lingering kiss or the multiple hugs or maybe it was the thought of Joshua.

His eyes cut to mine, but I avoided his gaze as he took down two plates and we started to spoon out a little of everything.

"Rice?"

I nodded, and he dumped some on my plate. Then, grabbing both our plates, he walked straight out of the kitchen. "Let's eat at the table. I'm tired of sitting at the kitchen island alone."

Wordlessly, I followed him and stood in the doorway as he stopped next to the dining table. I watched him put down our plates, pull out a chair, and look at me with a raised eyebrow.

"Will you join me?"

As a kid who had taken most of her meals in the kitchen, a dining room table always reminded me of one thing.

Family.

Which I'd never had.

I walked toward him and sat down as he pushed my chair forward.

He sat across from me, reaching for his chopsticks.

I was staring straight into his deep blues.

Shaking my head, I got up and just as I was going to walk past him, his hand gently curled around my wrist, his thumb gently sweeping up and down, effectively stopping my forward movement. My words got stuck in my throat and I just stared down at him, at his eyes.

"Rose." He spoke softly, as if he was talking to a kid. "Are you sure everything is okay?"

"I forgot the water."

Deeply conscious of the way his presence and his hand on my skin were making me feel, I waited for him to let go of me. It took a few seconds, but when he did, I almost ran to the kitchen.

Back in my seat, keeping my hands under the table, I rubbed my wrist, trying to get rid of the weird tingles.

The silence and familiarity calmed me down, and I realized it was normal now, being with him, like this. We were just two strangers who had gotten married for the wrong reasons sitting at a big, ten-person dining table, and it felt normal and good.

As soon as my plate was cleared, I rose, and Jack pushed up to his feet with me even though he wasn't done yet.

"You're going?" he asked, something that sounded very similar to disappointment in his voice.

"I...should go to bed. Tomorrow is going to be another long day. I've been getting these little headaches recently, so it would be better, I think, if..."

"I understand."

I took my plate and again tried to walk past him, but he touched me again.

"I'll take care of it."

"I can—"

"Rose. Go away. Get some rest."

I gave him a smile. Exactly when had my name become so...so effective in making me break out into goose bumps?

I felt the ghost of his touch and the warmth of his fingers on my skin almost up until I fell asleep.

The number of times Jack Hawthorne smiled: not even a single one.

CHAPTER TEN

JACK

F or two strangers who had met and gotten married roughly a month and a half ago, we had fallen into a routine faster than I'd expected. Day after day, I found myself helping Rose at her coffee shop. Even when I didn't intend to drop by, or let's say even when I knew I shouldn't drop by, I still found myself on her doorstep. I'd lost count of how many times I'd lied and said I had a meeting nearby or found other convenient lies. I don't think she believed them anymore. Maybe I needed the lies for my own sake.

By the time her place was ready to open, it had felt like she had destroyed the small barrier I'd tried my best to put up between us. Something had shifted. It was there in the way she looked at me, or sometimes the way she *wasn't* looking at me. I wasn't sure just yet if it was a good change or what it exactly meant, but it was a change nonetheless.

I woke up earlier than I was used to. After having received another text from Joshua Landon after Rose went to bed, I had some issues sleeping. I sighed and got up, going straight to the gym in the next room. I couldn't think of any other way to work out my frustrations with myself and the situation. This business deal, Rose, this marriage was the worst decision I'd made in my life because I was losing control and losing it fast. I was doing everything I'd thought I wouldn't do. Yet it was too late to back out. It'd been too late to back out ever since I'd met her at city hall.

I hated running, but I ran on that damn treadmill for over an hour, watching the night sky slowly change color as the sun replaced the moon. When I jumped off, I was still angry and frustrated to the point that I was ready to risk everything and come clean, even though I knew it wasn't the right time, that it might never be the right time.

I stopped and listened. As much as I didn't want to admit it, I'd been doing that ever since I woke up, but so far I hadn't heard a single noise coming from Rose's side of the second floor or downstairs. I kept telling myself I wasn't her chauffeur; if she wanted to walk to work when it was almost dark outside, she damn well could. I had to mind my own damn business. She had gone places without me just fine before we had made this goddamn deal and gotten married.

Yet my ears were still searching for the telltale signs of her stepping out of her room and rushing down the stairs as she did every morning.

Taking my shirt off, I walked to the small fridge in the corner and took out a water bottle. Draining it in one go, I threw it on the floor.

Guilt was a very strong opponent to go to war with, and I couldn't seem to shake myself out of the funk I was in. When you added ex-fiancés into the mix...

I started on the weights until I was dripping with sweat.

What was it with her? Why couldn't I stay away? What the hell was I going to do?

When I was done, I went back to my room to take a quick

shower. Maybe it'd been a good thing that I hadn't been able to sleep. If by the time I was dressed, Rose hadn't gotten up, I was going to have to wake her myself. With a towel wrapped around my hips, I checked the time as soon as I was out. She was late. I got dressed as quickly as I could and headed to her room, cursing myself for worrying the entire time. I was in this marriage for the property. I was in this marriage for the sake of looking like a family man. All I had to do was keep repeating it to myself.

Still a little worried, I wasn't exactly quiet as I knocked on her door.

"Rose? I'm not your goddamn alarm."

Provoking her and watching her reactions was probably one of my favorite things in life at the moment.

No sound. After hesitating for a second or two, I pushed open the door only to see her bed was made and she was already gone. Had she left while I was working out or when I was in the shower? I grabbed my phone from my room and went downstairs. I was tempted to call and ask her if she had made it to work okay, but I thought better of it. I left my phone in the living room and went into the kitchen to make myself a cup of coffee. What I brewed at home tasted just fine. I didn't need to go to her coffee shop every day just because she was my wife or because I enjoyed looking at her. I made a good enough coffee myself.

While I was still waiting for my coffee to be ready that I was sure wouldn't taste anywhere near as good as hers, I heard my phone going off in the living room. By the time I picked it up, it had stopped ringing. It wasn't a number I recognized so I let it be. Leaving the phone where it was, I headed back to the kitchen, only to turn back midway when the phone started ringing again.

"Yes?"

"Jack?"

"Yes. Who is this?"

"Jack, it's me, Rose. I...I'm calling you from...a...someone else's phone."

Not knowing what was going on, I tensed when I heard how her voice trembled.

"I was just wondering if—Jack, are you there?"

When she started talking to someone else, I lost my patience.

"Rose, tell me what's going on. Where are you?"

"Oh, you're there. Okay. Right. I...I just took a little tumble, and—"

"Are you all right?"

"Yes. Yes, I'm fine. Well, I wasn't, but I'm now...Henry?" I heard her address someone else. "Your name is Henry, right? Yes, I—" She let out a long breath. "Henry was out running, and he saw me trip and fall. He was kind enough to help me. My phone flew out of my hand and took a tumble of its own so it's not working at the moment. I was wondering if you could come and help me to work. Henry offered to wait with me until then. I'd go on my own, but I think—"

Somewhere in the middle of her ramblings, I had already opened the door and was standing in front of the elevators.

"Where are you? Tell me your exact location."

When she couldn't even tell me where she was, she asked Henry and related his exact words to me. I hung up on her. Then I put the damn phone back to my ear as if she could still hear me and I could apologize after realizing I'd been rude.

Out on the street, I considered grabbing a cab, but from what they were telling me, they weren't anywhere near the road. Before I could waste more time thinking of the best way to get there, I found myself running across the street, ignoring the blaring car horns as I avoided getting hit by oncoming traffic. I entered the park somewhere around 79th and ran as fast as I could in a suit. If Henry had described the place correctly, she was somewhere in between the Ramble and the Boathouse.

I slowed down to a brisk walk when there was almost fifty feet separating us and watched as Rose lifted her head and looked straight at me. She gingerly got to her feet with the help of the man standing next to her. My eyes ran over her, but I couldn't see any visible injuries. My heart was pounding from the run, or maybe it was just worry, or what the hell maybe it was just seeing her, but thankfully my brain was still working enough to remember that we were supposed to be husband and wife and we could and *should* act like a couple around other people.

"Rose."

I went straight for her and before I could try to think of what I could do or what would be appropriate, I found myself rocking back a step when her body hit mine. She was fine, and she was already in my arms. A little out of breath, I didn't hesitate to wrap my arms around her, squeezing gently since I wasn't sure where her injuries were. I closed my eyes for a second and let out a long breath. She was fine.

"What happened?" I asked, addressing the guy next to her, but Rose answered before he could speak, thinking I was talking to her.

"I probably shouldn't have called you. I was being stupid, I'm sorry," she whispered to my shoulder and pulled back. My brows snapped together as I studied her face. If she didn't think she should have called me, what was she doing jumping into my arms? Reluctantly, I let her go. Her gaze dropped to her hands, so I looked down as well to see her staring at her shattered phone screen. "It works enough that I could find you in my contacts, but it's not calling. I'm not sure what's wrong."

"It's broken to pieces, that's what's wrong."

"Henry thought I should call someone to pick me up."

I finally turned to Henry. He was maybe forty or forty-five with white streaks in his hair, wearing black sweatpants and a black zip-up sweatshirt. I extended my hand. "Thank you for helping my wife. Is there anything we can do for you?"

We shook hands as he gave Rose a once-over. "It's nothing. I'm just glad I was there to help." He glanced at his watch. "I need to go, but she took a bad fall so you might want to have someone look—"

My jaw clenched. "I'll take care of her. Thank you again."

Rose shuffled closer to me. "I have a coffee shop on Madison Avenue, Around the Corner. If you're ever around, please drop by—I'd like to buy you a cup of coffee as a thank you."

"Sure. It's not safe for you to walk around the park this early in the morning, so be careful in the future."

"I will. Again, thank you."

Giving us a nod and a quick wave, Henry jogged away toward the west side.

Rose took a deep breath and sighed. I looked her over from head to toe once again, trying to assess the situation. "I feel fine now, and when Henry insisted I should call someone, I couldn't protest. I mean, I was going to call Owen, but he probably already started on the baking and I didn't want to take him from—"

"Rose, stop talking." I picked up her hand, the one she was holding her phone with, and she winced. I frowned down at her, gently picking up the phone so I could hold her hand and look at the damage. The heel of her palm was scraped and there was some blood.

"Give me your other hand."

"It's fine."

My mouth tightened and I kept my hand open, waiting for her. Reluctantly she held up her palm—the same scrapes, more blood.

"The ring is fine."

"Do I look like I care about a fucking ring?" I snapped, too busy turning her hand over and gently pressing on her wrists to see if she was hurting.

"Nope, you don't. How did you get here so fast anyway?"

"I ran."

She was quiet for a few seconds as I examined her skin.

"You ran?"

I gave her a long look that made her lips twitch which broke my concentration.

"It's just a bunch of surface scrapes. It'll be fine once I wash and clean them, Jack. I'm fine. Really. No need to worry."

"I'm not worrying."

I ran my thumb across her palm, dislodging a few small stones that were sticking to her skin. She was right—they weren't so bad that I would consider taking her to the hospital, but I *had* considered it. There was more dirt on her jeans so I assumed there were more scrapes at unseen places.

I let go of her hands, my eyes scanning her body again.

I watched as she held her hands up to her chest, rubbed the center of one, and winced.

"How did you managed to fall?"

Shifting her feet, she looked up at me under her lashes. "I was feeling a little dizzy and I fricking tripped on something. I don't even know what it was, I wasn't paying attention and then my ankle turned and I fell hard on my knees and hands. Henry helped me up, and I was a little shaky so he made me call someone. I couldn't think of anyone but you. It's nothing, I just need a little help walking, that's all."

I couldn't think of anyone but you.

That shut me up for a second or two as I stared at her.

"You're fine?" I asked with my brows raised. I reached for her hands and gently held them between us. Her palms weren't dripping with blood, but the scrapes weren't nothing either. "This isn't nothing. Who knows what your knees look like."

"I'm sure they look fine. It does hurt a little when I bend them, but only because I landed pretty hard on them, not because they're scraped."

Kneeling down, I looked at the foot she was trying her best not to put weight on. I rolled up her jeans once and gently wrapped my hand around her ankle. Even this. Even an innocent touch like this was starting to affect me.

"Jack?" Rose whispered and snapped me back from my thoughts.

When I pressed on a spot that was slightly red, she jerked it back.

"Yes," I said dryly as I stood up. "You're completely fine. Can you walk?"

"Yes."

"Okay. Let's see how you walk." Slipping her bag off her shoulder, I turned left, but she turned right. I stopped. "Where do you think you're going?"

"To work, of course," she replied with a small frown forming between her brows.

"I don't think so."

"Excuse me?"

"Rose, I need to take a look at what else is hurt. We're going home."

"I don't think so. I'm already late so if you're not gonna help, I'm completely fine walking on my own."

She turned, getting ready to walk away.

"Because that turned out so well for you the last time, right?" I asked, stopping her in her tracks before she could take a step.

Her eyes were narrowed when she faced me again. "Yes, actually, it's worked out just fine these last few weeks. So, I'm thinking it's gonna be just fine now too."

I gritted my teeth and kept my mouth shut. She didn't give me a chance to say anything anyway before she turned around to leave again. Her first step looked normal, but the second didn't look smooth enough. She was favoring her left leg. What was I gonna do with her? Without even realizing it, she had just crumpled another wall I'd tried my best to put up.

Still just a few steps separating us, I called out after her. "Your bag."

She stopped and looked at me over her shoulder, her features tight. "What?"

Staying silent, I raised my eyebrow and showed her the bag in my hand. She limped back the few steps she had taken and held her hand up, eyes boring into mine.

She was something else.

I studied her face, thinking maybe I could intimidate her, but she wasn't giving an inch. I'd gotten to know her pretty well, and I knew she wouldn't give in, no matter what I said or did. Shaking my head, I threw her bag on my left shoulder and tucked her arm around my right.

She stiffened next to me and tried to pull away. I covered the back of her hand with my right hand to keep her still.

"I'm not going back to your apartment, Jack," she said through gritted teeth as a group of runners and their two dogs forced us to move to the edge of the road.

"It's not my apartment anymore, is it?" I asked distractedly. "It's supposed to be ours. Get used to it so you don't let something like that slip around your cousins or other people."

"Are you taking me to work or—"

"We're going to your precious coffee shop, goddammit," I burst out, and then I tried my best to gentle my voice. "You called me for help and I'm helping. Stop arguing with me and try to walk instead."

That shut her up. She gave me another look and bit down on her lip as she grabbed my arm with her left hand too. After a few slow steps, she rested a bit more of her weight on me.

She was as stubborn as a mule. Another thing that made me like her more.

"How are your knees?" I asked, completely aware of how surly I sounded.

Another fleeting look at me. "They feel a little tight. I'm sure it'll go back to normal in a few hours. We're closer to the coffee shop than *our* apartment anyway."

I gritted my teeth, glaring at the people walking past us. "Right." After a few minutes of shuffling and resting and wincing, I couldn't take it anymore. "Put your arm around my neck," I ordered. When she hesitated, I sighed and did it myself.

"I'm shorter than you, so we can't walk like that—Jack!"

"What?" I asked, grunting softly when I had her up in my arms.

"Have you lost your mind?"

I started walking at a normal pace, holding her tightly against my chest as she slid her other hand around my neck.

"Jack, you don't have to carry me, I can walk. Put me down."

"No. You can't put weight on your left leg. You're gonna make it worse."

"I can. I've been walking with your help. Jack, I can."

"With the speed we were going, you'd reach your coffee shop at noon. What's the problem? I'm doing all the work here, and I thought you were in a hurry to get there."

"Jack," she growled, her eyes shooting daggers at me. I kept my eyes forward and continued walking. "Jack, I'm warning you, you're not going to carry me all the way to the coffee shop."

"I'm not? If you say so, I'm sure it must be true."

"Everyone is staring at us," she whispered.

"We've only passed two people."

"And both of them were looking at us like we were crazy. I'm not gonna be in your arms while we're crossing 5th Avenue with all those people around. Everyone will look at us. The traffic! And Madison Avenue!"

"You will."

"I'm really regretting calling you right now."

"I couldn't tell."

I was enjoying it too much.

When trying to push off of me so she could get down didn't work, she gently slapped my shoulder with her injured hand and then winced.

I clenched my jaw so I wouldn't smile. "Stop squirming. You're not the only one who likes to get to work on time."

"Fine, have it your way. You'll put me down once we exit the park." Since we were almost out of it anyway, a lot more people started to pass us, some of them snickering, some of them giving us disapproving looks. I ignored them, but Rose wasn't exactly good at that.

"Hi," she shouted to a stranger walking by and staring at her. "I just hurt my leg, that's why he's carrying me. He's my husband. Everything is good." The woman just shook her head and quickened her steps. "Jack," she groaned, her voice muffled by her face being buried in my neck. "They think we're crazy. I'll never be able to walk through here again."

I hiked her up and, with a surprisingly satisfying squeak, she held tighter on my neck. That was fun.

"If you don't want them to think you're crazy, I'd suggest stop shouting at them. And you aren't going to walk through here again anyway, so stop complaining."

She lifted her head off my chest. "What the hell are you talking about?"

"I'll talk to Raymond. He'll come earlier and take you across then he'll come back and take me to work. It was stupid of you to walk through the park while it was barely light out. You're lucky you didn't break your leg or get mugged."

I could feel her eyes on me, but I didn't look at her.

"I have pepper spray in my bag. And I don't need a driver. I'm not the kind of person who has a driver. No offense to Raymond—I like him, and he's a nice guy—but I'm not like you."

Finally, we made it out onto 5th, where there were a lot more people. "Thanks for pointing that out. I hadn't noticed."

"I've been taking care of myself all my life, Jack," she said softly.

"I know and you've done an amazing job. Just because you can take care of yourself, you're not supposed to let anyone else help you? I'm sorry for committing this atrocity against you."

"You're insane."

"I think we covered that the first day we met. No need to rehash it all over again."

"You're also unbelievable, do you know that?" she asked softer.

"I can imagine," I murmured, a little distracted. Standing next to a group of people, I waited for the light to change.

"He is my husband," Rose announced to the group. "I fell."

There were some snickers from the school girls on our left when I hiked her up again and Rose squeaked.

As we made it across, she started up again, and I sighed.

"We're almost there—"

"You can hold on for a few more minutes then."

"Jack."

"Rose. You know some women would find this romantic."

"I'm not some women."

"You're telling me," I grunted.

Luckily, there was silence after that until we reached the front door of her beautiful coffee shop. I gently put her down under the roses and handed her bag to her. Keeping her gaze averted, she searched for a key and opened the door. I could see the light in the kitchen from where we were standing, meaning the guy, the part-time worker, was already there. With jerky movements, she unlocked the door and walked in.

"Let's take a look at your knees while I—"

Before I could finish my sentence and follow her in, she slammed the door in my face and reset the alarm. As I stared after her, she didn't even look back. Still limping, she disappeared into the kitchen.

Shocked and absurdly amused, I stood there looking into the empty coffee shop for another ten seconds. Then, turning around, my hands in my pockets, I walked for a block or two. I eventually hailed a cab and headed home so I could get to work myself. I wasn't sure what to feel about the smile that stayed on my face the entire morning.

LATER, I walked into my office and greeted Cynthia.

"Good morning, Jack."

I leaned against the edge of my desk. "Good morning. Any changes in my schedule for today?"

Her forehead creased, and she looked down at her tablet. "No, no changes."

"Then I need you to clear everything between..." I checked my watch, trying to decide what time would be better. "Eleven-thirty and two-thirty. A few hours would be enough, I think."

"Enough for what?"

"I have something I need to take care of."

"Jack, I can't clear those time slots."

"Why not?"

"Did you forget? You have the negotiations with Morrison and Gadd."

"The documents with the necessary changes are ready?"

"An associate is on it, and it'll be done in time for the meeting."

"Get them from him."

"But—"

"I'll get it done quicker. Get it for me."

"Done."

"Good, and push the negotiations to two. The other side, Gadd, didn't want to meet up that early anyway, so let them know first." I got up and moved to sit behind my desk.

"And Morrison? What am I supposed to tell him?" she asked.

I sighed and ran my fingers through my hair. "Did you read his email? The one he sent this morning?"

She nodded.

"Well, tell him we need to do more research on the new company he wants to invest twenty million in. I want to get both the negotiations and the new investment deal taken care of today. He won't mind the delay if we have everything ready."

"Okay. What about the rest of your schedule? We'll need to push everything back. You have a five PM call with Gilbert—you can't miss that today."

"Fine. I'll leave the office at eleven. I can get through my ten-thirty call by then, and I'll come back around one-thirty for the meeting so push it to then instead. That way I'll be done with Morrison and Gadd by the time I need to be on the phone with Gilbert. If everything goes as planned, we'll have Gadd sign the final papers at the end of the meeting and I'll be ready for the call with Gilbert. I'll stay late and catch up, don't worry."

"Okay, I can work with that. Where did you say you were going again?"

"I didn't say. Close the door, please, and don't forget to bring me those documents."

When I lifted my head up from my laptop, Cynthia was already gone.

An hour later, when I was going through the documents, making sure everything was ready for the meeting, Samantha appeared at my door. I glanced at Cynthia's desk, but she was nowhere to be seen.

Wanting to get it over with, I was the one who engaged her. "What do you want, Samantha? I need to go over these before I leave."

She shrugged and took my question as an invitation to walk in and sit across from me. "Something is not right with you—or maybe I should say something has changed."

"What the hell are you talking about?"

"You've been leaving early."

"And that's your business because...?"

"You're the last one to leave here, every day."

"And now I'm not." I put down the papers in my hands. "What do you want?"

She lifted her hands in surrender, her red lips curving up. "Nothing. I'm just making conversation and sharing my observations."

"What gave you the impression that I would be interested in your observations? I'm not going to explain myself to you. Do you need something from me?"

"Not really. I had a little free time so I'm just chatting with you. How is your lovely wife?"

If it had been someone else sitting across from me, they would've tucked their tail between their legs and left already, but Samantha wasn't like other people. She had never been scared of me, and I thought maybe it was time to change that.

"If you pull the same shit you pulled at dinner again, we'll have problems."

"Excuse me?"

"What you did at dinner—I'm letting you know if it happens again, we'll have problems."

"It's going to be like that, huh?"

"Cut the crap and don't act like you care about my life or my wife. We know each other pretty well by now, I'd think. You know I don't like having people in my business, so stay out of it."

Cynthia stuck her head in, interrupting before Samantha could give a response. "Did you call me, Jack?"

I hadn't, but Cynthia knew the trick. If there was someone in my office she was sure I wouldn't want there, she always ran interference. "Yes, I need you to get me the—"

Samantha rose to her high-heeled feet and I paused midsentence. "I'll leave you to your work. I didn't mean any harm, Jack, truly—not that night, and not just now. I'm simply pointing out that you've changed, and I'm not sure if that's a good thing. Plus, I was curious, obviously."

When she realized I wasn't going to answer, she released a long sigh, turned around, and gave Cynthia a smile before walking out of my office.

"You need anything?" Cynthia asked, and I shook my head. She left without another word. She was the best assistant in the entire firm.

Done with the papers, I got on with my ten-thirty call, and we wrapped up at a quarter past eleven. Rising, I put on my suit jacket and called Raymond so he could bring the car around front.

Leaving the office, I stopped in front of Cynthia's desk and dropped off the documents. "Can you have the copies ready by the time I get back?"

"Of course."

"Also, do you remember the charity thing you mentioned a few weeks ago? Something for kids?" I tried to remember where it was going to be held, but I couldn't come up with the name. "It was on the tenth, I think. I'm not sure."

"Yes, I remember. What about it?"

"I want to donate, so I'm going to attend with my wife. Can you take care of everything?"

"You're going to attend a charity dinner?" Her voice got thinner with each word as her brows rose higher.

"Try not to look so surprised. Can you handle it?"

She shook herself out of her disbelief. "Of course I can. I'll give you the info you need when you get back."

"Okay. Thank you, Cynthia. I'll see you later."

I managed to take a few steps away from her desk before her voice stopped me.

"Jack?"

I turned back and waited. She played with her glasses and looked away from me.

"I'm going to be late. What do you want?"

"Jack...it's not my place, and I know that, so don't bite my head off for saying this, but..." I knew nothing that started with those words could be something I'd want to hear.

"I don't bite your head off."

She smiled, relaxing in her seat. "Only every day."

"Surely not every day," I said seriously, but her smile grew, and then she slowly went back to being serious.

"You have to tell her, Jack."

"I have to tell who what? Samantha?"

She pinned me with her stare. "No. Not Samantha. I've known you for years now—don't try to act stupid with me. You have to tell her. That's all I'm going to say on the matter."

I opened my mouth, but she lifted her finger and stopped me. "You have to tell her."

It finally dawned on me what the hell she was talking about. Of course she was talking about Rose. If there was one person whose crap I'd tolerate, it was Cynthia, and even with her, I had a limit, yet I didn't respond the way I would've responded if it was anyone but her. "It's not the right time," I forced out through my gritted teeth.

"It's never going to be the right time, Jack."

As if I didn't already know that. As if I didn't know I was doomed.

I left before she could say anything else.

NOT EXACTLY SURE what I would face—because it always seemed to be a surprise when it came to Rose—I walked through the door. The day before, it had smelled like vanilla; it now smelled of cinnamon and fragrant coffee. With the bell's noise, Rose glanced my way while still attending to a customer. Her smile faltered, but she didn't lose it completely. Instead of heading over to her, I picked the table next to her little library and got comfortable. My seat was facing her, so I looked around and noticed, out of the twelve tables, nine were occupied. For her second day, she was doing amazingly well. Even the bar seats had a couple customers deep in conversation as they looked out on the street, drinking their coffees. Two new customers walked in and I settled down to wait. Taking out my phone, I started to catch up on emails.

The few times I glanced up to see if she was avoiding me or was simply busy, my eyes lingered on her, causing me to lose my train of thought. She always looked so lively, so vivacious and confident. In between customers, her eyes slid my way. I held her gaze to see what she'd do, but she managed to act as if I wasn't even there.

Holding back a smile, I waited. A few minutes turned into ten, and then finally she stood over me, waiting. I raised an eyebrow and lowered my phone.

"I was starting to think you were avoiding me."

"I didn't expect to see you here. Can I get you anything?"

"Why are you always so surprised to see me?" I asked, genuinely curious to hear her answer. Her expression didn't change, which told me she was still annoyed with me—not that I could understand her reasoning. Her leg had been hurt, so I'd helped her, end of story. Why did it matter what other people she'd probably never see again in her life or even remember if she saw them thought? I'd always been under the impression that women found it romantic when guys carried them. Apparently not this one.

"I'm not surprised anymore." She looked over her shoulder when one of the customers let out a loud laugh then turned back to me. "Can I—"

"Were you expecting to see me tonight?" I asked, again, just out of curiosity. I leaned forward and put my phone on the table.

She licked her lips, looking toward the kitchen. I followed her gaze and saw the girl she had introduced me to before—Sally, I believed—leaning against the doorframe and talking to someone in the kitchen, most likely the other employee, the guy. My eyes back on Rose, I waited to hear her reply.

"I was. You always come," she said, shrugging as if it was a given that I'd be there. I supposed it was now.

"Will you join me, please?"

She eyed the seat across from me but didn't sit down. "Can I get you anything before I do that? Coffee? Tea?"

"I wouldn't say no to coffee if you're the one preparing it."

She looked a little surprised then nodded and walked away, slowly. She wasn't limping exactly, so she was probably right that it hadn't been a serious injury, but she wasn't walking smoothly either. Point being, her ankle was hurting. I still didn't understand the fuss when I had only tried to help her.

Instead of getting back on my phone and finishing the response I had started, I watched her prepare coffee for both of us, discreetly glancing my way every now and then. A few minutes later, she came back with a small tray and put it on the table before sitting down across from me. Reaching forward, she put one of the mugs in front of me and held on to the other one. Between us sat a plate full of lemon bars.

I gave her a questioning look, but she was busy drinking from her mug, her eyes cast downward.

"No work today?" she asked into her coffee mug.

"I need to get back soon."

She nodded and we fell silent.

"So, we're not talking then," I concluded. "I'm not planning on apologizing for trying to help you, if that's what you're waiting for me to do."

"No, you're not the kind of person who apologizes, are you?" she asked, lifting her big brown eyes up to mine. "Do you ever apologize? For anything?"

"I try not to do anything I'll end up having to apologize for," I answered honestly. *Try* was the operative word here.

She sighed and took another long sip of her coffee. "I'm not angry at you for helping me. I would've preferred to walk on my own, but I'm not gonna stay angry at you for carrying me. I was a little annoyed by your last comment, that's all. Still, I'm sorry," she mumbled.

A little amused, I leaned forward, resting my elbows on the table. "Excuse me? I couldn't hear what you said to your coffee."

"I said—" she looked up and met my eyes. "You heard that."

Why did I enjoy provoking her?

Why did I enjoy when she snapped back at me?

"For what?" I asked, reaching for my own coffee.

Another long sigh. "For slamming the door in your face and leaving you out there. It was immature, but in my defense you know exactly which buttons to push."

I couldn't exactly argue with that. "Okay. Now will you tell me which of my comments made you annoyed with me?"

"It's not important."

"It is to me."

We looked at each other for a while.

"I said *I'm not some women* and you said, *you're telling me.*"

Hiding my smile behind the mug, I kept my eyes on her, and she chose to look anywhere but me. She appeared to be both annoyed and surly at the same time, and defiant, of course—definitely not someone who was regretting slamming the door in my face.

"I meant that as a compliment, Rose."

Her eyes came back to me.

"I...Good. That's great then. Thank you?"

"How's your ankle?" I asked, letting her off the hook.

"It's better. It didn't swell up, but I'm still taking it easy."

At least the stiffness in her shoulders had softened a bit.

"How are we? Are we good as well?"

Her smile was as sweet as it could get.

"Yes, Jack."

"You made lemon bars again," I commented in the hopes of changing the conversation to safer ground when I felt myself drawn to her even more.

She shifted in her seat. "Actually, that was why I was coming in early. I promised you I'd make more of them yesterday, bring a batch back to the apartment maybe, because I like them too. I thought I'd get them done before opening up."

"You made them for me?"

"I promised." She shrugged and pushed her hands under her legs. "And I thought it would be a good apology for slamming the door in your face."

I raised an eyebrow and took another sip of my coffee before reaching for one of the bars. Taking a bite, I watched her watching me.

Feeling eyes on me, I looked over Rose's shoulder, saw Sally keeping an eye on us from her spot with interest, and missed the end of Rose's sentence. I doubted we looked like a real couple from where she was standing, let alone a married one.

Maybe we should do something to fix that.

My focus shifted back to Rose.

"So we had our first married fight, huh? How do you feel about that?"

"The honeymoon stage is over for us, I'm afraid," I agreed offhandedly.

She nodded. "We made quick work of that. I don't see good things for the future of our marriage."

"You never know. Maybe we're one of those married couples who fight at the drop of a hat but never get a divorce. You might be stuck with me."

"Oh, that sounds exhausting, and annoying for other people. Let's not be like them. Let's find better examples and try to imitate them."

"Like who?"

Her gaze slid up to the ceiling as she tried to come up with an example. "Actually, I don't think I know that many married couples. You?"

"I'm afraid the ones I know aren't people I'd like to imitate," I answered.

"Evelyn and Fred?"

"They are more like partners than anything else."

"Oh, from the way Fred talked about her that night, I assumed they were in love."

"They do love each other, but I think if they didn't have a kid, they wouldn't have much in common other than work."

"Your parents? How about them? Are they still married? Do they have a happy marriage?"

After drinking almost half of the coffee, I put it down and leaned back. "The last people you'd like to imitate, trust me. Just look at how I turned out."

"I don't know. I think they did a pretty good job with you. Then how about we don't imitate anyone and just make our own rules?"

"What kind of a couple do you want to be then?"

She thought about it some, taking sips of her coffee every now and then. "I don't want to be one of those couples who are in everyone's face, being all extra touchy. We could be more subtle, you know what I mean?"

I nodded and she kept going.

"Let me give you a small example, just in case. Let's say we're standing and talking to someone—you can hold my hand or have your arm around my waist, just keep it simple and...maybe a small, intimate kiss. I don't know, just...simple."

"Any other tips you have for me?" I asked with a raised eyebrow.

"It wasn't a tip, exactly. You asked what kind of couple I wanted us to be, so I'm just saying. I like that kind of couple."

"What else?"

"I want to be the kind of couple that has traditions. Like... maybe Mondays are pizza nights. Thursday is pasta day. That type of thing."

"That's it?"

"Okay, give me a minute. I'm going to Google this and see what we're working with. Let me get my phone."

Before I could stop her, she got up and ran to the kitchen. Her movements were a little wobbly and she tried to tiptoe on her left foot, but in essence it would be called running. She waved

Sally off when she looked alarmed, and her return was calmer, no running this time.

Puffing out a breath, she took her seat again and focused on the screen of her phone. "Okay, let me see...okay, there are more formal types like traditional, disengaged, cohesive, pursuer, distant—we won't be that. I hate those types. Operatic...heated fighting followed by passionate lovemaking." Her head snapped up and she stole a glance at me then quickly focused back on her phone. "Nope. Romantic couple—that doesn't sound too bad, does it? Okay, let me try to find something more informal..."

I drained the rest of my coffee.

"Okay. Showoffs...basically PDA—this is what I meant. I don't like being all extra. Also, I don't see you as a PDA person," she mumbled. "Space-giving couple—I guess we're like that? Why are they married couple...we can't be this. That is not me. Even if this is fake, I don't want to be like that. If we're playing a part, let's do it right."

"That would be my parents."

Her head lifted again. "Really?"

I nodded.

"Yikes. Okay, what else...what else...honeymoon couple. Dammit, we just fought, so that doesn't work for us. Next, whining couple—nope. Always together couple...I mean..." She looked at me under her lashes, but neither one of us made a comment. "The rest is crap." She put her phone down. "Anything specific you want to be?"

"Let's stick with doing whatever needs to be done at the moment."

"That's leaving it very open to interpretation."

I ran my hand over my face. "How about just being ourselves and acting natural?"

"You're loads of fun. Being ourselves individually isn't the problem. How to be ourselves as a couple—that's the hard thing."

"What? Do you want to practice playing pretend?" She looked at me weirdly but didn't respond. I changed tactics, because playing pretend wouldn't be a good idea at all. Not with how things were going. This was fake and temporary. Period. "Am I allowed to ask about your relationship with your ex-fiancé? What kind of a couple were you? Why did you break up?"

She looked taken back but at least responded. "Where did that come from?"

"I'm curious."

"You're never curious."

"Today, it seems I am."

Looking all kinds of uncomfortable, she sighed. "We weren't a specific type of couple, I guess. We did our own thing. Sometimes he was into PDA even when I wasn't and it would bug me off, but other than that it was an easy relationship. Looking back at it now maybe it was too easy. And we just... God, I hate this. I was shocked when he ended things. Came out of nowhere, he dumped me in a text. I couldn't believe I was so wrong about him. Couldn't believe he didn't want to marry me anymore. Called him for days, trying to get in touch. Never heard back. Went to his apartment and his neighbor said he'd moved out. Just like that, he just disappeared." She lifted a shoulder and then let it drop down.

"I lost it there for a few days. Then sadness gave way to anger. I gave myself permission to cry and curse him for a week, but anyone who breaks up with me via text is not worth crying for. I stopped crying on day four. I don't have the luxury of pining after someone who doesn't want me. He had this way of making me feel less than without me realizing he was doing it. It was weird. I definitely thought he was the one for me, up until he broke up with me, but when he wasn't around anymore, the rose-colored glasses came off pretty quickly. He was really good at getting me to say yes to everything even when I didn't want to. Everyone loved him, especially Gary."

"I thought you didn't see Gary much."

"I didn't, but Joshua really wanted to meet him so I kinda had to... He knew exactly what to say to get you to like him, and as for being my fiancé...he did ask me to marry him, but he didn't give me a ring or anything like that, so now that I'm thinking about it, maybe he never meant to go through with it anyway? Who knows."

"What about now? Do you feel something for him now?"

She frowned. "Of course not. Sometimes all you need is a little time away to look at things with a new perspective. Joshua and I seemed like a great idea on paper, but in reality I don't think we would've worked in the long run. There wasn't much of a spark to keep it going, I think. I'm not sad it's over. Anyway... Jack, why did you say you came here again?"

I let the Joshua topic go.

This was fake. This was temporary.

"I wanted to see if you needed anything. And to see if you were okay."

"That's...really sweet of you, Jack."

Before I could say something, the door behind me opened, cold air rushing inside as the bell rang, a soft welcoming chime for the new customers.

I looked over my shoulder to see four women still admiring the flowers as Rose got to her feet. The smile I was getting too familiar with was already plastered on her lips and it was not just for me anymore.

"I'll be right back." Her mind was obviously focused on the newcomers as they slowly walked forward, their curious eyes taking everything in.

She turned toward the group of customers.

"Welcome," Rose said when the chatty women were finally

near her. My eyes dropped to her lips as her smile widened when the women smiled back and said hello.

"If you have work to do, I should leave. I have a packed afternoon and evening," I commented, distracted.

Her gaze flitted back to me. "You're not coming tonight? You don't have to, of course, but I—"

"I pushed back a meeting to be able to come here now, so I'm going to have to stay late to catch up with my calls after that ends. I'll send Raymond. You think you'll be able to make it back to the apartment in one piece?"

"Oh, that's funny, Mr. Hawthorne. I—"

"Rose!" Sally called out, catching her attention.

Instead of going behind the counter to work next to Sally, Rose stayed next to the customers, chatting with them and pointing at the food under the glass domes. I waited for a few minutes, feeling impatient; waiting wasn't my strong suit. Eventually, after a long discussion and several changed decisions, everyone had given their orders. I ate another of the lemon bars Rose had baked herself and rose from my seat. Reaching for my wallet in my back pocket, I took out some cash. She didn't notice me until I was standing right next to her.

"Oh, Jack, I'll be right—"

Everyone's eyes were on us, especially Sally's, so I tried to be careful. "I need to leave." I held out a hundred-dollar bill to Sally and instead of being a good employee and taking it from me before Rose could see, her gaze jumped from me to Rose.

"Ummm...Rose," she mumbled, causing Rose to take her eyes from me and glance at her and then at the money I was holding.

"What's that for?" Rose asked, fully facing me.

I sighed and, after giving Sally a cold look, met Rose's eyes.

"Let's not do this again. Take it," I ordered, holding it out to her.

"Don't make me hurt you, Jack Hawthorne," she said slowly,

and my lips twitched involuntarily. I could imagine she fully meant what she said. I had no doubt she could hurt me.

"I need to leave," I repeated. Then, thinking it would simply be a good distraction, a good show for her employee and even sort of a practice for the charity event we'd be attending, I slid my arm around her waist. Her eyes were slightly widened in alarm, her entire body stiff, but at least she wasn't jumpy like she had been at our first outing. Slowly her body relaxed, and she arched her back so she could look up at me with those big eyes.

A simple and meaningless touch would have to be acted out more naturally at one point in our fake marriage, almost as if touching her or kissing her in front of other people would become second nature. Practice was good.

"Thank you for the coffee. It's always the best," I murmured, having trouble looking away. Then I leaned down and hesitated for a heartbeat before I pressed a lingering kiss on her forehead as she was still looking up at me in confusion. That spot felt like it was the most harmless one and I took my time, breathing in her sweet and fresh scent. When I pulled back, one of her hands was resting against my chest, the other one clutching my arm. Her chest rising and falling, she blinked up at me.

Taking her hand that had ended up on my chest, I opened her fingers, my fingertip catching on her wedding ring. Why did such a simple and, in our situation, meaningless thing give me so much pleasure to see? She wasn't mine, but the idea of it...the possibility... I placed the money on her still red palm before gently closing her fingers around the bill. Surprisingly, she didn't say a word, just kept staring up at me as if she was lost. Was she just as affected as I was by our pretending?

"Don't take it off, okay? I like seeing it on your finger," I whispered.

I had already forgotten about the people around us. This wasn't so much for them but more for me, I thought, just so I could see that soft look on her face. I cupped her cheek and leaned down enough so I could whisper in her ear. "Was that the right amount of PDA for our fake marriage? A small intimate kiss, you said, right? Arm around the waist? Bodies close, but not touching?" I lifted my head up enough so I could meet her eyes and, in a louder voice, said, "Don't stay on your feet for too long—you're still limping."

She didn't look like she was going to say anything, so I pushed a little more.

"Can you at least say goodbye to your husband?"

"Uh...I should, shouldn't I? Goodbye?"

After wishing a good day to everyone who didn't have the decency to mind their own business, I left.

Yes, practice was good.

CHAPTER ELEVEN

JACK

A lmost an hour later, I was back in my office, eating lunch and answering emails when my phone vibrated on the desk with a new text message.

Rose: I'll give your money back to you as soon as I see you.

Sighing, I put down my fork and knife and picked up my phone.

Jack: You stayed quiet about that for long enough. It's been an hour. You're still on that?
Rose: It was lunch time. You're not paying me for a cup of coffee. Also, today's customer count is a total of 68. All the sandwiches are gone. Yay!
Jack: I'm not gonna keep talking about money with you. Congratulations on the new customers. You're counting them?
Rose: Of course I'm counting them. Who wouldn't? And what

about what other people think about the money? Sally asked a ton of questions about you after you left. Whose husband would pay for coffee at his wife's coffee shop?

It was little things like this that were slowly cracking my resolve against her. No one else would count their customers. No one else would smile as big and beautiful as she did when they saw me, simply because I showed up. No one else would work their ass off every day and night and still find a way to bust my balls. No one else would dare to slam the door in my face, but she did all of those things, and because of that—because of *her*—I wasn't sure how long I would be able to keep up my part of the charade.

Jack: And I should care about Sally because...? Your husband pays for his coffee because he wants his wife to succeed.
Rose: I hope you won't take this the wrong way, but I don't know what to say to you sometimes.

I smiled at my phone.

Jack: See, we're doing just fine as a fake married couple. That sounded a lot like what a wife would say to her husband. Also, you didn't get jumpy when I put my hands on you this time. I'd call that progress.
Rose: Yeah, because you came at me like a turtle.

I was drinking water when her text came in, and reading it started a coughing fit. It lasted long enough that Cynthia walked in to see if everything was all right. I sent her away and picked my phone back up.

Jack: I'll try to work on it.

Rose: There should be a middle ground, I think, but it was a good start. Definitely closer to the type of couple I'd want to be if I were really married.

Jack: Right. Hopefully I didn't embarrass you too much.

Rose: No, it was fine. They all thought it was very romantic. Everyone loves a good forehead kiss.

Jack: I'm guessing you don't.

I checked the time. I had another half an hour before I needed to head to the meeting room and get ready, and my lunch was still not done, not to mention I still had emails I needed to get back to. I didn't have time to text anyone, let alone get into a texting marathon, but when it was Rose on the other end of those messages, I couldn't seem to help myself.

Rose: I mean, there is nothing wrong with it, I guess. It's just a little weird sometimes. Why not kiss me on the lips instead? With the right guy, even a simple cheek kiss can make things happen, or a temple kiss, or a neck one, or one on the skin just below your ear. I just don't get the significance.

Jack: Make things like what happen?

It took her longer to respond.

Rose: Things.

Jack: I see.

Rose: That was not me saying I'd prefer you to kiss me on the lips instead of the forehead. The next time, I mean, when that kind of thing is necessary to do again.

Jack: I can try if you'd like to see how it'd work out.

Rose: I mean, it's your preference. You should do whatever feels right.

Her lips then—next time it would be her lips I would taste.

Rose: I just don't want you to think I was fishing for a kiss or something like that.

Jack: Is there a reason we're still texting and not talking on the phone instead? This is not efficient.

Rose: Like I said, I don't know what to say to you sometimes.

Jack: I think you're doing just fine considering the number of texts you've sent in the last five minutes. There is something I forgot to tell you when I was there.

Lately everything had started to slip my mind when she was close to me.

Jack: There is a charity event we need to attend this weekend. It's this Saturday. Do you think you can make it?

Rose: That was our deal. You held up your end, I'll do the same.

I thought that would be the end of our impromptu text conversation, but more kept coming.

Rose: So what are you doing?

Jack: Eating lunch. I have a meeting in half an hour.

Rose: You're out at lunch?

Jack: In my office.

Rose: You're eating lunch in your office by yourself?

Jack: Yes.

Rose: Why didn't you tell me? I make great sandwiches.

I looked down at my high-priced steak lunch and wished I had a sandwich instead.

Jack: Next time.

Rose: Okay. I'll let you go so you can finish eating before the meeting.

I wasn't sure what was wrong with me, because calling her was not what I was supposed to do next. She answered on the second ring right when I put her on speaker.

"Jack? Why are you calling?"

"After receiving all these texts, I'd say you're not annoyed or angry with me anymore, correct?"

Her voice sounded a little sheepish when she answered. "Not at the moment. I'm not the best at holding grudges, as you can see."

I'm gonna have to remind you of that when the time comes.

"I'm guessing things are not busy at the coffee shop if you can text for that long."

"And I'm guessing you hate texting." She was right; I really did. "We do have customers," she continued. "Wait, let me check." There was silence for a few seconds then her voice came back on the line. "Eight tables full and four more at the bar. I'm covering the front and talking to you. Oh wait, customer number sixty-nine just walked in."

"I'm hanging up then."

"Why? No. Stay on the line—I'll be right back."

I should've hung up. Instead, I listened to her take an order.

"Jack, you there?"

"You told me to wait."

"Good. I'm preparing two macchiatos. They're to-go. Are we going to do something tonight?"

"Like what?" I asked.

"Like any events, work dinners, client meetings?"

"I was under the assumption you weren't a fan of those."

"I'm not, but the last time wasn't so bad. We can have fun or make it fun—this whole make-believe thing, especially since I know you better now."

"You think you know me?"

"Oh, yes, Jack Hawthorne. I've pretty much figured you out. One second."

She went back to her customer and, like a fool, I kept waiting, anxious to hear what she was going to say next.

"I'm back. What was I saying?"

"You think you figured me out."

"Ah, yes. I actually have a pretty good idea what kind of person you are."

"Are you going to share or are you going to make me wait for it?"

"Oh, I'm going to make you wait. I think you'll like that more."

"I won't. Tell me now."

Her laughter rang in my ears and I closed my eyes, drinking it in.

"Nope. Oh, customer seventy and seventy-one just walked in. I'll see you tonight, Jack. Show someone some smiles for me. Bye!"

Just like that, she hung up, leaving me wanting for more. *Is this my life now?*

My mood only declined when I tried to focus on the documents in front of me and couldn't. All I could think about was how I could dig myself out of this grave I'd ended up in. When the time came, I left for the meeting. Thankfully, everything else was ready, so after doing a quick check on the documents just to confirm everything was in order, I stepped out of my office.

Cynthia greeted me, standing up.

"If you're ready, let's go."

She grabbed her tablet and followed me.

"Bryan Coleson called. Twice, today."

I gritted my teeth, but didn't answer.

"Did you tell her?"

I stopped moving. She took a few steps but, realizing I wasn't walking anymore, stopped and backtracked.

"You're going to stop asking me that question," I forced out, trying my best not to be too rude.

"I have so much respect for you, Jack. You know I do. I've been working with you for years and I've never done this, but right now you need someone to tell you you're doing wrong. I'm that someone. As foreign as that idea is, you know you're doing wrong."

"We're late to the meeting. If you want to—"

"No, we're not. Morrison called ten minutes ago to say he'd be late. Gadd is waiting with his lawyers."

I tried again. "I respect you, too, Cynthia. Like you said, you've been with me for years now, but this doesn't concern you, and I'd think after the years we've spent together, you'd know better than to push me on this."

"I care about you, so I'd say I should."

I started walking again, silently passing some of the senior associates as they greeted me. Cynthia kept up with my pace, not uttering another word. I thought she was finally done, but that changed when no one else was in sight and it was just us again.

"Just tell her. It's not too late."

I came to another abrupt stop. Ready for it this time, she halted next to me, a little out of breath. After glancing behind me, I pulled her into a small junior associate office and closed the door. Our voices would still carry outside, but at least it would be muffled and there would be some semblance of privacy.

"I'm not going to have this same conversation with you again. This is my last warning."

"You telling me not to talk about this again is not us having a conversation about it."

"What the hell has gotten into you today?" I asked, frustrated and not sure how to handle this side of my assistant.

"I told you: the day you made this ridiculous deal, I told you not to do it. This was the stupidest idea you've ever had."

"You think I don't fucking know that?" I growled, my temper boiling over. "You think I didn't figure that out the second she went along with my plan?"

"Then what's the problem? Just tell her."

"Tell her what, for fuck's sake? Tell her I basically stalked her and the more I learned about her, the more interested I became? Or should I tell her I don't give a damn about the property?"

"You didn't stalk her, Jack. You were trying to help her. She'll understand when you explain it to her."

"Trying to help by marrying her? There were a number of other things I could've done to help her, Cynthia. Getting married wasn't at the top of the list—it shouldn't have been on the list at all. I was being a selfish bastard."

"Your own gain—"

My voice had risen enough that George, who was just passing by, stopped and opened the door.

"What's going on here? I can hear your voices from a mile away. Aren't you supposed to be at the Morrison and Gadd meeting?"

"I'm heading there now," I gritted through my teeth. "We just picked up a file we needed."

Frowning at us, George accepted the lie and, giving us a final confused look, walked away.

Cynthia started on me before I could utter another word.

"You had me look into her a year ago. Why did you wait so long to introduce yourself?"

"I'm only going to tell you one more time, Cynthia: if you ever say another word on this subject, I will fire you on the spot and not even think twice about it. I don't give a damn whether you're the best or not."

Without waiting for her to even acknowledge what I had just said, I stormed out of the room and headed straight to the meeting.

———————

By the time the meeting was over, my head was pounding and I was ready to end the day and leave. It was only five PM, though, so I was stuck in my office for a few more hours going through more paperwork.

Cynthia was smart enough to stay out of my sight the entire time. I took all my frustrations out on work and didn't even think about anything else for the rest of the day, which is why when I ended my last phone call and lifted my head, I was so surprised to see Rose standing just outside my office door, talking to my assistant. Trying to keep my anger with Cynthia in check, I slowly rose from behind my desk and strode toward them.

When I pulled the glass door open a bit too fast, Rose jumped a little, her hand flying to her chest. "You scared me. How did you get here so fast? You were just sitting at your desk when I looked in."

"What are you doing here?" I snapped, my eyes going from her to Cynthia.

Cynthia gave me a disapproving head shake, which I chose to ignore.

Rose's eyes widened slightly, and I cursed myself. "I'm sorry. If this is a bad time, I don't have to—"

"Come in." When she didn't move, I tried to soften my tone.

"Please come in, Rose." As she moved past me, I gave Cynthia a long look. "You're done for the day. You can leave."

"I was just thinking I should do that," she replied coldly, and I gritted my teeth.

Closing the door and hoping Cynthia would leave as quickly as possible, I turned to find Rose standing in the middle of the room.

"Please, sit," I said, gesturing to one of the leather chairs in front of my desk.

"Jack, if you're busy—"

"I finished my last call. I'm not busy anymore."

Keeping her eyes on me, she slowly sat down, her eyes studying me. "You look extra grumpy. I can leave."

I sighed and ran my hand over my face, trying to get it together. "Extra grumpy?" I asked, my brows rising. She bit on her lower lip and shrugged. I had to force my gaze away from her mouth before I forgot about everything else and just acted. "No, you don't have to leave. Too many meetings, too many calls, that's all. I didn't mean to be harsh out there, I just wasn't expecting to see you."

"That's usually my line. You always show up when I'm not expecting you." I couldn't manage to smile back. "Ray came to the coffee shop when I was getting ready to close up, when he asked whether he should take me back to the apartment or pick you up first, I thought it'd be a nice change of pace—me picking you up, I mean."

Her lips curved up slightly, and my eyes focused on that. Her smile was what had gotten me into this mess that first time we were introduced.

I just stared at her as a frown replaced her smile.

"Jack? Are you sure everything is okay? Is there something I can help with?"

Unfortunately, everything wasn't okay. I was losing control, and it was all because of her, all because of the guilt I couldn't get rid of. If I kept going down the same path, all I'd accomplish would be making her hate me. Cynthia's words came back to me and I considered them for a second, considered telling Rose. Maybe if she heard everything, maybe if she knew what had happened and what I was thinking—I decided against it. I wasn't ready to lose her just yet.

If I could find the courage to tell her one day and hope she'd still stay, things would have to change—drastically.

I'd need all the time I could get to try to make her feel something for me, and maybe along the way I would come up with a good way to admit that I'd deceived her from the very beginning, to admit that the reason I offered to marry her wasn't to have someone to attend the parties with. I hated any and all events, rarely went to them. It wasn't to appear to be a family man to appease clients, and it definitely wasn't because I was interested in the property. I could've bought ten of them if I was so inclined.

But, to be able to tell her all of that, I'd have to forget about the guilt that was eating me up on the inside and focus on getting and keeping her attention.

Coming to a concrete decision, I focused on Rose. "Everything is great. Are you free to have dinner with me again tonight?"

That piqued her interest. "Takeout?"

"If that's what you want."

"Can we have pizza again?"

"If you'll let me take a look at your knees, I'll think about it."

The look she gave me...

"That's sounded a little kinky, Jack."

The sweet smile on her lips that I had craved to be on the receiving end of for so long...

I was ruined.

In the end, we had the pizza, but she didn't let me get a look at the damage to her knees. When it came to Rose, I knew I had my work cut out for me.

Good thing, after getting to know her and spending so much time with her, I had no intention of backing off anymore.

Grabbing my phone, I found Bryan Coleson's number from my contact list and hit call. Finally returning his call.

CHAPTER TWELVE

ROSE

B eing married to Jack Hawthorne had turned out to have its own advantages—apart from the broody eye candy and the almost daily arm porn, I mean. As much as I didn't care for the idea of having a driver take me to work, I didn't put up any fight when Jack forced me to go with Raymond in the mornings instead of walking through Central Park and getting myself into *situations*—his word, not mine—because I knew it was safer.

I still mumbled under my breath and put up the illusion of a fight to look more impressive and fearless in his eyes, which sounded stupid when I thought about it more, but I still did it.

Being the prickly, no-nonsense guy he was, with a hand on my back—literally—he pushed me all the way down from the apartment to the car where Raymond was waiting next to the passenger door, as if I'd run away from him like a kid if he wasn't keeping his hand on me. I was quite fine with the acting, because it kept his hand firmly on my back. So, joke's on him. I managed to mumble and mutter the entire way down in the elevator, and he didn't even utter a word.

There was something about his gruffness that I just loved. It would put some people off, it definitely had put *me* off, but the more I got to know him, the more I found it adorable.

As Raymond drove me to the coffee shop, I had an amused smile plastered on my face the whole time because Jack had looked so triumphant as he shut the car door in my face.

I chatted with Raymond to hide my giddiness and learned more about him. One particular subject that came up a few days into our morning rides was him trying the online dating scene for the first time in his life after divorcing his ex-wife, who he had caught cheating with one of his friends. Thank God they hadn't had kids. We were both happy about that, and the retelling of the horrible and awkward dates provided much amusement that early in the morning.

At the end of the week, we pretty much knew almost everything about each other, and it had stopped feeling like he was my driver and had turned into going to work with a friend. It also helped that he was the only person who knew about our fake marriage and never even mentioned what a weird thing it was.

There were plenty of times when I wanted to prod him about Jack, just little questions here and there, but asking him how long he'd been with Jack was as far as I'd gotten.

He looked at me through the rearview mirror in a weird way. "Six years. He doesn't let a lot of people in, but once you get to know him, he isn't as bad as he looks."

I thought he looked pretty great, but I was pretty sure Raymond wasn't talking about his appearance. He surely possessed a wealth of information on the man who was my husband, but it didn't feel right to pepper him with questions, so I chickened out. After a few days, I had accepted that I would have to personally experience the ultimate joy of learning about my fake one true love who hated sharing any kind of personal information willingly unless you hounded him about it for quite a while.

One thing I'd learned was that he hated when I asked and answered questions on my own as if speaking for him. That was a good way to get him all frowny and talking on his own. I didn't think he liked me much when I did that, but then again, I didn't think he liked me much most times.

I would have liked to think he tolerated me, and I thought that was at least a good starting point.

I, on the other hand, was actually getting used to his Grinch-like ways. The day he gave me a warm and genuine smile, I was going to celebrate with cake. I still didn't like some things about him, like barely managing to greet people around him and maybe a few other things, but we weren't in a real relationship so I didn't feel like I had the right to nag him about any of them. To be fair, I thought it was just his personality. He didn't go out of his way to ignore people. He couldn't help it if he had been raised in a stuffy, rich family.

The only time I hated him a little bit in the entire week leading up to the weekend where we'd have to attend our first big event as a married couple was when he gave me his credit card in the kitchen on Wednesday.

"About the event on Saturday—this is important," he started as he walked into the kitchen, startling me as I was reaching for the travel cups on the higher shelves.

"Jesus!" I sputtered as one of them came a little too close to landing on my face before it crashed to the floor. "What are you doing up so early?" I asked as we both crouched to pick it up. It played out just like in the movies. I was faster than him by a second and closed my hand around the cup just before he wrapped his big hand around mine. My head jerked up and I managed to hit his jaw with my head. All I heard was a grunt and then my cheeks were blazing.

"I had it," I croaked, wincing and massaging my head where I had hit his surprisingly tough and perfectly shaped square jaw while still on my knees on the floor.

When I peered up again, he was rubbing his jaw as well. I didn't know what else to add to the conversation when my eyes landed on him—he looked too good to be true for such an early hour even though he'd probably just rolled out of bed. I, however, had to wake up at least half an hour earlier than I was supposed to so I could make myself look somewhat presentable to the world.

Inwardly, I cursed myself for taking the extra ten minutes in bed that morning and deciding to do my makeup at the coffee shop. I tore my eyes away from him and got up on one knee. He extended his hand to help me get the rest of the way up. As soon as I reached for his hand and our skin made contact, we experienced a little zap of electric shock between us. I thought, just to be on the safe side, I should get up on my own, but he was still holding his hand out between us, so I gave it another go.

"I'd like to live through this day—don't zap me," I muttered, slowly taking his hand and letting him pull me up. When I was on my feet, I realized I was standing a bit too close to him, close enough to feel his body heat.

"Are you okay?" he asked, looking straight into my eyes with what looked like worry.

A little flustered by his closeness and his hypnotizing eye color, I remembered that I should probably let go of his hand.

"Yeah. Sure." I took a step back from him, plastering myself against the edge of the counter. "Good morning. Hi."

"Good morning."

"You're never up this early. To what do I owe the pleasure?"

"I *am* usually up this early." He checked his watch. "You're fifteen minutes late. Usually I don't see you in the kitchen. You like to run down the stairs and out the door every morning. I can hear you when I'm having my coffee."

"Oh, I didn't know that. If I knew you were in here, I'd say good morning before I left."

"That would be nice."

At his unexpected admission, I didn't know what to do with myself. Nodding and clearing my throat under his unflinching gaze, I looked away. When I noticed he was closing the cabinet door, I stopped him with a hand on his arm.

"I need the other travel mug, too."

"For what?" he questioned, glancing at my hand on his arm before he reached for it. I pulled my hand back and kept it behind my back so I wouldn't get myself in more trouble.

I thanked him softly when he put the cup next to the other one on the counter, close to the shiny espresso machine. "The other one is for Raymond."

"You two seem to get along well," he commented casually—perhaps a little too casually.

I gave him a quizzical look before trying to refocus on the coffee. "We spend every morning together, so yeah. I mean, we talk. Is that a problem?"

"Of course not." Looking a little uncomfortable, he shifted on his feet, surprising the hell out of me. "I was just trying to make conversation."

Feeling like a jerk, I dropped my head forward and felt something tickling my nose. Thinking I was getting a nosebleed because something was definitely trickling down, I leaned my head back. "Oh, Jack, Jack—paper towel. I think my nose is bleeding."

Keeping my head tilted back, I tried to blindly find the paper towel myself. Instead, I placed my hand on what felt like his forearm and held on.

I was *not* good with seeing blood. I didn't faint or anything dramatic like that, but I wouldn't have called myself a fan of it either.

"Here," Jack murmured, and I felt him gently cup the back of my head. "Stay still." Then he pushed the paper towel into my hand and I curled my fingers around it.

His hand holding my head up and my hand gripping his shoulder, I held the towel up to my nose and slowly, with his help, started to straighten myself. Something definitely did run down my nose, but when I looked down at the paper, I felt like a complete moron.

My face flaming and my ears ringing, I loosened my death grip on his incredibly muscled shoulders and turned my back to him, wishing the floor would open up and I could just disappear.

"What is it?" he asked, his voice coming from right over my shoulder, his breath tickling my neck.

Dear God. I closed my eyes.

"Nothing. It's not bleeding—false alarm," I croaked and stationed myself back in front of the espresso machine, sniffling constantly—because something was still coming down—and trying to hide my red face the entire time.

"What's wrong with your voice?"

The croak hadn't been just because of my embarrassment. My throat actually did hurt a little when I swallowed, but I'd thought it was nothing when I first woke up. Add my runny nose into the mix, though, and maybe it was something more.

"My throat is hurting a little. It's probably nothing, just a little cold."

"Are you going to be sick?"

"No, it's nothing. I'll be fine for the event." It was neither attractive nor helpful when I had to sniffle a few times right at the tail end of my sentence.

"That's not why I asked, Rose."

I gave him a quick look before touching the screen for the espresso. "Oh, well, still...I'm fine. I'll be fine."

"You've been working too hard."

"You work hard, too. You lock yourself in your office even after we get back here every night. What's that got to do with anything?" I shrugged, still trying to keep my head slightly tilted back to avoid any liquid coming down my nose. "It's probably the cold weather. I never get sick for too long. It'll go away in a day or two." The espresso stopped dripping, so I started steaming the milk. "Were you saying something about the event on Saturday when you first came into the kitchen?" I raised my voice so he could hear me, but he was already one step ahead of me because he had gotten even closer and was now standing right behind me.

His chest touched my back as he leaned forward and pushed something in front of me. One hand holding the milk jug in place, I looked down to see a credit card.

"What's that?"

"My credit card."

"I can see that. What is it for?" When the steaming was done, I swirled it for a bit so the bubbles would settle down. Pouring the espresso into the travel cups, I followed it with the steamed milk. Securing their tops, I faced Jack, waiting for his answer.

"The event is going to be a big to-do, so I'd like you to buy something appropriate for the evening."

It was him saying things like this with that unreadable expression of his that made me not like him sometimes.

"Did I do a bad job last time? At the dinner with your partners?" I asked, avoiding his gaze.

"No. Stop putting words into my mouth."

"Then what is this?" I pushed the credit card back toward him.

His forehead creased, and since I'd dropped my gaze from his eyes, I watched a muscle in his jaw twitch. "So you can buy a dress for an event you're going to attend because of me. You don't need to spend your own money. Save it for the rent you're eventually gonna be paying me." He pushed the black plastic back toward me.

"I can buy my own dress and pay rent, Jack."

"I didn't say you couldn't, Rose, but I'm saying I'd like to buy this one."

It was the fact that I couldn't argue further that got to me the most, I thought, that I really couldn't afford to buy a dress that would be appropriate for someone who would be on his arm for a big charity event. We were worlds apart. If we had met under different circumstances, we would have had nothing in common. A 'we' wouldn't have been a possibility. So...we really were playing pretend, and I had to get that into my head whenever I was looking into his eyes and starting to catch feelings.

No more feeling mushy when he came to the coffee shop—which happened often.

No more jumpy heart whenever he walked through the door.

No more of those excited little butterflies everyone kept talking about being all fluttery in my stomach.

This was a business deal between two adults, nothing less, nothing more.

Logically, he was right. I wouldn't be going to such a high-profile event if it weren't for him, so it made sense that he'd buy the dress, but I couldn't ignore how small it made me feel around him.

"Okay, Jack."

Without another word, I picked up the credit card.

I was more than ready to leave for work and get far away from him. I was quietly passing Jack when his hand on my arm stopped my movement. I was expecting him to ask me his favorite question: *What's wrong with you?* I was trying to come up with an answer that would let me get out of the kitchen quicker when his other hand gently nudged my chin up and my surprised eyes met his. His thumb gently swiped back and forth on my jawline as if he had no control of it. Then it stopped and his hand slowly cupped my cheek.

My heart jumped in my chest—even though I'd decided mere moments ago that it wasn't allowed to do that—and then slowly started to pick up speed as I realized I couldn't look away from his searching eyes. My lips parted because I wanted to say his name, wanted to tell him to...not look at me so intently, as if we weren't as fake as it got. I wanted to say I didn't think I could take it anymore.

His expression softened, the creases on his forehead smoothing out.

"Buy whatever you want, for me."

For him? I nodded, incapable of stringing two words together. His gaze moved across my face, pausing on my lips, and I simply forgot how to breathe. What was he doing? What witchery was this?

First you breathe out and then in. No, you need to breathe in first. You need air in your lungs first to be able to breathe out.

"Something white, maybe, or nude," he continued, unaware of my flustered state. "You look good in those colors."

I do?

What in the world was happening?

I tried to fire up my brain so I could think if he'd ever seen me in white, but other than maybe a white blouse I wore over my black jeans, I couldn't think of a single outfit.

I swallowed and managed another nod.

If at that moment he had smiled at me, I was fairly certain it would have pushed me straight out of my trance because I would've been sure this was a copy of Jack Hawthorne—a really gorgeous one, but just a copy—but he didn't. When I didn't stumble after he let go of my arm, I thought I could survive anything, but then he tucked the longest part of my bangs behind my ear and started leaning toward me. He was only a tad quicker than a turtle this time, but it still gave me time to slightly lean back with widened eyes.

"What are you doing?" I whispered.

He completely ignored my attempt to protect myself and gently pressed a kiss right under my jawline on my neck.

I forgot how to breathe, how to exist in this new world.

"Let me know the customer count sometime. Text me."

If I had tilted my head back any more, I'd have toppled over.

"But you said you don't like texting."

"Text me anyway."

Breathing was still a problem, because when he pulled his hands off my body, I didn't know what to do with myself. Did I leave now? Did I just stay and stare? He must've realized I was frozen, but he didn't make any comments as I stood stock-still trying to figure out what had just happened.

He casually looked down at his watch and I realized how tightly he was holding himself.

"Raymond must be waiting for you," he commented, turning to the espresso machine, probably for his own morning coffee. I finally got unstuck.

"Er...right. Yes. I am late, aren't I? You should, umm, have a good day at the office." He faced me, leaning against the counter, hands gripping the edge of the white marble. "Happy...day!" I added at the end, as if that would make anything better, and then I turned around.

I closed my eyes and wished myself a quick death as I quickly got out of there. I was only three steps out of the kitchen when his voice stopped me in my tracks.

"Rose."

I didn't answer. Words were still precious to come by, in my case.

"You forgot the coffee."

I closed my eyes, turned, put one foot in front of the other, and strolled back into the kitchen, keeping my eyes safely away from his.

I mumbled a quick thank you as he handed me the stainless steel cups. I tried my best not to touch him in the process, but it was unavoidable, and my eyes flew up to his when his fingers skimmed mine.

He tilted his head, eyes on my finger. I knew what he was looking at.

"You're wearing it."

I brought the mugs closer to my chest, trying to hide my ring finger. "I've been wearing it all the time. You know this."

"Good," he mumbled, his eyes holding mine.

"What is happening here?" I asked suspiciously, because I really couldn't tell and I really needed to know what was going on so I could somehow take cover.

"Nothing. Have a good morning, Rose."

Even more suspicious and a little off-kilter, I turned around and left without saying anything else. Too busy in my own thoughts, I didn't say much to anyone for the rest of the morning.

The number of times Jack Hawthorne smiled: none. (I've lost hope. Help.)

CHAPTER THIRTEEN

ROSE

The rest of the few days leading up to the event was just as weird as that morning. We were both very busy and didn't catch each other alone that much, but in the evenings when he came to pick me up, if there were people around, he made a show of touching me. It was nothing big, nothing that made me jump out of his arms in panic, but even a simple kiss on my cheek as a hello or a hand at the small of my back got to me. He would casually pull my hair out of my coat and would offer me his hand when there was a puddle in my way while we were walking to the car, as if I would slip and drown in that little puddle of water if he wasn't holding on to me. I very well could have, but that wasn't the issue. He was opening my doors, giving a gentle push at my back when I just stared at him with a small frown, and the way he said my name while looking into my eyes, the way it fell from his lips...the way he listened to me so intently whenever I managed to say something...had he always listened to me like that or had I started imagining things?

I couldn't be sure.

Almost every night he asked if I was free for dinner, and

almost every night we ate takeout in the dining room where he actually made a big effort to talk to me, and I enjoyed every minute of it, but if I said I wasn't confused, it'd be a lie. That didn't change anything; even when he received one-line answers, he kept going. I usually went up to bed as soon as dinner was done, not entirely because I was running away from him, but because I was getting these vicious headaches almost every other day.

I bought the dress the day before the actual event. I'd put it off as long as I could, but leaving it to the very last day was pushing it even for me. I chose the cheapest dress they showed me, though that wasn't saying much of anything because it was equal to two months of my rent.

As much as I'd hated the experience, the dress was beautiful and worth it—so beautiful, in fact, that you'd want to randomly take it out of your closet and wear it in your home while binge-watching *The Office*. To say I was nervous to go out in public wearing it was an understatement.

It was an embellished tulle dress with a short tan lining beneath it that ended a little over my knees. The bell sleeves and low back were a statement on their own, but my favorite part of the dress was the fitted bodice that gave way to a full skirt and the thin gold metal belt. The skirt made you want to sway from side to side like a five-year-old with a new princess outfit. It almost reminded me of a dreamy wedding gown.

I loved it, but I was mostly worried about what Jack would think. Would it be too much? Would it be too simple? When Raymond picked me up on Saturday, it had just started raining, and because of the impossible traffic, it took us longer than usual to reach the apartment. When I asked where Jack was—because I'd gotten so used to Jack always coming inside to pick me up—Raymond said he had work to do but would be at the apartment on time.

We were supposed to leave at seven-thirty. It was now seven-forty, and not only had Jack already arrived, he had also knocked on my door twice. I'd tried my best to pull my hair up into an effortless ponytail that would look elegant and messy, but my hair wasn't having it. In the end, I had to put a few waves in my hair with the curling iron and just leave it down. My makeup was as simple as it got. I only added a bit of concealer to what I already had on. I pressed brown eyeshadow onto my eyelids with my fingers then added more blush, and finally I swiped on a burgundy-colored lipstick, again with my finger. Standing in front of the elegant full-length mirror, I put the dress on and found myself staring at the reflection.

To be fair, I didn't look so bad, but I felt uncomfortable, like I was in way too far over my head. A deal was a deal, though, so, trying not to overthink it too much, I bundled myself in my dark grey knee-length coat and flew out of my room. High heels weren't my best friend, so I ran barefoot down the stairs and put on the only pair of heels I owned in the foyer.

I found Jack right in the middle of the living room, staring down at his phone. I didn't make a sound as I took him in. His stubble was in great shape as always and demanded your attention when you first set eyes on him, but add a tux to the mix and Jack Hawthorne had become deadly. I swallowed down my groan and cleared my throat. My husband glanced up and met my gaze.

I didn't give him a chance to comment. "Yes, I know we're late and I'm sorry, but I'm ready now, we can leave."

He gave me a sharp nod, eyes moving up and down as he put his phone up to his ear. "Raymond, we'll be there in a minute."

My coat was all buttoned up and I had my hands in my pockets, so the only thing he could see was a few inches of the hem of my embellished skirt. He made no comments as he joined me. Trying to avoid his gaze, I walked ahead of him, and we took the elevator down.

"Good evening, Steve," I said as we passed the doorman and my now friend.

He winked at me and, as nervous as I was, I couldn't hold back my smile. "Have a fun night out, Mrs. Hawthorne." He always called me Mrs. Hawthorne whenever Jack was around, but in the mornings when it was just me and him chatting for a minute or two as I waited for Ray to pull up, I was always Rose. Jack's hand found my back and I straightened.

"Have a good night, Steve," Jack added, and my surprised gaze flew up to him. Since when had he started talking to Steve? Evidently it was a fairly new thing because for a moment there, Steve didn't know what to say.

"Ah...you too, sir."

Then we were out in the cold evening air, the rain now only a drizzle. I was very conscious of Jack's hand on my back up until I got in the car and scooted all the way to the other end. Nothing changed once he got in after me. I was still very aware of his presence, his scent, his eyes whether he was touching me or not.

"Hello again, Raymond."

He looked over his shoulder to offer me a smile. "You look beautiful, Mrs. Hawthorne."

I blushed and, out of the corner of my eye, noticed Jack tense.

"We're already late as it is. Let's go," he ordered in a harsh tone, cutting me off before I could respond to Raymond.

I would've apologized again for making us late, but he was being a jerk to Raymond so I chose not to say anything during the entire car ride to where the event was being held downtown. It took us an hour to get there, and being quiet in a car for an entire hour required some serious patience on my part.

Exiting the car, we stood side by side at the bottom of the stairs leading up to the brightly lit building.

"Why do you sound weird?" Jack asked into the silence.

"You and your compliments. Always sweeping me off my feet." I said, distracted, my eyes still on the building.

"I'm being serious, Rose."

Surprised at the tight tone of his voice, I peered up at him. "What?"

"Your voice sounds different. Is the cold getting worse?"

"Oh." I touched the side of my nose and looked forward again, a little embarrassed that he'd noticed. "The cold, yes. It's not that much worse, actually, but I do have a small cotton ball in my nose. I thought it would be a better idea than sniffling the entire time."

"You need to see a doctor."

"I will."

"Ready?" Jack asked, holding his hand out in between us.

I stared at it for a few seconds and then, left with no other choice, had to put my hand in his very big one. I took a deep breath and took a step forward only to be tugged back gently. When he shifted our hands and linked our fingers together, causing my wedding ring to shift slightly, I had to close my eyes for a second and ignore the heavy thump in my chest. Every single time he touched my wedding ring, my heart did a happy little jump.

We were ready to go, but neither of us was taking the first step. Our hands gripping each other, we stood motionless.

"What is it, Rose?" he asked softly, and I closed my eyes tighter this time. He was standing too close, smelling too good, and being nice again.

I couldn't think of a legitimate lie, so instead of just straight-up admitting that simply his presence was affecting me, I blurted out the first thing that came to my mind. At least I was telling the truth.

"I don't like it when you act like a jerk."

When I said the words out loud, I wasn't looking at him. As a couple passed us, climbing the stairs and, from the looks of it, arguing with each other, I had to wait for Jack's answer since I had no intentions of meeting his gaze to see what he was thinking.

He only spoke up when the couple's voices had trailed off and we couldn't be heard either.

"When was I being a jerk?"

That had me looking back at him. "You can't be that unaware of it. You were a complete jerk to Raymond, Jack."

"Is that why you didn't say a single word to me during the ride?"

Perplexed, I just peered at him. "You snapped at him for no reason."

"He complimented my wife," he argued. "We didn't have time to sit around and chitchat for an hour."

"Your fake wife, and he knows that."

Fascinated, I stared as the muscle started ticking in his jaw.

"Is that supposed to help your case? I do—"

"He just said one sentence as he was starting the car." I lifted one finger up to make my point. "He was being nice, and he is my friend. You're the one who acted like a jerk. I think it's expected that I wouldn't want to talk to you."

"Great," he bit out.

"Great," I shot back, terser.

He stared down into my eyes and I stared right back, not backing down. I must've imagined the lip twitch, because a second later he barked out another order for us to head inside and we were trotting up the stairs.

Still hand in hand.

It was a big problem that I didn't mind holding his hand.

The second we stepped through the doors, the soft classical music hit my ears, replacing all the horns and sirens.

Here we go.

We stopped in front of the coat check as the couple who had just passed us was still lingering in the corner, arguing in hushed tones.

"I'm sorry," Jack grumbled, stopping right next to me, eyes focused on the couple. "It wasn't my intention to be a jerk. Forgive me?"

Shocked at his words and the softness I heard in his voice, my head snapped to him and I took in his profile. God, he was so good looking. I really had no chance, not from the very first day.

"That's okay," I mumbled back still a little surprised at what I felt when I looked at him, and his hand gave mine a quick squeeze. Just when I was pretty sure it was going to be easier not to like him, he did something like that and left me at a loss for words.

"You don't have a purse?" he asked, leaning into my ear. I had to lean away just a little so I wouldn't burrow myself against his chest. For that little piece of idiocy, I blamed his breath, which I'd felt on my neck, causing a shiver to move up my spine.

He let go of my hand and stood at my back, ready to help me take off my coat. "I don't have anything that matches," I answered softly, angling my head to the left so he could hear me as I slowly started to unbutton my coat with cold fingers and then gently shrugged it off.

"Why didn't you buy something?"

"You said to get a dress, and I don't need a purse. Don't worry, the dress alone cost a fortune already."

He handed off my coat to the girl and when he forgot to say thank you, I spoke for both of us and offered a small smile. A second later I heard Jack grumble a thank you too as he was taking off his own coat.

It made me smile and I walked ahead.

Thankfully, inside the ballroom where the event was being held, it was much warmer, so I didn't think I'd have much problem with freezing in my dress. Discreetly, I touched my nose to make sure the little cotton ball I'd pushed in back at the apartment was still there. How fun was it that my runny nose had decided to stick around? Tugging the bell sleeves of my dress and trying to make them look good, I stood still and waited for Jack to stand next to me again.

When he reappeared at my side, I caught him staring at me. I looked down at myself.

"What? Is it too much?"

"Rose."

I met his piercing gaze with an arched brow and waited for him to go on, but he just stared. Starting to feel worried, I tried to pull down the tan lining underneath my dress.

"No. No, it isn't," he whispered. "You look incredible," he said, and my eyes snapped up to his.

This time when he offered his hand, it was a welcome distraction.

"I...you look incredible too, Jack. You always do," I murmured feeling myself blush a little.

He opened his mouth to say something, but right at that moment, an older man put a hand on his shoulder and drew his attention away from me.

Jack introduced us, but after the initial shock of hearing Jack had gotten married, the guy wasn't really interested in me. They started talking about a company I believed Jack was representing. Keeping the fixed smile on my face, I tuned them out, taking the opportunity to look around the room.

When I spotted two tables full of kids toward the back of the room, I couldn't hide my curiosity. Some of them were talking to each other, while some of them just stared around in wonder. Their clothes didn't fit in with this snazzy crowd, so I doubted they belonged to anyone who was in this room. It looked like each table had one adult sitting with them.

As Jack finished his conversation with the guy, Ken something, I leaned closer to him so nobody could hear us. He leaned down at the same time to make it easier for me, and my nose got a pretty good whiff of his cologne when my nose bumped his neck. It was the one I hated because it made me go all wonky around him—not a good look. "What charity is this event for?" I asked, managing to focus after the initial shock of the smell.

"An organization that supports foster kids."

I pulled back and looked up at him in surprise. "You didn't tell me that."

"I didn't?"

Slowly, I shook my head.

"I thought I did. Is that a problem?"

My entire childhood spent with the Colesons was rough. I was unwanted. For a kid that age, that knowledge was a hard pill to swallow. I knew what these kids were going through, how alone they felt, how abandoned and sometimes worthless. I'd always have a soft spot for kids and probably would have for the rest of my life.

Steeling my voice, I whispered, "I'd like to donate too. Where can I—"

Jack cleared his throat and looked away from me, his eyes moving across the crowd. "I'm already donating."

"I understand that, but I'd like to donate as well."

"I'm donating, so you don't have to."

He started walking, but this time holding hands worked in my favor and I was the one who tugged him back. He gave me an incredulous look as I raised my brows and waited for him to give me the answer I was looking for.

I didn't know why he chose to lean down and whisper it in my ear, but I couldn't exactly push him away. Before I could stop myself, I was tilting my head to the side and closing my eyes. Savoring the moment.

"We're married, Rose. My donation is in both of our names. Let me do this."

I heard his unspoken words as if he had spoken out loud.

For you.

Let me do this for you.

As he was pulling back, I reached up with my free hand and held on to his neck so he would stay put and listen. "Married or not, that's your money, Jack. I love that you're doing it in both our names, that means the world, but I want to help, too. We can both donate."

For a long moment there was no answer, but he stayed bent like that, looking into my eyes. After a few more seconds passed in silence, feeling awkward I started to drop my hand from his neck, but he captured my wrist with his left one before I could and kept it on his shoulder.

I swallowed as I realized we were basically standing in an embrace in front of everyone, though it didn't matter much to me whether anyone was watching or not. When I felt Jack's nose brush my neck, my fingers tightened on his shoulder and a small shiver went through my body. I smiled.

"Does everything have to be a battle between us? Do you despise me that much? I'm taking care of it, Rose. Trust me. I'll be donating one hundred and fifty thousand dollars in both our names."

He finally pulled back and peered into my eyes. Like a fish, I opened and closed my eyes. Despise him? What gave him that idea?

"I could never despise you, Jack," I whispered, feeling out of my depth.

Satisfied, he nodded once. "Let's find our table."

I closed my eyes for a quick second, trusting him to steer me away from any obstacles, and let out a deep breath. For the time being, playing the role of husband and wife was going to play some real tricks with my mind, and I wasn't sure if I was gonna handle it all that well come the end of the night.

I opened my eyes and noticed we were passing the kids' table. One of the little girls—she couldn't have been over eight—was looking up at us with wide eyes, so I winked at her and watched her quickly drop her gaze back to her lap as she played with the edge of the white tablecloth.

When I faced forward again and Jack came to a halt, I still had a smile on my face. *Maybe tonight won't be so bad after all,* I thought, but then when I saw who was standing in front of us, I wasn't so sure about that anymore.

Bryan smiled at us, not a happy smile like you'd expect from someone you'd considered family for long years, but a mocking one.

"What a great coincidence to run into you two here!" Bryan exclaimed, looking from me to Jack. "Oh, this is a good night indeed."

"Bryan," Jack returned tightly.

I couldn't say anything because I could see the couple standing right behind him, talking to an older woman. I was paralyzed.

As Bryan leaned forward to press a kiss on my cheek, Jack pulled me slightly against him so my shoulder was leaning against his side. I didn't react. I was shocked into silence.

"Congratulations on your marriage again. I know we started on the wrong foot, but we can't let little things like that get in the way of family, right Jack?" he asked. Bryan's fake smile slid off his face when neither Jack nor I responded, and he followed my gaze and looked over his shoulder. "Jodi, look who I found here."

Jodi turned to face her brother and her...companion turned with her.

I felt the remaining blood drain from my face, and as they strolled toward us, Jack's hand tightened around mine. I was thankful that I was leaning against him because otherwise I didn't think I could've stayed upright for too long.

Jodi and my ex-fiancé, Joshua, who had his hand around her waist, stopped in our little circle and greeted us as if nothing was wrong. It was the first time I was seeing him after he had broken up with me via text. It felt like it'd been ages, and now he was at a charity event with Jodi.

Even though I had no feelings left for my ex-fiancé anymore, I felt my heart break into little pieces all the same. Jodi smiled at me as if this was all normal and congratulated me on my marriage and apologized on missing the opening of my coffee shop, just like Bryan had. It seemed just as fake and forced. I couldn't even nod in return because I couldn't take my eyes off of Joshua. He spared me one glance and then looked anywhere but me.

I think Jack and Bryan exchanged a few more words, I could hear Jack's clipped and anything-but-happy tone, but the pounding in my ears prevented me from making out specific words. Starting to feel a little dizzy, I took my shocked eyes off of Joshua when Jodi leaned up and whispered something in his ear, earning a low chuckle from him. I'd been on the receiving end of that chuckle before, and I had loved the warm sound. Now it made my stomach turn.

I leaned harder on Jack, thankful that he was so big and strong next to me. He moved our joined hands from between our bodies and rounded his arm around my waist, my hand still very much attached to his, my arm bent.

I didn't exactly know what to do with myself, so when I felt Jack's warm lips against my temple, I looked up at him with a dazed look.

"You want to go find our table?"

I studied his face, his beautiful but angry eyes. He looked so good in a tux, so unattainable, yet there he was, not mine but still holding me up.

"Yes," I whispered. "Please."

Jack bid good evening to my cousins and Joshua, and I managed to force a faint smile on my lips. Jodi and Joshua were already walking away.

"Looking forward to hearing back from you, Jack," Bryan said and touched my arm which made me instinctively jerk and then he walked away too. I couldn't even make sense of his words.

"What's he talking about, Jack."

"Don't worry about it. Would you like to leave?" Jack asked, and I turned my unfocused eyes back to him.

"Yes."

My husband, the strong man who was still holding me up, started to gently turn me toward the door we had just come in through. Two steps later, I put my hand on his arm and stopped him.

"No. No, wait. We made a deal. I'm sorry. I'm not going to leave."

I was talking to his chest, but he nudged my chin up and looked deep into my soul.

"There is no deal, Rose."

"Yes, there is. This is a business deal. There is no reason for us to leave."

"Rose—" he started, but I cut him off.

"That was Joshua, my ex-fiancé, with my cousin."

His lips tightened. "I know who he is."

"I was surprised, that's all. I'm okay now."

"I didn't know," he ground out after a few seconds of searching for something in my eyes. God, his eyes were beautiful. "If I had known they'd be here, your cousins and... I didn't know, Rose."

I smiled, just a little. "I know that."

"What was wrong with Bryan? He called me just a few days ago, still threatening. Why would he talk like he just did?"

"You didn't tell me he called."

"It wasn't important."

"It is. If he bothers you again, tell me."

I nodded.

"Rose... I thought you'd enjoy this one, the cause—that's why I chose it."

My smile widened and resembled something more genuine. "You're right. I will enjoy this one because of the cause."

He shook his head, his expression hard. "I'm messing this up every step of the way, aren't I?"

I wasn't sure what came over me, but something in his tone didn't sit well. So, as if it was the most natural thing for me to do, still looking into his eyes, I rose up on my tippy toes, placed my hand on his stubbled cheek, and kissed the edge of his lips. That was as far as I'd allow myself to go. His hand tightened on my waist, pulling me at least a few inches closer to him. It didn't close the gap between us, but I was aware of his hand and where it was the entire time.

"Thank you," I whispered as I dropped down to my heels, busying myself with fixing his bow tie.

He let go of my waist. "For what?"

I didn't have a straight answer for that. "Just thank you."

He ground his perfectly square jaw and sighed. "You sure you want to stay?"

I wasn't sure, but I wasn't going to leave. I wouldn't give them the satisfaction, no matter how much I wanted to tuck my tail between my legs and flee. "Yes. Completely."

As we broke out of our little private bubble, I started to hear everything else around us: a man's robust laughter, plates clinking, someone coughing, a woman's giggle, and the low classical music. Jack guided us as he always did, with a gentle hand on my back, and I made sure not to look anywhere but forward. It was very hard not to flinch at every loud noise as we walked around tables and finally came to a stop in front of one that was tucked at the very edge.

Jack pulled out a chair and I sat down. Obviously, I didn't know anyone at the table, but I didn't think Jack did either. For a long while, we were quiet. Then I made the mistake of looking to my right, just to see if I could see the kids from where I was sitting, but my eyes met with Joshua's instead. They were two tables to our right and a little behind. It didn't look like Jodi was with him at that moment, but Bryan was there, sitting to his right, talking to someone else who was seated at their table. Joshua didn't break eye contact with me, his brown eyes watching, calculating. Then, so subtly I almost missed it, he raised his champagne as if toasting me.

I turned back around, feeling sick to my stomach and promising myself I wouldn't look over my shoulder again during the entire event.

"How do you feel?" Jack asked, and my eyes slid to him. He was staring ahead, his jaw ticking again.

In a way, I knew he wasn't asking how I felt about the situation. I believed he was asking what I was feeling toward my ex-fiancé.

I answered honestly in a steady voice. "Sick to my stomach." That was exactly how I felt, though somehow I also felt relieved that I hadn't made the mistake of marrying someone like Joshua—someone who told me how much he loved me so easily and so often and yet, in the end, apparently didn't mean it at all. I couldn't even begin to comprehend how he could be with Jodi. They knew each other through me. We'd had dinner together a handful of times with *the* family when Gary had invited him over and they'd chatted every now and then when we bumped into each other, but I could've never, ever imagined...this—not even from Jodi, and definitely not from Joshua. He'd always told me he thought Jodi was like an ice princess and he didn't care for that type.

My hands were in my lap, almost frozen, so when Jack's hand covered mine, I dropped my eyes, watching him slowly link our fingers together again, just as he had done so many times in the last hour. I was fascinated by it enough that I let go of every single thought about Jodi and Joshua evidently being together and focused on the only thing that was warming me from the inside out.

"Your hands are cold," Jack muttered under his breath, and I realized how close we were sitting to each other.

Had he moved? He kept our hands on my thigh, mine tightly grasped in his, and I decided I liked the feel of it, the heaviness, the warmth. So I held on just as tight. "I know."

His thumb started rolling my wedding ring around my finger. Back and forth.

Back and forth.

It was such a weird sensation, feeling his skin on mine. Did he feel the same? The tingles?

He nodded once and I peered at him under my lashes, trying not to be too obvious. So what if he was just pretending? I could do the same. I could take this comfort from him and let myself feel loved. I could just stop thinking and enjoy my seconds and minutes with him. I didn't have to analyze my every move. I could just be whatever I wanted to be with Jack while we were out in public like this. I could fool myself, happily, before we had to step back into the real, harsh world.

Lifting my head, I looked at him. Two spots were open at our table to Jack's left, the other four seats taken by two women and two men who were talking among themselves.

"Jack, talk to me," I urged as the emcee of the night took the stage and the lights dimmed just slightly. A hush fell over the crowd in the room, but there was still quiet chatter here and there, which was why I didn't feel guilty about my lack of attention.

Jack's eyes were on the stage, but they turned to me and I repeated my words.

"Just talk to me."

He sighed. "What do you want to talk about?"

I shrugged, glad he didn't put up much of a fight. "Anything. Everything. Whatever you want."

A line etched between his brows as he studied me for a quick moment. "How many cups of coffee did you sell today? You didn't text."

I smiled, my heart settling down a bit more. As much as he insisted he wasn't good at small talk, I always enjoyed his company. He had his own way of doing things. He rarely lost the frown, for one thing, but in my eyes, it only made him look more attractive. He could frown at me an entire night and I still wouldn't mind it. I relaxed in my seat, finally starting to thaw out.

"One hundred eighty-six."

"That's a few more than yesterday, isn't it?"

I nodded.

"Are you happy then?" he asked.

I gave him a bigger smile. "I am. It's going to be cinnamon week next week and I'm very excited about that. Do you have a special request? I might be able to make it happen."

His gaze moved away from mine for a brief moment when the entire room erupted in laughter and then applause. I noticed an army of waiters swarming around the tables, two of them rounding ours with plates in their hands. Jack let go of my hand and leaned back so the waiter could do his job. The loss of his touch settled over me, and I wasn't sure how I was supposed to feel about that. They took our drink orders: white wine for me and whiskey on the rocks for Jack.

As soon as they left us alone with our weirdly colored risottos and went to get the drink orders, I leaned back in.

"Any specific cinnamon orders?"

I would've preferred him grabbing my hand again, but instead he casually slung his arm across the back of my chair and turned his body toward me.

"Anything you make yourself, save some for me."

"I make this braided cinnamon thing. It's a Swedish recipe and I love it. I can do that if you want."

"I'd like that," he said simply, and we had to pull away a little when our drinks arrived. I wasn't a fan of alcohol and rarely drank, but it felt like it would be a necessity on this night.

I took a sip of my wine, and he took a sip of his whiskey.

"Do you know a lot of people here?" I asked, pushing my glass away.

He looked over his shoulder and his features hardened. Curious, I followed his gaze and saw Joshua staring again, even though Jodi was sitting right next to him. His arm was around her chair, almost exactly like Jack's had been on mine. I tore my eyes away and put my palm on Jack's stubbled cheek again. Applying a little pressure, I turned his head back to me.

"Jack, do you know a lot of people here?" I repeated as he drained the rest of his whiskey in one go. "It's just gonna be the two of us tonight, okay? We're not gonna focus on anyone else. We need to look like a happily married couple so it's just gonna be the two of us." It felt as if I repeated enough times maybe I'd believe it myself as well.

"A few. I know a few people," he responded finally, his voice rough from the alcohol.

When the waiter was close enough, he ordered another one. I took a small sip of my own wine and tried a small bite of the risotto. It wasn't the worst thing I could've been eating. I glanced at the people sitting across from us and noticed none of them were interested in what was happening on the stage either.

When I noticed something drip from my nose onto the table-cloth, my whole face heated, and I quickly reached for the napkin, cursing myself for not having a small handbag I could've stashed a few things in. Mortified, I hoped Jack—or anyone else, for that matter—hadn't seen my runny nose. Trying to be discreet about it, I dabbed the napkin on my upper lip and slightly on my nose. I could already feel my cheeks flushing as I started to panic. I looked down at the napkin and just saw clean liquid saturating the cloth. Pushing my chair back, I got up, and Jack rose with me.

I sniffled quietly, my hand going to my nose. Our height difference worked in my favor since I could keep my head tilted back as I looked up at him. "Just going to the bathroom. You don't have to come, Jack."

He didn't listen and followed me all the way to the back of the ballroom. I rushed inside and, thankful that no one else was in there, stood in front of the mirror. Reaching up, I pulled the cotton out of my nose and just stared at it. It was saturated to the point that I could squeeze it and watch it drip. I had no idea what was going on exactly, but I was pretty sure this wasn't just a runny nose anymore. I must've been allergic to something. I already had an appointment with the doctor on Monday so he could give me some nose spray to stop this from happening, but until then I was going to have to be careful about not dripping around other people.

When a knock sounded on the door, I opened it halfway and just pushed my head out.

"Everything okay in there?" Jack asked, trying to look over my head.

"Yes, of course. I'll be out in a minute."

I didn't give him a chance to say anything else and let the door close in his face. After tearing up some toilet paper and rolling it into a shape that I could tampon my nose with, I quickly looked myself over in the mirror and noticed how pale I looked. The burgundy lipstick I was wearing stood out too much in contrast to my skin. Grabbing some more toilet paper, I dabbed some of it off, turning it into just a tint of color. Finally exiting the bathroom, I rejoined Jack.

"We can go back," I muttered as I tried to walk past him, but he stopped me.

"What's wrong?"

"Nothing. We can go."

"Were you crying?"

I frowned up at him in confusion. "Why would I cry?"

"Your ex-fiancé is here."

"I noticed."

"With your cousin," he added helpfully.

"Really? Where?" I asked in mock outrage.

He sighed and ran his hand through his casually styled hair. "We should leave."

"You keep saying that, but we don't need to."

"Why not? And if you say we made a deal one more time, I'll carry you out of here over my shoulder."

His unexpected words pulled a laugh out of me. "You could try and see how that goes for you this time around," I offered with a little grin.

He didn't grin back. "You sure about this?"

"Why should I be the one who leaves? I didn't do anything wrong, so I'm not going to give them the satisfaction. Stop asking me. I'd like to try to enjoy this night."

"I don't want you to get hurt, Rose."

I stared up at him. It wasn't fair. It wasn't fair that he was randomly saying things like that when I was feeling so off-kilter around him. "You won't let me," I said, choking a little and having trouble finding the right words. "You won't let anyone hurt me." I knew—somehow I knew he wouldn't let anything hurt me.

He released a breath. "As you wish. Ready to go back?"

I nodded then hesitated after a few steps.

"I feel like everyone is looking at us, in there."

"That's because they are." Jack's eyes moved on my face, then my body. I felt my cheeks heat up. "Look at you. How could they not."

Oh, geez.

While I was trying to come up with something to say he covered my hand with his. A little surprised, I looked down and then up to him, but he was looking straight ahead. As another round of applause broke out in the room, we stepped back in again. Because of all the waiters rushing around, we were walking really slowly, and that's how I felt a small hand on my leg as I was passing a table.

"Jack, what a surprise to see you here!" someone said from our left, blocking our way back. As Jack was shaking hands with the man, I glanced back to see a little girl quickly turn her head away when our eyes met.

When I tried to pry my hand away from Jack's, he stopped talking and looked down at me questioningly. "I'll be right back," I whispered, smiling at his friend before retracing my steps back to the little girl. She was stealing little glances at me, and the closer I got, the more she couldn't look away. When I was standing next to her, she looked up at me with these big beautiful blue eyes. It wasn't as deep as Jack's blue, but a lighter shade, a sweeter one.

I gently dropped down to my knees, holding on to her chair with my hand.

"Hi," I whispered, leaning toward her.

She bit her lip and looked at someone I assumed was either a social worker to keep the kids in line or just a chaperone, but the woman was busy listening to whoever was on stage and didn't notice me and the little girl talking.

Both hands on the seat of her chair, the girl leaned closer and whispered, "Hi."

I grinned at her and she gave me a crooked smile.

"I love your dress. Is it new?" I asked. She looked down at herself. She wore a simple long-sleeved pink dress. It wasn't anything special, but its owner was, and that was all that mattered.

"They gave it to me today," she explained. "It's pink. It's mine now, I think."

"It looks gorgeous on you. I wish I had a pretty pink dress like that, too."

"You do?"

I nodded enthusiastically. "I don't have such beautiful blonde hair like yours, though, so I'm not sure I would look that good in pink, but I'm jealous just the same."

She gently touched my arm with one single finger and quickly pulled it back.

"My name is Rose. What's yours?"

"Madison, but my friends call me Maddy."

"Nice to meet you, Maddy." I held out my arm so she would feel free to touch me again. "Do you think my dress looks okay on me? I'm not sure."

"It's so pretty," she whispered longingly, and this time she felt okay enough to run her hand up and down the embellishments on my sleeves. She looked at me and then to the chaperone, and when she saw the woman still hadn't noticed us, she crooked her finger at me. I had to take two steps on my knees to get there and then she leaned in even closer, speaking into my ear. "I'm sorry I touched you. I'm not supposed to touch anyone tonight."

I tried to force a brighter smile on my face. "That's okay. I won't tell anyone."

"Okay. Thank you."

The girl sitting on her right, who could only have been a few years older than Maddy, turned to us too.

"Hey, what are you doing on the ground?"

"Hey yourself," I said, smiling. "Just chatting with your friend."

"I like your hair."

"Oh, really? Thank you."

"I love yours. I wish I had curls like that."

She swung her head from side to side, her tiny, frazzled curls flying everywhere. "I don't have to do anything to mine."

"You're so lucky."

"Sometimes other kids make fun of it though."

My heart ached. I'd also had kids make fun of me when I was her age. Kids could be brutal. "Don't listen to them. Trust me, they're just jealous."

"What's your name?" she asked, leaning over the back of her chair.

"Rose."

"It's a pretty name. You're pretty, too."

My heart melted. "Thank you. You're so sweet. What's your name?"

"Sierra."

"Really? I had a friend named Sierra in college. It's a beautiful name, just like you."

The pretty blue-eyed Madison touched my arm, and I turned to her. "I really like your dress. Was it a lot of money?"

"It was a gift to me. Maybe when you're a little older, you can buy something like this, something shiny."

"Who bought it?"

Thinking I would point Jack out, I looked over my shoulder. I was assuming he would have his back to me since that was how I'd left him, but he had switched places with his friend and was talking to him while facing me. He glanced my way over his friend's shoulder and our eyes met.

I bit my lower lip and turned to Madison. "You see that guy over there talking to the man wearing a navy blue suit?"

Both girls craned their necks to see who I was talking about.

"Which one? The old one?" Sierra whispered.

I looked back again and got caught in Jack's gaze. Since he was already looking our way, even though I could see his mouth moving as he talked to his friend, I pointed at him with my finger so the girls could see him. "Not the old one, the one in front of him. He has blue eyes and he is looking at us." Turning back to them, I asked, "Did you see?"

The girls giggled loudly.

My head whipped back to Jack, but he was focused on his friend. I also noticed a few other people from the tables around us sending me disapproving looks. I couldn't understand why, so I ignored them. "What? What is it?"

"He winked at us," Maddy said, still grinning. "He is so big."

"Is he your boyfriend?" Sierra asked, now sitting sideways on her chair.

"He is my...husband." I touched her nose with my finger.

Her grin got bigger.

"I don't have a boyfriend," Maddy chimed in. "I'm too young."

"Believe me, you're not missing out on anything."

"Boys can be stupid sometimes," Sierra added, nodding.

"Yeah, so stupid, and jerks, too," I admitted. It was something they'd learn soon enough.

When they started to giggle again, I started laughing with them, not caring that more heads had turned our way this time.

"You tell your husband he is stupid, too?" Maddy whisper-yelled.

"I told him he was a jerk tonight, right before we walked in here."

Both their eyes got huge. "You didn't!"

"I did." I shrugged. "He was being a jerk so I told him to stop it."

"But he is so much bigger than you."

"He is pretty big, isn't he? Well, it doesn't matter. Just because he is big doesn't mean he gets to be a jerk."

Sierra nodded enthusiastically. "He is kinda cute, though."

"Yeah, cute," Maddy mumbled.

As I was about to say something, I felt a hand clasp my wrist and pull me up not so gently. Surprised, I gasped and almost lost my balance.

"You're embarrassing us," Bryan hissed, leaning in close and pulling me toward him at the same time.

I tried to jerk my hand away, but his hold on me was tight and was starting to become painful. My brows drew together as I met his eyes. "What are you doing?" I whispered in confusion when I could find my voice again. Before I got an answer, I felt a broad chest pressing against my back, and just like that, Jack's hand was on Bryan's wrist. I didn't know how much pressure he was applying, but Bryan let go of me immediately.

Acting like nothing was wrong, my cousin looked around and smiled. "Try to control your wife, Hawthorne." Then, pushing one hand into the pocket of his pants, he strolled away from us.

Confused, hurt and more than a little surprised, I just massaged my wrist.

That broad, warm chest that was plastered behind me moved slightly so he could lean down and whisper into my ear. "What did he say?" he growled, and that gravelly voice did things to me —lots of things.

I let go of my wrist and involuntarily pressed myself back, absorbing more of his heat so I could whisper back. "Nothing."

"Rose—" he started in a low voice, his palm pressing against my stomach, keeping me in place.

Keeping me with him.

"It's okay," I interrupted, looking over my shoulder and into his eyes. His jaw clenched, but he didn't say anything else.

I remembered where we were—or more importantly, who I had been talking to just a few seconds earlier—so I turned back to the girls, who were staring up at us in confusion.

"I'm sorry about that," I apologized, shifting in place and facing them again. Jack stayed glued to my back, moving his body with me. It probably should've bothered me, his closeness, but I would've been lying to myself if I'd said it did. His hand curled around my waist and gave it a squeeze.

"Uh..." It was so hard not to fidget under his touch. "Girls, I'd like you to meet my husband, Jack. Jack, these are my new friends, Maddy and Sierra."

They both waved up at him, and I peered back to see him nodding at them with a serious expression on his face.

"It's a pleasure to meet you girls," he said, so smoothly my heart went crazy in my chest. Those pesky little butterflies were back in my stomach, too.

The girls were grinning again, so all was well.

"Did Rose really call you a jerk tonight?" Sierra enquired boldly, staring up at him.

I put my hand over Jack's, which was still on my waist, and looked back at him, too. He sighed and managed to change his expression to a really guilty one. I couldn't hold back my smile.

"I'm afraid she did."

"You didn't get angry?" Maddy quipped with big eyes.

"She was telling the truth. I *was* being a jerk, so I couldn't get angry at her."

"Rose said boys are stupid and jerks," Sierra put in.

I feigned a shocked expression. "You're telling on me to my husband, Sierra? I told you that in secret."

The giggles started again and I couldn't keep a straight face. My smile got bigger when Jack played his role perfectly by leaning down and pressing a soft kiss on my cheek.

"I'm afraid I'm going to have to agree with my wife. Boys are stupid. And sometimes jerks, I'm afraid."

God, who was this man exactly?

Both of them had heart eyes as they stared up at Jack. I was afraid I had them as well.

"Would it be okay if I stole my wife for a little while?" Jack asked the girls. I didn't want to leave, but they needed to eat their dinner, and I didn't want to attract any attention to myself and embarrass Jack in any way.

"Will you come back?" Maddy asked, and I nodded.

"I will. Promise."

"Okay. Bye!"

We got some more waves then, with his arm still around my waist and my hand on his, Jack guided me back to our table. I realized the emcee wasn't on the stage anymore and there were no other speakers. I felt and, more than that, noticed curious eyes on us, some of them likely disapproving, but I kept a small smile on my face and made sure not to glance at the table where Joshua and the rest of them sat.

When we reached our table, instead of sitting down like I'd assumed we would, Jack pulled me over, a little to the left, out of the way of the waiters changing out plates and delivering more drink orders. We were still out in the open, and we could still be seen clearly by everyone.

"What did he say to you?" he asked as soon as he was standing in front of me. None of our body parts were touching anymore. I didn't know about him, but I certainly felt the loss.

"He didn't say anything important, Jack," I assured him,

putting my hand on his arm then pulling it back. "There is nothing to get angry about."

"Then you can say what he said."

"But it doesn't matter."

"I can be the judge of that."

I tilted my head and sighed. "Jack." He just waited with that same cool expression on his face, and I released a long sigh. Knowing him, he could keep that expression for a long time. "If you promise you won't go over or say something to him, I'll tell you."

I got a sharp nod and nothing else.

I sighed, more heavily this time. "He just said I was embarrassing them. The girls were laughing, and I think some of the tables that were close by got annoyed. I don't think I did anything to embarrass you, but if I did I'm—"

His eyes bored into mine as his jaw tightened. "Don't even finish that sentence, Rose. You didn't embarrass anyone. You made two little girls' night." He looked away for a moment and I watched his features soften. Then he lifted his hand in a wave and, curious, I followed his gaze to see the girls waving at us enthusiastically with big smiles on their faces. I smiled back and turned to Jack, the smile still strong. "They think you're big, and cute—and Sierra thinks I'm pretty."

"You *are* pretty." His eyes were still on the girls, and he didn't even realize he was making my heart do a little somersault. "But cute?" he asked as his eyes came back to me with my favorite frown on his face. "I'm offended."

"Aww, don't be. You *are* cute, in a grumpy sort of way."

I laughed, and his eyes dropped to my mouth, causing me to bite on my lower lip as I quickly lost the big smile. His eyes flicked up to mine, the blue somehow looking even deeper in the low lighting of the room, then his stare went right back to my lips.

Completely mesmerized, I watched a smile tug at the corners of his mouth.

I swore I didn't breathe for a few seconds and just stood there gawking up at him, entranced.

Finally, *finally* his mouth curved into a smile. It had only taken us a bit more than a month. It was probably my own fault, but my God! It'd been a long wait, a pretty long wait that had been worth it because when he smiled...when the skin around his eyes gently crinkled, turning his expression into something completely different than what it was when he was frowning...I simply couldn't stop staring. My heart soared as if I had just accomplished something big, and for me, it *was* big—so big that I couldn't stop myself from beaming up at him.

"Is that a smile I just saw, Mr. Hawthorne?" I asked, still a little stupefied. "This is the first time you've smiled at me. I've been trying to count them since week one, and this is number one. A smile...I can't believe it. I wish I had my phone with me so I could capture this moment. We need to have cake to celebrate."

I looked to my right and left to confirm that I wasn't the only one witnessing this, but even though I was glancing around, I didn't see anyone. The entire room could've been staring at us, including Joshua, but I didn't see a single person other than Jack Hawthorne. This was actually not good news for me, the fake wife, but I didn't care one bit about that. I'd consider that later, much later, when I was over that smile.

His smile softened, but it was still there. "You've been counting my smiles?"

"'Trying' being the operative word here since you like to hoard them like a squirrel hoarding his nuts."

"I've smiled at you, Rose." He lifted his hand and tucked my hair behind my ear. I didn't think much about it because I was busy shaking my head at him.

"You haven't."

"Maybe you weren't looking."

"Are you kidding me? I've been looking nonstop." I lifted a finger between us and his gaze dropped to it. "One time—there was one time I thought I saw your lips twitch, but it was a false alarm, and that's it."

I was still grinning, but when I looked at his lips, he had lost the smile and the expression on his face was much more intense. He took a step forward into me and my pulse quickened. When his big, warm hand cupped my face, covering almost the entire left half, I noticed the shift in the air and stood still.

Oh, this is not good.

Eyes locked on mine, he lowered his head just a few inches away from my lips and whispered, "I'm going to kiss you now, Rose." His eyes were still open and on mine.

I swallowed.

"What?" I croaked, and then I cleared my throat, stuck in place, staring into the depths of his eyes. His gaze moved from my eyes to my lips. "I knew this was a possibility tonight, of course," I whispered. "But is someone looking?" We needed to put on a show and I supposed the time had come, but why was I suddenly freaking out on the inside? It wasn't like we were gonna suck each other's faces in the middle of a charity event.

"Do you care if someone is looking?" he asked.

I mean...that was the whole reason for the kiss, wasn't it? But did I care? Not really, I supposed. A peck on the lips was nothing. I took a deep breath and nodded, letting it out in a whoosh. "Okay. Right. Lay it on me. Let's do this." As his eyes swept over my face, I steeled my voice. "A little faster than that," I whispered, keeping my voice as low as possible. "Not like a turtle, remember?"

A smile danced on his lips again as if he found what I said extremely funny, but he managed to drop his forehead against mine and our noses touched.

My heart started beating in my throat when his arm rounded my waist and he pulled me just a little closer. Made sense too, I supposed, because I couldn't just keep my face close but my body away. Closing my eyes, I swallowed hard. My hands were instinctively resting on his chest. This was going to be one epic peck, and I hoped the people around who were watching—whoever they were—appreciated our acting.

His hand was still covering my cheek. "Are you ready for me, Rose?" Jack whispered in a low, insistent voice, and I smelled the whiskey and mint on his breath.

"You're still taking it too slow—you need to—"

I didn't get the chance to utter another word because Jack's lips were on mine, and we were not sharing a nice little romantic peck. No, his tongue was already sweeping in and teasing mine. For a moment, I wasn't sure what I should do. We hadn't done this even on the day we'd said *I do*. My eyes were still open, and I felt a little desperate to end whatever he had started. I even tried to, twice, both times thinking *Okay, this is it, he is stopping now so you need to stop too*, but the more he teased me with the way he slowly coaxed me into the kiss, pulling me deeper, the more I felt myself slipping. Finally, my eyes started to close on their own. It wasn't that I wasn't responding—I was, had been from the moment his lips touched mine—but up until that point, I'd been doing it reluctantly, thinking the entire time it would end in the next second, thinking he'd stop after just one more beat. I was doing my very best to hold myself back, trying my very, very best not to enjoy our kiss.

Then when he suddenly stopped, I could've cried. I wasn't sure if it was from relief or sorrow. Thankfully, he didn't pull back completely, and I only swayed toward him a little. I forced myself to open my eyes.

"Am I doing okay?" he asked against my already swollen lips, his eyes staring straight into mine. The hairs on my arms stood up and his eyes became my entire focus. They looked darker, deeper, and deep ocean blue became my absolute favorite new color.

I cleared my throat and tried to move my head up and down in a nod. "I mean, it depends on what you're going for, but much better, er, than a turtle...I think."

"You think so?" His gravelly voice caused my eyelids to droop, and the way he used his left hand to swipe some of my bangs out of my face, the backs of his fingers gently grazing my temple...

Biting on my lip so I wouldn't do something stupid, I took a deep breath, nodded, and forced my eyes to open. In the same second, he was on my lips again. As slow and sweet as it had started with his first kiss, with this one, the more his tongue swirled in my mouth, the more he tilted his head and tried to get in deeper, the further I slipped into a dark hole I never wanted to come out of. His hand at my back pulled me forward, a barely noticeable inch or two, but it made it impossible for me not to arch my back and help him along. I wasn't into public displays of affection at all, but I forgot about every single person that was in that huge ballroom with us. I could've been standing in the middle of a stadium in Jack's arms going at it full force and probably still wouldn't have cared in that moment.

It was a little rough, our kiss, and somehow I think I knew it'd be like that with him. Rough and demanding and consuming. Knew it even before this madness had started.

When my tongue got its own idea and started to get more into it, I rose up on my toes, basically climbing him with my arms to get more of *him*, this prickly and rough-around-the-edges man who was apparently mine in public for the better part of the next two years. Leaning in harder to get more, his hand slipped from my cheek to cradle my neck. I felt his other arm go around my waist, bringing me flush with his chest. Maybe he wasn't that good at communicating with me, but he sure was good at this.

Something I couldn't exactly identify was rising up to the surface inside of me, and to be honest, more than happy to be that close, I wrapped my own arms around his neck and a groan slipped from my lips. That was when he suddenly stopped and pulled back. He wasn't as out of breath as I was, but he was definitely breathing hard. Flushed, I just stared up at him in wonder. What the hell had just happened? Was he trying for an Oscar or something? Had he felt whatever I had felt there for a second? A minute? Or had it been an hour?

I quietly cleared my throat and dropped my arms, fixing my dress under his stare. Turning my head slightly to the right, I wiped my mouth with my fingers because I didn't think it was a good idea to keep licking my lips trying to taste him again.

Facing him, I started, "Jack, I—"

"Your ex-fiancé is staring," he said in a calm voice. His breathing didn't appear to be labored anymore, so opposite of what I was feeling.

I stiffened but didn't look back to where I knew Jack had just glanced or had probably kept glancing while he was kissing me. So, this *was* just a show. My stomach dropped and I let go of what I had been about to say. His kiss had been just a show. I mean...of course it was a show. I already knew that—he had given me a warning, for Christ's sake. It wasn't like he had smiled at me and then lost control and kissed me because he just couldn't stop himself. Nope. He had given me plenty of warning, but...but for a second there, I had lost myself in the kiss and had forgotten. For a second there, I had thought he was actually, maybe... It had probably just been a fluke. I shook my head, trying to get rid of the haze clouding my brain and return to reality. Jack was a good kisser—so what? Maybe I could simply wait for the next public event when he thought we should lock lips again, just enjoy it for what it was, and not think too much about it.

When Jack pulled my chair out for me to sit down, I studied

him a bit more carefully out of the corner of my eye as I took my seat. His face was as it always was: set and aloof, his expression cool and unreadable. If his lips hadn't been a little more reddish because of my lipstick transferring onto them, I wouldn't have even guessed he had just kissed someone—kissed me. There was absolutely no evidence left of what we had just shared.

Feeling confused, I picked up my fork and didn't even realize my plate had been switched out for some sort of chicken dish as I dug in without another word. Jack and I were quiet for a long time, letting other voices fill the heavy silence between us.

"You think that was better than a turtle?" he asked after the better part of fifteen minutes had passed in silence. The event was plenty loud, and he had to lean toward me so I could hear him. The other two couples sitting across from us weren't exactly silent as they laughed out loud in a way that made me cringe every time it started up again. I had to lean toward Jack as I had him repeat his words. My stomach still wasn't sitting right after the whole thing.

"Oh yeah, that was very professional." I winced and tried to salvage the moment. "As in I think we did a very good job of making people believe this is a real thing between us." It had almost fooled me, too—almost. "Hopefully I wasn't too bad either?" I asked lightly, trying to look like I didn't care much about it either way but at the same time regretting the words as soon as they left my mouth because I *was* curious, dammit.

I broke a piece of bread in half and stuffed the whole thing in my mouth.

"No, you were fine."

My chewing slowed down as I processed his words then I forced myself to swallow the bread that tasted so much like cardboard.

"Great," I mumbled, low enough that he didn't hear me. I was *fine*.

He leaned in again, his arm carelessly slung on the back of my chair. "What did you say?"

I leaned away, nothing obvious, just a little, as I reached out for my second glass of white wine. A hell of a headache would be waiting for me when I woke up the next morning. I just knew it.

"Nothing," I mumbled into my wine, and Jack leaned in closer, his shoulder on my back. I couldn't lean away because the damn wine glass was already in my hand.

"You need to stop talking into your beverage. Is everything okay?"

I put the wine glass down, took a breath as I did so, and then set my eyes on his jaw. "Everything is fine, just a little tired after all the excitement—not the kissing part, obviously. That wasn't much of a workout. Easy peasy." *Stop moving your lips, Rose.*

"Why are you not looking at me?"

"I'm looking at you." I looked down at his pants and then at the table where his left hand was resting, turning the whiskey glass around and around—anywhere but his eyes. Then I got pissed at myself and looked straight into his eyes with a raise of my eyebrow.

He stared at me in silence for a good twenty seconds, and I stared right back. Nothing was going on between us. This was Jack. This was temporary. I was the one who was making things awkward by trying to put some meaning behind something that didn't...well, it didn't mean anything. He had told me he was about to kiss me and then he'd kissed me. It wasn't anything new. Everyone kissed with their mouths and tongues; we hadn't done anything special.

His jaw tightened and he stood up.

"I need to check on a few clients then we can leave."

I opened my mouth to say something, but he had already walked away. When the waiter presented the dessert, I gave him a forced smile. It looked like some sort of eclair with three dots of something green on the side. A jam? Sauce? I had no idea. Making sure certain people weren't looking at me, I looked over my right shoulder and found Maddy and Sierra; they were six, seven tables behind us. When I caught Maddy's eyes, I smiled warmly and waved at her. She enthusiastically waved back.

My gaze searched for Jack next, and I found him talking to an elderly man a few tables away from the girls. I faced forward and accidentally met the eyes of one of the guys sitting at our table. The ladies were absent, and the other man was busy talking on his phone quite loudly. The one whose eyes I'd met gave me a sly smile and lifted his red wine glass in a salute. I looked away.

"Are you enjoying your night?" he asked. He was the one sitting closest to me on my right, and since the other guy was still on his phone, he couldn't have been talking to anyone but me.

I forced a small smile and nodded at him.

"I'm Anthony."

Because I was the most intelligent person alive, I acted as if I couldn't hear him, pushed my chair back, grabbed my plate with two hands, and found myself heading back to the table where the girls were sitting. Obviously, you never leave your dessert behind. When they noticed me coming, both Maddy's and Sierra's subdued faces broke out into a smile.

This time, because I didn't want to embarrass Jack, I asked a waiter if they could bring me a chair, and while standing between the girls with a dessert plate in my hand, I asked the chaperone if she'd mind if I joined the girls. When I got the okay and the chair, I sat between them and started chatting.

When they asked me if my husband had left me behind, I found Jack in the busy ballroom in a second and pointed him out. He was standing with his hands in his pockets again. He actually looked really good in a tux. His eyes found mine and, having been caught, I quickly looked away.

When I found the girls contemplating how to eat the eclairs

on their plate, I reached for mine with my fingers. It was easier, and also, I'd left everything else at my table and had nothing else to use. The girls relaxed when they saw me and attacked their own eclairs with such joy that I smiled at them. As we talked about random things and ate our desserts, I snuck glances at Jack, acutely aware of where he was the entire time.

When he finally got back to my side, it was hard to say goodbye to the girls. I kissed them both on their cheeks and waved goodbye as they giggled behind our backs. I was sure the giggles were all for Jack, who had actually kissed their little hands and bid them a good night, stealing more pieces of my heart in the process.

As we were waiting for our coats to be brought out, Jack pointed at my lips with his fingers. He was smiling softly. "There is chocolate around your lips."

I closed my eyes as I felt a rush of heat hit my cheeks.

Way to go, Rose. Way to go.

"I'll be right back!"

"Rose, no, we need to—"

"Just a minute!" Yelling at him over my shoulder, I rushed to the bathroom and looked in the mirror. Sure enough, on the left edge of my mouth were the tell-tale signs of chocolate, and even worse than that, my runny nose was starting to make an appearance again. At least he hadn't noticed that in the dark.

Pulling the completely soaked—yet again—tissue paper out of my nose, I tilted my head back when I felt a rush of liquid trailing down. Groaning, I made another ball of paper and pushed it up my nose, hoping it'd hold until we could reach the apartment. The last thing I wanted was for Jack to see me with a runny nose.

When I was done I rushed back to him. "Sorry, sorry."

"You don't have to apologize to me. It's fine," he murmured.

A lot of things were *fine* this evening.

He held up my jacket and when I hesitated for a second, he

raised an eyebrow and just waited. I pushed my arms in and let him settle the heavy weight of it on my shoulders. I turned to face him so we could leave and bundled myself tighter in my coat, knowing I was about to freeze my ass off the second I stepped outside.

Jack was right beside me as he opened the door, and I took my first step into the cold and busy night. With my right hand, I held the collar of my jacket closed and breathed out, watching it puff out in a cloud in front of me. On my third step, a warm hand gently slipped around my left one without a word, and I climbed down the stairs hand in hand with my husband as if it was the most natural thing in the world.

The number of times Jack Hawthorne smiled: three. (VICTORY IS MINE.)

CHAPTER FOURTEEN

ROSE

I woke up in the middle of the night with a loud gasp and a light sheen of sweat covering my body. My breathing was labored and my heart rate was a little faster than I would've liked it to be. Feeling dazed and not sure where I was exactly, I looked around. The room was dark, but as my eyes adjusted to the sliver of light coming through the terrace doors thanks to the moon, I realized where I was: in my room at Jack's apartment, where I had gone to sleep, but... I closed my eyes and groaned, letting myself drop back to my pillow. I turned to my side, facing the terrace doors, and just stared at nothing. It was...Sunday night, the night after the charity event.

And I had just dreamed of Jack.

I was so incredibly aware that what I had just seen wasn't real, but it had *felt* real—real enough that I felt a vast emptiness inside me. I swallowed and turned onto my back, staring at the dark ceiling, trying to rein in my emotions. I could still feel his arms around me, his touch, could feel and hear his voice right next to my ear. I couldn't remember the words, but I'd remember that low, gruff sound anywhere now, and when I'd looked back over my shoulder, Jack had been right there smiling at me.

I lifted my hand and touched my cheek where I could still feel the prickly sensation, a remnant of his stubble rubbing against my cheek. It felt so real that I had to close my eyes and try to feel the ghost of his touch.

I was screwed.

It all had felt so real.

In my dream, I was in love with Jack, and I was pretty sure he was in love with me too. When he kissed me, just a slow graze of his lips on mine, there had been no one around. It was just us. Then he smiled against my lips. We had *both* smiled, and I'd wrapped my arms around his neck and forced him into a longer, more satisfying kiss. I'd never felt a happiness like that. When we'd come up for air, we had both been smiling, him pushing my hair out of my face with his hands, our foreheads resting against each other as we caught our breaths.

There had been no one around.

No one to show off for.

Just us.

My feelings hadn't just disappeared suddenly like the dream, though. They hadn't changed. I could still remember what I'd felt. I still wanted him and that, more than anything, scared the hell out of me, because it wasn't real and yet I could still feel it.

I breathed in and out of my mouth and kicked off the covers. It was too hot inside the room.

After a few minutes of just staring into the darkness of the ceiling, I closed my eyes and desperately tried to go back to sleep in the hopes that I could pick up exactly where I'd left off.

I tried and it didn't work.

When I realized it wasn't happening, I dropped my legs from the bed and gripped the edge of the mattress, just sitting there for a few minutes, trying my best to clear my mind.

This was all happening because of that damn kiss and all that touching and smiling at the charity event. I knew it, but the dream had been too much. Feeling so good about something, feeling so happy and then having that feeling just be a lie? The moment I'd woken up, I had felt the physical loss of him intensely.

Saturday night had ended as soon as we got back to the apartment. Jack had disappeared into his study or office or whatever the hell he called that place, our car ride having been just as uneventful. He hadn't mentioned the kiss or seeing Jodi and Bryan and Joshua. And I...instead of sitting down and trying to process the fact that Joshua was now with my cousin and maybe —probably—had left me for her, I had been stuck on the kiss I had shared with Jack. Joshua hadn't occupied my mind for more than a few fleeting minutes.

It had been all Jack.

Sunday morning when I woke up, thinking maybe we could have breakfast together since I wasn't opening the coffee shop, I'd looked for him. I even went as far as knocking on his door and going into his room, only to find him already gone. If someone asked, I wouldn't admit it, but I had waited around until two PM, and when he hadn't shown up, I'd decided to go to the coffee shop and spend time in the kitchen baking instead. I'd picked up my phone countless times, thinking maybe sending a quick text asking what he was doing wouldn't be such a bad idea, but I hadn't ever gone through with it.

He hadn't contacted me either.

Heading back to the apartment at eight PM, nothing had changed. I didn't think I had anything specific to say to him, but I *wanted* very much to see him and be around him. When I had gone to bed at eleven, he still hadn't been around.

Massaging my temples, I sighed and blindly reached for my phone on the nightstand. I didn't know why my heartbeat quickened when I took a quick look at the screen and scrolled through a few messages from Sally; there was nothing from Jack there, no calls, no texts—and why would he call or text me anyway? We weren't that. We weren't ever going to be that, no matter what dreams I had.

Thoroughly annoyed with myself for being so affected just by a simple dream, I got up to my feet and looked for something I could wear over my panties. I left the simple short-sleeved thin grey t-shirt on and quietly left my room. The only positive thing for the night was that my nose wasn't running at that particular moment, and it looked like I was over whatever allergic reaction or flu had crossed my path.

When I made it to the staircase, I paused and glanced toward Jack's room but didn't dare go anywhere near it. Slowly going down the stairs, I decided a cold glass of water would be just the thing to wake me up from stupid and pointless dreams, but then I saw the light coming from under the door of Jack's study and turned that way instead.

CHAPTER FIFTEEN

JACK

The last forty-eight hours had been hell. I'd spent my entire Sunday at the office dealing with an unexpected crisis that took me away from Rose and when I had successfully handled that hoping I'd get to go home, I'd faced a much more annoying situation in the name of: Bryan Coleson. But it was done. Rose was done with them. I'd made sure.

As if that wasn't enough for the day, before I could leave the office Joshua had showed up. Everything was piling up and I was slowly getting buried underneath it all.

So I was in my study at three AM, doing nothing but making myself miserable instead of going to bed...just a few doors down from her.

When there was a hesitant knock on the door, I snapped out of my thoughts.

"Come in."

First, her head peeked in, her shoulders and body hidden behind the door.

"Hey, Jack."

"Hey."

"Am I bothering you? Can I come in?"

If I'd been sure it wouldn't startle her, I'd have laughed out loud. She wasn't bothering me enough—that was the problem.

Just in case, I closed the lid of my laptop, hiding the email I had just received.

"Please, come in," I repeated, and she finally showed her entire body and stepped in, closing the door and leaning her back against it. I wasn't sure how long I could keep my hands off of her or how wise it was to be in a secluded room together like this, but I didn't care.

"I woke up," she said, softly smiling at me. "Couldn't go back to sleep."

Rose was wearing black leggings and a light grey t-shirt that did nothing to hide her yellow lace bra underneath it. I had lost my tie somewhere when I'd walked into a quiet apartment, but I was still wearing the white button-up and black slacks I had put on that morning. She looked beautiful even disheveled, whereas I must have looked like a mess.

"What are you doing?" she asked when I didn't say anything.

"Something came up that I had to deal with."

She pushed herself off the door, slowly approaching with her hand behind her back. "You still have work to do?"

I gave a sharp nod.

"I didn't see you today."

Had she been hoping to see me? I didn't think so. "I was at the office. There was a crisis with a client, but I dealt with it."

"I thought you didn't work every weekend." She was a few steps closer, and I was aware of each and every one of those steps. Her gaze slowly took in everything in the room but me.

Rising from my seat, I rounded my desk and sat on the edge of it. I had to shove my hands into my pockets so I wouldn't grab her, but I needed to be closer. I sat still on my perch and watched her slow movements as she walked up to the bookshelves and strolled the length of them, pausing once or twice to check a title, her fingertips softly grazing each spine.

"No, not every weekend. Did you need something?"

She stopped perusing the books and focused on me. "If I'm bothering you..."

"You are not bothering me, Rose. Did you want to talk about something?"

She lifted one shoulder in a shrug and kept her eyes on the books. "Nothing in particular. Like I said, I couldn't sleep."

"Okay."

She turned to me, keeping her back against the bookcase. "Will you go to bed?"

"At some point, yes."

"Good. That's good. Sleep is good."

With even slower steps, she drew closer to me, her eyes moving around the room.

"You have a beautiful apartment," she murmured, and I frowned at her.

"Rose? Are you okay?"

She hated when I asked her that question. I knew that, but I loved her reactions too much to quit asking.

She sighed. "Yeah, sure. Why?"

"You're acting weird."

She waved a hand in front of her, dismissing my words. Then, standing next to me, she put her hand on my desk. "This is a beautiful desk," she said.

Something was definitely wrong with her.

"It's a desk," I agreed in a flat tone.

Her lips twitched, and my gaze focused on that tiny movement. I was losing my mind. Being so close yet so far away from her was wreaking havoc on my self-control.

She released a deep breath and finally met my eyes, no trace

of the smile I had become so enamored with. "So...at the event...
we...did a good job, right?"

"A good job? Of what?"

"Of being husband and wife. I need to try something, so can
you just stay still?"

My eyebrows rose in confusion, but I simply gave her a sharp
nod, not having any idea where she was going with this.

She licked her lips and puffed up her cheeks before letting
out a long breath. Then she took two more steps forward until her
chest was only an inch or two away from my shoulder.

I stiffened, my hands twitching in my pockets. Not sure what
she was about to do, I had to take my right hand out and grip the
edge of my desk. Her focus was on my lips, and I watched her
bite down on her bottom lip then lean in close.

Her eyes flitted between my eyes and my lips.

"It's just...I'll..."

Then she leaned forward, and I covered the remaining space
between us until her lips finally touched mine, pressing a soft kiss
on the edge of my mouth. Her eyes still closed, she pulled back
and made a noncommittal sound.

"Huh."

To say I was surprised would be an understatement, but I
didn't dare move, scared I would break the spell of whatever was
going on. I just kept my eyes on her beautiful face and tried to
read what she was thinking. Then she took another step forward,
and I swear to God I felt her nipples press into my chest.

She swallowed and put her hand on my cheek.

"What are you doing, Rose?" I asked, unable to hold back
anymore. My voice sounded rough to my ears.

"I'm just trying something." She looked into my eyes. "Could
you close your eyes?"

I raised an eyebrow in question.

"Just for a quick second. Promise."

I sighed, slightly annoyed that she didn't want me to watch her, to take in her features when she was standing so close to me. My fingers gripped the desk tighter, but I did as she'd asked.

"It's just...you're making me nervous when you frown at me like that. This'll only take a second, I promise."

My lips parted to give her an answer, but no sound came out because her lips had found mine again. I responded to her gentle kiss and opened my eyes anyway so I could watch her. She had already closed hers, and her hand was slightly trembling against my cheek. Tilting her head, she deepened the kiss, her left hand pressing on my chest as she rose higher. I dipped my head down and closed my eyes, feeling drunk with her kiss.

She pulled back before I could take over completely, and we just stood there a few inches apart, her breath coming out in little pants. My heart hammering in my chest, I studied her as her eyes slowly opened and she made a face like something wasn't quite right.

Scrunching her nose, she gave me a look I couldn't interpret.

I cleared my throat. "Not good?"

She lifted her hand between us, rocking it from side to side. "Ehhh."

"I see. Turtle again?"

Another noncommittal sound.

"Right. And this was important...why?"

She huffed and thought about her answer for a second. "Kinda like practice, maybe? Saturday was a little weird, so I thought we could work on it, so it looks more natural?"

"So Saturday was bad? I didn't realize you had a problem with my kiss. You seemed okay with it then, but now you think we should work on it?"

"I mean...I didn't have anything better to do, so..."

"Right."

I waited, my eyes on her.

"Maybe one more time? Just...you know, to see what we're doing wrong."

"Sure. Any pointers you'd like to give?"

She took me seriously and thought about it some more. I was having trouble keeping a straight face but decided to play along. I didn't buy into her bullshit, but if she wanted to kiss, I wasn't gonna argue.

"Would more tongue be weird for you?" she asked.

My lips twitched, and I smiled.

"What?"

Clearing my throat, I shook my head. "Nothing. I'm not sure about the tongue," I ventured. "If you think that's a good idea, I'll have to give it a try."

"Okay." She sighed and put a hand on my shoulder. "Then... yeah. Okay, let's try that."

After another deep breath, she took one small little step. Her eyes were already closed so she missed my smile. Taking my other hand out of my pocket, I brushed her bangs away, relaxed my hand that was gripping the desk to death, and gently placed it on the small of her back so I could bring her closer in a soundless order. She obeyed and licked her lips, eyes still closed, face slightly tilted up.

"Let me know if it gets worse," I whispered against her lips, and she nodded quickly. "Relax." My voice was even lower this time, and her hand tightened on my shoulder, fingers digging into my shirt.

There was only a breath separating us, and her breathing was already too loud. I kissed the edge of her lips first. They parted and the tip of her tongue swiped the bottom one. I released a breath. I was in so much trouble.

Impatient, I took her upper lip between mine and slid my

tongue in, gently licking and sucking, getting reacquainted with her mouth. She took a step forward and fell into my chest. I fisted her t-shirt in my fingers and sat up straighter, my dick already straining in my pants as I pushed my chest against her. There was no doubt she could feel it.

Her mouth opened wider with a wild moan, and I tilted my head to the right as she went for the left, the kiss becoming something more in just a quick second. I brought my hand up to her neck, feeling her skin against mine, her pulse wild just under my fingertips. I pushed in and took as much as I could from her, thirsty for more, for everything I could take from her. I wanted her to drown in me like she'd never drowned in someone else before. If I had thought it was the right time, I would've planted her ass right on my desk and fucked her until she couldn't take it anymore.

Her hand slid from my shoulder around my neck, and her fingers grabbed hold of my hair, her other hand gripping my bicep. I didn't think she realized what she was doing or the fact that she was moaning and melting into me, pressing and pulling at the same time as I took her mouth ruthlessly. I'd been so hungry for her touch and taste.

The more I demanded she give me, the quicker she responded with more. Maybe this marriage thing hadn't been the worst idea I'd ever had. Maybe things would work out just fine.

We were both reaching the point where we'd need to take a breath, but I wasn't sure I could let go. She abruptly pulled back, deciding for me as she let my hair go and rested both her palms against my chest. We were still standing close enough to breathe in each other's air, our heads tucked in together, still close enough for me to go for her lips and pull her back into the kiss so she wouldn't have time to think about it.

"Yeah." She cleared her throat. "That was better, I think," she croaked, her chest rising and falling rapidly as her breasts and hardened nipples rubbed against me with each and every breath. I was seconds away from lifting her up onto my desk and taking her little fake experiment further.

"You want to try again?" I asked, my own voice just as rough as hers had sounded. I used my thumb to caress her jawline.

"Uhh..." She swallowed and unfortunately remembered that she was touching me. She took a healthy step back, causing me to reluctantly let go of the back of her t-shirt. "I think we've got it down now. We should be fine, I think. I'm guessing, I mean."

I shoved my hands back into my pockets so I wouldn't grab her and pull her back against me, starting something we would have even more trouble stopping. I noticed her eyes drop down to my waist, where she could clearly see my outline, and then she was backing away. I had to lock my body to stop myself from tracing her steps and asking for another go.

She cleared her throat. "I have to wake up early tomorrow, so I'm going to try to get some more sleep. You staying up late?"

I forced my body to relax and straightened, walking behind my desk. I sat down. It was the only way I could stop myself from going after her. I opened my laptop.

"I'll come up as soon as I'm done here."

"I'll see you tomorrow, right?"

I looked up from the screen and into her glazed eyes. Yes, she'd see me the next day, and hopefully every day after that. I was going to make sure we finished what we'd started soon enough. I was going to do everything in my power to make sure she wouldn't want to let go of me. The guilt I had for deceiving her was still there, but I would tell her everything when the time was right, no more holding back. I'd be anything and everything she would want and need me to be.

"Yes, Rose," I replied softly. "We'll see each other tomorrow."

She nodded and, while still trying to back away without

breaking eye contact, bumped into the floor lamp next to the door. When she winced, I stood up.

"Are you okay?"

Her hand shot up. "No, sit. I'm fine."

"You sure?"

"Yes. Yes, I'm fine. I've bugged you enough, so you just get back to work."

"You could never bug me, Rose."

She froze then laughed, and for the first time, it seemed forced and tight. Her eyelids drooped and she glanced at the floor. Pushing her hand behind her back, she moved it around until she was able to grasp the door handle and open it. Eyes on me, she backed out of my room.

"Nice touch—a very husbandly thing to say. So, good night then."

"Sweet dreams," I said, and she hesitated as she was closing the door.

"What did you say?"

"Sweet dreams."

"That might be a very, very bad idea, so let's all have normal dreams instead—normal and alone dreams."

I tilted my head and narrowed my eyes, studying her expression. "You sure you're okay?"

"Perfect. A little flustered, actually, because kissing you is a little weird, so excuse my weird behavior."

I raised an eyebrow, confused. "Kissing me is weird?"

"Yeah. You know, you're my husband, blah blah blah, but also you're not, blah blah blah." Sniffing, she gasped and suddenly tilted her head back. "I'm going to sneeze. Okay. Bye." She slammed the door shut, leaving me staring after her, confused.

I crossed the room and opened the door, listening to her running up the stairs and then hearing another door slam shut.

I walked back to my desk with controlled steps and took my

seat. The email was still open, waiting for me to send a response. I was feeling much better than I did just five minutes before. My mind consumed with Rose, it took me a while to gather myself enough to form one simple sentence and press send.

You even think of threatening me again, I'll turn your sorry excuse of a life into a living hell, Joshua.

CHAPTER SIXTEEN

ROSE

I t was caramel week, and Owen had baked four different caramel treats while I had tackled our basics—sandwiches, brownies, and berry muffins. Even our basics tended to change day by day since we were such a new place, but in a month or so we'd have a more set menu after we got to know our customers and learned what they enjoyed more.

On Monday, I had taken my usual ride with Raymond at five and had joined Owen in the kitchen as soon as I got in. Sally had come in an hour after me, earlier than her usual time. The mystery was solved when she started trying her best to flirt with a straight-faced Owen.

"You think you could teach me how to make this salted caramel banana bread? It's really good."

Owen just grunted and kept working the dough in his hands. He was making cinnamon buns, my absolute favorite.

Sally gave me a wide-eyed look and rolled her eyes. She was relentless. Resting her elbows on the marble workspace that dominated the center of the kitchen, she pushed him some more.

"I'll cook you something. What's your favorite food? I can't bake to save my life, but I can cook."

"If you can't bake, what makes you think you'll be able to make banana bread?" Owen asked, his eyes and hands busy, busy, busy.

Sally just slid a little closer to him. "You can teach me. I'm sure if you teach me, I'll get the hang of it, and from what I understand, banana bread isn't that hard to make."

"Can you back off a little? You're gonna be covered in flour if you come any closer."

Barely holding back my burst of laughter before I attracted Owen's fierce frown, I turned away from the doorway and focused on stacking up the sandwiches under the glass dome. Owen didn't like anyone messing with his routine. He barely tolerated me working alongside him for a few hours in the mornings, so even though he sounded rude, it was just his way, not to mention he was also a very private person.

"Would you like me to make you coffee?" I heard Sally push on, ignoring his rudeness.

As Owen grunted a nonverbal response that didn't quite reach my ears, I couldn't help but lean back to take a peek into the kitchen. Sally had been dismissed to her original starting point right across from him.

"How about cinnamon buns then?" Her voice was still upbeat and positive.

"What about them?"

"Can you teach me how to make cinnamon buns? It looks like a lot of fun, all the rolling and cinnamon stuff."

"Stuff... Don't you have work to do at the front? It's almost opening time."

I bit down on my lip and got back to my own work. Owen was somewhat like Jack— essentially, not a fan of using a lot of words. Speaking of Jack...I was still experiencing the effects of my dream and then everything that had happened after it. I wasn't exactly sure what I'd been thinking when I'd decided to work on our kissing technique, but at the time, trying to see if what I had felt at the charity event was a one-time thing or not seemed like a good idea. Maybe my dream was the driving force behind me having the bravery to face him, but I couldn't complain. The second kiss was just as good as the first one, maybe even better because we'd been all alone in his study, away from all the curious eyes. It was still temporary, this thing between us, but the dream had shifted something inside me, I felt it with every fiber of my being.

For a second there, I thought I had felt his erection against my stomach when he grasped the back of my shirt and pulled me in closer. I had encountered them in the wild before. I wasn't imagining *that*. I might have imagined—because of the damn dream— that he was really into the kiss as well, but I hadn't conjured up that erection in my mind.

He was a great kisser; there was no arguing with that. He was just a little rough and completely consuming, just as I had imagined he would be, and I thought I had a completely different stance about PDA after the weekend. I didn't think he'd fall for the 'practice kiss' again, so I was going to have to make the kissing in public thing...well, a thing for us—only to make our marriage more believable, not for myself or anything.

Then again, who was I kidding? Everything about Jack was starting to become too appealing for me. I was starting look forward to seeing his stony and sometimes aloof expression at the end of the day...every day. I chatted more than him, but he was talking, too, much more than he had in the beginning. I hardly did the 'talking to myself as Jack' thing anymore, and when I did, it was for the fun of seeing his troubled expression as if he was considering his life choices of ending up in a fake marriage with me. I wasn't making fun of him or anything even remotely close to that. I just enjoyed the way he glowered at me a little too much.

It was the highlight of my day.

And that smile...gosh, he had finally smiled, and it had absolutely been worth the wait to see his face transform. You could fall in love with that face, with that smile, even if the package came with the frown and the prickly personality. I just couldn't decide which expression I preferred more on him, because I thought you could easily fall for that stony, grumpy expression just as hard. Then again, the way I was feeling after that dream, my unexpected attraction to Jack had tripled overnight. Clearly I couldn't be trusted to be around him until the effects wore off.

"What are you smiling at? That was a complete disaster," Sally mumbled as she sidled up next to me, licking her fingers, presumably after snacking on sticky banana bread.

I stopped daydreaming about Jack and tried to focus on Sally. She wasn't exactly pouting, but she was getting there.

"I didn't realize you were interested in him," I replied, ignoring her question.

She reached for a mint from a small bowl next to the cash register, unfolded the wrapper, and popped it in her mouth.

"I can see how it might be a little too late to ask after what you just witnessed, but do you have a rule against employees dating?"

Stacking the last turkey sandwich, I put the glass dome back in its place and turned to Sally, thinking about my answer for a moment. "I mean...you two are my only employees, obviously, so I've never even thought about it. You're into him that much? I thought maybe you were just messing with him."

"Why would I do that?"

"Because it's fun to get him all riled up?"

Sometimes I thought it was fun to rile Jack up.

"Nope." She shook her head and glanced toward the kitchen

over my shoulder. "I mean, he is really attractive, don't you think?"

I looked over my shoulder to try to see what she was seeing. Owen was rolling the dough, his biceps flexing. He actually was attractive when you took a long look at him, not in the sense that Jack was attractive, but in a more...different way. He looked more like a French guy without the romantic and charming part. His brown hair was curly and fell over his forehead, and you could see the edges of the tattoos on his strong arms curling under his shirt. He was skinnier than Jack but still lean. Jack felt stronger to me. When I looked at Owen, I didn't feel like *You know what, I think I would like to hug that*. He was just...Owen, a friend. When I looked at Jack, I was very interested in hugging him and staying in his arms for as long as possible.

Sally waved her hand in front of my face. "Earth to Rose?"

I snapped out of my Jack haze.

"Sorry. I guess he is attractive."

"And he has this intense air about him. It seems to be working for me. I don't know, I wouldn't say no to a date."

"Well I think it looks like you'll be the one asking in this case."

I reached for the brownies and pushed them in front of the chocolate muffins, rearranging things so the sandwiches would be on the far left next to the register, tempting the customers.

"So you have no problem with this, then? I really like working with you, and I won't risk that for a guy, but if it's okay with you, I might go for it one of these days."

How the hell was I supposed to decide on something like this? "As long as it doesn't affect your work, I think I'm okay with it? You sure about this, though? I don't want him to feel uncomfortable if he isn't interested." It probably wasn't one of my finest ideas, but I didn't know how to say no. I was still a romantic at heart, despite my own marital status.

"Oh, no. He isn't ready yet. I'm gonna have to work on him little by little, which is the fun part, to be honest." She gave me a blinding smile, bouncing twice on her feet. "Okay, I'll go wash my hands and unload the last batch of coffee cups then get everything else ready."

Before I could say okay, she was already back in the kitchen, her eyes lingering on Owen as she walked past him.

If I wanted something real with Jack, would I have to work on him little by little? Not that it didn't sound fun. But would I even want to complicate things like that? He wasn't the romantic type; he was a whole different type of his own. Sure, he was my husband, but that was all just an act, nothing more, and the erection...well, I thought it was pretty much involuntary when kissing someone. He didn't have a special erection for me. It wasn't a special erection.

There was a hard knock on the glass door that jolted me out of my thoughts and I turned to find a young guy, maybe in his early twenties, looking inside the coffee shop with a huge bouquet of roses in his arms.

With a big grin blooming across my face, I rushed to the door and unlocked it, the cold air hitting my cheeks a refreshing welcome after all my thoughts of Jack Hawthorne and his not-so-special erection.

"Rose Hawthorne?" the guy asked. He was bundled in a blue jacket and was jumping in place, presumably to keep warm.

"Yes, that's me." I could barely keep my hands to myself as he checked something on his notepad then finally handed me the flowers wrapped in brown paper, but there was no note. "Who are they from?"

"It says Jack Hawthorne."

The grin still going strong on my face, I hugged them to my chest then signed where he was pointing at.

"Have a good day," he offered before running back to the white van that was apparently waiting for him.

"You too!" I shouted, waving even though he wasn't looking back.

I pushed the door closed with my hip and locked it back up, my eyes on the roses as I made my way back toward the kitchen and Sally appeared in the doorway.

"Did I hear a kno—oh, Rose! Look at them!"

I was. I was looking and trying to contain the smile on my face while also trying to ignore the lightness I was feeling in my heart.

"They are gorgeous," I mumbled, almost to myself, as I touched a few rosebuds. This week there were pinkish purple and white roses.

"Okay, I'm officially in love with your husband. He is too cute."

I laughed, feeling all happy from head to toe. "He doesn't like it when people think he is cute, but yeah, I wholeheartedly agree." Still smiling, I looked around the coffee shop. Some of the roses he had brought in the previous week were still going strong, but I had switched the ones that had started fading with fake ones just half an hour earlier. I was going to switch them all out for the fresh ones.

"Do you want me to help?" Sally asked, leaning in to smell the roses.

I didn't know why I was feeling protective, but I wanted to handle the roses myself and only barely stopped myself from snatching them away from her nose. As stupid as it sounded, I tried not to think about it too much. They were all mine.

"No, I got it, but can you gather the fake ones and bring the mini vases to the back so I can change them all out?"

"Of course."

It took me ten minutes to have them all out on the tables, and the remaining twelve were set on the counter next to the cash register so I could constantly see them and maybe put a little smile on the faces of my customers too. Placing the last one on the table in front of the bookshelf, I reached for my back pocket and took out my phone. We still had eight minutes before I would unlock the doors and welcome our first customers.

Not wanting to wait any longer, I quickly typed a text.

Rose: Hi.
Jack: Something wrong?

I laughed and sat down in the chair closest to me.

Rose: Nope, just saying hi, and thank you.
Jack: Hi. Thank you for what?
Rose: The flowers. I still can't stop smiling.
Jack: Glad you liked them.
Rose: I love them, but I might have liked the ones from last week more.
Jack: Did they mess up the order again? I'll call them.
Rose: No! Wait.
Rose: They didn't mess it up. It's just that...last week you brought them in yourself, and that was more...something, I guess.

I closed my eyes and groaned, loudly. I couldn't possibly be cheesier, and I was officially flirting with my husband, officially poking the beehive, knowing it couldn't possibly end well.

Jack: I see.

I see. That was all he gave me. I took a deep breath and slowly let it out.

Rose: Will you drop by before work? I make good free coffee.
Jack: I'm afraid I'm already at work. We have an early meeting.

I tried not to feel disappointed, but it was hard.

Rose: Ah, okay. I'm sorry, I know you don't like texting so I'll shut up. Hope you have a good day. Again, thank you for the flowers. They're beautiful.

I hit myself on the forehead with the side of my phone a few times. I needed to get it together. I was not in love with Jack Hawthorne, and he was most definitely not in love with me either. It had just been a very, *very* convincing dream and kiss and touch and...that was it. Also, I just found him attractive —any woman would. That wasn't a crime. Deep down, as prickly and cold as he seemed, he was actually a very good person.

Just as I was getting up to finally unlock the front door, my phone buzzed in my hand with another text. Glancing at the screen as I was walking, my heart soared when I saw his name, and I stopped next to the cash register.

Jack: Do you want to see me?
Rose: What?
Jack: You said you liked the flowers I brought in more and you offered me free coffee. Am I assuming...

He was flirting back. As unbelievable as that sounded, I still hoped.

Finding it—*him*—stupidly charming, I quickly wrote back.

Rose: I mean, you're my husband, so I think I'm bound to look at you. Thankfully you're not too bad-looking, so I wouldn't cover my eyes if you showed up.

The second I pressed send, I wanted to take it back, delete it, and write something more...smart and witty, but it was too late.

"Hey, again, earth to Rose. Can you hear me?" Sally yelled from somewhere behind me. "We have two customers waiting—maybe we should open a few minutes early."

I looked up in surprise and only then noticed the two girls waiting for me to open the door. I rushed forward and invited them in, apologizing.

As Sally started on the coffee orders, I served them one sandwich and one blueberry muffin. As the next customer and the next started to file in, my phone buzzed twice in my pocket, causing an irrational excitement in me as I tried to ignore it and chatted with the customers.

When the last customer in line left, Sally and I looked around the place. Some were on their laptops, some just chatting with their friends. One person was reading a book they had picked up from the bookcase, and nine tables were already full.

"This is a great start to the week," Sally commented while wiping down the counter.

"It is, isn't it? I think we're doing very well. Oh, by the way, I forgot to tell you—I have a doctor's appointment at two PM, so I asked Owen to stay until I get back. Do you think you two can handle it? I'll get back as soon as I'm done."

She stopped and turned her worried gaze to me. "Something wrong?" Then her eyes widened comically. "Are you pregnant?"

I frowned at her. "No! I just got married! What are you talking about?" My frown deepening, I looked down at my stomach. "Do I look pregnant or something?"

"No, you don't look pregnant at all. My mistake. With that

husband of yours you could get pregnant just by him looking at you, so I'd say watch out."

I just stared at her in something close to horror, and she laughed.

"Fine. Pretend I didn't say anything. Of course I'll handle it. The lunch rush will be over by the time you leave so we'll be fine until you come back. Everything all right? Still the cold?"

"Yeah." I gingerly touched my nose, glad it wasn't runny at the moment. But it had been when I first woke up. "I think it's just allergies if not a weird cold. I just need to get a nose spray or something. I won't take long."

"Okay. You go do whatever you gotta do." Her smile turned into a grin. "It'll give me time to start working on Owen, so great timing on your part."

As soon as Sally headed to the kitchen, I reached for my phone to read my texts.

Jack: I'm glad I'm considered not too bad to look at.
Jack: Are you free for dinner tonight?

It didn't seem like he was flirting, because he asked if I was free for dinner every night anyway. My excitement slowly deflated, and before I could type something back, a new customer walked in.

AFTER I WALKED out of the doctor's office, I took the train to Midtown instead of heading straight back to Madison Avenue. I was still feeling a little dizzy, but if I was being honest with myself, I'd started feeling dizzy the moment the doctor had started talking.

One time I'd been prescribed antibiotics for my sore throat

when I was twenty-years-old, and I'd ended up at the emergency room. As it turned out, I was allergic to penicillin. Giving my blood was a whole other...experience. To say I didn't like needles, doctors or hospitals of any kind would be an understatement. Because of all that, I could do nothing but feel dizzy, thinking the worst.

As to why I was standing in front of Jack's building near Bryant Park, I didn't have a straight answer for that. I walked through security, got in the elevator with six other people, and got off on Jack's floor. I walked up to the blonde-haired, blue-eyed receptionist, the same one I'd seen the only two times I'd been there.

"Hi. I wanted to see Jack?"

"Hello, Mrs. Hawthorne. You don't have to stop here—you can go straight to his office."

Dazed, I nodded and thanked her. I had forgotten I was the wife for a second there. While heading to his office, I bumped into Samantha, who was walking next to two other suits.

"Rose?"

I stopped moving my legs one in front of the other. "Oh, hello Samantha. I'm here to see Jack."

Her perfectly shaped and perfectly arched eyebrows drew together. "Are you okay?"

I held on to the bag on my shoulder tighter. "Yes. Good. Thank you. Do you think Jack will be in his office?"

"I think he is out, actually, but check with Cynthia and she'll let you know." The two suits kept talking and walking without her so she glanced at them over her shoulder then faced me again. "Are you sure you're okay? You look a little pale."

Surprised that she sounded genuine, I forced a smile onto my face. "Oh, yeah. Just a little sick. It was nice to see you again." Without waiting for another question, I walked toward Jack's office, taking the left turn at the end of the hall. Cynthia was on a call so I cast a quick glance into the office as I got closer; it didn't look like Jack was in there.

"Hello, Rose. How nice to see you here." Cynthia's voice made me turn back to her.

"Hey, Cynthia. I just needed a few minutes with Jack. Is he around?"

"He had a lunch meeting with a client." She looked down at her wrist, checking the time. "Did he know you were coming?"

"Oh, no. I just dropped by. I need to head back to work soon. If you think he'll be much longer, I can just leave. I'll catch him tonight."

"He should be here in five or ten. You can wait in his office. Would you like me to bring you some tea or coffee while you're waiting?"

I shook my head and managed to offer her a small smile. "I'm good. Thank you."

When she pushed the heavy glass door open for me, I walked straight toward the two comfortable chairs in front of his meticulously organized desk and sat down.

When I looked back, Cynthia was gone.

Having a moment to myself, I grabbed a clean Kleenex from my bag and, holding it tightly in my hand, leaned back and closed my eyes, trying to calm myself down and give my wildly imaginative mind a break.

I couldn't believe this was happening. I didn't even know how many minutes had passed when the office door behind me opened and I looked over my shoulder. I wasn't sure how or what I was feeling when Jack's head lifted up from the phone in his hand and he noticed I was waiting there.

"Rose?" His brows snapped together in confusion as he paused with one foot through the doorway. "What are you doing here?"

I lifted my hand halfway up in a weak wave and then dropped it.

Cynthia appeared behind him, a little breathless. "I've been trying to catch up with you to tell you Rose was waiting for you. Do you want me to call George and push back that meeting?"

"Oh, no. Please don't," I cut in, standing up before he could answer her. "I just dropped by. I don't want to mess up his schedule. I'll leave." I bent down and collected my bag from the floor. Keeping my eyes down and feeling like I was about to break down at any second now that Jack was actually standing in front of me, I tried to walk past him, but he used his body to block me and gently gripped my wrist before I could do anything else.

Jack turned his head toward Cynthia but kept his searching gaze on me. "Give us a few minutes before you do that, okay?"

"Of course."

My eyes met Cynthia's and she gave me a small smile right before Jack shuffled me inside and she closed the door on us.

"What's wrong?" Jack asked as soon as it was just the two of us in the spacious office.

I pulled my hand away from his warm, gentle grip, massaging my wrist. Any kind of touching would just cause me to break down faster.

"Nothing. I just dropped by. I should leave." I checked my watch and then set my gaze on his shoulder instead of his eyes. "It's pretty late. Owen is covering for me with Sally, but I think I should head back so he can take off. So, I'm just gonna leave."

Despite my repetitive words, I couldn't make a move to leave, and Jack wasn't getting out of my way anyway. A few seconds later, I felt two of his fingers gently tilt my chin up and remain there.

We looked at each other for a few heartbeats. I really was affected by the dream I'd had the night before. It still felt like there was something real between us, and it was quite possibly the worst time to feel the leftover effects of being in love with him —or, more accurately, the effects of *him* being in love with me.

"Tell me what's wrong, Rose," he said simply, his voice soft and worried. "Have you been crying?"

I winced a little then bit on the inside of my cheek as he waited patiently. "Just a little, but it's nothing big. I just went to the doctor and—" My voice started breaking so I stopped.

"When? Why?" He let my chin go.

"Now. I mean I'm coming from the doctor's office. I had an appointment. I wanted to get a spray or something for the allergies." I touched my nose and his gaze followed. "For my nose. Obviously." I smiled, but I didn't think it reached my eyes.

"For the cold, right?"

Lately, I was always walking around with a Kleenex in my hand or had some nearby, just in case it started up when I wasn't expecting it.

"Yes, the one-day sore throat and the...um, runny nose and the headaches. Anyway, it doesn't feel like a normal cold. I feel completely fine if you don't count the headaches and the nose issues, which is why I thought suddenly I'd become allergic to something. It's like water dripping from my nose." I let out a small groan and looked away. "Talking about my nose is not what I want to do with you at all."

He ignored my discomfort. "I never saw you have any problems like that other than a few times."

"That's because it's not dripping 24/7. Sometimes it's okay if I'm standing up, but when I sit down, it starts dripping. Lying on my back is obviously fine, and so is keeping my head tilted back, but sometimes when I sleep on my face, I wake up in the middle of the night because I can feel something trailing down and... You get the point. Also, when it starts up when I'm working or like when we were at the charity event, I have to push a cotton ball or some tissue paper up there, *something* so I don't have to hold a tissue under my nose like this all the time." I lamented my words when I had to hold the Kleenex up to my face again. "In any case, whatever I do, it gets drenched too quickly anyway."

"Why didn't you tell me all of this before, Rose? Why did you wait?"

"I was working, and I thought it would go away on its own. Plus, I don't like doctors. Sometimes it starts up and doesn't stop for hours. Sometimes it disappears after half an hour or so. I try my best not to tilt my head down, because that triggers it too. Thankfully in the mornings it's slow, for some reason, so it hasn't been a big issue when I'm baking, but I never know when it's going to happen. Speaking of..."

I felt it coming down again, and the Kleenex in my hand was done already. Holding on to the chair, I slowly got down to my knees, my eyes looking up at the ceiling. Blindly, I tried to reach for my bag, but suddenly Jack was on his knees too, reaching for my hands. I felt my eyes blur a little.

"Can you get me a tissue, please?" I asked, keeping my chin up and away from his gaze.

He let go of me and got up to leave.

"Wait, I have some in my—"

He walked out of his office before I could tell him I had some more in my bag. I stood up. He came back with a pretty box of Kleenex and held it out for me. I pulled one out and, sniffling, held it under my nose.

"Are you okay?" he asked again, looking straight into my eyes. I nodded and tilted my head back a little more to stop the flow a bit. Sometimes that helped. Now that I'd learned what it could be, the feeling of that warm trickle was freaking me out more than it had only hours earlier.

Jack massaged his temple, walked a few steps away, and then came back to stand in front of me. "Okay. Okay, tell me what the doctor said. I'm assuming it's not allergies from the look on your face."

"Nope. Turns out it's probably not allergies or a cold. He wants to run some tests, wants to get a CT scan and an MRI, but he thinks I might have cerebrospinal fluid leak, especially because it's only coming from one side of my nose." I twisted my lips and tried my best to hold back my tears. His eyes studied my face, and the longer I looked into his gaze, the more his image started to blur.

"Don't do that," he ordered, his face unreadable.

I nodded. Given the kind of guy he was, I didn't think dealing with a crying female would be his favorite thing to do, but even hearing his gravelly voice was breaking the tight hold I'd had on myself ever since I left the doctor's office.

I'd put my bag on the chair as I was standing up, so I grabbed it and hitched it higher on my shoulder then nodded to myself. Tightening my fingers around the Kleenex in my grasp, I dropped my hand down. "I should leave, really. I should've gone straight back to work in the first place. I just thought I'd drop by and tell you I might not be able to join you—" When the first tear slowly slid down my cheek, I angrily swiped at it with the back of my hand. "I might not be able to join you at events for a while. I think they need to do surgery so I'm not sure if I'm gonna…"

He looked at me for a long time as the tears I had promised myself I wouldn't shed started to come more rapidly after the word surgery. Then I felt the now familiar feeling that something was running down my nose, so I quickly tilted my head back. The last thing—the *very* last thing I wanted was for him to actually see something coming down my nose. I felt like I couldn't come back from that.

"Okay." He rubbed the bridge of his nose, his cool demeanor cracking just slightly in front of my eyes. "Okay. Let's just sit the fuck down for a second." It was the first time I'd heard him curse. "And stop saying you need to leave. You're not going anywhere."

I nodded as much as I could with my head tilted back, because what else could I have done? I didn't want to interrupt him at his office, but I didn't have it in me to leave either. As I turned around to head back for the chairs, he stopped me with one hand on my arm and opened the office door again with the other one.

"Cynthia, call George and tell him I won't make it. Send him the junior associate I worked with—she should have the details he needs. I'll get back to him later."

"Jack," I broke in as he closed the door without even waiting to hear Cynthia's answer. "I don't want to keep you from your work."

"What did I just tell you?" He pulled me toward the couch that was next to the floor-to-ceiling windows and sat right next to me. He was still holding the Kleenex box in his hand. I didn't know why I focused on that so much, but him holding that box along with the intense and slightly scary expression on his face while wearing one of his many expensive suits would always be a good memory for me after this whole marriage business was over.

"I don't think I know how to do this."

"Do what?"

"Rely on someone. Lean on someone. I feel like I'm messing it up."

"I want to be that person to you, Rose. I want to be the person you lean on. You and I, we're the same. We have no one but each other. You'll lean on me and I'll do the same. We'll learn how. We're in this together."

I was speechless.

"Now tell me what the hell a cerebro..."

"Cerebrospinal leak," I finished for him.

"Whatever the hell it is. Tell me what needs to be done. How did it happen? When are you scheduled for the MRI and CT scan? Tell me everything, Rose."

I managed to stop the tears, but my nose was still leaking. "Can you give me another tissue, please?"

He pulled another one out and handed it to me. I mumbled a thank you and quickly held it under my nose as I pushed the used one into my bag. There were more than a few like it in there already. He turned his body so he was sitting on the edge of the leather couch, his knee pushing at the side of my thigh, and then he finally placed the box on the glass square table in front of us. Sniffling, I wiped my nose and held it in place.

"Are you sure you're feeling okay?"

"I'm fine—that's the weird thing."

"Okay. Now tell me everything he said, from the beginning."

"So, I went in and told him what was happening, and he just looked into my nose and then my throat because I said I had a sore throat a week or so ago, but now I think that's totally unrelated. Then he asked me if I've been in an accident recently or had any kind of surgery, a head trauma, a hard hit to the head. I haven't, and I told him that. Then he asked about the taste of the liquid and I told him I had no idea because I didn't taste it, obviously. I was fine at the doctor's office so I couldn't show him, but I told him it especially starts dripping whenever I lean down for too long, look down, bend down, or when I sleep on my face at night—which is every night."

"Did he tell you what it is exactly? Explain cerebrospinal leak to me."

I blew out a breath and swallowed. "He wouldn't tell me much, said he wanted to schedule an MRI and a CT scan right away to make sure, but I kept asking, and apparently the CSF—cerebrospinal fluid—leak occurs when there is a hole or tear in the membrane that surrounds and cushions the brain. Apparently it can be around the spinal cord too. Ah, anyway...so the fluid, just a clear liquid, in the membrane protecting the brain starts leaking through the nose. Since I didn't have a head trauma, I don't know how it happened." My eyes started watering again. "And I feel so icky just talking about this. I was sure it was allergies even though I've never had them before."

"And he is sure this is CSF?"

I shook my head. "No, that's why he wanted to schedule the MRI and CT scan. Apparently they'll be able to see where the leak is coming from, if there is a hole, and things like that."

"When are you going in for the scans?"

This was the bad part, or the worse part. I winced. "I didn't schedule them." My nose seemed to take a break so I rested my hands in my lap.

His forehead creased. "What do you mean you didn't schedule them?"

"A CT scan, I can do, Jack. I googled it and it's only a minute, plus only my head would go in. The MRI, which is what he said they needed to see if there is a hole and where it is—that one I can't do."

He looked at me in confusion. "What are you talking about?"

"I'm not okay with closed spaces."

"You're claustrophobic? You never panic in an elevator."

"Elevators are fine, as long as I don't get stuck in them. Plus, I can move. I don't have to stay still. I talked to a nurse when I exited the doctor's office and apparently their MRI machine is old and the type of scan he wants takes over fifteen minutes, and I can't move at all during it—as in I'm not allowed to move or twitch any part of my body. If I do, they'll have to start all over again." I could feel my eyes burning with tears. I felt so stupid. "Thinking about it is already giving me anxiety, and she said they will need to close a cage on my head because apparently it needs to be stable." I shook my head more vehemently. "Trust me, I know how stupid it sounds, but I can't do it, Jack. I can't."

He stared at me for a few beats and I hoped he'd understand. "There are open MRI machines. You wouldn't have to be closed in."

A tear escaped from my eye and I let it be. "She said the scan he wants is complicated and those machines don't take that scan. It has to be closed."

He watched the tear slide down my cheek and abruptly got up to pace in front of the couch as he ran his hand over his face. He stopped and took a deep breath. "Wait." Opening his office door, he leaned toward Cynthia. "Call Benjamin for me, tell him it's urgent." Casting a quick look my way, he headed for his desk and lifted his phone as soon as it started ringing. "Okay. That's fine."

Then I listened to him talk to Benjamin, who was apparently a doctor from what I could tell from Jack's side of the conversation. A few minutes later, after he had explained my situation, he had made an appointment for me for the next day with an ENT specialist this Benjamin guy recommended. More doctors—just what I needed.

When he set the phone down, I got up to my feet. He met me halfway as I was headed for the door.

"We'll meet him at eleven tomorrow morning and see what he has to say. Maybe we can get out of it without an MRI."

"Okay," I muttered, trying to walk past him. "I really need to leave." The more I thought about doctors and tests, the more anxious I was starting to get, and I needed to just get out and breathe in the cold, fresh air.

"What's wrong?" His hand curled around my wrist again, stopping me.

"Nothing," I said, my tone a little harsher than necessary. "I need to leave. I'm already late."

"Hey." Dropping my wrist, he covered my cheek with his palm, and my lips started to tremble. I was one of those who couldn't handle kindness when I was already teetering on the edge, and the gentle tone of his voice was the worst thing he could've offered to me in that moment.

"Are you gonna die?" His question was too much of a contradiction with the tone of his voice and his warm hand resting on my cheek, which was why I couldn't find my words for a moment.

I blinked at him. "What?" I stuttered, shocked out of my tears.

"I asked if you're going to die." He pulled his hand away from me and dropped it to his side. "Is it something like cancer?" he continued. "Did the doctor say anything like that? Is it not treatable? If that's the case, let's sit down and cry together and break things."

I just kept blinking up at him, drawing a blank as to how to respond. A few seconds later, I just burst into laughter. I was aware that it probably looked like I was losing it in front of him, but it couldn't have been further from the truth. Jack actually must have thought I had indeed lost it, because the line between his brows got deeper by the second.

"Something funny?"

"Oh, the things you say to me, Jack Hawthorne." I sighed, wiping tears of laughter from under my eyes. "I think this might be why I found myself in front of your building, because I probably knew you wouldn't cuddle me and allow self-pity. If I'd called any of my friends or gone straight to the coffee shop, I would have just felt sorry for myself the entire day."

When his expression didn't lighten up, I decided to go ahead and answer his question.

"No, I don't think I'm going to die. I hope not, at least. He didn't say it was anything that bad—if I have what he thinks I have, that is. There is always the possibility of ending up having surgery and dying on the table, but then again he might have skipped that part because I don't think it'd be a very positive thing to tell a patient."

Jack tilted his head and gave me an impressively exasperated look. "How about we don't jump to any conclusions yet? We don't know whether it is CSF or something else. Let's see the ENT specialist tomorrow and then start to worry about tests and scans and surgeries."

I nodded and took a deep, deep breath, having gotten a better handle on my emotions thanks to his brand of tough love. "I'm not good with doctors," I told him, repeating my earlier confession. "I'm not good with stuff like this."

"I really couldn't tell." His beautiful and gentle smile was the last straw for me, and the tears just started to roll down my face.

He must've misunderstood my tears, because he rushed to explain. "You have to stop crying. I can't take it. We'll deal with it together, if it comes to it, but we're not going to worry about it before we know what it is exactly. It doesn't make sense to do so. Agreed?"

"Now you smile at me?" I blurted out, ignoring his support. His face was already blurring as my eyes started to fill with tears, but I managed to hit him on his chest once, lightly. "Now?" I didn't even realize my voice was rising, but I felt his entire demeanor change as he kept my hand against his chest and pulled me in closer, which only made things worse.

I rested my forehead against his chest, near his heart, and tried to get myself together. When his deeply masculine scent started to mess with me, I grabbed the lapel of his jacket in my fist and pulled back so I could look up at him.

"This is the worst timing, Jack. If it really is brain, spinal cord fluid leak, or whatever the hell it is, he said I'd need to have surgery. I'm afraid of needles! Needles, for God's sake. Surgery? And that close to my brain or spinal cord?" I took a breath and continued. "I know this is going to sound extremely vain and I hate myself for it, but does this mean they're gonna cut my hair off? Go in through my skull? How would it even work? I was going to google it on my way over here, but I couldn't even manage that."

Both his hands went up to my cheeks this time as he cleared my rapidly falling tears with his thumbs. "We're not gonna do that." He leaned down so he could be eye level with me. "We're not gonna start worrying before we know what's going on. I told you this already and you're not hearing me."

"I just know it's CSF." I stared into his eyes. "With my luck, I know it is." To have something to hold on to or maybe because I wanted to keep him connected to me as long as I could, I lifted my hands and placed them over Jack's wrists. "I don't want this, Jack. I have the coffee shop. After years of dreaming, I have it, and I can't close it if I have to have surgery. We just opened."

He took a step closer and I released my hold on his wrists. "Who is talking about closing? You have employees—they can take care of it. If not, we'll hire someone else to help. Are you even listening to what I'm saying? We don't know what's going on yet, Rose. Let's see what they say tomorrow and we'll start thinking about the coffee shop then."

My breath hitched as I managed a small nod with his hands on my cheeks. I must've looked like a mess, and I knew I felt like one. I tried my best to stop being stupid and listen to him, but my heart was clenching and I was starting to have trouble breathing. I forced myself to take a deep breath as Jack tilted my head back so he could look into my eyes.

"You're not alone in this. I'm right here, Rose. We'll figure it out together. We have each other now."

Cue more tears, because this Jack was too close to the dream Jack. As a result, I couldn't help but lean forward and rest my forehead on his chest again. His hands fell from my face even as I burrowed closer, deeper into him. Both my arms were flat against his chest yet his arms stayed limp at his sides. I didn't say anything, just stood there and breathed in his scent, and for a good long while, at that. As my breathing slowly returned to normal, he didn't say anything either.

I closed my eyes tight. If he didn't wrap his arms around me in the next few seconds, I'd have to pull back and walk away from him, otherwise it was going to be too awkward. Then I felt his arms embrace me.

"I'm right here, Rose," he whispered, his rough voice washing over me like a caress that fired something up inside me. "I might not be what you wanted or needed, but you got me anyway. I'm right here."

There was a tightness in my chest when I answered him. "You said that, in the beginning, said you weren't good at this kind of stuff. You're doing wonderful, Jack." I managed to push myself even closer to him as his arms tightened around me.

Maybe I would start to be greedy with this man.

I didn't know how long we stood like that, right in the middle of his office, but when there was a soft knock on the door, I reluctantly stepped back and tried my best to wipe under my eyes. I could only imagine what I must look like. I glanced at my fingers and held back a groan when I saw the black smudges of what was left of my mascara.

Jack had turned halfway to glance at the newcomer so he couldn't see me as I reached for a Kleenex and furiously started wiping at my face. The damage was done and he'd already seen the worst, but that didn't mean he had to keep looking at it.

When I heard Samantha's voice asking if everything was all right, I quietly groaned, still hiding behind Jack's big frame.

"Yes. Do you need something?" Jack asked, his tone much more businesslike.

"No, I saw Rose earlier and was concern—"

"Thank you, Samantha, but I'd like to be alone with my wife if there is nothing else you need."

I paused the wiping as a heavy silence followed his words.

"Of course," she said tightly, and then the door gently closed.

I hurried and pushed the Kleenex into the pocket of my jeans before Jack could face me again.

"Feeling better?" he asked, eyes moving across my face. I hoped I was at least a normal shade of human.

"Mhmm."

When he closed the distance between us with an unexpected smile on his face, I was surprised.

"Why did you really come here, Rose?" he asked, pushing my hair away from my ruined face. "Just to tell me you weren't gonna be able to attend events with me? Just because you knew I wouldn't let you break down?"

I stood still as he reached up and his thumb started a gentle stroke on my cheekbone, my skin breaking out in goose bumps.

I couldn't answer a question I didn't have a real answer to. "Don't smile at me. Now is not the right time. I don't want to lose my count," I said instead, and he chuckled.

He actually *chuckled*—a low, deep, manly chuckle that caused a slow shiver to run up my spine when coupled with his touch.

"You look awful," he said in a low voice, eyes boring into mine.

I repeated the same answer I had given him the first time he had paid me that specific compliment. "Thank you for noticing. As you know, I always try my best."

With his left hand, he brushed my hair back again and pushed it behind my ear. When he lowered his head and pressed a kiss on my forehead over my bangs, I stilled. "Okay, Rose," he murmured. "Okay."

As I was still trying to process the aftermath of the low and deep sound of that chuckle and then the kiss, my eyes slowly widened as he leaned down farther and pressed a soft kiss on my tear-wet lips. My eyes closed on their own and my lips parted—partly in shock, partly because the response was automatic. He didn't kiss me like he had the night before, didn't leave me feeling hungry for more, but as soon as he had the opportunity, he molded our lips together and kissed me longer, gentle and soft. I tilted my head up, my heart hammering in my chest, and returned his slow kiss. As we kept going and the kiss became more than just gentle, bit by bit, I started to rise up on my toes to deepen it.

My hands found his wrists again because I needed to feel anchored to something—that something being him, specifically. When I felt him pull away, I reluctantly pried my hands off. Biting down on my lips, I swallowed down a protest and, with a little trouble, managed to flutter my eyes open.

"Is someone watching?" The question was nothing more than a whisper falling from my lips.

Eyes intently on mine, he shook his head.

I swallowed, not sure if I wanted to hear the answer to the question I was about to ask. "Then why—"

"Are you free for dinner tonight?"

"What?" I asked, frowning up at him, the fog his kiss had caused slowly dissipating. I was having just a little trouble following, that was all.

"You never answered my text."

His... *Oh.*

"We got busy and then I...Jack, I don't think I'd be good company tonight. Is it an important dinner?"

"It'd be just the two of us."

"It's not a...work dinner?"

"No."

"Then I'd rather get some takeout as usual or actually cook something at your apartment as a thank you for dealing with me."

"Our apartment. Stop calling it mine. And I'd like to take you out, Rose. We've done takeout enough. If you're not feeling up to it tonight, tomorrow then?"

My brows drew together as I tried to understand what he was saying. "You...uh, you don't mean as in a date, right?" I laughed nervously, searching pretty hard for an answer in his eyes and maybe hoping he said he did mean it that way.

He gave me his fifth smile and I got distracted.

"It can be called a date. It's dinner. You can use any words you like."

I wasn't exactly sure what to say or what to think. Frozen in place, I just kept staring up at him. "I mean..." I mumbled, taking a step back. "Like a real-life date?"

He looked at me for a long beat, and I realized the smile on his face had disappeared. His expression was back to being unreadable. "If I read things wrong and you're not interested..."

"No. No. No." I was. I really, really was. "I just... Do you think that would be a good idea?"

He arched an eyebrow. "Who cares whether it's a good idea or not?" That was not an answer I expected to hear from a guy like Jack. "It's dinner, Rose. Say yes. Takeout or a restaurant, nothing much changes. We can just try, and if you think—"

"Okay," I blurted out before he could say more.

"Okay?"

I gave him a nod. "Yeah. Yes. Okay."

He opened his mouth, but my nose had had enough of a break. I instantly tilted my head back, eyes on the ceiling, and my hand latched onto his arm. "Jack—Jack! It's coming again. Kleenex!"

In less than three seconds, I had another one in my hands.

"Thank you."

"Come on. I'm taking you home."

"What? No. I need to go back to work and forget about all of this until tomorrow."

He gave me a sharp look, which I could only see out of the corner of my eye as I kept my head tilted up.

"I mean the leak, not...not everything else."

His gaze only softened a fraction. "Let me take you home, Rose."

As sweet as that sounded, I couldn't just sit at the apartment by myself with nothing to do. "I can't. I need to work, Jack. I can't sit around and obsess about what the doctor will say tomorrow."

He shook his head and sighed. "Then I'm coming with you."

"You don't have to drop me off. I'll take a cab—an Uber. It'll be fine."

Ignoring me, he walked over to his desk, closed the lid of his laptop, and picked up his phone. As I watched him, he made his way back to me and, to my surprise and delight, reached for my hand. I had to tighten my fingers around his to keep up with his strides before we stopped in front of Cynthia's desk.

"I'm heading out. I'll still take calls, but I won't be here for the four PM client. Let's try to reschedule that, or if he can, have him meet me at Around the Corner. You know the address. I'll be going with Rose to the ENT specialist at eleven tomorrow morning, so try to get in touch with Fred and have him take care of whatever we have going on. Better yet, I'll call you when I'm at the shop and we'll reschedule things."

Cynthia's eyes moved from me to Jack and back again and then to our joined hands.

"Everything okay?"

He glanced down at me. "Yes. Everything is good now."

Everything did feel good. Apart from my nose.

While we were standing at the very back of the elevator, heading down to the lobby with five other people, he called Ray to tell him to bring the car to the front of the building. When he pocketed his phone, I couldn't hold it back anymore.

Leaning against him, I tried to be as quiet as I possibly could and asked, "Jack?"

His hand gave mine a squeeze, which was his version of *I'm listening*, I supposed. My heart rate picking up, I whispered, "That just happened, right? You want to...you want us to date? As in be boyfriend and girlfriend?"

He gave me a long look. "More like husband and wife, don't you think?"

CHAPTER SEVENTEEN

JACK

The remnants of whatever guilt I was still holding on to that seemed to keep me back or make me hesitate when it came to Rose had disappeared overnight. I didn't care about anything I'd done to be with her. I knew the truth, and that was enough.

She was sitting next to me on the spacious couch, leaning over a small cup she was holding in her hand. She didn't want me to see her like this, but I wasn't budging from her side no matter what she said. So, as a result of that, I was watching drops of a clear liquid—which was quite possibly brain or spinal cord fluid—very, *very* slowly drop into the cup. It'd already been twenty minutes since the nurse had brought us in there, and we still had at least another two inches to fill before it reached the point where it'd be enough for them to test the sample.

"If I tap the other side of my nose it comes out faster."

I leaned forward, resting my elbows on my thighs, watching her nose intently as her eyes flitted to me and then back to her slowly filling cup. I was so consumed with my thoughts that I didn't understand what she had meant, so I didn't think to stop her until I saw what she was doing. When I realized she could be harming herself, I caught her left hand before she could start tapping on her nose again.

"Stop doing that."

She heaved a long sigh and leaned back, her right hand, which was holding the cup, slightly trembling, her left one tightly held in mine. She didn't pull away, and I didn't plan on letting her go.

"What's wrong? Does it hurt?" I asked, trying to understand what was going on.

Her eyes glanced to me and then back to the ceiling. "My head is spinning too much, Jack. I think I need a break. How long has it been?"

"You chose this instead of the MRI. It was either this or that." Our shoulders brushed as I let go of her hand and reached over to take the cup from her.

"I know, Jack. I didn't mean anything by it. I'm sorry."

I closed my eyes and took a deep breath. She had no idea how angry I was, how helpless and useless I felt because there wasn't anything I could do to help her in this situation other than sit my ass right next to hers and make her understand that I would be there no matter what happened, which didn't seem to do anything.

"You're sure you don't need to be at your office?" she asked to the ceiling.

"I'm not leaving, so you can stop trying to send me away. Come on. We only have a little more then we can get out of here." I glanced at her, waiting with the cup in my hand. I wanted to get out of there just as much as she did, if not more.

"This isn't an allergy, Jack. I am leaking CSF. You know that, right?"

I agreed with her. I'd never seen anyone go through anything like this before, but I was smart enough to keep my mouth shut. "We don't know that yet. You heard what the doctor said."

She shook her head from side to side, slowly. "Actually, I didn't. I just zoned out when you started asking all those questions."

I reached out and pushed her hair behind her ear. "Come on, just a little more. Then we can go." She licked her lips and I noticed her eyes getting all glossy again. "If you start crying, I'm going to lose it and we're going to have a problem."

She chuckled, wiping at her eyes. "I'm not crying. I'm not gonna cry."

She tried to take the cup from me, but I held it up for her, my arm resting across her leg. "Let me hold it for you. Come on."

Her eyes met mine and I gestured to the cup with my head. She dropped her head forward and the first few drops started coming. A few seconds later, her left hand curled around my wrist. At first I thought maybe she was trying to line up the cup right under her nose, but when I looked closely, she had her eyes tightly closed and was biting her lip.

I cursed myself for not being better in a situation like this. My family hadn't been any better than hers. Not as bad maybe, but still not better. I had a family, but not really. I didn't know exactly how to be there for someone because I hadn't seen anything like it in my family. This felt much like trying to find my way in the dark. But it was Rose. I didn't mind if I crashed into everything as I tried to find my way, the only thing that mattered was being there for her. She had me now.

I wanted her—that was crystal clear to me. That first time I'd seen her at the party, I'd been intrigued by her, but it had been different then. It wasn't love at first sight. Like she had said the day I proposed our business deal to her, I wasn't romantic enough for that, but that first night, seeing her with her fiancé, and not even that...just seeing her smile at him—I'd wanted that smile she had for her fiancé to be mine. That was it. That was everything.

That was how it all had started, me wanting her in my life,

and now after our fake marriage, things had started to change. It was more than *I should help her out of this situation*. I was starting get to know her—her quirks, her likes, dislikes, the way she reacted to the things I said. It was now more than just wanting to have her in my life. I wanted her to *want* to be in my life. As much as I knew I was a bastard for lying to her and knew I was going to keep lying to her, I wished I could be someone different, someone who would know all the right things to say to make her stay.

I knew that wouldn't be the case when it was all said and done, because I was not that guy. She deserved someone warm and open, and yet, selfish bastard that I was, I couldn't and wouldn't think of her being with someone else. Cold and distant was what I'd grown up with, and cold and distant was what I had become. It didn't bother me in any other part of my life, but with Rose, it did.

When her hair dropped and curtained her face, I pushed it back again and curled it behind her ear. Instinctively, I ran the backs of my fingers along her jawline, and her fingers tightened around my wrist. My jaw clenched, and I moved my hand behind her neck, trying to massage her muscles and help her relax. The more our skin stayed in contact, the more I had trouble keeping myself in check and not pulling her head up so I could kiss her again. Both times we had kissed, I hadn't gotten enough of her taste. She somehow left me wanting more, each and every time, and she was like that with everything, not just the way she kissed. It was even that way with her smiles. Ever since that first night, this whole thing had started because I'd wanted more. Would I ever get enough?

"One drop every seventeen seconds," she murmured, drawing me out of my thoughts. "A single drop comes every seventeen seconds. We'll be here for hours."

Her tight hold on my wrist hadn't loosened a bit. "It'll be over soon," I murmured, my hand still on her neck.

"My head is spinning so much," she whispered, her voice barely audible.

I couldn't help it. I slid closer to her and found myself pressing a lingering kiss on her temple. Her head snapped to the right and we lost one drop to the ground. When she caught my eyes, she looked down again, clearing her throat.

"Talk to me, Jack."

I gentled my voice as much as I could. "What do you want me to talk about?"

"Just let me hear your voice. Distract me. You never talk about your family."

"There isn't much to talk about. We don't talk."

It wasn't that I was uncomfortable talking about my family, I just didn't see the point. Rose had been closer to me these last few weeks than they'd ever been. I wouldn't lie and say I never wished to have a more close-knit family, but wishing didn't change anything.

"Why?"

"No specific reason. We all work a lot, and none of us have time to spare or the inclination."

"What do they do?"

"My mother is a psychologist, and my father is an investment banker."

"No siblings, right?"

"No siblings."

"Why did you want to be a lawyer?"

I thought about it and realized I didn't have a straight answer. "I don't know. It was always something I found intriguing. Lydia, my mom—her dad was a criminal lawyer and I used to think the world of him, so it felt natural to go into law. Plus, I'm good at it."

"You call your mom by her first name?"

"Yes. She preferred that, I think, after a certain age."

"You didn't want to go into criminal law like your grandfather?"

"I considered it for a time, but turns out it's not my thing."

"Is your grandfather still alive?"

"Unfortunately, no. He passed away when I was thirteen."

"Oh, I'm sorry, Jack. You're not so close with your family, then?"

"No. Like I said, we grew apart."

A few minutes passed in silence.

"How much more?" Rose asked.

"Just a little. You're doing great."

She snorted, and when more liquid came rushing down, her grip on me tightened. "You have no idea how weird this feels."

"I can imagine."

Another twenty minutes passed much the same way. With each passing minute after the one-hour mark, she started to get paler.

"How are you doing?" I asked, my voice coming out gruffer than I wanted.

"Not so good. I feel nauseous and I'm starting to get a headache."

"That's normal. You've been hanging upside down for an hour now. Do you want to take another break?"

As an answer, she pushed her head up, and I had to let go of her neck so she could rest it on the back of the couch.

I studied the cup as she took a few deep breaths. "Another ten minutes or so and you'll be done."

Opening her eyes, she also examined the cup, which was almost three inches full. "When do you think they'll be able to tell?"

I frowned at her. "Didn't you hear what the doctor said?" When she gave me a blank stare, I continued. "He'll rush it for us.

Thankfully they can do the test here so we'll come back tomorrow and learn what's going on."

Sniffing, she nodded and took the cup from me. "Your hand must be going numb. I'll hold it."

"I'm fine. I don't mind."

"I know, but I do." Closing her eyes, she took another deep breath and bent down again, making sure the cup was aligned correctly.

When her left hand curled around her knee, without thinking I grabbed it and linked our fingers together. This time, she didn't look at me, and she didn't try to pull away either. We just held on.

I wasn't sure which one of us was holding on tighter, but we stayed like that for the rest of the ten minutes and then finally the cup was full enough to stop.

"Okay. Okay, Rose. It's done."

She opened her eyes. "Done?"

"Yeah." I took the cup from her and snapped on the cover they had left us. I kissed the back of her hand, but had to let it go as I stood up. "You rest for a few minutes and I'll get this to the nurse."

Wordlessly, she nodded and leaned back.

It took me a few minutes to track down the nurse and hand the cup to her. When I got back to the room and gently closed the door, Rose's eyes opened. "Can we leave, Jack?"

"I think you should sit for a few more minutes. Here, take a few sips of this." I handed her the water bottle I'd gotten for her.

She downed a third of the bottle. "What time is it?" she asked in a rough voice as she was tightening the top back on.

"It's one PM."

Before I could stop her, she was up on her feet, and almost just as quickly she swayed back and forth. "Whoa."

"For fuck's sake, sit down!" I grumbled as I caught her arms before she could fall. "You've been sitting with your head between your legs for longer than an hour. You're not gonna get up and start running around." I tried to soften my rebuke. "Take it easy for a second. For me at least."

She just kept her grip on my forearms and, as always, ignored what I'd just said. We had reached for each other at the same time. "I need to get back. I don't want to keep Owen longer than necessary."

"I know, and you will, but right now you need to sit your ass down and get well before you attempt to work for the rest of the day." As much as I admired how hard she'd worked to get that place up and running, this was not the time for her to run around and get herself even more sick.

She looked up at me and nodded. That usual light, spark— call it whatever you want—was gone from her eyes. She looked scared and tired, and *that* pissed me off even more.

I helped her sit down and lean back as I took my spot next to her and managed to pry the water bottle out of her hands.

"I was going to drink that."

"You'll have it after you've rested enough that you can stay up on your own two feet and hold a water bottle at the same time."

That earned me a sideways glance that I ignored. I was hoping for her to snap back at me like she always did. That was why I always provoked her, because I loved seeing that heat in her eyes, but she didn't respond, and for her, even that side eye had been pretty weak.

As she was resting with her eyes closed, I leaned back too, my shoulder brushing hers. I ran a hand up and down my face, my stubble pricking my hand, having grown longer than what I was used to. Now, we'd have to wait twenty-four hours. It didn't sound like much, but I didn't know how I was even going to make it through the day yet.

Rose leaned to her left and hesitantly rested her head somewhere between my shoulder and chest. My body froze for a quick heartbeat. When it looked like she was settled, I gently pulled my arm away so she could get more comfortable and rested it on the back of the couch.

"How do I look, Jack?" she asked.

I couldn't see her or her eyes, so I kept my gaze straight ahead on the white wall with the red poster.

"Like death warmed over," I said.

I could hear the smile in her voice when she responded a few seconds later. "I can always count on you for compliments, can't I?"

"That's why I'm here, isn't it?"

I wasn't clear on how long we sat there like that, me breathing in her scent, but after a few minutes passed, my dick started stirring in my pants. It wasn't the first time it had happened around her and I was sure it wouldn't be the last either, but the timing was wrong, as it always was when it came to her. I didn't know if her eyes were open or not, but to be safe, I rested my left arm across my lap in the hopes of hiding the rapidly growing hardness I knew was noticeable through my pants.

When her hand came on top of mine, adding more weight to what was already a painful situation for me, I groaned and closed my eyes. I was aware of every inch of her that was pressing against my body, and I couldn't fucking do anything in that room.

She turned my watch enough so she could see the time then started playing with my wedding ring, just like I'd played with hers plenty of times.

"You never took it off," Rose whispered.

I closed my eyes and tried my best to ignore what I was feeling. No, I never took it off. Didn't *want* to take it off.

"I'm feeling a little better. We should leave," she said after a few minutes.

When she was around, I felt like I had no control over myself.

So, leaving worked just fine for me—if she really felt fine, that is. "Are you sure?" I felt her head move up and down on my chest in a nod, because her rubbing her face and scent all over me was exactly what I needed so I could think about nothing but her when I was back at the office. "I'll drop you at Around the Corner then I need to go to the office."

"Jack?"

"Hmm." Finally, she lifted her head and looked up at me. With her warmth gone, I felt colder. Swallowing the lump in my throat, I gave myself permission to touch her, in the name of helping her. I pushed back her hair that would not stay in place behind her ear. "Listening."

"This wasn't the deal."

My forehead creased. "What deal?"

"Our marriage deal," she said slowly.

Right. My brilliant idea. "What about it?"

"I'm aware that this isn't what you signed up for. Let's not fool ourselves—this is probably what they think it is. Two doctors, one of them a fancy ENT specialist, think this is most likely CSF, so I don't know how or when I'll be able to accompany you to your work events and dinners, but at least if the coffee shop tanks you'll get the property faster and you won't have to do the free rent—"

"Let's not worry about that now. I can get away with not attending by saying my wife is having health issues, and we'll pick it up from where we left off once you get better." I didn't plan on going to any dinners, but she didn't need to know that.

She looked away from me. "Okay. I just know I'm breaking the rules, and if there is anything else I can do to make up for it, you can just—"

I stood up and, with my back to her, quickly rearranged myself to hide my uncomfortable erection. I faced her and met her confused gaze as I offered my hand. She took it after a short pause.

"We didn't set any rules, Rose. If necessary, we'll make them along the way. Let's just focus on your health for now. I wouldn't take you anywhere like this even if you wanted me to."

She got up with my help then stared at me with her piercing eyes, a smile breaking out on her face, which didn't help what I had going on in my pants at all. I frowned harder.

"I think you're nothing but bluster sometimes, and I also think I might have gotten the better end of the deal by marrying you."

I arched an eyebrow at her as I opened the door to the hallway.

"Come on, Jack Hawthorne, help me end my day with a high. Let me count to six. Show me that smile. You can do it—I know you can. It's in you."

I couldn't have held back my laughter even if I'd tried. Then she just kept staring up at me as we started walking. She had this crooked but beautiful and expectant smile on her face as she tried to keep up with my steps. That was what I'd wanted from day one, wasn't it? To be on the receiving end of that smile?

I would fight for her when the time came. I would fight with everything I got. "Stop grinning and walk faster. I can't wait around for you the entire day—you're making me late to work."

When we exited the building, Raymond was waiting for us. It took us almost an hour to get her to work, and when we finally made it, I walked her up to the door.

"Looks like we have a full house," she commented, staring inside before turning back to me. "So...I already made you late. You should leave."

I had my hands in my pockets, my best protection against reaching for her. I nodded. "Yes. I need to leave."

We didn't move.

"How are you feeling?" I asked, trying to stay longer.

She winced and took a deep breath. "Still a little nauseous, to be honest, but better. The headache feels like it's a permanent thing now." She gently touched her nose. "This stopped for the time being."

"When we know for sure tomorrow, you'll feel better. Eat something as soon as you get inside."

"I'll do that."

When the door opened behind her and two customers walked out, we had to move to the side, to the right of all the flowers she had put up. Her eyes caught on them as well.

"They look good, don't they? I wanted people to take photos in front of it and post on social media so it can be its own advertising."

"That's smart."

She smiled shyly, and even that looked beautiful on her. She hugged her coat tighter to herself. "It's going to snow soon. It's getting colder. I want to change out the roses for a winter theme with big beautiful wreaths on every window, and something for the entrance too. It would look gorgeous for winter and Christmas, but if I end up having surgery—"

"There are easier ways to ask for my help. You don't have to resort to histrionics."

She chuckled, and finally some warmth returned to her eyes.

"Okay. Will you help me? I'd like to do it with you again. Maybe that could be like a little tradition too. Not for show, for us."

"I will."

I looked over her shoulder and saw her two employees watching us with concerned faces. They were probably anxious to hear what had happened.

I gestured inside with my head. "Sally and your other employee are watching us."

"Owen. His name is Owen."

As if I didn't already know.

She looked back and sent them a quick wave with a smile.

"So you have to work from your office today, huh?"

Did she want me to stay? If she asked, I would.

I checked my watch. "I rescheduled yesterday's meetings for today, so I need to get back to them."

"Oh, okay. Yeah. Then I shouldn't keep you."

I wanted her to keep me forever.

She pulled her hands out of her grey coat's pockets and took a step forward. Placing one of her hands on my shoulder, she reached up and pressed a kiss on my cheek. "Thank you for today. It means the world to me," she whispered into my ear.

"I didn't do anything."

My control, already frayed as it was, could handle neither her sweet kiss nor the whisper. I wrapped my arm around her waist and held her against my body before she could back away.

Her wide eyes were staring straight into mine while she was still holding on to my shoulder, so I kissed her like that. As I held her waist tightly, I parted her lips with my tongue and kissed her until she slowly relaxed in my arms letting me have her. When I tilted my head and sucked her tongue, a small gasp escaped her and she closed her eyes, pressing her body into mine even more. Then her tongue slid against mine and she turned eager. As the rush of pleasure started to get too intense for an outdoor kiss as people walked by us, I had to slow it the hell down, but even with that, I took my time and kissed her swollen lips a few more times, just for myself, just little pecks, just to hold me over until the next time I could get away with tasting her.

When her eyes opened lazily, I explained, "Your employees—"

"Are watching," she interrupted, a little out of breath and flushed. "I guessed as much. Good kiss. You're getting better and better. Practice seems to be working. No sighting of a turtle, but was it maybe a little bit because you wanted to kiss me too?"

I chuckled, and her eyes dropped to my lips.

"Yes, it wasn't just for your employees," I admitted, leaving it at that.

It was only because I wanted to kiss her. The only thing I had been about to say was a reminder that she had people waiting.

"Six." It was just a soft whisper, but it was more than enough to stir my dick even further after our short-lived kiss.

"Go inside, Rose. Try to sit down for a while before you jump back into everything."

Nodding, she turned away.

"Don't work too much," I added.

"I'll talk to you later?" She opened the door halfway and looked back at me.

"Yes."

Her smile was another favorite of mine, sweet and happy. "Okay then."

When I came back to Around the Corner two hours after dropping her off, the smile she gave me, the one that made her eyes sparkle in surprise and happiness—it became another favorite as I guided my client to one of the corner tables and had my meeting, feeling Rose's eyes on me the entire time.

I hadn't been able to stay away after all.

———

THE NEXT DAY we were sitting at the ENT's office again as he gave us more information about Rose's sickness. He said everything the other doctor had said to Rose before, and whenever I cast a quick glance her way where she was sitting next to me, her eyes were glazed over. I didn't know how much of it she actually heard. Her hands were grasping the arms of the chair in a white-knuckled grip, so I didn't think my touch would be welcome. Instead, I asked every single question that came to my mind about her upcoming unavoidable surgery.

"After we see the results of your MRI and the CT scan, we'll schedule your surgery."

Rose cleared her throat and interrupted the doctor. "I'm sorry for interrupting you, but I'm claustrophobic—is there any way we can avoid the MRI scans if we already know from the samples that this is a CSF leak and I'm gonna have surgery anyway?"

"I'm afraid not, Mrs. Hawthorne. Since you didn't have a head trauma or any other injuries that could cause a CSF leak, we need the MRI to see if..." The doctor's eyes flicked to me and then back to Rose again. "We need to see if there are any tumors that would create pressure on the membrane and ultimately cause the leak. We'll also need to see where exactly the leak is. We need to know everything before we can go in."

My body tightened, my anger boiling over. A brain tumor?

Rose crossed her arms against her chest. "Can I have an open MRI? Is that possible?"

"I'm afraid the specific scan we need, the open MRIs can't take."

"Okay, I understand."

"I'll see you tomorrow and we'll have a better game plan on what the next step will be."

Much to Rose's and my horror, they managed to squeeze her in for the MRI and the CT scan as soon as we were out of the doctor's office. We took the elevator down to get to the radiology department in complete silence. I didn't need to ask her if she was okay; I already knew she wasn't. I wasn't either, but I still felt the need to hear her say something...anything. The doors opened and we got off after an older couple holding hands.

"Rose—"

Her eyes slid my way and then she quickly looked down.

"Brain tumor sounds fun, huh? That was something I hadn't thought of. Oh, there's radiology."

She didn't even give me a chance to say anything, and in a few minutes she was guided into a small room where the radiologist, a young girl with round glasses and an easy smile, told her to take off her shoes, bra, jewelry, and belt along with any metal objects and place them in the secure locker. When she came out after a few minutes, she looked paler than she had when she'd gone in. Her hair was down in soft waves around her, the hair tie that had been holding it up gone.

I could only focus on the way her hands were trembling. When she noticed it herself, she hid them behind her back. I tried to catch her gaze more than a few times, but it looked like she was purposely avoiding me. The shimmer of tears in her eyes was another issue, and my chest tightened at the sight of her trying to be brave.

She followed the technician into the room, her steps faltering when she saw the tunnel-shaped machine. I watched as she hugged herself with one arm and then quickened her steps.

The technician was holding a weird contraption in her hands, waiting for Rose next to the machine.

"You can lie down on the table now. We'll need to place this on your head so we can keep it stable in the machine."

Rose stood still in her spot. "I...I'm a little claustrophobic. Is there any way we can skip that thing if I promise I won't move my head?"

"I'm sorry, but we have to use it."

A cage—it was a cage for her head.

Rose nodded but didn't make a move to get on the table.

The technician pushed forward. "It'll only take fifteen minutes or so to complete the scan, and I will be right on the other side of the glass." She held up a small button connected to a long wire. "You'll be holding this in your hand, and if you start to panic, you can press it and we'll stop and take you out."

"But then we'll have to start again, right?"

"I'm afraid so. Ready?"

My jaw clenched, my hands forming fists on their own. I didn't like this, and Rose wasn't moving.

She laughed, the sound broken and wrong. "I'll move any second now, promise."

The technician smiled.

"Can I stay in the room with her?" I asked, the anger in my voice loud and clear, only I wasn't angry at anyone there. I just hated that my hands were tied and no matter how much I wanted to, I couldn't help her. Me staying in the room wouldn't change the fact that she was gonna have to go in there, but I figured it would help me, if not her.

Rose's head snapped up to me, her lips parting. "Jack, you don't have to do that."

I ignored her. "Is it safe?" I asked the technician, trying my best not to growl at her. I didn't think I was that successful because her eyes grew large and she nervously reached up to push her glasses up her nose.

"Erm, yes. It's safe, but you'll need to take off your—"

"Got it." I turned away and walked out of the room to take care of everything. Less than a minute later, I was back.

Rose was still standing on her two feet and not on the table.

"Okay?" I asked when I was standing too close yet not close enough.

She took a deep breath, let it all out, and nodded. I offered her my hand and waited as she ran her palms up and down her leggings and then slowly grasped mine. It was cold. I helped her up, and right when she was about to lie down on her back, the technician stopped her.

"Oh, I'm gonna need you to lie on your stomach."

Rose straightened up to a sitting position immediately, one of her hands still in mine, her grip as tight as possible. "What?" she sputtered.

"The scan your doctor wants is taken facedown."

"But my nose—it's—and..." Her eyes came to me as her face started crumpling, her breathing too fast. "Jack, I won't be able to breathe, not facedown. I can't—"

I gave Rose's hand a squeeze and she stopped talking. Without shifting my eyes from hers, I addressed the technician. "Could you give us a moment, please?"

Rose's gaze followed the technician as she stepped out of the room and closed the door. She was on the verge of hyperventilating, and the scan hadn't even started.

"You're going to be late to the coffee shop, and on top of that you're making me late, too. We have to do this, right? You heard the doctor."

She swallowed, her throat moving.

I caught her chin between my fingers and forced her gaze to meet mine. Arching an eyebrow, I asked again, "We have to do this. I need you to be okay, so we can't avoid it."

Licking her lips, she nodded. "I won't be able to see anything. The room is closing in on me even right now."

Her chest was starting to rise and fall faster; she was seconds away from a panic attack, so I leaned down until we were eye level. "You can do this, Rose. You *will* do this, and then we'll get out of here. It'll only take fifteen minutes—surely you can hang on that long. I'll be here the entire time, and once it's done, we won't look back."

She closed the distance between us and rested her forehead against mine. "I know I'm being stupid. I'm sorry. I'm scared, that's all. I—" She took another deep breath and closed her eyes. "I'm gonna have surgery, for crying out loud—if I freak out with this, I won't make—"

My left hand, the one that wasn't in Rose's death grip, clenched. "Let's worry about this hurdle, and then we'll start freaking out about the surgery. Take the time to think about your coffee shop. Make plans."

Pulling back from me, she sniffled and nodded, her eyes suspiciously wet.

"You ready now?" I asked.

"You'll really stay here?"

"I said I would, didn't I?"

The edges of her lips moved up. "Yes, you did." Another deep breath out. "If I didn't worry about what you'd think of me, I'd try my best to run away from this right now."

I gave her a long look. "I can run faster than you. I'm calling the technician back in and we'll get this done."

Another stiff nod and she pulled her hand back to rest it on her thigh.

I called the technician back in and she moved to Rose's left side. "All set?"

When Rose didn't answer, I gave the girl a curt nod.

"Since you were worried about the leaking, we'll put this paper down under your nose so hopefully it won't distract you too much. Also, it's going to be loud in there, so here are your ear plugs. The sounds are completely normal, so don't let them panic you."

The technician offered another pair to me as Rose took them without a word and placed them in her ears.

"Ready?" the girl asked, her gaze moving between mine and Rose's.

Rose cleared her throat. "Yes."

She secured her head in the contraption, and I helped her lie down on her stomach. Her eyes were already tightly closed.

Before the technician could disappear behind the door, I got her attention.

"Can I touch her?"

"Yes, but try not to move her."

The door closed, and Rose and I were alone—if you didn't count everyone else on the other side of the glass, that is.

A few seconds later, the technician's voice filled the room as she spoke into a mic from the other side. "Okay, we're about to start, Rose. I'll be talking and letting you know how many minutes are left. Here we go."

Just as the machine started up, I put my hand on the only part of her body I could reach without pushing my arm into the tunnel: her ankle. I forced myself to relax so my grip wouldn't be painful, but I wasn't sure how successful I was with that. At first I could hear her erratic breathing as she tried to inhale and exhale in an effort to calm herself down, but when the noises started getting louder and louder, I couldn't hear anything.

As minutes passed and I started to get more anxious by the second, all I could do was gently run my thumb up and down under the edge of her legging. I closed my eyes and tried to ignore the way my heart was hammering in my chest. I wasn't supposed to feel this way. It was just a simple, painless MRI scan, but her panic had affected me as well, and I had trouble just standing still when all I wanted to do was pull her out so she wouldn't hurt and I wouldn't see that scared and worried look in her eyes again.

As the machine's jackhammering sounds picked up and all the banging and thumping and beeping started to get to me, I just circled my fingers around her ice-cold ankle and held on, hoping she was doing okay in there and hoping that I was waiting for her.

"We have just a few minutes left. You're doing great."

"It's almost over, Rose," I said in a normal voice. I didn't think she could hear me over the maddening sounds or through her ear plugs, but just in case she could, I kept talking to her, saying the same thing again and again. "It's almost over. I'm right here. You're almost done. I'm right here with you."

"And it's done," the girl said cheerfully through the speakers. "I'll be right in to get you out."

The loud beating in my skull stopped and I realized the machine had as well. The technician opened the door and walked in. I let go of Rose's ankle and clenched my hand a few times as I stepped back to let the technician do her job and get Rose out of there so I could get to her.

The moment the table started to slide out of the machine, Rose started moving. Just as her head cleared the opening and I saw her profile, my heart sank. She looked worse than I'd expected, and I'd expected it to be quite bad already. I took a step forward then stopped, clenching my fists at my sides. The second she could, she got up to her hands and knees, her eyes wide open, tears rapidly coursing down her cheeks in rivulets. Her entire body was shaking, her breathing frantic, as if she couldn't quite remember how to breathe. Other than the shallow and harsh breathing, she wasn't making a single sound. Sitting back on her heels, she started to push back the contraption on her head until the technician helped her and released her from it.

"Give me a minute and we'll help you down."

Rose didn't listen to her. I doubt she even heard her. She pushed her legs out from under her and tried to put her foot on the little ladder they had, but her legs didn't hold her up and she stumbled. I rushed forward and caught her before she could fall on her face. She fisted my button-up shirt in her hands, but with her eyes swimming with tears, I doubted she could even make out any of my features.

My jaw set, I got my arm under her legs and lifted her off the table and into my arms. The fact that she didn't protest only wound me up tighter. Her arms rounded my neck and she pushed her face into my neck, her tears running down my skin.

Without a word to Rose or the technician, I quickly walked out of the room with her clinging to me and moved back into the small space where we had gotten ready. I closed the door behind us with my shoulder and gently sat down on the bench next to the wall. I stayed quiet until her breathing was finally on its way to getting back to normal.

"It's over now. Calm down."

Her head moved just a fraction, but she still stayed put. I closed my arms a little tighter around her, just holding her close.

She pressed her palm high on my chest and held it there. "I can't...I can't seem to catch my breath, Jack."

I closed my eyes. Her voice was scratchy, and it bugged the hell out of me. "You're doing fine. Just keep breathing and that's enough for now."

Her chest moved against mine when she released a small snort. "That's enough?"

"That's enough."

She burrowed in closer. "I'm sorry—for embarrassing you, for freaking out, for not being able to move right now even though your shirt and skin are soaked with my tears and some brain fluids."

My eyes still closed, I dropped my head back with a small thud against the wall. She was killing me.

"I was fine the first ten minutes or so," she whispered, pushing her forehead into my skin. "But then I couldn't breathe. My head started spinning like crazy and the tears just started coming down on their own. I was afraid they were gonna stop and start it all over again, so I don't even know how I stopped the shaking."

I kissed her temple. "You did fine and it's done."

"I should get up."

"Yes."

We didn't move, I kissed her temple again. I couldn't stop myself. She was still trembling slightly, but when a knock sounded on the door, she stirred in my arms.

"Give us a second," I called out, raising my voice only enough that whoever was outside could hear me.

Pressing her hand on my chest, Rose pushed herself off of me before I was ready to let go and slowly got back up on her feet. Tucking her hair behind her ears, she opened the locker and grabbed the tissue she'd apparently left inside, quickly wiping under her nose and tilting her head back. Holding the tissue and sniffling at the same time, she started to pull out the rest of her things. Still sitting down, I watched her eyes dart around, her face blotchy and wet. I caught sight of her blue lacy bra and rose to my feet.

"I'll wait for you outside."

As I was moving to go pick up my own things—my watch, belt, and wallet—from the desk, her voice stilled me.

"Jack?"

I pressed my lips together and glanced back at her over my shoulder, waiting for her to go on. She was standing in front of the locker with her socks on, hugging her bra and her coat to her chest. For the first time, she really looked ill, not to mention lost and alone, and that image didn't sit right with me. No, it pissed me the hell off.

"This isn't enough, I know, but thank you. Thank you for being here when I know you... Thank you."

"I didn't do anything," I muttered, my tone harsher than I intended, before giving her a curt nod and stepping out of the room.

When she stepped out a few minutes later, she looked better. She even offered the technician a smile before walking out the door. She had licked her wounds and was ready for the rest. I believed that was why I was starting to fall for her.

I placed my hand on the small of her back, maintaining whatever contact I could with her all the way to the car.

THEY HAD SCHEDULED her surgery for the following Tuesday after her eventful MRI. That one week was hell on earth for both of us. On Monday they needed us to come in so they could do the last few tests that were necessary for the surgery to go smoothly. An eye exam, an echocardiogram, and a pre-assessment with the anesthesiologist were just a few of the things we—*she* had done. Rose thought all of it was *fun*. That was her go-to word the last few days leading up to the surgery, and she was laying it on thick with the sarcasm. For me, it had been anything *but* fun.

She was all smiles when she was working—welcoming the customers, laughing and joking around with Sally and the other one—but as soon as she closed the place down with me standing right next to her, she turned mute.

She barely talked to Raymond and didn't ask about his latest date, which I had gathered was her favorite thing to do in the mornings and in the evenings as he drove us back to the apartment. She barely said hello to the doorman, Steve, and left me to do the talking.

Me.

The days after the MRI, as soon as we got home, she disappeared into her room, mumbling a few things that ended up with her saying something about having a headache and being tired. I believed her. I knew she was tired, could see she was having headaches more frequently, but on Monday when we got back from the hospital and she ran straight up to her room without a word, I finally reached my limit and couldn't take it anymore. I wasn't going to let her revert back to the way we'd been when she'd first moved in.

I'd managed to convince her to skip going to the coffee shop the day before the surgery. It would be her first day off of many until she felt all right enough to get back on her feet.

She looked heartbroken when I had to gently keep her moving toward the car with my hand on the small of her back as she kept looking back at the coffee shop over her shoulder as if it'd be the last time she'd see it. I felt like I was taking her baby away from her. When she went straight up to her room, I let her be for the time being.

I took off my suit jacket, rolled up my sleeves, and walked straight into the kitchen.

An hour later when it was six PM and the table was ready, I reached for my phone and sent Rose a quick text.

Jack: Can you come downstairs?
Rose: I don't feel so great, Jack. If it's not anything important, I'd like to stay in bed.

Other than the simple fact that I didn't want her to be alone, she also hadn't had anything to eat the entire day, and no matter what she said, I wouldn't let her spend the next however many hours hungry. She had three hours before she needed to stop eating.

Jack: I'd really like your help with something if you could just come down.

I knew that would get her moving, because it was probably the first time I'd asked for her help with anything. Just the curiosity alone would get to her.

Sure enough, two minutes later, I heard her door open and close. Then footsteps started down the stairs and she came into the living room. Her hair was up in a simple ponytail with a few strands of her hair framing her pale face. She was wearing a chunky and oversized sand-colored sweater that fell way past her hips, and under that she had on what looked like simple black leggings and some cozy socks. Her sweater's arms were pulled down, and in one hand she was grasping a tissue, something that had become a constant for her these last few weeks.

As soon as she saw me standing next to the dining table with my hands shoved in my pockets, her steps slowed down and her eyes darted between the set table and me.

"Jack? You need my help with something?" she asked, holding the tissue up to her nose and sniffling.

"Yes." I walked around her and pulled out the chair she was standing next to. "I need your help with finishing this food."

She glanced at me over her shoulder, fidgeting. "Jack—"

"You haven't eaten anything today, Rose." I softened my tone and looked into her eyes. "You only have three hours then you won't be able to eat or drink anything anyway. I don't want to eat alone, so you're going to eat with me."

She worried her lips between her teeth and nodded. "You're right, I should eat something. Just give me a minute so I can do something about my nose."

Turning around in her socks with a *whoosh*, she hurried away to the bathroom.

When she came back with a cotton ball in her nose, she sat down on the chair, and I helped her get closer to the table.

I took my seat across from her and reached for her plate, only to have her grasp it midair.

"What are you doing?" she asked.

"I'm trying to wrestle the plate away from you." I gave her plate a gentle tug and she let it go. "Tonight, you get to be spoiled."

Finally the smile that touched her lips was genuine. "Pity night, huh?"

I shrugged. I wouldn't have called it that, but if she wanted to think of it in those terms, keeping my mouth shut would be a better option. I reached for the big serving dish and started to pile spaghetti onto her plate.

Rose leaned forward and reached for my hand, placing her fingers on my wrist when I was about to go in for more spaghetti. A small smile was blooming on her face. "I think that's more than enough for me, don't you think?"

I took another look at her plate and decided it would do. I could always sneak more onto her plate when she was done. I let go of the spaghetti spoon and reached for the Bolognese sauce. She tried to stop me after the second spoonful, but I sneaked another one in.

When I lifted my eyes, she was smiling at me. It was a lot closer to what her usual smile looked like, so I started to relax.

"Fresh thyme?"

Her grin got bigger, and she nodded again.

"I like this side of you."

"Which side?" I asked distractedly.

"This domestic side. It suits you."

When her plate was ready, I handed it to her, and she had to hold it with two hands before she could put it down in front of her. Leaning over the food, she closed her eyes and took a deep breath.

"This smells amazing. You were right, I'm starving."

I couldn't take my eyes off of her even as I grabbed my own plate and started the same process.

"I'm always right."

She arched her eyebrows at me, her grin turning more playful. "Easy there. I wouldn't say always."

"I would. Come on, time is ticking. Start eating."

"You are always bossy, though—that's definitely true."

After giving her a pointed stare, I waited for her to start, and she took her time, getting more comfortable in her chair and then finally started eating.

After chewing for a few seconds, she closed her eyes and groaned before finally swallowing. Satisfied that she would keep eating, I started on my own.

"Where did you get this from? It's incredible."

"Glad you like it."

"Is it a secret place? God! This is so good, Jack!"

I kept chewing and then swallowed under her expectant gaze.

"I made it. It's not takeout."

She stopped with her fork a few inches away from her mouth and lowered it. "You cook?"

"Sometimes, if I have the time."

That earned another beautiful smile, and I decided I would always cook for her on Mondays, pasta or whatever she wanted.

"You're amazing." She had started chewing but stopped. "Meaning, this is amazing—the pasta."

"I'll cook on Mondays."

She swallowed, hard. "You cook on Mondays?"

I shook my head and reached for my water glass. "No, I'll start cooking for us on Mondays. I enjoy spending time in the kitchen."

"Can I watch it? Next Monday? Or do you not like company? Oh, and of course if the surgery goes well and—"

My eyes met hers. "You don't want to finish that sentence. I don't like company, but I like you. You can watch."

"Jack I believe we're flirting."

I grunted.

"Every Monday, promise?"

I looked into her eyes. "Whenever you want, Rose."

"Then I should pick a day to cook, too."

We continued eating.

"If your cooking is as good as your baking, I'll be there."

"I enjoy cooking when it's not just for me. Are Mondays gonna be pasta day?"

"Do you want to make it pasta day?"

She smiled, her head bobbing up and down. "I think I'd like that. It'll be our first tradition."

Her tone of voice had changed with her last words, so I looked up from my plate to find her smiling at me. My night was already made.

"Pasta day it is then."

"So, tomorrow—"

"Nope. I don't want to talk about tomorrow tonight, if that's okay." Slowly she put down her fork and steadied her eyes on me. "I'm completely aware that I'm being a complete—let me correct that, I *have* been a complete diva about this whole sickness thing. I'm also well aware that compared to some illnesses, this is nothing, but my issue is that I'm simply scared. It's too close to my brain for my liking and it's really bothering me. I don't like that I'll be under anesthesia and I won't know what's going on, not that I would want to know or want to be awake even if that was an option... I'm especially grateful that it's going to be endoscopic surgery instead of cracking open my skull like they used to do back in the day, because *that* would probably kill me, but...I'm still scared. I told you, I'm afraid of giving blood, so a surgery..." She shook her head vehemently. "And the timing couldn't have been worse."

I parted my lips, but she stopped me from saying what was on my mind.

"Like I said, tonight I want to act like tomorrow will be just another normal day. I just want to enjoy this amazing dinner you very sneakily cooked for us and then try to see what else I can milk out of my situation. I'll deal with the rest tomorrow."

"*We'll* deal with the rest tomorrow," I corrected her, and received a nod in response. "What else did you want to milk out of your situation?" I asked, trying to look only mildly curious. I already knew I would do whatever it was she wanted to do.

Her smile came back in full force. "I thought you'd never ask. So..." She scooted forward in her seat, rolling spaghetti onto her fork, eyes on mine. "Remember how you said you'd never watched *You've Got Mail*? I thought a cozy movie would be perfect for tonight. It's not a wishy-washy film either. I promise you won't be bored. Any movie that has Tom Hanks in it is amazing, and his on-screen chemistry with Meg Ryan is absolutely perfect. I'm sure you—"

"Okay," I agreed, keeping my hands flat on the table and my eyes on her.

"We can watch it?"

"I said okay, didn't I?"

Her laughter took me by surprise, but I wasn't against it.

"Happy?" I asked, smiling back at her.

Her gaze dropped to my lips. "Yes, Jack. Very. Thank you."

"You're welcome. Now stop talking and keep eating."

She had a big smile the entire time she chattered and pulled me into conversation after conversation during dinner. As good as I was at not showing what I was thinking or feeling, I wasn't sure if I did a good job that night. I was too worried about what the next day would bring and what I would do if something happened to her when she was out of my reach.

CHAPTER EIGHTEEN

JACK

We got up from the dining table around seven-thirty PM. It had been one of the longest dinners I'd ever had, but since Rose looked happy, I didn't and couldn't have complained. She insisted on getting all the dishes in the dishwasher, and I kept her company until she was done. Her smile never wavered, and it made me happy to see it.

I prepared her some tea and made myself a cup of coffee. I had bought her some truffles on Friday because I knew her weakness for chocolate but hadn't ended up finding the right moment to give them to her, so I took the elegant box with me and set everything up on the coffee table.

I found the Apple TV remote and started to search for the movie she was talking about. When I came upon it, I charged it to my account and pressed play.

"Wait, wait." Rose jumped up and ran over to get the lights. "That's better."

She came back, sat down, and immediately pulled her legs under her as she reached for the big knitted blanket she had brought down from her room. I handed her the tea mug.

She grabbed my wrist with her right one and tugged me down next to her. "It's starting, sit down."

I managed to reach for my own coffee mug and her box of truffles.

Feeling a little uncomfortable about it, I thrust the box into her hand and leaned back against the couch. When she glanced at me in confusion, I focused on the movie that had just begun and took a sip of my coffee.

"What is this?" Balancing her mug on the flat surface of the couch, she sent me a quick look then started opening it. "Chocolate? For me?" she asked, her voice high.

"A client brought it on Friday, and it was just sitting in the office so I thought you might want it." The lie rolled off my lips so easily, I surprised even myself.

Out of the corner of my eye, I could already see her taking a bite out of one of them. "You want one?" she asked when she was done driving me crazy and moaning about it. She held the box toward me. "Don't you like truffles? Come on, take one."

I gave her an exasperated look and took one, holding it in my hand. "Will you let me watch this movie or are you going to talk the entire time?"

She winced. "You're one of those. Be prepared for me to talk. I'll keep pointing things out you can already see for yourself. I'm just excited because you've never seen it. Is it past nine?"

I kept my eyes on the screen as Meg Ryan's character started running toward her laptop to check her email. "Not yet. I'll tell you when you need to stop. It's only eight."

We sat in silence and just watched the movie. Around the ten-minute mark, Meg Ryan finally made it to her shop. The Shop Around the Corner.

I slung my arm across the back of the couch, toward her.

A few minutes later, I glanced at her. The box containing the truffles looked like it had six missing ones, and she was still holding the tea mug tightly in her hands as if trying to warm them.

"Are you cold?"

"Just a little. Would you like to share?" she repeated, and my brows drew together.

Then I realized she was holding the edge of the blanket up and away from herself.

It wasn't cold—the apartment was plenty warm—but I took the opportunity to move a little closer to her, and she put it over my legs. When she leaned her head back, it was almost resting in the crook of my arm.

She took a deep breath and let it all out.

Her voice was quiet when she spoke up again. "Thank you for tonight, Jack."

Leaning down, I pressed a kiss to her temple. "You're very welcome, Rose."

At ten to nine, I took her now cold tea mug away from her and put it down on the coffee table. A little more than halfway into the movie, she'd fallen asleep, and her head had dropped on my shoulder. I watched the movie till the end without moving an inch so she could rest. The more she tucked herself closer, the harder it had been for me to not wake her up and take her mouth. It seemed like she had invaded the entire apartment and I could smell nothing but her.

I enjoyed every second of it, both the movie and Rose's warm body against mine.

Scooping her up into my arms, I straightened up, letting the blanket fall off of her.

She started coming around once we were halfway up the stairs.

"Jack?" Her hands tightened around my neck. "What time is it?" she mumbled.

"A little past ten."

Sighing, she rested her head on my shoulder.

"Did you like the movie?"

I didn't have to lie. "Yes, you were right, it was good."

"They don't make movies like that anymore," she murmured.

I opened the door to her room and walked in, gently putting her down on the bed. She curled up on her side and I pulled the already open covers over her.

"Good night, Jack," she whispered. "I'll see you tomorrow."

"I'll wake you up at six-thirty. We need to be at the hospital at seven-thirty."

"Okay."

I was rooted to my spot but didn't know what else to say that would allow me to stay with her longer, to spend this night, at least *this* night with her.

"Good night, Rose." I leaned down and pressed a lingering kiss on her forehead and then her lips. It was such a natural move for me that I didn't even hesitate. She closed her eyes with a smile on her lips. I was pretty sure she had never woken up fully.

My mind on her, I walked out and headed to my own room.

Later that same night, hours had passed and I was still wide awake. My mind was running in all directions, but it was especially running in the direction of where Rose was sleeping a few doors down, which was why I was surprised when my phone pinged with a new text.

Rose: Are you asleep?

Jack: No.

Rose: Me neither.

I took a deep breath, ran my hand over my face.

Jack: Everything okay?

Rose: Yes. Just can't sleep.

Rose: Why are *you* still up?

Jack: Couldn't sleep either.

Rose: Can I still milk my situation or did I miss my chance?

Jack: Depends on what you want.

Rose: It's a weird one.

Jack: Try me.

Rose: I was wondering if I could kiss you.

Rose: And before you say no, it doesn't have to mean anything but that, just a kiss. The truth is you've slowly become this adept kisser and I think I wouldn't mind kissing you right now. I'd like to call it a pity kiss. If that's not okay since no one would be around to see it, I understand that.

The dots were still dancing around, but I left my phone on my nightstand and walked away. I chose not to knock and just walked into her room.

She seemed to be still typing but stopped when she saw me. Clearing her throat, she got up to her knees to get out of bed, but I made it to her before she could.

"How do you want to do thi—"

I didn't give her time to finish her sentence. In the next breath, I was holding her head in my hands after having pushed her hair back. Her cheeks were warm and slightly wet.

"I don't want you to cry anymore," I muttered with a tinge of anger coloring my voice. That was the last thing I wanted for her. "I'll kiss you, but only if you promise not to cry anymore. I can't take it, Rose."

She nodded.

I lowered my head down to hers, parted her lips with mine, and watched her eyes as they closed the second our lips touched. She placed her hands over mine on her cheeks and tilted her head up, deepening the kiss. I slowly dropped to my knees on the bed, tightened my hands around her face, plunging my fingers into her hair as her arms moved between us to wrap around my neck. I pulled her tongue into my mouth and happily swallowed her quiet groan.

If I had to describe our kiss, I would say it was a gentle violence. I couldn't get enough of her, couldn't get close enough. I let one of my hands travel down her back, memorizing every inch and how her body dipped at her waist. When I had a good grip on her shirt, I pulled her flush against me. She grunted but didn't stop, didn't ask me to stop.

I could feel her chest rising and falling against mine, her heat burning me up already. I fisted her shirt in my hand and deepened the kiss, forcing her to arch her back at the same time, gripping her waist tightly with my other hand. Her head dipped back with the force of my kiss, her tongue playing with mine.

Then her hands were braced on my chest and I felt a slight push.

I managed to wrench myself away, and she quickly jumped out of my arms and the bed, running straight to the bathroom.

My whole body was wound up tight. I sat down on the edge of the bed and dropped my head into my hands. My breathing was heavy, my heart beating in my throat like a teenager making out with his girlfriend in her house.

While I was contemplating getting up and leaving or staying, Rose re-emerged from the bathroom, her face flushed, lips red and swollen, hair all messed up.

She looked perfect.

She slowly made her way back, stopping in front of me when her knees were almost touching mine.

I didn't want to apologize for pouncing on her like a beast, but I had completely forgotten she was ill.

"Sorry," she muttered, her voice thick. Her index finger tapped the side of her nose. "It was starting up again so I had to..."

I sighed a breath of relief and nodded. I swallowed down the lump in my throat and was about to get up to leave, but Rose put both her hands on my shoulders and climbed into my lap, not sitting, but she had put one of her legs between mine and was standing on her knees. My hands found purchase on her hips and I held her still.

"What are you doing?" I asked in a harsh whisper as I stared into her alluring eyes.

She smiled down at me. "I'm getting the rest of my pity kiss," she whispered back in a low and steady voice, much steadier than mine, to my surprise. "I'm not done with you yet." Her hands smoothed my hair back as her eyes closed on their own and her head descended.

I met her halfway and took her mouth in a deep and scalding kiss, giving her needy laps of my tongue as her fingers combed through my hair and she gripped my neck to hold me up to herself. I kissed her like that for a long time, trying to be gentler and more considerate than I was feeling, but she disarmed me. Her taste, her little moans, her hands tightening on my neck, her body moving restlessly against mine—everything about her disarmed me.

When she moved her lips to the right and tried to breathe against my cheek, I watched all the emotions playing on her face. Knowing I couldn't stop, I held her waist and gave her a tug so she would sit down. Her eyes opened and found mine. Moving her leg to straddle me, she wordlessly followed my lead, sitting right on my dick. My eyes closed and a groan escaped my lips. When I looked back at her, she was biting her lip, staring at me intently. I rounded my arms around her, letting one of my hands slowly slide up her back to hold her neck, and dove in for another kiss. I kissed her once then pulled back, then again and again and again. It was maddening, the way her lips fit mine.

With my other hand, I gripped her waist. She tilted her head and pushed her tongue into my mouth. I could barely think as it was, but I met her exploring tongue with my own and leaned forward, forcing her to arch, going deeper, trying to take more and more.

The pain and pleasure that seared through me when I felt her heat slide across my cock through her thin pajama bottoms only tripled with the way she was kissing me, so out of control and hungry.

We pulled and pushed as if we were starving for each other. I grabbed her thighs and tried to somehow pull her even closer. When she rocked against me, some sense started to trickle back in. My hands still hard bands around her, she managed to pull back and, in an instant, took off her shirt. Her eyes glazed and her breaths coming out as shallow pants, she leaned toward me again, but when my eyes dropped to her full tits enclosed in a pale blue bra, I leaned back and gently deposited her on her back.

"Jack?" she gasped, surprised.

I made sure I wasn't looking at her, because if I did get another look, I would forget myself, forget that she was sick, forget everything. I reached for her t-shirt and handed it back to her. She held it up against her chest, covering herself.

"The doctor said no sex. You can't have too much pressure in your head." I heard my own voice, hoarse and raw. I dared to meet her eyes. They were still dazed, but she was coming back to herself. She licked her lips and my stomach dropped because it wasn't my own tongue on them.

"But Jack, I—"

"You have surgery in a few hours, Rose. I'll wake you up when it's time to leave."

She sobered and quickly put her shirt back on, getting under the covers. "You don't need to do that. I'll wake up when it's time."

"Rose—"

"Good night, Jack. Thank you for the kiss."

I gritted my teeth and backed away. Before I could close her door, she'd already turned off her bedside lamp, and I could barely make out her form in the bed. The door clicked shut and I let go of the handle, leaving something very important to me behind.

CHAPTER NINETEEN

ROSE

The next morning, I woke up on my own, just as I'd said I would, and I met Jack downstairs. Maybe because of the nerves that came with the surgery or because of what had happened just the night before, neither one of us said a word to each other.

When Steve, the doorman, wished me good luck and told me he couldn't wait to see me again with all good news, I was ashamed to admit I got a little teary-eyed and only managed to give him a small smile and a nod. He understood I wasn't trying to be rude, though; I could see it in his own smile. The car ride was similarly quiet. When Raymond pulled the car up in front of the hospital, Jack got out and held the door open for me. I followed after him, but before I could step out, Raymond's voice stopped me with one foot in the car and the other one out on the pavement.

He slung his arm over the passenger seat and turned his body so he could meet my eyes. "You will be fine," he assured me, his voice soft and quiet. It was the second time I teared up that morning. Everything else had been just automatic. I'd woken up, taken a very quick shower, gotten dressed, grabbed my hospital bag, and walked out of Jack's apartment. It had almost felt like I was just going to travel somewhere I didn't necessarily want to go to.

"Okay," I replied.

Raymond arched his eyebrows. "You can do better than that."

"I'll probably be fine."

"No probably about it. I'll come up when you're out of surgery to say hi, all right?"

I wasn't sure if I wanted anyone to see me after the surgery, but I didn't say that. "I'd like that. Thank you, Ray."

"See you soon."

"Okay. See you soon."

I got out and, with Jack by my side, walked into the hospital. I cast quick glances at him, but his face looked all stony, like the first day I'd met him. I didn't know what to say to him. That wasn't true—I actually did know what to say to him, but it wasn't the time for it. After we checked in and they confirmed our surgery time, a nurse took us up to a hospital room, apparently not the one I'd be staying in, but a different one.

Jack stayed in the corner with his hands in his pockets. I now knew what that meant: he was nervous about something, unhappy.

The nurse gave me my hospital gown and asked me a whole lot of questions: my name, my age, my weight, the things I was allergic to—all things they already knew, but double-checking never hurt anyone. I was allergic to penicillin. That was the one thing I remembered I kept saying. She put the identification band on me, walked me through what was going to happen next, and left me with Jack so I could change into the gown.

I was like a robot. I went into the little bathroom and took off my clothes, all but my underwear, and put the gown on. My heart hammering in my chest, I stepped out of the bathroom and met Jack's hard gaze.

Spreading my arms, I tried to sound cheerful when I asked, "How do I look?"

He didn't answer, just stared into my eyes.

I took a step toward him, because now was the time to say what I needed to say to him. The same nurse who had been in just a few minutes earlier popped her head through the doorway, and both Jack and I glanced at her.

"Is she dressed? Oh, good, you're ready. I'm sending someone in to get you in the wheelchair."

"I, uh, can I have just a quick minute with my husband?"

Her eyes darted to Jack then she checked her watch. "Just one minute. We need to get you to the OR on time, okay?"

I nodded, and she left.

Letting out a deep, deep breath, I walked over to where Jack was leaning against the wall, his arms crossed against his chest.

"I have some things I want to say to you," I started, feeling a little sick and very small in front of him. It could've been the thin hospital gown, the surgery, nerves, or simply because of what I was about to tell him. I ran my hands up and down my arms and his eyes followed my movements.

He was silent for a full minute as we took in our fill of each other.

"Okay," he finally said, looking all miserable.

"Jack, I want us to—"

"I'm sorry, but they need to take you now," the nurse said, walking into the room with someone else trailing behind her with a wheelchair.

Oh, dammit! Things just got real.

The fear that spiked in me wasn't much different than my panic attack in the MRI machine, and I looked back at Jack with fear in my eyes. I really wanted to talk to him.

He straightened up off the wall. "We'll need another minute."

"We're already running behind. She—"

Jack walked over and took the wheelchair from the other woman's hands then turned to the nurse, gritting his teeth. "I need just a moment with my wife. Please."

A shiver worked its way through my body when I heard him call me his wife, which was stupid on its own, but coming from his mouth with that growly tone, it was unexpected.

Not so surprisingly, they left us alone with only one disapproving glance toward Jack. He rolled the wheelchair toward me and gestured with his head for me to sit down.

If he wasn't using words, we had problems.

Before the nurse could come back, I rushed into my impromptu speech. I could already sense that it wasn't going to be elegant.

"Jack, I want to stop pretending."

He came around and kneeled in front of me, his hands resting on my thighs. His face looked a bit softer, the harsh scowl he had flashed to the nurses not there anymore, but there wasn't a smile in sight either.

He opened his mouth, but I leaned forward and shook my head.

"When I wake up from this, I want us to stop pretending."

Those beautiful blue eyes I couldn't stop looking at whenever I had the chance bored into my ordinary brown ones. I had no idea how this was going to go, but we didn't have much time.

"You like me," I continued, and he arched an eyebrow. I pushed forward despite that. "You probably won't want to admit this out loud, but you like me. I know it, so don't lie to me, and I like you. So, Jack Hawthorne, you asked me out on a date, which I know got lost with everything else happening, but we're still pretending, and I want us to stop doing that, okay?"

He looked at me for a long moment and I started to think this really wasn't going to go how I wanted it to go.

"How do you know I like you?"

"You have to. Yesterday...that kiss wasn't just a pity kiss. A pity kiss would be a quick peck on the lips or just a minute of something a little more, maybe. Neither was the kiss in your office at home." I shook my head. "Even if it wasn't that kiss, it's the things you do. The dinner yesterday, the flowers you bring every week—everything. You must have started liking me at some point during the last two months. I'm not stupid, and I like you more and more with each passing day."

"No, you're not stupid. You like me then?"

"Yes. So...I want to stop pretending and start...something real. More than just a date." As lame as that sounded, I wanted that right to him. He was my husband on paper, but that was it. I wanted a real claim on him.

"Okay."

"I—what? Okay? Just okay?"

He smiled at me and reached up to tuck my bangs behind my ear. It was smile number ten or maybe twenty, and it was such a good one. Hesitantly, I returned his smile, my heart soaring.

"I already asked you out on a date, didn't I? You just like to steal my thunder. Why do you look so surprised?"

"You weren't really committed to the date thing when you asked me out for dinner. You said we could try and see if there is something there. I'm being bold and saying there *is* something there. I thought you'd put up a big fight and deny liking me."

"Why would I do that when all I want is you? I want us to stop pretending too."

The nurse came back in with a stern face. "Time to go, Mrs. Hawthorne."

Jack's smile melted and he glowered at the nurse who had taken hold of my wheelchair. He grabbed the armrests and pulled me toward him as the nurse tried to wheel me back.

"Mr. Hawthorne!" she exclaimed in shock. "Let go of your wife, please."

"We're still talking here."

Nervous laughter bubbled out of me as they continued to push and pull for a few seconds. I put my cold hand on his cheek, and he stilled. "It's okay, Jack." Leaning forward, I kissed his cheek and took a deep breath through my nose so I could keep his scent with me for as long as I could, and then the nurse wheeled me away.

Jack walked with us all the way to the elevators.

I looked up at him from my seat and he reached out to hold my hand. "Will you come back from work before I wake up, or...?"

"Don't be stupid. I'm not going anywhere," he growled, softening his words with a squeeze around my hand. He was still glowering at the nurse.

"Okay. I was just testing you. I'd really like to see you when I come out." He must have heard the tremor in my voice, because his eyes met mine and he lowered himself to my level as we waited for the elevator to get there. He looked so ridiculous in a hospital with his perfect suit and perfect face and perfect stubble. My eyes started to well up and he became a blur in front of me. Then his hands were cupping my face and he was wiping away my tears. He rested his forehead against mine.

"Jack, I'm a little scared, I think," I admitted, quietly so only his ears could hear.

He sighed. "I don't know what the right words are here because I'm more than a little scared, but I know you're going to be fine. You have to be. It's going to be fine, Rose. I'll be waiting for you when you come out, and then it'll be just us."

I bit my lip and let him clear more tears from my cheeks. "Okay." My voice was nothing more than a croak. I looked down at my hands. "Oh, here." I took off my ring and opened his palm, placing my wedding ring in the middle. "Hold on to it for me." More tears started to come down and I couldn't look into his eyes.

"Rose," Jack started, his hands holding my face.

The elevator doors pinged open and there was a long sigh.

"Mr. Hawthorne, please let go of your wife."

He did—reluctantly—right after he pressed a soft yet somehow still hard and desperate kiss on my lips.

I looked at Jack over my shoulder once I was in the elevator and found him back up on his feet. He was so handsome. I tried to smile, but more tears blurred my vision of him.

"I'll be right there when you wake up, Rose. I'll be waiting for you *right here*, so you come back to me, okay? Make sure you come back to me."

I knew I was being a baby, but I didn't care. Pressing my lips tightly together, I nodded and the doors closed, taking him away from me.

Everything after that was a big blur. I was taken down to the OR area. They scanned the band on my wrist and took me into another waiting room where I was told to get in a hospital bed. More questions came that I answered absentmindedly. The anesthesiologists came in and again asked more questions. I couldn't even tell you how many times I repeated my name, my birth date, my weight, my allergies, and which side of my nose I was leaking from, and I wasn't sure how long I was in that room before they took me into the operating room. When I got there, it was already filled with all kinds of people: the anesthesiologists, the surgical assistant, the nurse anesthetist, my doctor, and a few more people who I had no idea what they were doing in there.

Smiling at me the entire time, the nurse anesthetist put my IV in and reassured me that everything would be okay. I realized I'd started crying again at one point, so I angrily wiped at my cheeks and tried to play it off by laughing at myself. She just smiled at me.

When they secured my hands and legs, I started to get dizzy and my vision started to darken. I hadn't realized that was going to happen. No one had told me that. I started to panic in earnest, my breaths coming in faster. I heard the nurse say she was pushing in the anesthesia, and a few seconds after that I started to feel sick to my stomach, fleetingly thinking it was a really, really bad time to puke. I thought I opened my mouth to let them know I really wasn't feeling all that well, but then suddenly everything went black.

CHAPTER TWENTY

JACK

It was one PM and still she hadn't come out. I'd been in that waiting room for several hours already and still she wasn't out. I felt like a caged animal, not only in that room, but in my own skin.

I paced every inch of the space, stopping next to the windows and staring out without seeing anything. I sat down on the green chairs I now hated, closed my eyes, and leaned back...opened my eyes, rested my elbows on my legs, and put my head in my hands...yet still she wasn't back.

A family of three was waiting with me, a dad and two kids. One was a small girl who wouldn't let go of her father's hand, and the boy, maybe nine or ten, would pat his sister's head every now and then and try to make both the dad and the girl laugh. When they got the good news that their mom was out of surgery, I felt a surge of relief for them, but when no one came to tell me about Rose, I sank farther down in my seat.

At one-fifteen, my eyes on the door waiting for a nurse, to my surprise, Cynthia walked in.

"What are you doing here?" I asked when she made it to my side.

She sat down in her own ugly green chair and settled in. "Wanted to check on you." The bewilderment must have shown on my face because her expression softened and she patted my arm. "Any news?"

"No," I grunted, resting my elbows on my parted legs again. "Just waiting."

"That's the hardest part."

My eyes on the door, I nodded. "Aren't you supposed to be at work?"

"My boss didn't come in, so I'm taking a very long and late lunch break. Is there anything I can get you?"

I shook my head.

"She'll be fine, Jack. You'll see. You just hold on so you can take care of her when she gets out."

I had no idea what she was talking about. I was fine.

We didn't talk for at least thirty minutes. Finally, she sighed and got up. "I better get back. I'm trying to get all the urgent stuff to the partners."

Clenching and unclenching my hands, I looked up at her from my seat, taking my eyes off the door. "Anyone making things hard for you?"

She patted my cheek, and we were both surprised by the gesture. "You worry about yourself and Rose. I'll handle the partners."

I jerked my head in a nod. "Thank you, Cynthia. I appreciate your help with everything these last few days. I know I dumped everything on you."

"She is changing you, you know."

My brows drew together. "What are you talking about now?" Distractedly, my gaze caught on the big clock on the wall right over the door: two PM.

Starting to get angry, I got up and started pacing right next to the windows.

"Nothing," she murmured with a weird smile on her face.

I only paused long enough to give her a quick look then continued with my pacing.

"You're gonna wear a hole in the ground."

Another look thrown her way, this time more menacing—at least I hoped it was. "Then I'll wear a damn hole in the ground."

"Okay, I'm gonna leave you to your pacing now. Jack?"

I stopped with a frustrated sigh and faced her. "What?"

"Try not to lose her, okay? Don't wait to tell her till it's too late."

I ground my teeth together to keep my mouth shut. My gaze must have finally worked because she raised her hands in the air then started putting on her coat, gloves, scarf, and finally the bright red coat.

When she shouldered her bag, she turned to me. "I'd appreciate it if you could let me know how the surgery went when she comes out."

To my own horror, I muttered, "If she comes out." Luckily, Cynthia didn't hear me and finally left.

I spent another hour in my own unwanted company, and more people trickled out of the room as they got their good news so they could be with their loved ones.

Around three PM, Raymond walked in with balloons. Balloons. I didn't know how I felt about that, but my body tightened to the point that I couldn't have moved even if I'd wanted to. I knew she had a good relationship with him since he drove her almost more than he drove me lately, but I still didn't know how I felt about him being there for her.

With *balloons*.

I hadn't brought anything, and I didn't think I could manage to leave the hospital. The fact that she wanted to be with me and stop pretending cooled me enough that I didn't demand he leave the second his eyes spotted me and he moved to my side with his ridiculous balloons.

He left an empty seat between us and sat down.

I couldn't keep my mouth shut. "Balloons, Raymond?" I asked, the words coming out as a low growl, unintentionally...or maybe not.

He cleared his throat. "Not from me."

I linked my hands together, glancing at him and then the balloons. There was a big blue one that said *Get Well Soon* and a few more colorful ones around it.

"I came from Around the Corner." He thrust a brown paper bag at me with Rose's shop's little logo on the side.

Curious, I took it and looked inside: one cup of what smelled like coffee, one sandwich, and a muffin. I put it down on the floor. Rose made the sandwiches herself every morning. She used a spread she'd come up with on her own, as she'd told me countless times. Knowing she hadn't made these, even though I hadn't had anything since our dinner the night before, I couldn't even stomach eating them. I picked up the coffee since I could've used a little more energy for more pacing.

Raymond continued, "I thought I could drop by and see if they needed any help with anything, and the girl—Sally, I think— she handed me the balloons when she heard I was coming here next."

I grunted unintelligibly. That was better.

"How is it? Are they busy?" I asked a moment later.

"Yes. There was a line at the register. She is doing great. Oh, they also said they'd be here as soon as they closed down, to check on her."

I nodded; I had expected as much. Since she wanted to be with me, I didn't have to worry about the other one who worked with her early in the mornings anymore, whatever his name was.

We fell silent.

"Any news?" he asked after a few moments.

I ran my hand over my face. "Not a goddamn thing."

"When did they take her in?"

"Eight. I don't know when they started, though. She must've waited for a while."

"How long is this surgery supposed to last?"

That was what was scaring the hell out of me. When we'd spoken to the doctor and I'd asked him how long these surgeries usually lasted, he hadn't given me a straight answer, which was expected, but he'd said other times it had lasted anywhere from forty-five minutes to three hours. We had passed the three-hour mark a while ago, so I knew something must have gone wrong.

I rubbed a hand over my heart when I felt it tighten painfully. "She should've been out by now."

Raymond took a look at me and didn't say anything else.

All I could do was play with her ring, which was a dead weight in my pocket, and hope she was doing fine and holding on. We sat like that for another two hours until *finally* a damn nurse made her way toward us instead of going to someone else.

I sprung up from my seat, my limbs prickling from all the hours I had sat on that uncomfortable chair.

"She is out of surgery now and in the recovery room." She smiled at us, as if everything was perfectly fine. She should've come down there hours ago.

"When can I see her?" I growled.

"We'll go up to her room now, and you can wait there."

"I think I've waited enough," I snapped. "Take me to see her."

The nurse lost her smile and scowled back at me. That was fine.

"She's been in surgery for quite some time now, so we're just anxious to see her," Raymond spoke up. "Waiting for her in the room would be great, thank you."

The woman, probably somewhere in her fifties based on her black and white natural hair, lost some of her stern look, which I didn't care for, and then she sighed.

"They'll bring her up to the room as soon as she is ready. They need to keep an eye on her until she starts coming around from the anesthesia."

"Is she okay?" I rushed the words out, taking a step forward. "Did something go wrong?"

"I'm sure she is fine. The doctor will come to her room to check on things later and he'll be able to give you more information. Now follow me, please."

Up in her room, nothing changed. I barely took in the surroundings as we walked into the private room I'd paid for. There was a big TV mounted on the wall right across from the hospital bed, a leather couch right under the big window where the whole city was laid out in front of you, and then two comfortable enough chairs on the left side of the bed. There was also a door to what looked like a private bathroom on the left side as soon as you walked into the room. Raymond stood closer to the door with his ridiculous and cheerful balloons and wisely stayed out of my way as I started my pacing again.

"Tie those stupid things to a chair or something. You look ridiculous, for God's sake," I growled when he just stood there. I ignored the twitch of Raymond's lips.

An hour—it took them another fucking hour to bring her up. As soon as they rolled her in, I rushed to her side. I was having trouble keeping my distance as they transferred her onto the bed.

Her eyes were barely open, she had a white tampon-looking thing in her nose, and she had slight bruising under her right eye. I moved my gaze over every inch of her face and her body, but other than that, I couldn't see anything wrong with her. She looked tired and worn out, but she seemed to be okay.

"How are you feeling?" I asked as soon as the guys who had brought her in left the room.

She reached for my hand, and my goddamn heart skipped a fucking beat. I grabbed it with both hands and held on tight.

Her eyes were suspiciously wet. "I feel really tired. My head hurts and my stomach is stinging, but I think I'm fine. How did it go? What time is it?" she croaked, her voice barely audible.

I brushed her messy bangs out of her face and leaned down to press a lingering kiss on her forehead.

"You took ten years off of my life, Rose," I whispered right next to her ear, resting my temple against hers. "I don't know how you're going to pay me back for this, but you better think of something."

She tried to frown, but even that she couldn't manage fully. "What? What are you talking about?"

"You've been in surgery for seven, almost eight hours."

"Oh. It's been that long? I didn't realize."

She slowly lifted her hand, which still had a little needle taped to it, and gingerly touched the side of her nose.

"There is a tampon in there, I think," I commented unnecessarily.

Her eyes darted around the room and spotted Raymond a moment later. "Oh, Ray. Hi." She paused as if waiting for the right words to come to her. "I'm sorry. I didn't see you."

Ray.

I gripped the bedrail, wondering what the hell was wrong with me that all of a sudden I was acting very unreasonable, especially since it wasn't the first time she had called him Ray.

He stepped forward with the damn balloons, and Rose's smile got wider.

"You brought me balloons? Thank you so much." She looked up at me. "Jack, he brought me balloons."

I hadn't brought her shit. I gave Raymond another murderous look.

"They're not from me, I'm afraid," Raymond started. "I dropped by your shop before I came here, and Sally wanted me to get them to you so you could see them when you woke up. How are you doing, kiddo?"

I relaxed further at Raymond's nickname for Rose and watched as her smile got all wobbly. "I'm okay, I think...a little dizzy, and I feel a little off. My head hurts...did I say that? Still better than what I expected. I must look like hell," she mumbled and tried to chuckle, the sound nothing like her warm laughter.

I squeezed her hand, and her eyes came to me as I softly said, "You look beautiful."

She groaned, trying to sit up a little straighter. "Uh oh, I really must look like hell." She looked back at Raymond. "Jack's usual compliments are more like *You look awful*, *You look tired*, *You look like hell*, or *You look like a mess.*" I scowled at her and she flashed me a small and tired smile. "Did I miss any?"

"I'll give you new compliments you can add to your list as soon as you're out of here. Don't worry."

"Thank you for trying to make me feel better."

Raymond's suppressed laughter got my attention, and I looked up from Rose.

He patted her leg, two gentle thumps. "He isn't lying. For someone who just came out of a seven-hour surgery, you look great. I'm going to leave you two alone. I just wanted to say hi and see how you're doing." His eyes met mine. "If you need anything, I'll be waiting close by."

I nodded and, after another look at Rose, he left.

Her eyes were starting to close on their own, but when I gave her hand a gentle squeeze, she turned her head toward me.

"Jack—"

"How are we doing?" An older red-haired nurse named Kelly

walked in, and she started checking Rose's blood pressure. "Everything okay?" she asked with a generous smile.

"I think so," Rose replied.

"Your blood pressure looks good. Let's see if you have any fever."

"Is the doctor coming?" I asked, and she turned her smile toward me.

"He'll be here soon enough. We need to start another IV on you, so you can just sit back and relax now. If you have pain, I'll get you a painkiller after you have your dinner. Sound good?"

"Okay."

"You don't have a fever, so that's great. I'll come back and check everything every hour. Okay?"

The nurse walked out, and Rose's head rolled toward me on the pillow. "Hi, Jack."

Looking into her eyes, I reached out with my right hand and ran the backs of my fingers across her cheek. "Hey."

"How bad does it look? You don't have to lie." Her voice was still cracked and hoarse.

"Bad enough."

Her lips moved up an inch or so, her eyes closing.

"That's more like you."

The nurse walked in with the IV bag, so I had to pull my hand back from her face.

The doctor came in two hours later when Rose had had small naps with her mouth open in between the blood pressure and fever checks. Every time she woke up, she'd look around the room and say my name when her eyes found mine. Every one of those times I got up and went to her side to assure her I hadn't left.

I looked like hell. Even more than that, I felt like I was living *in* hell. I wasn't cut out for stuff like this. I didn't know the right words to say. I was more likely to mess things up.

"How are we doing?" Dr. Martin asked.

Rose had just woken up so she pushed herself up in the bed.

"Not too bad," she said. "My stomach hurts a little."

"Yes. You remember what we talked about before, right? To patch the leak, we needed cartilage and other tissues from either your nose, your stomach, or the back of your ear, and—"

"I thought you said it was going to be from the nose," I cut in.

"Yes, that was the initial plan, but the tear was bigger than what we'd hoped for."

"Is that why it lasted over seven hours?"

"Again, yes. The tear was bigger and farther back than we expected, so it took a while to patch it, and if we had taken the tissue from the nose, it wouldn't have been enough. I didn't expect the operation to take that long either. Like we discussed before, it's usually a few hours at most, but it was successful, and that's what's important."

"I can't really breathe through my nose," Rose said, getting the doctor's attention.

"That's normal. You have packing in it right now and it'll have to stay in at least two, maybe three more days."

"When can I get out?"

He flashed Rose a smile. "Trying to get away from us so quickly?"

"No, I just—"

He patted Rose's arm. "That's fine. You'll be our guest for a few more days, maybe a week. We need to keep an eye on you for a while and see how things are going."

They had operated so close to her brain and because of the tear in the membrane, there was no protection. "Is infection a concern?" I asked.

"Infection is always a concern with any operation. Because we were so close to her brain, we just need to keep a close eye on her to make sure everything is healing smoothly."

"When will we know if it's still leaking?" Rose asked.

"I'll order another CT scan in a few days after we take the packing out and see how things are looking. After you get out of here, I'll need you to do another MRI scan in a few weeks." Rose stiffened in bed. "I know you have trouble with that, but we need to see if everything is okay."

She nodded and I took her hand. It seemed like I couldn't control myself anymore.

"Okay. I'll be checking on you every day, but a few things you need to know before I go: I need you to take a few pills morning and night. The nurse will get them to you before you take your meals. Also, there will be a syrup for constipation that you need to have two times a day."

Rose groaned and I tightened my grip around our linked fingers.

"We can't have you straining in any way. You need to keep taking the syrup even after you leave us, probably for about a month. Do not bend forward because we don't want any pressure in your skull. After you get out of the hospital, you need to stay in bed for at least another two weeks and keep your head high with two or more pillows. You'll visit us for check-ups in the meantime, and we'll talk about these things in more depth when you're ready to leave. For now, no tilting your head down, no sneezing."

"I'm guessing I'm not allowed to sleep on my face then?"

"No. I'm afraid that's not gonna be possible for quite a while. A few months. If you don't have any other questions, I'll see you tomorrow."

Another round of blood pressure and fever checks happened right before her employees and now friends showed up with cinnamon rolls, brownies, and two sandwiches.

As Sally approached, Owen stayed back, at the foot of the bed. I was standing on her left side.

"Hi," Rose whispered to Sally's smiling face.

"Hey," she said back. "Sorry we couldn't come before. We got all the good news from Raymond though. How are you doing?"

She rocked her hand in a so-so gesture. "How did it go at the coffee shop?"

"Everything went well. Don't even worry about a thing on that front."

Her eyes went to Owen. "Thank you for saying yes to working full-time, Owen. I don't know what I would've done if you hadn't accepted."

"We would've found you someone else," I interrupted, but she seemed to ignore me.

They stayed for another ten minutes and then left after promising to call her a few times the next day with updates on how things were going. Her dinner arrived a few minutes later.

"I don't want anything," Rose protested.

"You'll eat so you can have your pills. You heard the doctor."

"Just a little then."

"Yes, just a little." I moved the rails down and sat on the edge of the bed after we adjusted it so she could sit upright enough to have a few bites of the beef stew and rice. She could barely lift her arms, let alone feed herself. "How do you feel?"

"Still a little loopy, I think, and very, very tired."

"Do you want to have some of the sandwich Sally brought in or this?"

She scrunched up her nose. "I don't think I can handle the sandwich right now. Soft is better."

I cut a small bite off of a potato and gently placed it in her open mouth. She chewed it very slowly.

"I can't breathe through my nose, Jack."

"Dr. Martin said that was normal."

Next, I gave her a piece of beef, following it with some rice.

I felt like a true bastard, because there was something about feeding her that was getting to me. It was an intimacy we hadn't shared before.

"Would you like some water?"

"I'm sorry," she said, still chewing as she looked away from me for the first time.

"Sorry for what?"

"You're doing a lot more than what we agreed to."

I tried not to stiffen and just kept feeding her small bites. "I thought we were done pretending—or did you forget what you said before surgery?"

"I—" I forced another forkful of rice and potatoes into her mouth before she could respond. "Of course I remember, but still, this is—"

"If you remember then stop saying stupid things and keep eating."

A smile tugged at her lips. "Okay."

Eventually, the nurses changed shift, and after the last check, I turned the lights off.

Rose's eyes followed me as I made my way back to her side, her body slightly turned to the right, her head facing up.

"What's wrong?" I asked, pulling the covers higher so her shoulders were covered.

"My nose is a little tender. It hurts when I touch it."

"Stop touching it then. Do you want water?"

"A little."

I helped her up and she sipped from a straw, only a few pulls. "Enough?"

She nodded and settled down.

I turned away to put the water bottle on the bedside table.

"Jack?"

"Right here, Rose."

"Maybe we should talk more."

"About?"

"You know…"

"Some other time."

"Will you stay?"

"What?"

"Are you staying tonight?"

It wasn't completely dark in the room, but it was still hard for me to see her eyes and try to understand what was going on in her mind. Her eyes always gave her emotions away.

"You didn't bring anything with you—no clothes, no bag—so I wasn't sure if you'd stay tonight. You have work tomorrow so if you can't…that's okay."

All I could hear from her tone of voice was that she wanted me to stay with her. They couldn't have kicked me out even if they'd tried to anyway.

"I forgot to bring a bag. I wasn't thinking about that," I muttered.

We fell silent for a few moments.

"So then you are staying?"

I leaned down, pressing a gentle kiss on the edge of her lips as she closed her eyes. "Always," I said, my voice raw. "Even when the time comes that you don't want me anywhere near you."

She smiled a little. "I like having you around, so I doubt that will happen."

I wished that were true.

"Okay. Now shut up and get some rest."

CHAPTER TWENTY-ONE

ROSE

The next few days I spent at the hospital were hard. More tests and doctor visits resumed, and I felt like I was about to lose my mind. I'd never appreciated the outdoors as much as I did in that hospital room.

The only good moments came at night, with Jack.

I wasn't sure if I was feeling extra vulnerable because of the surgery and my sickness, but what I was starting to feel for him seemed like it was tripling every night we spent together in that spacious hospital room I couldn't possibly have afforded on my own.

It was the second or third night, I was having trouble sleeping because of all the mouth breathing I had to do, and I just couldn't get comfortable with the fact that I couldn't breathe through my nose.

The room was dark when he spoke, and the world outside my room was quiet other than the footsteps of the nurses walking by to check on patients every now and then.

"You're not sleeping," Jack said quietly. It wasn't a question.

I had my back to him because I wanted him to get some sleep

and not have to worry about me. He worried about me quite a lot, and just realizing that fact had made me so extremely happy. I rolled over slowly, making sure I wasn't lying completely on my side and my head was tilted toward the ceiling.

It wasn't completely dark in the room, not with all the city lights and the light slipping in underneath the door from the hallway, but it wasn't as clear as day either. He was lying on the couch, his legs crossed at the ankles. He was wearing pants and a thin, navy blue sweater, which were his casual clothes. I didn't know why he didn't wear something more comfortable.

"No," I replied. "But I'm trying."

"Do you need anything?"

"No. Thank you. Are you okay there?"

"I'm fine. Try to go to sleep."

We were silent for a long time. I was staring up at the ceiling when he spoke again.

"It started snowing."

I rolled my head and looked out the window. Sure enough, you could make out the white flurries flying around. It looked beautiful, and if it held, the city would be covered in white. Winter in NYC was my favorite time of the year, and Christmas would arrive soon—not that I'd be up and running then, but still... Christmas was coming.

"First snow...it's beautiful. I wish we could go outside and actually feel it. I love snow."

"There will be more."

"Jack? Can I ask for something?"

"Of course."

Before I could even say what I wanted, he was up and by my side. I looked up at him in the dark. I couldn't make out his features clearly, but I was sure he looked amazing. He always did. He was always so put together, and more than that, there was something about the way he carried himself, so confident and aloof. It pulled you in and kept hold of you. The fact that he looked like a movie star—a really grumpy one—was just an added bonus.

"Do you need water?"

He ran his fingers through my hair and waited for me to answer. He'd been doing that a lot the last few days, which was why I didn't think he'd turn me down when I made my next request.

"Could you lie with me?" His fingers stilled in my hair. "I know it wouldn't be comfortable, but just for a little while."

"Are you cold?"

"Nope."

Before he could say no, I scooted back to give him a little space. Thanks to the private room, the bed wasn't as small as the usual hospital beds. Without another word, he lay down next to me.

I turned to my side.

"You're supposed to lie on your back, not on your side."

"Thank you for reminding me, doctor, but the back of my head is tingling, and I can barely feel my head. I'll just stay like this for a few minutes, that's all."

He finally turned his head to look at me. "How are you feeling?"

"Better. I don't have much pain, which is surprising. The headaches aren't so bad either. I think I could go home."

I noticed his lips moving up an inch. "Not so fast. We're here for a few more days."

So that didn't work.

"You haven't been going to work."

"And?"

"Can you take so many days off like this?"

"I can do whatever I want."

"But don't you have clients and whatever stuff that you need to get back to?

"Are you trying to get rid of me, Rose?"

I scooted closer to him and pushed my hand under my cheek. "Nope." I didn't want to get rid of him at all. I pulled on the cover he was lying on top of, and as soon as he moved to the side and it was clear, I threw it over him, leaning over and making sure he was covered.

"What's going on here?"

"Just so you won't be cold," I muttered, securing him to my side. It was more like *Just so you can't leave*.

He turned to his side as well, staring straight into my soul.

"What's going on?" he repeated, softer.

"Please tell me this is real," I whispered. "What I'm starting to feel for you...what I think we have. Please tell me it's real and I'm not just imagining it."

My right hand was resting on my hip then a second later it was resting on his broad chest, our fingers linked together. "You're not imagining it."

"Do you think it's smart?"

"You and I?"

I nodded.

"Who cares about being smart. We're already married so... there is no reason why we shouldn't go there."

"Right?" I agreed, perking up. "I was thinking the same thing. It'd be a waste of a marriage."

"And if you don't think it's working or you don't think I'm what you want, it'll go back to what it was."

"Same goes for you, of course. Sometimes I can be an acquired taste. I know that."

He chuckled, and it warmed something inside me. He let go of my hand and cupped my cheek. The hairs on my arms stood up, and I could do nothing but close the distance between us, needing to get closer to him. Only a few inches were left between us.

"I'm the one who is an acquired taste in this relationship, and we both know that," he said.

Gently, I laid my head on his shoulder, but then he lifted his arm so I could lie on his chest. We settled in better after that.

He moved his hand under the covers and came out with something between his fingers.

My heart jumped in my chest when I saw what he had for me. "My ring!"

"I thought I should hold on to it until you were feeling better," he explained.

"I'm good. I'm okay." I held up my hand between us, impatient for him to put it back on. His fingertips slid along my ring finger and he pushed it back until it was securely in place. I stared at it for a little while in the dark.

I closed my eyes and let out a deep breath from my mouth. "How do you feel about Thursdays?"

"How should I feel about them?"

"Like pizza, maybe? We can do pasta on Mondays and pizza on Thursdays."

"We can argue about the toppings."

"Sounds fun to me."

"Good. Now go to sleep."

With a smile on my face, I snuggled in closer. "I have a good feeling about this, Jack Hawthorne. I have a really good feeling about this."

I smiled even bigger when he whispered, "It'll work. I promise you, Rose."

Jack and I, we were made in a crappy hospital bed, whispering our secrets, dreams and promises to each other. We were holding each other close as if what we had, what we were forming and building would be taken away from us with the sunlight.

Four days after the surgery, they finally took out the packing in my nose, and to say it was an experience would be an understatement. I'm not ashamed to admit that I cried for a solid ten minutes after it was done as Jack let me hold on to him tightly in our room and told me to stop crying. Everything seemed to be catching up with me, and then when they took out the damn thing—which I'd thought was only a few inches in but actually reached all the way up to my forehead, if not higher—I couldn't keep it together any longer. I hadn't cried since the surgery, so I supposed I was due.

The nights with Jack continued to be the only highlights of my day. I was secretly hoping we'd get to sleep in the same bed when we went back to his apartment, because I was already getting used to feeling his body and touch right next to mine.

When I had first met and married this man, I hadn't understood him, but he had surprised me at every turn from day one. I couldn't believe I'd thought the man lying next to me was cold and detached. He had proven otherwise with his actions countless times.

With all of that in my mind, I was feeling surprisingly torn about leaving the hospital, feeling afraid things would change once we got back to the real world as Dr. Martin gave me his last warnings on the day I was set to be discharged.

"You're on bed rest for two weeks, Rose."

"Can I get back to work after that?"

"You have a cafe, right?" he asked.

"Yes. I won't work too much, but I'd like to get back out there as quickly as I can."

"Fine. You can go back to work, but you can't work like you used to. Don't overdo it. Sit down and look over things, and only a few hours at first. Listen to your body—if it tells you it's tired, you stop doing whatever you're doing. No heavy lifting, nothing more than a few pounds. No sneezing whatsoever. No sex, no alcohol. You have to take it easy."

I only latched onto one thing. "No sex?" I could feel Jack's eyes burning into me, but I maintained eye contact with the good doctor.

"Yes, no sex for quite a while."

"What's quite a while exactly?" I pushed, probably surprising everyone in the room.

"At least three months. No alcohol for at least three months either, and no plane rides, because that kind of pressure can undo our work. Anything that can create pressure in your skull is to be avoided."

"Okay. No sex for three months."

Dr. Martin let out a loud laugh, and I couldn't help but smile back at him.

"I want to see you back here next week, and in another two weeks, we'll take out the stitches in your stomach." He turned his attention to Jack. "You have my private number if anything happens or if you have any questions, and don't hesitate to call me. I'll see you two next week."

The doctor left and we were alone once again. Jack turned to me with a scowl on his face.

"I'm sorry," I started before he could say anything. "I know you can't keep your hands off of me, so this is gonna be tough for us. After all the sex we've had so far in our marriage, three months will feel like an eternity. I hope you can survive."

"Smartass," he muttered. Shaking his head, he went to the little closet and took out my bag so I could change into my clothes. I slid down from the edge of the bed and took it from him, but only after I leaned up and kissed him on the cheek. There was something about being able to kiss him when there was no one around that appealed to me. He thought I was being ridiculous, but I didn't see him try to stop me even once. He always put his hand around my waist, holding me to him for longer. I was pretty sure he liked it too.

"How do you not sneeze, by the way?" I asked while rummaging around in my bag without looking down into it, trying to find some socks to wear.

"I have no idea, but you're not allowed to sneeze, so I suggest you figure it out fast."

After an hour of sitting around and signing stuff, we finally walked out of the hospital and straight into the cold. The sidewalks were muddy and wet with melted snow, but the air...*God*, finally being hospital-free and outside, holding Jack's hand all the way to the car...it was indescribable.

After saying a quick hello to Raymond, the first thing I asked him to do was take me to Around the Corner.

CHAPTER TWENTY-TWO

JACK

We had just stepped into the apartment. I dropped her bag right next to the door and helped her out of her coat. Then I couldn't hold it back any longer. I gripped her waist and pulled her toward me, gently. She braced herself with her palms on my chest, but she didn't push me away.

I stared down into her eyes. "Hi."

Her lips twitched. "Hi back. I'm angry at you."

"I know." She was annoyed with me because I hadn't let her take a quick look at Around the Corner. Before a protest could leave her tongue, and I didn't doubt it would, I slipped mine into her mouth and stole her breath, again being gentle. Her fingers slowly curled in and she fisted my sweater in her hands. Slowly easing the kiss even more, I sucked her tongue into my mouth and then just let myself have little nips at her lips so she could get her breath back. I knew she was still having trouble breathing through her nose.

"I kinda like it when you're angry at me."

Her closed eyes slowly peeled open.

"That didn't make it any better."

I let go of her and she swayed a little. "I imagine it didn't. Too much turtle?"

"Just the right amount of turtle, actually, but I'm not forgetting about the fact that you didn't let me take a quick look at my place."

She seemed to be loving picking a fight with me, and when it frustrated me to no end, she seemed to enjoy it even more. I just enjoyed every minute I got to spend with her.

I decided to change the subject. "What do you think about changing out the roses for something more green and Christmassy? It's that time, isn't it? It's going to be December soon."

She stayed put in her spot and I watched as her eyes got big then she lifted her hand up to her nose.

My adrenaline spiked and I was right back next to her, holding her face up for my inspection. "What's wrong? What's happening, Rose?"

She lifted her hand up and made me wait another full ten seconds. "I just learned how not to sneeze."

I swallowed and my sluggish heartbeat picked up again. "You're gonna be a difficult patient, aren't you?"

"What? What did I do?"

I couldn't stay away from her or keep my hands and lips off of her for too long, it seemed. I walked back and cupped her face, pressing a lingering kiss on her temple. "Come on, let's get you off your feet. Can you walk upstairs?"

"Do you have work to do?"

"Yes."

"If you can work in the living room, I'll lie down on the couch and keep you company. I'll be quiet, promise."

Instead of heading for the stairs, I guided her toward the living room and helped her lie down on the couch.

"Okay?" I asked when I noticed she was a little breathless.

"Yeah, I'm fine. How is it that I feel so tired after one car ride and then coming up in an elevator?"

"Other than walking up and down the hospital corridors, you didn't move much the past week, and you had a major surgery. This is normal. You stay here while I go get a few pillows to keep your head raised and something to cover you up."

I bent down at the waist and touched her lips with mine.

Her eyes were partly closed, her lips curved up. "By the way, I can't believe the word Christmassy came out of your mouth."

"It only came out of my mouth because I was repeating your words."

"Sure, you keep telling yourself that."

She managed to stay quiet for an hour and a half before she started talking to me, and she was asleep for eighty of the ninety minutes. Turned out, I could work just as well in the living room while listening and talking to Rose as I did in my office.

WE SPENT another week cooped up in that apartment. I went to work, and she stayed home and, according to her, did a lot of planning for her coffee shop. She wanted wreaths up on the windows—big ones. Not just any wreath would work, apparently. I told her I'd take her there and put them up right in front of her eyes. I told her we could only do that the following week if she was feeling better, and we got into an argument about how she was going to go crazy cooped up inside and could handle going to work for just a few hours to check things out. I loved every second of it and if our kiss after the short argument was anything to go by, she loved it just as much. Soon after, she fell asleep, proving my point that she wasn't ready to go anywhere.

The first few days we were back from the hospital, she would get dizzy and out of breath just from climbing the stairs. After that, she started to spend most of her time on the couch until I'd get done with work—which I was still playing catch up with—and then I'd carry her upstairs.

At the end of that first week, we went to the hospital and they cleaned out her nose. There was still blood coming down, but despite that, she was looking better and better every day.

Toward the end of the second week of her bed rest, she started crying at least once a day. "Jack. I want to go out, *please*."

"Do you even realize how much you're breaking my heart with all this crying you've been doing?"

She kissed me after that. She kissed me for a long time.

Georgie and Emma, two of her friends, came to visit and see how she was doing. I'd missed them at the hospital but met them when they came to the apartment. I felt like a lovesick idiot for hovering around her just in case she needed something and went to work while they stayed with her. Every day I would leave for work, I couldn't wait to come back to her, knowing I'd get to see her smile as soon as she saw me and got up to greet me halfway into the living room.

As soon as her two weeks of bed rest were complete, she demanded to go and check on things at the coffee shop.

"You heard what the doctor said: two weeks of bed rest then I could go to work."

"Rose, you still can't go up the stairs on your own without getting dizzy—how do you think you'll be able to work?"

"Maybe I just like you carrying me upstairs. Ever think of that?"

"Is that it?" I asked with a quirk in my eyebrow.

"I do like you carrying me..."

"But..."

"I'm not gonna overwork myself, Jack. Trust me. I'm not gonna risk going through the same stuff again. I'm just going to sit behind the counter, only for a few hours."

"If you want to come back, call me and either I'll come pick you up or I'll send Raymond to get you."

"Deal."

She walked over to me, grabbed the lapels of my jacket, and did her best to pull me down. After giving me a quick peck that did nothing to quench the unending thirst I had for her, she whispered against my lips. "I think I like it when you worry about me. It's really hot, Jack."

With a new sparkle in her eyes, she bit her lip, and I realized she was both seducing me and backing away from me at the same time. Stopping that nonsense, I pulled her back against me and met her waiting lips with a better and longer kiss than she'd given me. We were both out of breath, and my cock had very different ideas about how we should spend the day. I forced myself to let her go and took her to her beloved coffee shop.

During lunch time, I found myself on her doorstep with three damn bouquets full of roses. She was sitting behind the register, chatting and laughing with Sally. The shop was full of people, both at the tables and at the bar. She came alive in this place, looked perfect with a smile on her face, and I was happy I'd had a part in giving it to her—no matter *how* I'd had a part in doing so.

It was then, right at that moment, that I decided I wasn't going to tell her anything, because I couldn't bear the thought of losing her, not when I could see she was starting to fall for me as I was starting to fall for her too. I'd happily hide the truth and feel no regret if it meant I got to make her happy and keep her in my life.

A few people who were occupying the table in front of her small library trickled out of the coffee shop, walking around me to do so and I came unstuck. The second the bell on top of the door chimed, her head turned just so slightly, and her eyes came to me. I smiled at her, and her smile turned into a big grin. Then she noticed the flowers in my arms. Gently, she slid down the stool and came around the counter, meeting me halfway. Even though I'd dropped her off just a few hours earlier, I could hardly take my eyes off of her. I didn't think I was ever gonna get enough of that smile.

We were only inches apart when she stopped and whispered uncertainly. "Is it okay to kiss you?"

I lost my smile and frowned down at her. "What kind of question is that?"

"We haven't kissed in public since we decided to be..." She moved her hands back and forth between us. "This."

I held the back of her head and bent down to whisper into her ear. "How about we try it and see what happens." When our eyes met, hers were smiling at me. Finally, she tipped her head back, her lips met mine, and she opened her mouth to me. A few seconds into the kiss, right when it was getting better, we had to stop when a new group of customers walked in.

"There," I said, my voice hoarse.

"There," she echoed, her own voice husky. She grinned up at me and pulled me to the side as Sally took care of the newcomers. "The roses are for me, I assume?" she asked, bouncing on her feet a little.

Finally I remembered the damn things and handed them to her. She took them from me with a gentleness that broke my heart. The first time I'd brought her flowers on the opening day, she had done the same thing with an expression that read like she couldn't believe all of them were hers. It both pissed me off and broke my heart. I'd buy her flowers every day if it meant that look would disappear from her face in time.

Closing her eyes, she smelled a white rose. "Can this be your Monday thing? If you're gonna buy them every Monday, that is. I mean, if you do, can you be the one who brings them over? Instead of the florist?"

"If that's what you want, I can do that, Rose," I said softly.

She nodded slowly; I knew she didn't like to jostle her head too much.

"Can you wait for a second? I'll leave these in the kitchen and come right back. Wait, all right?"

"I'm not going anywhere."

She rushed away at a slower pace than her usual and came back out a moment later.

"Just put them in some water. Also, they delivered the wreaths this morning. Garlands and other stuff for the front door to replace the roses will be delivered tomorrow."

I looked at the windows but didn't see anything hanging.

"I didn't put them up yet," she clarified.

I focused on her. "And you're not gonna put them up."

She laughed. "No, I won't. I know. I meant I didn't let Owen put them up. I thought maybe you and I could…"

I couldn't help it—I leaned down and kissed her again. "Yes. You and I. It's always you and I from now on."

To my surprise, she rose up on her toes and hugged me. Carefully, I wrapped my hands around her waist and plastered her to my body, holding tight. Her hair smelled of pears, it was her new shampoo, and I found myself closing my eyes and breathing in her scent. Too soon, she let go and dropped back down to her heels.

"What was that for?"

She ran her hands down my chest, adjusting my tie as she shrugged. "Just because. And I feel fine. You don't have to take me back to the apartment just yet. Sally and Owen are doing all the real work."

"That's not why I came," I lied. I *had* come to check up on her and see if she wanted to go back home. Just in case she wanted to leave or wasn't feeling okay, I wanted to be the one who took care of her, not Raymond.

"Oh?"

"I wanted to have lunch with you, but if you're busy—"

Her eyebrows rose and her smile widened. "No, not busy at all. It can be like a date—our first date."

"Date?" I asked in an uncertain tone. I wasn't so sure about that.

The bell over the door chimed and her smiling eyes shifted in that direction. In just a second, right in front of me, all the color in her face drained and her expression went blank until she looked nothing like my Rose. I looked over my shoulder.

Joshua Landon.

He was staring at Rose, and she was staring right back.

I couldn't believe what I was seeing. Rage like I'd never known rolled through me. It took a lot for me not to pummel him where he was standing.

When Rose moved, my hand shot out and I caught her elbow. She met my eyes, her hand covering mine. "It's okay, Jack."

No. No, it wasn't okay.

Joshua made it to our side.

"Hawthorne." He inclined his head to me then turned his entire focus on Rose. When my fingers were starting to curl, forming fists, I had to let go of Rose's arm before my grip could hurt her. Instead, I linked our fingers together and faced Joshua like that. He noticed it, as I wanted him to, but his only reaction was a fleeting grin I was just itching to wipe off of his smug face.

"Rose."

"What are you doing here, Joshua?" she asked, her grip around my fingers just as tight as mine around hers.

"I heard you had a little health problem. I wanted to see how you were doing, and, well..." His hands in his pockets, he looked around the coffee shop with an appreciative smile and shrugged. "I also wanted to see your place. You wanted this for such a long time, and I'm glad you finally made it happen, honey."

I started to draw in slow and steady breaths. The endearment coming from his lips kept echoing in my brain. He was goading me. It was only by sheer luck that I was holding myself together when I wanted to kill him.

"I had surgery, and I'm fine. Where did you hear about it?"

"Here and there."

Roses's fingers tightened around mine.

"If I had known before, I would have visited you at the hospital. I hate to think you were going through that alone. But then again, you like to be alone, don't you."

Rose took a side step and rested her shoulder against my arm. We looked like an unbreakable unit in front of him, and I liked that. "Thank you for your concern, but I wasn't alone. My husband was with me."

The son of a bitch tilted his head and fully took me in. When the smug bastard smiled, my jaw clenched, and without even realizing what I was doing, I took a step forward, only to feel Rose's arm wrap around mine to keep me in place.

"Your husband. Right. I can see that," he murmured with amusement.

"How is my cousin, Joshua?" Rose asked, surprising both me and Joshua, it seemed.

"She..." He faltered, eyes flitting my way. "She's good. Rose, I want you to know it wasn't anything we had planned, and it had nothing to do with—"

"I don't need or want your explanation. It's not my business what either one of you does."

More customers trickled in, and Sally called out to Rose. After a quick look shot my way, she went to see what Sally wanted. Leaving me with Joshua.

I fisted my hand, my eyes fixed on him.

"You son of a bitch," I whispered.

He chuckled and shook his head.

"If I were you, I'd watch my words. The next time I show up

you might not be here and who knows what will come up. So if I were you, I'd answer my calls."

Before I could slip in a word, Rose came back to my side.

Joshua turned his attention to her. "You seem to be busy so I won't keep you any longer. I just wanted to see that you were okay with my own eyes. I know I made a mistake in the end Rose, but you can't even imagine how hard it was for me."

He leaned forward, and every muscle in my body tensed.

Rose leaned back before he could get to her, and Joshua somehow feigned a very believable hurt expression as he sighed and said, "I deserved that."

Rose chuckled and I turned my confused gaze to her. "You're a joke. Seriously? I mean seriously? God, you have no idea how thankful I'm that you dumped me. Have a good day," Rose said, ice in her tone.

"I deserved that too," Joshua murmured, but there was a hardness in his eyes. He didn't like what he heard at all.

He nodded to her once and then to me. Without another word, he walked out the door. The blood in my veins was boiling. Him showing up had been a show for me. A warning.

If Rose hadn't been holding on to me, I would've followed him.

"Wait for me," Rose ordered firmly. "I'll be right back."

I looked down at her in confusion.

"Sally needs my help. You don't have to leave yet, do you?" she asked, mistaking my silence for something else.

"No," I grumbled, and then I cleared my throat. "No, I'll wait."

After the new customers had grabbed their orders and were heading to the empty table, Rose got back to me.

"I don't want to talk about it. I don't even know why he thought coming here would be a good idea, but I don't care. I won't spend a single second talking about him."

"I wasn't going to say anything," I lied. "Only...I don't want you to talk to him again."

"You'll hear no arguments from me. Good. So...do you want to wait for a table to open, or do you want to eat with me in the kitchen?"

"What do you want to do?"

The smile that had been missing ever since Joshua Landon had walked in came back out for me again. "Kitchen. I like having you all to myself."

It was one of the best things I had heard in all my life, if not the absolute best.

In the following days, Rose and I never talked about her ex's sudden appearance, but *I* did have a private talk with him without her knowledge, for the last time.

CHRISTMAS EVE WAS nothing special compared to how others celebrated it. It was just the two of us, as neither one of us had family to celebrate it with. There had been an office party I could've taken her to, but she wasn't completely back to herself yet, she still got headaches if she skipped her medicine, and I didn't want her on her feet for more than a few hours.

As a last minute surprise, I brought in a small Christmas tree and enough ornaments to decorate the whole damn house if we wanted. It was a tradition I wanted to share with her. The smile that bloomed on her face when she saw me and Steve hauling the tree into the apartment was priceless. Her laughter that rung through the apartment as we decorated it together made it one of the best days of my life.

So, it was just us in front of the TV after we cooked together and then ate together. She fell asleep with her head on my shoulder around nine PM, twenty minutes into the movie she had picked for us to watch. When it ended, I woke her up with a kiss on her neck.

She walked in front of me all the way up the stairs, and I followed. We were both quiet. I shoved my hands in my pockets and stood in front of her door as she leaned back against the wall.

Neither of us wanted to say goodbye, so we stood there, looking into each other's eyes and waiting for the other to do or say something that would keep us together longer.

"It was a good day. I really enjoyed cooking with you."

"You didn't cook, Rose. You sat on the counter and stole my carrots and roasted potatoes."

"But you fed them to me yourself."

"You stole more than what I gave you."

"I shared my roasted chestnuts with you."

I nodded and my eyes fell to her lips. "You did."

"So do you want to make it a regular thing?"

"You mean where I cook for you and you steal from my preparations?"

She grinned and nodded enthusiastically.

"Sure. Why not."

We stared at each other for a few seconds. I had no idea what she was thinking, but there were a few things crossing my mind.

"I should go," she mumbled, but she didn't make a move to leave. "Merry Christmas, Jack Hawthorne." She leaned up, placed her hand on my chest, and softly kissed my lips. It was over in three seconds. It was over too soon.

"Merry Christmas, Rose Hawthorne." Then it was my turn to kiss her. It maybe lasted five, six seconds.

"Good night Jack." She leaned up again, and we went for another kiss as I tried to hide my smile and kiss her back at the same time. On this round, she let her tongue tangle with mine and cupped my cheek. When I opened my eyes, hers were still closed. She sighed and licked her lips. They were already red. They were perfect.

I smiled down at her, but she missed it.

She fisted my sweater with one hand and dropped her forehead to my chest. My smile widened and I wrapped one of my hands around her waist, using the other to tilt her chin up.

"What are you thinking, Rose?"

She let out a long breath and then grimaced. "That I really want you."

I arched an eyebrow, the admission coming out of nowhere and kicking me in the stomach.

"And we are married, but we haven't even gone out on a real, official date yet. I really want to have sex with you, but I'm not allowed to do that yet. I feel like everything is going the wrong way with us. It's all backward, and it's frustrating the hell out of me."

"You want to have sex with me?" I asked, still stuck on that. Evidently we were thinking the same thing. She didn't realize I'd taken a step forward and she was now backed up against the wall.

"Really, really bad."

My heart hammering in my chest, I leaned my head down and whispered in her ear. "Tell me how bad."

She arched away from my lips, and I noticed the goose bumps on the skin of her arms. Mirroring me, she put her hands on my neck and pulled me down to her so she could whisper back. "I don't think I can put it into words, Jack."

It struck me that even though we were alone in this big apartment, we were acting like we were quickly running out of space. It was just the two of us, yet still we were whispering as if we wanted to make sure no one could hear our thoughts.

No one could hear our wants.

No one *but* us. We didn't want to share anything.

We wanted it to be just us.

Rose and Jack.

"Your suits make me go crazy. Your frown?" She let out a small groan and pulled me down farther until her lips were grazing my ear with each word out of her mouth. "Your frown kills me, Jack. Every time you frown, it does things to me, and then you roll up your sleeves and I feel like I'm watching porn specifically made for my eyes. You kiss me...you kiss me and you're not a turtle anymore. You're so good at it that whenever you kiss me, whenever I think about you kissing me, I get so wet and I don't want to stop. I don't ever want to stop kissing you."

"Rose," I growled, my cock already hard.

My arm still around her waist, I pulled her flush against my body. Her shoulders still pressed against the wall, she arched her back and kept whispering into my ear.

"That's not even half of it, Jack Hawthorne. Whenever we're walking somewhere or just walking next to each other, you always put your hand on the small of my back, and even that little gesture turns me on. I get the goose bumps just because you're touching me."

My hand *was* resting at the small of her back, so I curled my fingers, bunching her soft sweater until I heard her gasp. I nuzzled her cheek and she moved her hands from my neck up into my hair, keeping me in place. We were both breathing hard and when I took her lips, our kiss was nothing like the innocent ones we had shared just a few minutes earlier. We both took from each other, our tongues ravenous, our lust unending.

When I swallowed her groan, I put my hand right under her ass and she lifted her legs, one by one, wrapping them around my hips. After I was sure she wouldn't drop them, I put one of my hands behind her head so she wouldn't get hurt and crushed us into the wall, my cock pressing right between her legs.

She turned her head away, her breathing almost as ragged as mine. I kissed and nipped her, tracing along her jawline and neck and then gently sucking on her skin. She moved her hips and I had to push harder into her so she couldn't, which didn't help at all. My control was shot to hell, and I was afraid if she rolled her hips one more time, I would have no choice but to take her—to hell with what the doctor said.

"Jack." She moaned my name as if she had done so her entire life, and I buried my head in her neck so I could at least try to control my breathing.

"Stop talking," I ordered.

She didn't listen. I didn't think she ever listened to me.

"You feel so good against me," she whispered, sliding her temple against mine, adding more fuel to my fire.

Involuntarily, I rocked my hips, and her moan spurred me on. She was in my arms, I could smell her need, could smell her skin, and I still couldn't have her, not yet. Seemed like this was my life story when it came to her.

"How many months since the surgery?" I managed to get out in a hoarse voice.

"What?" she asked dazedly.

I looked into her eyes and they were already glazed, much like what I expected mine looked like. I took her mouth in another long kiss until I couldn't remember my own name.

"How many months, Rose?"

"Not three yet," she whispered, out of breath. "Not three."

My breaths coming out in short bursts, I pressed my forehead against hers and tried to gain some sort of control back. She didn't let me.

"You bring me flowers every Monday." She gasped, one arm wrapped around my neck, the other one grasping my hair. "And every time you come in with your arms full of such beautiful roses, I just want to grab your hand, dump the flowers, and take you into the bathroom in the back so you can...so I can..."

"Don't say another word," I growled.

"Everything you do is starting to drive me crazy. I see you in my dreams and I wake up so frustrated because it feels so real and I can't have that in the real world. I can't have you."

I pulled back, my chest heaving. Hers was too, but I wasn't sure if my heavy breathing was because of her words or her tongue and taste.

"You have me, Rose. You've had me the entire time." She didn't even know how true my words were.

She made a guttural sound in the back of her throat, a frustrated and lust-filled sound. "I don't have you. I have nothing. I'm your wife, but I can't have you."

"Just a little longer," I whispered, pressing hard kisses against her lips. "Just a little longer, Rose. Then you'll have everything and more."

"No. Now. Please."

"No."

"Jack."

"No."

Groaning, I kissed her, hard, one last time for now, and gently put her back down on her feet. My hand was still protecting the back of her head, so I dropped my forehead against hers and just breathed her air in, trying to calm myself down. Looming over her, invading her space, there was nowhere else I'd have rather been in that moment.

"I want you," she said, her voice so small I could feel something breaking inside me. "I want you more than anything I've ever wanted in my life."

"That's a lot of want. Mrs. Hawthorne." I cupped her cheeks with my palms and closed my eyes. "I've been craving you for so long I don't know what to do with myself anymore."

She was the first to speak after both our breaths had somewhat returned to normal again.

"What are you doing on New Year's? We should do this again."

Despite the painful situation I was in since my cock hadn't given up that easily, I laughed and took a step back.

"I'm spending it with my beautiful Rose," I said, and then I finally walked away.

AFTER SPENDING ten minutes out on the terrace in the freezing cold, I'd just lain down on the bed when my phone pinged.

Rose: Are you awake?
Jack: Yes.
Rose: Me too. Thanks for asking.
Jack: Rose.
Rose: Fine. You need to sleep with me.
Jack: Rose.
Rose: You don't have to Rose me. I don't mean like that. Ever since the hospital, I've wanted to ask you to stay with me. I got used to it back in the hospital, got used to sleeping next to you, but when you didn't get in bed with me the first night we were back...
Rose: I couldn't ask. Now I'm asking.

I didn't feel the need to write anything back.

She didn't realize she wouldn't have had to ask me every day. Once would've been enough. I didn't intend to spend my nights in a different bed than she was in.

Getting up from the bed, I opened my door and came face to face with my Rose.

"Hi, fancy seeing you here. My room or yours?" she asked as if this was completely normal.

I sighed and shook my head. "Let's go to yours then."

As soon as she was in bed, she turned to watch me.

Lifting the other end of the covers, I got in after her. She settled on her back and stared at the ceiling.

I was in the same position, the only difference being that she had two pillows to keep her head high during the night and I only had one. Raising my right arm, I put it under my head and rested my left hand on my stomach.

"We're going to sleep," Rose said.

"Yes," I agreed. "We're only going to sleep. Just like we did at the hospital."

"Yes," she echoed in a small voice.

Seconds passed in silence.

She scooted an inch closer and turned onto her side, tucking her hands under her face. She had gotten the go-ahead from the doctor to sleep on her side just the week before, and she'd been over the moon about it for two full days.

"Jack?"

Closing my eyes, I sighed. Her bed smelled like her, her pillow smelled like her, the room smelled like her, and she was too close to stay away for too long—not that I wanted to, but more like had to.

"Hmmm."

"We didn't sleep this far apart at the hospital."

"That was a small bed—I didn't have anywhere else to go."

"Why would you want to go anywhere else?"

Great question.

She scooted even closer. Then, before I could do anything about it, she rolled over and gave me her back, fitting herself against the length of my body. I rolled over and threw my arm over her stomach, tucking my hand under her waist, keeping her as close as possible.

Around her, there was no concept of self-control.

I hid my face in her neck and breathed her in.

"This is better?"

"It's perfect. Thank you."

A few minutes passed in silence then she was back at me again.

"Jack? Are you asleep?"

I sighed, sure there would be no sleeping in my future. I didn't mind it at all.

She grabbed my hand and placed my palm on her stomach. Her shirt had ridden up, and my hand connected with her hot, smooth skin. She didn't take her hand away.

"Rose," I groaned.

"You can say it as many times as you want, Jack," she whispered. "I love your voice, so please keep going."

Smiling, I kissed her neck and pressed my forehead against the back of her head. "You have no idea what you do to me, do you?"

I had made sure to keep my hips away from hers, but she moved her lower body back until her butt was nestled against my hard cock.

"I can feel it."

It wasn't just my cock, though—it was everything. She was wreaking havoc everywhere.

Her hand still on top of mine, she started to push it down, and when my fingers touched the edge of her panties, I pressed my hand harder into her stomach and stopped the descent. When had she taken off her leggings? How had I not noticed it before?

"What are you doing, Rose?"

"Nothing. You showed me yours and I'm showing you mine."

"What are you talking about?" I whispered, my fingers digging into her soft skin.

In the name of getting closer, she backed up into me, making her meaning clearer.

I was dying to touch her, so when she pushed harder on my hand, I didn't have a good enough reason to stop her a second time.

Holding my breath, I let her move my hand to wherever she wanted. She was having mercy on me—either that or she wanted to torture me. Instead of pushing my hand under her panties, she lifted her leg just slightly and pushed until my hand was resting right over where I wanted to bury myself deep. Her panties were soaked. *She* was soaked, for me.

I closed my eyes tighter. I couldn't stop myself from wanting more, not when we were like this.

"Don't you want me, Jack?" she whispered into the dark room, and it broke the hold I had over myself.

I gripped her ruined panties in a tight hold and just ripped them off of her.

Her little gasp of shock did nothing but spur me on.

"Don't I want you?" I asked, my voice raw and harsh. Tossing the now completely ruined panties aside, I placed my hand back on her sensitive skin. Resting the heel of my hand on her mound, I let my fingers part her folds and just lazily ran them up and down in her slickness.

"Happy now?" I asked, harsher than I expected.

"Are you scowling at me?"

"Are you making fun of me?"

"Never," she whispered, pushing her top leg back and over mine, opening herself up to me, letting me have what I was craving. "I love it when you scowl at me."

I nipped her neck, dragging my teeth over her skin. She shivered, causing her butt to push harder against my hips.

"I won't fuck you, Rose. I won't give you more than this." I found her clit and moved the tip of my finger around it, barely grazing.

"I'll take it," she gasped out. "Whatever you can give, I'll take it."

"What do you want then? Tell me."

"You—I want you."

My fingers stopped moving and I cupped her.

She turned her head, her shoulders almost flat on the bed, and looked into my eyes. She was halfway there; I could see it in her gaze, in what I could make out of her flushed cheeks. I pushed two of my fingers inside her and her body tightened, eyes falling closed. God, she was slick, so slick and tight.

"I want to feel your lips against mine, Jack," she whispered.

I closed the distance between us but didn't kiss her. "The way you kiss me makes me lose my mind," I whispered back. I wasn't even sure if my words had been audible or in my head, but my lips were against hers and I was only a man. I pulled my fingers out and plunged them back into her, slowly, catching her breathy little gasp and drowning her in my kiss. The tip of her tongue touched mine and I was lost. I wanted to grab her chin and hold her mouth where I wanted it, but my hand was busy between her legs and I had already lost my head.

When her fingers grasped my forearm in an unforgiving grip, her fingernails biting into my skin, I knew she was getting closer, and it hadn't even been a minute yet. I curved my fingers up and found the spot that caused her to kiss me deeper and harder, the spot that made her groans wilder. I responded back in kind, lost in everything that was Rose.

She was a mess down there, her wetness running down my fingers. She widened her legs, giving me more room to play with her. My thumb found her clit and I pressed hard.

She wrenched her mouth away from me, panting. "Keep

them in," she moaned. "Please, not yet. Just keep your fingers in me. Deeper, please."

I pressed as far as my fingers would go, which was *deep*.

I listened to the sounds she made, mesmerized—how could I not? *Why* would I not?

"My brain is tingling," she murmured, clearly half out of it.

I was moving my fingers in her in small, light movements but stopped at her words.

"Rose we sh— "

She covered my hand with hers before I could think or gather the strength to pull out. "If you stop, I'll kill you in your sleep, Jack Hawthorne. Don't you dare."

"Rose, if you feel—"

"I'm being serious, Jack. I'll murder you. Please make me come on your fingers. Please. Please."

"You're a vicious little thing, aren't you? And all mine."

I took her begging lips and fucked her with my fingers like I couldn't fuck her with my cock. I was still being as gentle as I could, but I went as deep as possible, and her body got tighter and tighter against me.

And when she came...

God, when she came it was the most beautiful thing I'd ever seen in my life. Her little gasps and moans were killing me, but I took them all from her until the only things heard in the room were our labored breaths and the sound her now even more soaked pussy was making.

Her body slowly melting in my arms, she twisted her upper body toward me, held my head, and kissed me in slow, maddening nips. Her hips were still twitching as I pulled my fingers out and wiped my hand on the sheets. When she turned completely, I hauled her up against me and renewed the kiss until we were on the verge of passing out.

We rested our foreheads together, just breathing. Hard.

"How is your head?" I managed to ask.

"Perfect."

"Are you sure?"

"Yep. Thank you, Jack. If you hadn't given me that, I think I was going to die."

I was dying a slow death so I understood what she meant.

Her hand sneaked in between us, right under my pajamas. I didn't intend to stop her. I didn't have the strength anymore.

Her palm brushed the slick head of my cock and she ran it up and down my length, her eyes boring into mine. She bit the edge of her lip, and I could do nothing but stare. Was she really mine? Was she really my wife?

"Take me out," I whispered, and she hurried to obey, using her other hand to pull my pajamas down.

She swallowed hard when she had all my length to take care of.

"You're not gonna try to stop me?" she asked.

"What's the point? You never listen to me and we already screwed up. I want your hands on me too much to try to resist you."

"Are you saying you can't resist me?"

"I haven't been able to so far."

She nuzzled her nose against mine and breathed out my name. "Jack...I want you in me."

I grasped her head and pressed a hard kiss on her forehead. "No."

Her grip on me tightened, her fingers not quite connecting with her thumb.

"Be rough," I hissed.

There was a fire burning in her eyes, and I couldn't have looked away even if I'd wanted to.

"Is that how you're going to fuck me? Rough and deep?"

"If that's how you like it, yes—as deep as I can get." She

moved her tight grip all the way to the base and then moved all the way up to the top agonizingly slowly. After the second tug, she tried to slip under the covers, but I stopped her. "No."

"Why?"

"As much as I'd love to have your mouth on me, you can't do that, not yet."

"You're killing me, Jack Hawthorne."

"You already killed me when you came all over my hands. We'll call it even."

Her tug danced on the edge of being painful and I loved it. She picked up her pace, staring straight into my eyes.

"I can't wait to be in you," I whispered, holding her head in my hands. "I can't wait to take you in any way I can, to make love to you for hours until I know you're truly satisfied and make you moan and cry out my name. I can't wait, Rose. I can't wait to have you, to push into you and feel you come around me."

She groaned. "We should do it now."

"No. You're gonna love it. I'll make sure of it." My eyes on hers, I whispered, "Faster, Rose. Just like that. Come on. Make me come."

She slowed down, her thumb brushed the head, and my eyes dropped closed.

"I want to taste you so badly."

"One more month," I forced out. "One more month and I'll let you."

With slow but sharp thrusts, I started to thrust into her hold, and suddenly she wrapped both her hands around me to keep her grip tighter.

"Yes," I hissed out then dragged my lips along her jaw. She turned her head and started another kiss. I sucked on her tongue and kept moving my hips. Ending the kiss, she kept her already glazed eyes on me, watching me intently as I asked, "Do you want me to come?"

She hummed in her throat and nodded.

"Yeah? Keep going," I moaned, already on edge. I wrapped my hand around hers and she dropped the other one. I slowed down our strokes, making our grasp tighter and pulling harder. A second later, I came all over her stomach with a loud groan, and it was more than I'd ever come. I let go of my cock as soon as I was done, but she didn't. She kept her strokes light until I had to pull her hand away because instead of losing my size, I was starting to get hard again.

"I think you've had enough of that," I whispered against her lips.

"I don't think I'll ever have enough of that." She let me breathe in and out in silence for a moment as I caught my breath. "I'm going to count the days till you can take me, Jack."

My countdown had already started.

CHAPTER TWENTY-THREE

ROSE

It had been two months and twenty-five days since my surgery, and it was a Friday.

So, we had finally reached the end of three months. Some days I'd thought we'd never get to see the day, and I'd told Jack exactly that. I'd never in my life told another guy I wanted to have sex with them as much as I'd told Jack. In the beginning, I had thought my constant pressure was affecting him and he'd soon fold, but nope. Jack was nothing if not in control of his emotions.

He had slept right next to me every night without me having to ask for it again. If I went to bed earlier than him, he always found his way into my bed, but he hadn't touched me the way I was dying for him to touch me again. He said *no* and nothing else.

I came back down to earth when Sally snapped her fingers in front of my face.

"Are you here?"

"Yes. Yes, sorry. I just got distracted. What were you saying about Owen again?"

Owen was currently in the kitchen so there was no way for him to hear us, but Sally still leaned in closer. "I think he likes me."

"I thought he wasn't talking to you."

"Technically he isn't."

I laughed. "Your logic scares me sometimes."

A couple walked in hand in hand so we had to break up our little gossip bubble. Suddenly, I wasn't so sure if it had been a good idea to give the go-ahead to Sally about Owen. I kinda felt sorry for him.

As I got the orders of the newcomers and cut two pieces of apple pie for them, Sally prepared one cappuccino and one macchiato. They picked up their orders and sat down at the last table available in the left part of the coffee shop.

"I'm thinking of getting two or three more tables. Most days we barely have any space left, and I think we can easily squeeze in three more—one more on this side, maybe even two, and another two on the other side."

Sally leaned her elbows on the counter, humming. "I think you're right. Ever since that blogger posted about us on Instagram, we've started getting even more customers, and even if they don't come in, they keep taking photos outside the front door."

Right then the bell chimed and our heads turned that way.

"Jack!" I called out, perhaps a little too enthusiastically, and he paused in the doorway. Half of the customers who didn't have their earbuds in turned to look at me.

Ignoring Sally's snort and chuckle, I gave the customers an apologetic smile and rushed to Jack's side as he closed the door and met me halfway. I was half running, half trying to appear like I wasn't running at all, and he was just walking, in no hurry.

"What's going on?" he asked with an arched eyebrow and a suspicious look around the coffee shop. Even that look and that lifted brow turned me on. To be honest, lately, everything Jack did turned me on. He'd give me a look, a strong look that said he didn't find me amusing at all, and I'd become a puddle on the ground. It was becoming a thing for me.

"Come, come." I reached for his hand and when he linked our fingers together, my smile turned up a notch, making me look like an idiot. I didn't mind it at all.

"Hello, Sally," Jack said as I took him behind the counter.

Still with that knowing grin on her face, Sally waved at him. She thought I'd scored with Jack. I thought so too.

"He's going to steal me for a few minutes," I told Sally then pulled him to the back.

"Who said I wanted to steal you?" Jack murmured into my ear, amused. I barely managed to stop a shiver.

"I'm saying it because you *should* want to steal me—all the time, regularly. Just a friendly reminder from a wife to a husband."

Owen looked up from the paper he was scribbling on and straightened up. "Hey, man."

Jack nodded and they formally shook hands. For some reason, he hadn't warmed up to Owen yet.

I leaned against Jack's arm, our hands still tightly clasped. "Can he have a minute alone with me, Owen? I told him a million times that it's not appropriate in the coffee shop, but he just looks at me..." I peered up at Jack and looked at his frowny face with a happy heart. "Just like that. You see that frown? So yeah, I can't resist him when he is glowering at me. Plus, Sally might need help if someone comes in."

Owen didn't even blink at my statement. "Yeah, sure." He picked up the paper he was working on—another list.

"Why don't you like Owen?" I asked once he was out of earshot.

"Who said I didn't like him?"

"I do. You barely say a word to him."

"He gets to spend entire days with you in here."

"So?"

"I don't," he grumbled, leaning down, his mouth entirely too close to mine.

"Jack?" I whispered, my nose bumping his.

"Hmm."

"That might be the sweetest thing you've ever said to me. Let's go crazy in the back—we have to after that comment."

He straightened up, taking that beautiful mouth away and giving me a blank look. "No."

I pulled Jack forward and stopped with my back against the island.

"At least give me a lift up, or is that too much touching for you?"

His lips twitching, he shook his head. "Always ordering me around," he murmured as he put his hands around my waist. I had instant goose bumps when he lifted me up on the island, and I pulled him between my legs.

My hands grabbing the lapels of his jacket, I pulled him closer and pressed my forehead against his. "Hi. How are you? I missed you."

His hands squeezed my waist once, moving down to my hips, sliding me an inch or two forward. "You saw me a few hours ago when I dropped you off this morning."

"I know. It's been ages." He gave me that precious smile I couldn't get enough of and my own lips mirrored his. "And you're supposed to say you missed me too. That's what husbands say."

He hummed, and the warm sound traveled all over my body. "Is that what I'm supposed to say?" His hand made its way down my thigh and he unwrapped my leg from his waist, which I hadn't even realized I had placed there...kind of. His face softened and he cupped my cheek. "You look a little tired."

I scooted forward a bit to make up for the unwrapping. I

wanted to be as close as possible. "You know how much I love it when you compliment me on how good I look. Tell me more."

He pulled back and gave me a pointed look that pretty much said he wasn't having it.

I hauled him back. "I'm fine. I promise I sit down before I get dizzy, and I'm sitting right now too. I haven't baked a thing either. Would you like to know what else good husbands do?"

"Good husbands," he mumbled, his hands moving up and down on my back. I did my best not to squirm.

"They kiss their wives when they see them."

"They do?"

"Yeah. I'm told it's a tradition."

He licked his lips, and because I was trying to fuse myself to him, his tongue touched my lips too. Letting go of his jacket before I could wrinkle it too much, I wrapped my arms around his neck, already having trouble remembering how to breathe like a normal person.

"Good thing I'm not your real husband then," Jack said.

My mouth dropped open and I let go of him, feigning shock. "Jack Hawthorne, did you just make a joke?"

"Smartass," he muttered with a smile, his eyes dancing. It seemed I was making him happy. Every time he smiled it loosened something in me.

"You may kiss me now," I whispered, ready for it, desperate and impatient for it, and then he finally did so. I quickly wrapped my arms back around him again and gladly returned his kiss. Unfortunately, he put a stop to it in no time.

"Hello, my beautiful wife," he whispered, and I felt a little better since he was out of breath too. It wasn't just me who was affected.

I heard the bell chime and more chatter trickled into our private little bubble. We weren't alone, though I kept forgetting that when he was around.

"That's slightly better," I commented, my hands on his shoulders.

"Are you ready?" he asked.

"I'm buying new tables," I announced instead of responding to his question.

He frowned. "What?"

"New tables—we need them. We're always full and we have the space too, so I'm buying new tables." I smiled widely. "Yay!"

"That's good, baby, but—"

That word, that *baby*—hearing it for the first time from his lips caused a full body shiver. It was something about his voice that just added to the endearment. I'd never even considered that I would love to be called *baby*, but this...*this* specific one coming from this specific guy, it stopped me in my tracks. I could've spent the rest of my life just being called baby by Jack Hawthorne.

"Hmmm," I moaned in the hopes of distracting him. I leaned in and nuzzled his nose with my own, whispering against his lips, "Should I even let you know how much I love your voice? Or the way my name sounds when it comes from your lips?" I gently kissed his top lip then his lower lip, and then I went in for a deeper kiss, searching for his tongue. "That *baby* just about killed me, Jack."

"You're trying to distract me," he muttered, and I smiled because it was exactly what I was doing and it was working perfectly. I tilted my head to the side and took a big breath before going in again.

No one had ever kissed me like Jack Hawthorne did, and I didn't think I ever wanted to find out if there was anyone else out there who could.

"Why would I do that?" I whispered, my lips still touching his. I bit my lip. "Don't get angry, I'm not saying we should act on it, but I really want you, Jack. Just so you know."

I felt his smile against my mouth and then his warm chuckle. The sound made my heart sigh in happiness.

"Really? I had no idea. You only say and text it every day, a couple times a day."

"And you never say it, or text it, or do it."

"Because I can control myself."

I kissed him again, taking it slow, coaxing him. "You're very good at that."

He smiled into our kiss, nipping at my lips.

I leaned forward until my lips were right next to his ear. "But I want to hear you say you want me. Tell me you want me, Jack. At least give me that much."

I drew back and looked into his eyes. I could see the sparkle in his beautiful deep blues.

"You think I don't want you?"

Keeping my eyes on his, I slowly shrugged. His jaw clenched and he looked toward the doorway where I could hear Sally steaming milk and Owen talking to a customer. I didn't care about where we were, not really, not when I was with Jack. Whenever he was around me, I felt like I was on top of the world, and the fact that he always brushed me off because he was genuinely worried about my health only intensified my need for him. I didn't think he was indifferent at all, but I liked pushing him. I especially liked watching his eyes flare up every time I told him I wanted him.

"You make me forget my name when you kiss me," he whispered into my ear. "Wanting you is all I've been doing, and when I finally fuck you like I've wanted to—"

Every time he said fuck with that rough voice of his, my eyes fluttered closed on their own. Before I could learn what was going to happen when I was finally fucked by my husband, Sally walked in on us.

"Rose, do you think you could—oh, I'm sorry. Sorry. Ah, I'll wait out here."

I rested my head on Jack's shoulder and groaned.

He cleared his throat and tilted my chin up. "We need to be at the hospital in an hour."

"But I thought today—"

He arched an eyebrow. "I reminded you just this morning, before you ran out of the car, so don't try to act like you don't know what I'm talking about. They scheduled your MRI and your antibiotic shot for today. We need to be there in an hour."

I cupped his face with both my hands. It was on the tip of my tongue to tell him I loved him, and I didn't even know where the thought had come from. I knew I was falling for him, but I hadn't realized I was already there. "Okay. All jokes aside, I love that you're taking care of me," I said seriously. "I've never had that before. I'm sorry if I'm pushing you too much. You know I never really had family, but you—"

He kissed me, a quick and hard and fierce kiss. "What am I? Chopped liver? You could never push me too much. Don't ever stop pushing me."

I smiled and let him put me down back on my feet. "I'll go see what Sally wants and then I'll get my bag so we can leave."

"I'm sorry, Rose."

Something in his voice made me turn back to him. "Sorry? For what?"

"I know you don't want the MRI, but they need to see if everything looks okay. I need to know if everything is okay."

I walked back to him and rose up on my toes so I could press what was my version of a quick and hard kiss on his lips, and I melted a little when he put his hand on the small of my back and pulled me against his body.

"You'll stay with me again?"

"Always."

"Then it'll be okay. I know I'm being stupid about it. It helps that you'll be there when it's over to carry me away."

The car ride was fun, and I tried my best to look as if I wasn't freaking out about the fact that I was going back in that casket again. We sat hand in hand the entire time, and Jack even made a comment or two about Raymond's love life when we were having a very serious talk on that very subject. Too bad I was too anxious to enjoy it all.

But then the MRI scan...it was no better than the first time. Even though I was required to lie on my back this time, they still put the cage thing on my head, and this time around I got much dizzier than the first time. I had to keep my eyes closed the entire time as I tried to focus only on Jack's touch on my ankle. As soon as they took me out and I got rid of the thing on my head, he carried me off to the small room, and just like the previous time, he let me cry on him for a good two minutes. The last time I'd done that, we hadn't been real. This time, we were, and it made me feel better because he kissed every drop of my tears away, stealing more pieces of my heart in the process.

"Where do you want me to take you?" Jack asked once we were back in the car.

The needle part hadn't been fun either; it had hurt like hell, which you could easily tell from my ashen face and the hand I kept pressing on my arm. Since my brain had been kind of exposed with the tear, preventing infection was important. That'd been what they kept telling me, so I knew there was no way to get out of it—not that I had tried to get out of it or anything. I'd never.

"Rose?"

This time, we weren't sitting so close.

I looked at him. "Home. I want to go home. I'll text Sally and Owen. I don't feel like I'd be any help there, and I don't want to bring the energy down."

"Okay," he said simply and then told Raymond where to take us.

Back in the building, Jack said hello to Steve and asked him how he was doing. I couldn't help it—I cracked my first post-MRI smile. To think I'd been the one to tell him what his own door-man's name was.

"How is the kid doing?" I asked, wrapping my arm around Jack's and standing in front of Steve.

"She's good, back at the new school."

"No more problems I hope."

"So far it's been okay."

"That's good."

Steve's daughter, Bella, was this beautiful and smart fifteen-year-old who had been bullied at her old school and ended up changing schools midyear.

"Please tell her I'm looking forward to seeing her again."

"She'll love hearing that. She adores you."

Even though I had heard about her situation from the heart-broken Steve and obviously already knew some about her, we'd only met twice when she had come to visit her father for a few hours. We'd bonded over our love of baking and rain, of all things, because it had been pouring in New York both days. We'd come up with over twenty-five reasons why we loved rain and rainy days when I had wandered down from Jack's apartment because I'd been bored out of my mind just sitting, sitting, sitting.

Jack had found me on the floor with Bella and had taken me back upstairs because it was 'cold' and I wasn't healthy enough to sit my *ass* on cold floors. That had been original, especially hearing the word ass coming from his mouth.

"And I adore her. She is a smart cookie. If it's okay with you, I'd love it if she could come to my coffee shop. Maybe we could bake together if she feels up to it? Then I'd bring her back here, of course."

"You don't have to do that. I know how busy you are."

"Of course I don't *have* to do it. I *want* to. We'll bake and spend a few hours together. It'll be fun."

"Thank you, Mrs. Hawthorne. She'll love that."

Back in the elevator, Jack was the first to break our silence. "Does he call you Mrs. Hawthorne every time you talk or is it just my presence that changes things?"

I gave him a sheepish grin and he just shook his head. "I like the sound of it, though."

"The sound of what?"

"Mrs. Hawthorne. I like it when you say it too."

The doors opened to his floor before he could respond, and we walked into the apartment.

All I wanted to do was go upstairs, take a shower so I could feel like a normal human being again, and take a long, long nap. So, that's what I decided to go ahead and do. I took off my shoes next to the door and headed straight for the stairs.

"I'll jump in the shower and just try to get myself back together." I turned around and started walking backward, my eyes on Jack. "Would you like to join me?"

"Rose."

One word, my name, which had gained a new meaning lately. It meant no.

"I meant for cleaning purposes only, but suit yourself, buddy. Do you have work to do? You came to the hospital with me and now you're here so I'm guessing you need to catch up with things because of me."

"I'll be in my office."

"Okay. I'll come bug you as soon as I'm done." Waving at him, I finally turned back around and trotted up the stairs.

"Rose?"

I looked down at Jack, my husband who was in fact not my husband, who had held my ankle during the entire MRI scan and then wrapped me in his arms while whispering that I was okay, that we were okay again and again in the privacy of a little hospital room. I didn't think he understood how much it meant to me. It was getting harder and harder with each passing day to hold myself back and not tell him what I was feeling for him, what I had been feeling for him for quite a while now.

"Yes?"

"You're good."

It wasn't a question. I wasn't sure if it was a statement or not, either. He wanted me to be good, so I'd be good, for him, so he'd feel good.

I gave him a small smile. "Never better."

"You should try harder—it doesn't seem to be working."

My smile got bigger and I saluted him, disappearing from his sight.

THERE WAS a small knock on my door before it cracked open. "Rose?"

"If you don't want to have sex with me don't come in," I warned the only person who could be knocking on my door.

Despite my warning, he opened it and stood there in all his glory. Same suit, same everything, face and frown and all.

I stood there in my thankfully matching sky blue bra and panties. I was standing with the towel in my hands, and I kept standing there as his hungry eyes took in every inch of my half-naked body. I had hips, but I liked them. I liked that there was a curve to me, a curve that loved the touch of his hands. While my boobs weren't anything too spectacular, Jack didn't seem to agree. I'd never been happier to have almost C cups as I'd been when I'd caught his eyes on them a time or two. In any case, we stood just like that, him in the doorway with eyes glued to me, me in the middle of the room with my body heating. I didn't think anyone would describe me as shy, but I felt a touch of heat on my cheeks when the seconds ticked by and Jack didn't say anything.

"Hi?" I managed to croak out.

His eyes snapped to me and his jaw hardened, making him even hotter. I truly loved it when his face turned all prickly and frustrated and angry and arrogant and heated and hungry and annoyed and *all* the things. "Hi," he forced out.

Gulping, I brought the towel I had been using to dry my hair to my front and somewhat tried to conceal my nakedness. It wouldn't help much with anything because it was only a little bigger than a hand towel.

"How can I help you?" I groaned on the inside. Me being horny was all the doctor's fault. I'd never in my life asked any of my boyfriends if they were in the mood to have sex, let alone begged someone to have sex with me as much as I'd begged Jack.

There was something about him. Maybe if we had done it once, I would have stopped thinking and talking about it all the time. Maybe he'd be excruciatingly bad—but I knew he wouldn't be. I knew what he'd do to me, and I couldn't wait.

"Are you free for dinner?" His voice was still tight, as was his grip on the door handle, and that was a question I hadn't heard in a while.

"I'll have to check my schedule."

I didn't move. Then I smiled, making my way to him. It wasn't a seductive smile or anything like that; I wasn't trying to be sexy at all. I honestly wouldn't have known how or what to do to begin to seduce a guy like Jack. I'd imagine for a guy like him to be impressed, you'd have to pull out all the stops, maybe do a light striptease as you were walking toward him and then just go for it. Or, what would be even better...you'd be so spectacular that he'd just couldn't stop himself and go for *you*.

He hadn't gone for me, hence why I kept mentioning it. Basically I was trying to seduce him by badgering him on the subject and hoped he'd get frustrated enough to actually do it just to have me shut up, because I figured that worked too.

I stopped in front of him, looking up at him and smiling. "I checked."

He arched an eyebrow, his eyes not even dipping to my boobs once. I didn't find that reassuring at all. "And?"

"I'm free. I'm free every day."

"Finally. Get ready. We're going out on a date."

As soon as he got those words out, he took a step back and slammed the door in my face. I stared at the door in shock then broke into happy laughter.

I opened the door to see his retreating back.

"Our first official date?" I yelled after him before he could get to the stairs.

"Yes," he yelled back, his voice angry. A shiver worked through my body.

"Where are we going? Can I ask?"

"No."

"Where are you going? Can I at least ask that?" I was lucky he wasn't looking back because my face was sporting the most ridiculous smile in the world.

"Out," he snapped, making his way downstairs.

"Out? Where are you going? What about our date?"

He paused on the last step and finally looked at me. I was hanging from the rail, still in my underwear, face flushed and happy.

His gaze was piercing. "I'll wait for you downstairs."

"But why are you leaving?"

"Because you're pushing me."

My mouth dropped open.

"I'm pushing you?" I took a step down the stairs. "I didn't say a thing."

"Don't come down here, Rose."

I paused.

"I'm pushing you?" I started again. "How about you coming into my room and staring at me like that?"

"How did I—never mind. I'm waiting for you downstairs. I don't trust you."

I started laughing in earnest, so happy, happy, happy. I caught his lip twitch.

"Take as much time as you need. I'll wait for you downstairs."

"Okay. Promise I won't be long. You can keep Steve company."

"Yes. How did I not think of that? I'll just go do that."

When I couldn't see him anymore, I shouted after him from my perch on the stairs. "What should I wear? What kind of date is it?"

"It's a date—what else do you need to know? And I don't care what you wear as long as you cover yourself up, neck to toe."

I did exactly that. I wore a black dress that wasn't too flashy. Short sleeves, open V neck, a relaxed fabric that gently hugged both my boobs and my hips and ended four or five inches above my knees. I roughly dried my thick hair and straightened my bangs because I wasn't interested in getting a cold from walking out the door with wet hair on a snowy New York night. I did my makeup, focusing heavily on the eyes. I wore my thick black coat and wrapped my scarf around my neck, also donning my black leather gloves. Grabbing my cream ribbed beret from the top shelf of my closet, I put it on my head and walked out of the apartment in a hurry. I couldn't exactly run yet because of my brain and nose thing, but I came close to it.

My heart jumping in my chest and my tummy filled with those excited butterflies, I felt like I was going out on my first ever date with a boy I'd had a crush on for years. It was a strange feeling being so excited about a simple date, but this was Jack

Hawthorne, my pretend husband who knew how to kiss me exactly the right way. How could I not have been excited?

When the elevator doors opened, I forced myself to take smaller steps just in case Jack was waiting for me in the lobby. He wasn't. I stopped in front of Steve.

"How do I look?"

He smiled at me and I beamed back at him. "As beautiful as ever."

"Maybe I should tone down the happy a little?"

He let out a roar of laughter. "Don't ever tone down the happy, Rose. It suits you well."

I melted a little at his words. "You're the best, Steve."

He inclined his head. "So? What's the special occasion?"

"My husband is taking me out for a date," I said proudly.

"Lucky lady. That's as special as it gets."

"Oh, you have no idea."

"Mr. Hawthorne said he'll be waiting for you outside."

"Okay." I ran my gloved hands down my coat now that there was some unexpected nervousness trickling in. "Thank you, Steve. I'll see you later?"

"I'll be right here. Have fun."

Saying a quick goodbye to the kind doorman who had become my friend, I walked out onto the street. It had started snowing again, adding to the snow- and slush-covered sidewalks. I looked up at the skies and closed my eyes, little snowflakes melting on my face, tickling me. I smiled. I felt so giddy and free. I looked around to find Jack and he was right there, on the left side of the building. He leaned against his car, right next to Raymond, studying me.

My heart soared at the sight of him, as it always did lately, and I truly felt like I hadn't ever felt any happier in my life. I couldn't help myself—I ran to his side just as he became alert and straightened up. He said something to Raymond and after nodding at Jack, Raymond opened his door and got into the driver's seat, leaving Jack to me.

I stopped right in front of him, just a tad out of breath.

He pushed my bangs out of my eyes, the tips of his fingers gently trailing the contours of my face. "You aren't supposed to run, Rose."

I moved my head up and down, and he sighed as I grinned. "So?"

"What am I gonna do with you?"

I shrugged. "Keep me?"

He reached for my beret and fixed it on my head then, with his hands cupping my face, he leaned down and kissed me. His hands were warm on my cheeks, his lips even warmer and more addictive. I grabbed his wrists to hold him there just a little longer. When we'd had a taste of each other, not enough of a taste but a small sample, he pulled back and looked into my eyes.

"You're going to be the death of me," he said with all the seriousness in the world.

And I think I love you, I wanted to say, but instead I gave him my biggest smile.

His laughter was everything to me. My eyes and heart warmed just looking at him.

He was all mine.

"Get in the car."

I repeated his own words back to him: "Always ordering me around."

He gave me a blank look with an arched eyebrow and I smiled sweetly. He opened the door and slid in right after me. I rarely sat on the other end anymore. Usually, he wanted me to be right next to him, and what do you know, so did I. At that moment, my thigh was resting against his. We were sitting that close, and I couldn't have been any happier.

I shivered a little once he closed the door, and I ran my hands up and down my arms. "It's really cold tonight."

One at a time, he picked up my gloved hands and rubbed them between his own.

Oh, I really wanted to keep him.

The car ride didn't take long, and when we were dropped off in front of the cutest little Italian restaurant, I was pleasantly surprised. To be honest, I hadn't been looking forward to heading to a crowded, fancy place. This place, however, was anything but fancy. Jack had my hand in his as we walked down two steps to enter the restaurant. All the cute little tables had those red checkered tablecloths, every table that was occupied had two small candles burning on it, and I couldn't wait to get my own candles. Jack talked to the woman who came forward to greet us, and she took us to one of the tables right in front of the big window. At the table right next to us sat a grandpa and his grandson, and they were biting into their first slices of pizza.

I could hear my stomach growling. I took off my gloves first then my beret and my scarf, and then finally my coat. Jack was in the process of pulling my chair back when he stopped moving. I pressed my lips flat and tried to keep in my smile. He cleared his throat and came unstuck. I sat down, and he took his spot across from me.

He looked at me for a long moment before he let out a long breath. "You take my breath away, Rose Hawthorne."

Whoosh—there went my own breath. That was as real and as perfect as it got. "Is this one of those times?"

"Yes."

Clearing my throat, I leaned my elbows on the table and rested my head on my hands. "That's a good start. Keep going."

He smiled then his eyes slowly dropped to my boobs.

Finally!

"I thought I told you to cover yourself up, head to toe."

"And I listened to you," I agreed easily. "I wore my coat, my scarf, my gloves, my beret. I wore everything I could wear."

"Nice try," he countered, shaking his head. "It's freezing out there—you're gonna get sick."

"I won't. It's all cozy and warm and perfect in here."

A kid who barely looked sixteen dropped off our menus, cutting into our conversation. I dropped my elbows from the table and started checking out the options. The kid next to us was chattering away and making his grandpa laugh, and it just lifted my mood even more. I looked up from the menu and around the restaurant, noticing the other few customers, and I realized we were extremely overdressed.

I leaned in toward Jack, and he looked at me quizzically. "Come here," I whispered.

"Why?"

He looked so suspicious and adorable in a grumpy way that I had to laugh. "Just lean in closer."

He did so carefully.

"I think we're a bit overdressed."

His shoulders relaxed before he looked around, and I had to bite my lip to hold in my laughter. Did he think I'd jump on him?

"I like it though," I continued before he had a chance to say anything, and his eyes came back to me. "I feel special. I know this isn't your usual type of place at all, so I appreciate that you're doing this for me even more. Thank you."

"You don't have to thank me, Rose. It's as much for me as it is for you, and it's just dinner. It doesn't matter where we are as long as we're together."

"Ah, you just killed me, and that's true. That's really true."

"I'm still glad you approve."

"Yes, you did well. You might get lucky. Eventually."

Another head shake as he put his menu down. "You don't give up, do you?"

I groaned and hid my face behind my hands. "It's not me, I promise. It's the doctor."

"What do you mean it's the doctor?" He reached out and pulled my hands down as if he couldn't not have eyes on my face —at least that was what I liked to think.

"I do want you, I'm not gonna lie about that, but I'm not like this. I'm never like this. This is only happening because he said..." Looking at the grandpa and grandson next to me, I whispered, "It's because he said I can't have sex. Now I want all the sex. You can't tell me I can't do something. Then all I wanna do is...well, it. It's the allure of the forbidden. You're not like that?"

"You either want something or you don't. What does what other people say have anything to do with it?"

I leaned back. "Of course you'd say that."

"What's that supposed to mean?"

I waved my hand in the air. "You're...you. You're very disciplined. I don't think anyone or anything can affect you. Like you love to say, you can control yourself."

"*You* affect me."

I smiled. It was a slow and happy one. "You affect me too."

"So, correct me if I'm wrong: if the doctor had said it's okay to have sex, you—"

"Jack!" I snapped, reaching across to put my hand over his mouth.

"What?" he muttered.

Tilting my head to the side, I gestured to the duo sitting next to us with my eyes.

Jack looked up and sighed. I supposed it was his version of asking for deliverance.

"Just skip the word, but keep going," I prompted as I sat back down.

"If he had said it was okay to...do it, you wouldn't be asking me to do it every day?"

"Well, I imagine I'd still want you, but I'm not sure I'd say it out loud, and definitely not this much. Two months after the surgery...well, since then I'm extremely...whatever." Feeling my face flush, I pressed the back of my hand to my cheek.

"What's wrong?"

"Nothing, just a little hot in here."

"Finish your sentence."

We locked eyes and I managed to hold his intense gaze for a whopping ten seconds.

"Horny," I said, my voice frustrated and maybe a little louder than I was anticipating. "Horny," I repeated, more to myself this time.

The hostess, the girl who had walked us to our table, came back. "Hi. Welcome again. What can I get you folks?"

Jack and I were still staring at each other, and I didn't want to be the first one to break eye contact. It was him doing stuff like this that was making me fall for him more and more. His intense gaze managed to touch all sorts of places, and when he was looking at me like that, I lost my mind a little.

"Hi," I said brightly, and Jack finally moved his gaze to the girl. I sighed in relief and slumped in my seat. I'd just told him I was horny. Nice choice of word, for sure.

"You want to share a pizza or are you going with pasta?"

I quickly returned back to the world. "Pizza."

"What do you want on—"

"Mushrooms," I blurted out. "And maybe artichokes too."

"That's it?"

"No, you add something too. What do you want?"

"Pepperoni. You'll have water?"

I nodded and let him finish our order then, just as the girl left after promising to get our drinks ASAP, my gaze caught on an empty booth toward the back.

"Did you hear anything from your cousins?"

When I gave him a confused look, he continued.

"About your surgery. Did they call you to check on you?"

"No. I'm not even sure if I want to hear from them. I'm surprised that Bryan never showed up again though. Did he call you? I feel like he gave up too easily."

"No."

Because I wanted tonight to be just about us, I changed the subject and didn't think too much about his angry expression.

Pointing with my finger at the booth in the back, I waited for him to follow my direction.

"Yes...that's a table, I believe."

"Ha ha." Giving him a pointedly blank look, I ignored his dry comment. "Can we sit there?"

"You don't like it here?"

"No. No, I do, but a booth...I don't know, it feels more intimate."

Jack caught the attention of the girl as she was bringing a soda to the cute little kid next to us and then helped me out of my seat and carried my coat. The touch of his hand on the small of my back practically seared me through my dress. I got in first and scooted.

Instead of sitting next to me as I had assumed he would and wanted him to do, he went to sit across from me again.

"What are you doing?" I asked, perplexed.

"What does it look like I'm doing?"

"Jack, you're gonna sit here." I patted the seat next to me. "That's why I wanted a booth."

"To sit next to me," he echoed.

I nodded slowly.

"We could've moved our chairs closer to each other."

"It's not the same thing. Come on. Move."

"No touching, Rose. I'm serious. Do not drive me crazy in public."

Hearing that I had *any* kind of power over him was exhilarating. Happy and excited, I laughed and raised my hands. "No touching—got it. Come on, I won't bite. I promise."

And what do you know...as soon as he settled next to me, he reached for my hand and tightly clasped it in his, playing with my ring the entire time. *He* was the one who couldn't stop touching me, and I loved every second of it. We talked for hours in that little Italian restaurant, accompanied by some romantic Italian tunes. If Jack wasn't touching my face, he was holding my hand. If he wasn't holding my hand, he was offering me bites of pizza as I chattered away at him. When he wasn't making me laugh with his dry comments, he was resting our linked hands on his leg. When I wasn't smiling or laughing, I was melting.

He also kissed me. I didn't know why I was surprised, but he kissed me so many times. Every time he leaned forward and I felt his lips moving against mine, asking for entrance, my heart lost its steady rhythm and I felt excitement bubbling up inside me, the kind of excitement you don't know how to hold in, an excess of happiness. I loved it. I completely fell for him on our first date.

It was the most perfect first date I'd ever had in my life.

My husband was perfect. With all his arrogance and prickliness, Jack Hawthorne was perfect for me.

He wasn't what I'd had in mind or even what I'd wanted for myself, but he was perfect and already mine, truly mine. There was no doubt of that in my mind.

CHAPTER TWENTY-FOUR

ROSE

It was after the official first date, not days after, only hours when I woke up with a weird feeling.

It was so hard to sleep in the same bed with Jack after I'd started feeling better from the surgery. As much as I talked about wanting to get him into bed naked, I never actually did anything about it, at least not when we were in bed like this.

That being said, I wasn't actually surprised to find Jack spooning me—that happened a lot. I woke up in a lot of different positions in the morning, usually with my face tucked under his chin, my hand across his chest. Sometimes my face was on his chest with his arms wrapped around me, and there had been a few instances where we had woken up fused to each other just like we were right then.

Little spoon, meet big spoon.

In the hospital, that had been the only position we had slept in, but that was only because the bed wasn't big enough for any other positioning. At the hospital, sex had been the last thing on my mind, but out of it...the last two months, things had been different. In those instances where we had woken up with his front pressed to my back, he usually got out of bed as quickly as possible and I said a silent goodbye to his lovely erection that had been pressing into me from behind.

Those mornings were my favorite, because it was something else to wake up wrapped in his arms. I felt protected, cared for, and maybe for the first time in a very long time, like I belonged somewhere: in his arms. Those times, I wasn't brave enough to tease him, and I just closed my eyes and took my fill instead.

When we were both vertical and wearing actual clothes, that was when I flourished in making him squirm. So much for my bravery.

"Jack?" I mumbled, peering over my shoulder. His lips were right there, only inches away, and I shivered when those same full lips pressed a kiss on my bare shoulder. He was already awake, apparently. I tried to turn onto my back so I could look at him, but with his body covering mine, it wasn't possible. I only managed to turn halfway, craning my neck back the rest of the way. "Is everything okay?" I croaked out, my voice heavy with sleep. Apart from the city lights casting a shadow on his face, there were no lights on, just us.

"Go back to sleep," he whispered.

Jack's hand found mine and I held it up, palm against palm, his skin warm against my fingertips.

"What's wrong?" I asked.

"Nothing."

Watching our hands dance as he gently tapped his fingers against mine in the low light, I linked my fingers with his, tightly, and listened to him release a long breath.

"You want me to believe you just woke up to hold hands with me?"

"I talked to your doctor today."

I turned my body a little more toward him and cautiously watched his face.

"When?"

"After dinner. I called his private phone."

"And?" I prompted anxiously when he didn't go on. I was starting to hate the word doctor.

"He sent the email today with the results, and I thought it was a bill so I opened it. The MRI was clean. The surgery worked. There is no tear in your membrane anymore."

I closed my eyes and dropped my head back onto the pillow, releasing the biggest sigh in the world. I was feeling a little dizzy with relief. A weight had been lifted off my chest with his words, the equivalent of a baby elephant. I felt worlds lighter.

"But you still need to be careful—you know that, right?" Jack reminded me.

That I did. The doctor had warned me that usually when a CSF leak happens out of nowhere, there is a high chance that the same issue can pop up in a different part of the membrane. If the pressure is constantly high, it really is inevitable.

I opened my eyes and looked at Jack with a big smile. "I know, I know, but I'm still happy to have good news." However, Jack didn't look all that happy. My brows lowered. "Is everything else okay? You don't look very excited." I touched the space between his brows with my fingertip after I pulled my hand out of his grip. "Why this frown?"

Catching my finger in his hand, he leaned down and pressed a soft kiss on my temple that caused my eyes to fall closed and my entire body to wake up and take notice of the man looking at me with such an intense expression on his face.

"Jack," I mumbled. My brain was screaming *Danger!*—the good kind.

"I asked if we were cleared for sex."

That shut me up. My heart rate slowly picked up, and suddenly the room felt hotter.

"And?"

I swallowed and held my breath.

His victorious fingers found a way to link mine with his again, and he gave them a squeeze as he stared into my eyes. "He said if we took it slow, it'd be fine."

"Huh."

That was all I could come up with to say. *Huh*. I was a genius for sure.

I gave him my back but kept my tight hold on his hand so he was forced to spoon me again.

"Why didn't you tell me before?"

"I thought we should wait the last five days."

"Now? Now you don't think we should."

"No, I don't think we should."

"What are you thinking?" he whispered into my ear in a hoarse voice, causing all the hairs on my arms to rise. "I thought you were waiting for this. I thought you wanted this."

I worried my teeth over my bottom lip. I could hear every little noise in the room. His breathing was low and deep, and the sound the sheets made when he tucked his legs behind mine was a soft swoosh, caressing my senses.

I was on the edge of whimpering like a little girl when I felt his tongue on my neck, kissing me, tasting me.

"I do want to," I whispered, my eyes fluttering closed as if I was afraid he'd hear me.

Silence followed my words for at least a full minute.

"It's okay, Rose. Go back to sleep," he whispered back.

How could I when his hard-on was getting harder and harder to ignore? I squeezed my eyes shut and went for it.

"I didn't think you'd ask me."

"Ask you what?"

Groaning, I turned my head and burrowed it into the pillow, trying to be careful with my nose. "It sounds weird when I say it out loud."

"How would you know that if you don't say it? Come on, let's hear it."

Releasing my breath, I opened my eyes and looked out the windows in the terrace doors. "I thought when it happened, it'd just...happen."

His hand let go of mine and he started stroking my waist and then my arm. "What do you mean exactly?"

How could I think of anything when he was touching me?

"I'm not sure if you've noticed that I talk a big talk, Jack, but I'm not exactly an expert when it comes to getting busy. I'm not saying I'm bad or anything, I'm just saying I'm nothing special when it comes down to it. I've only been with three and a half people—"

"Half? No, I take it back. I don't want to know. I already want to kill all three and a half of them."

"Cute. You know I'm a romantic, so I thought when the time came, you'd just wake me up in the middle of the night and take me, you know, because you couldn't wait any longer...or we'd walk into the apartment and you'd just lift me up and I would wrap my legs around you and you'd say *fuck it* and we'd go for it, or you could push me against a wall and do it like that. I didn't think you'd ask my permission to have sex with me. It's making me feel nervous."

"Sounds like you've been thinking about the logistics of this."

"Of course I have."

"I didn't ask your permission."

"It was implied."

"You feeling nervous about something? I wouldn't believe it if I saw it with my own eyes."

Frowning, I turned my head so I could look at him as his fingers pressed into my skin, holding me at my waist. "Are you making fun of me?"

I caught his smile right before he captured my lips in a deep kiss and my eyes closed on their own. I slowly slipped my tongue in, brushing it against his as I turned onto my back so I could kiss him deeper. This time he let me, and his response was glorious. His fingers lifted the bottom of my shirt and, with no hesitation whatsoever, he pushed his hand right down into my underwear, going straight for my core.

I moaned into his mouth and let my thighs fall open. He growled right back and pushed one finger inside me then he slowly added another. My body offered no resistance, already wet for him. I made a low sound in the back of my throat when he pushed his fingers as deep as they would go, moving excruciatingly slowly.

I just kept kissing him through it, holding his face to me with both of my hands, hungrier by the second. I was so ready for this, for us to be a real thing, and this was sealing the deal. We had done everything backward—I'd even fallen for him before having an official first date—but this...this would make everything right.

When I was sure he wasn't ending the kiss before I wanted him to, my hands managed to find their way down into his pants, and the kiss turned into something much different once I had my hand wrapped around the base of his cock.

Still kissing him uncontrollably, I took a deep breath through my nose and whimpered into his mouth when he started fingering me in earnest, his thumb firmly pressing on my clit. I moved my hips as much as I could, his hand driving me out of my mind.

My body burning and tingling at the same time, I tore my mouth away from his and bit on my lip to hold in an embarrassingly long and loud moan. My hand tightened around his cock. I could hear all the noises him fingering me was making, and it was only getting me more worked up.

"You're dripping all over my hand again," he murmured, and

I was happy to see that he was just as out of breath as I was. He nipped my jawline, my neck, my earlobe.

All I could manage in return was to hold on to his cock, giving it a very rough pull every now and then when I could remember to do so.

My entire focus was on his fingers and then his lips were trailing along my neck, biting softly and licking. I was seconds away from coming on his hand. I worked my hips, pushing them down to take more of his fingers even though he was giving me everything. I wanted more, deeper, harder.

I only realized I was saying my thoughts out loud when he said, "Okay. Whatever you want, Rose, I'll give it to you."

When he pulled his fingers out of me, I sobered up a little.

"But..."

"Shhh."

I closed my legs, trying to find some kind of relief, and started pulling on his thick cock a little faster now that I could use my brain again, but he put a stop to that pretty quickly by sitting upright and gently pulling my hand out of his pants.

When I tried to sit up too, he softly pressed a hand on my shoulder and kept me in place. "Stay still for a second."

I huffed but stopped squirming when he went for my underwear and pulled them off.

"Shit." When his fingers parted me and I felt the cool air between my legs, I was already panting. My entire focus was on Jack and what he would do next. He put his big hands on my inner thighs and opened me wider for his perusal.

Two possessive fingers entered me again, and then those two quickly turned into three scissoring inside of me. For the life of me, I couldn't keep still, and the more he didn't take his eyes away from where his fingers were disappearing into, the hotter and brighter the fire inside of me burned. He leaned down and started licking my clit and all around it with a firm tongue.

"Jack," I mewled embarrassingly.

"Right," he mumbled, and after one final delicious lick, he stopped again.

I groaned and tried to close my legs with his fingers still inside. I was pretty sure that would help me get some relief.

His palm pressed into the sensitive skin on the inside of my thigh. "No, keep them open."

"I want to see you too," I admitted. "I don't feel particularly patient at the moment."

"Neither do I," he agreed, his eyes devouring me. The next thing I knew, his fingers left me and he was taking off his shirt. I was still trying to get over his pecs and abs that were just out of my reach. He had insisted on being fully clothed at all times when he was in bed with me. I had disagreed wholeheartedly, but he had won. He got off the bed. I sat up straight and got up on my knees in the middle of the sheets.

"Jack," I started, but I didn't get far as he got rid of his pajama pants next. I couldn't take my eyes away as his thick, veiny cock bobbed in the air, almost reaching his navel.

Oh, this was really happening, and I was all for it.

Holding his eyes with my own, I reached for the bottom of my shirt and took it off. Clothes were overrated anyway. Then I reached behind my back and took off my bra, throwing them both on the floor. A second later, Jack released a long groan and he was back in the bed with me, slamming into me and going straight for my mouth.

Compared to the kiss he gave me then, all the kisses we had shared so far would be considered innocent. I tilted my head to the side and let him go in deeper. One of his hands cupped the back of my head, the other gripping my waist in an almost bruising hold. I didn't care. All that mattered was that he was holding me to himself so he could take as much as he wanted. His cock was pressed between us, the wet and swollen head brushing my stomach. His other hand released its hold on my waist and trailed up, the drag of his skin on mine tipping me even further into delirium as he found my breast and molded it into his hand, squeezing and pulling on my nipple until I was moaning and making all kinds of noises.

The second his lips gave mine a break, he went for my ears, licking and nipping his way down my throat to my boobs. I arched my back, offering myself to him. He latched onto my nipple with his mouth and started sucking with deep, sensual pulls as his other hand moved to caress and knead the other, getting it ready for the same treatment. I let my head drop back and tangled my fingers through his hair, gripping tight.

My heart felt like it was beating in my throat, my pulse all over the place. There was one thing I was sure of: I would never forget Jack Hawthorne and his touch in this lifetime.

When he sucked my nipple into his mouth deeper and harder than I was expecting him to, I had to steady myself with one hand curling around the hard muscle of his shoulder as I tried my very best to catch my breath. I'd never in my life come from just that, but I was surprisingly close.

"Jack," I murmured on an exhalation as he hummed and sucked my nipples, sending electricity all over my body. I wasn't sure how I was even staying up on my knees. "Jack," I repeated. "I want you. I can't wait. I don't want to wait."

When he lifted his head to look into my eyes, I was still moaning, my body twitching. I hadn't come, but I was pretty damn close to it.

"Hmmm," he murmured, kissing me again, tangling his tongue with mine. Even though I was naked, I felt warm all over, tingly. "Are you sure it's not just *talk*? You really want me to fuck you?"

I reached between us and gave him a few luxuriating pulls that, as far as I could tell, he enjoyed since he nipped my bottom lip. I used my thumb to spread the warm liquid around the head and before I could do anything else, he tore himself away and went for the bedside table. I watched in awe as he ripped open a condom packet and slowly rolled it onto himself. I'd put them there myself to give him a hint. The second it was done, he was by my side. He turned my body until I was facing the headboard and he was on his knees right behind me.

"Open your legs as wide as you can for me, baby," he muttered, his lips licking and biting my neck. Every kiss caused a full body shiver, and I was sure I would die happy after this. "Hold on to the headboard if you need to."

I was turned on like I had never been turned on before. I would do whatever he wanted me to. I moved on my knees and opened my legs wider, balancing myself with one hand on the headboard. When he put both of his hands on the insides of my thighs and spread me even wider, his fingertips grazing my wetness, I thought I experienced a very tiny orgasm.

My throat was already hoarse when he finally settled himself between my wide open legs, his knees resting right beside mine, keeping me open. "Lay your head back," he whispered into my ear, causing another shiver to go through my body.

"Jack," I moaned. It seemed like I couldn't come up with any other word.

"I need you so badly," he whispered, his lips moving against my skin as he spoke, his hot breath keeping me on edge. I'd take it —I'd take him needing me any day.

I felt his left palm covering my stomach and then his right hand guiding his cock between my legs, moving it up and down my slit, spreading my wetness all over his shaft.

"Jack," I repeated again.

"Hmmm."

"Please...enough."

"You want me."

"I do."

"Tell me. Say the words."

"I want you like crazy, Jack."

"Just me, Rose. I'm the only one."

I closed my eyes. He wanted me to die a slow death then. "I've never wanted anyone as much as I want you."

That seemed to satisfy him.

"Kiss me then. Give me your mouth before I take you," he said.

The back of my head was already resting against his shoulder so I turned it to the left, and his mouth took mine in a rough kiss. The next thing I knew, before I could take in my next breath, he was pushing inside me in a slow and never-ending slide. I ripped my lips away from his and released a long, long moan, my head pushing back, my eyes closed shut.

"Okay?" he asked, and all I could do was bite my lip and nod. "You feel so good," he murmured, pushing the rest of his cock in. He was stretching me wide open and I was loving it. My muscles quivering, my moan started up again.

I could already see colors dancing in front of my eyes. "That's so good, Jack."

"Yeah?"

His left palm pushed harder on my stomach, pulling me against him, and finally I took all of it. I tried to open my legs wider to get more comfortable because my right thigh had started shaking, but the little bit of pain that came with his size and our position made everything feel a hundred times better.

He started pulling out and I gripped his forearm to hold on to him. One of my hands was still grasping the headboard, but I needed to feel his skin against my fingertips. "Easy," I groaned.

"You want me to stop? So soon?"

"I'll kill you if you stop," I gasped out.

"Then what? It hurts?" he asked, his nose nuzzling my neck.

"Good hurt," I managed to get out.

"Good."

Slowly he pulled out only halfway and then pushed in again. This time, I took him in more easily. I'd never had sex this slowly, had never known it could feel that good and also deliciously painful in a way.

"Is that good for you too?" I asked, feeling bold.

"You have no idea," he groaned, starting steady thrusts as I got comfortable with his size. I was soaking him in my wetness. "I could fuck you like this for hours."

Feeling overwhelmed, I chuckled, but then he thrust up all the way in and it turned into another moan. "I think I'd die from pleasure."

"I would never let you die, just trying to fuck you good."

"I'd love to die like this."

He started a slow rhythm that had me moaning constantly. Every time my head dropped forward, he warned me to keep it tilted back against him, and his worry for me helped build my pleasure higher and higher.

"Was this what you imagined all those times you teased me?"

"Better," I whispered, and his fingers dug deeper into my stomach. My breath and heart out of control, I tightened my grip on his forearm. We'd both leave our mark on each other by the time we were done, and I wouldn't want to have it any other way.

"Jack," I gasped, a little panic trickling into my voice only a few short minutes after he had started fucking me.

"What? We're stopping again?" he asked, not slowing down his thrusts. I held the wrist of his left hand, which was still pressing on my stomach.

"No, no, no," I chanted, and his thrusts started to go deeper and faster. I backed my hips up, trying to somehow take him even deeper. His right hand wrapped around me too, grasping my hip as my butt bounced off the tops of his thighs. "Jack...Jack, I'm gonna come. Don't stop."

"Come on, Rose. Come all over my cock, baby. Let me feel how much you want me." He bit on my earlobe and I lost it. "Yes, baby. Just like that. Ride it. Take my cock."

I closed my eyes, and listening to his rough voice push me right over the edge and into oblivion. Gasping his name, I felt heat burst between my legs, and all the muscles in my body tightened. I let go of the headboard and threw my right hand back, gripping Jack's hair, pulling involuntarily. I moaned long and hard as my body shivered in his arms and he kept riding me hard through my orgasm, his lips tracing an invisible line on my neck.

When my body started relaxing around him, he slowed down.

"Was that good enough?"

I could do nothing but nod. I had been too loud and had come too hard. Anywhere he was in contact with my body was burning, but I felt the heat in my cheeks even more.

"Do you feel how slick you are for me? How hard you came on my cock?"

It was impossible not to feel it. My only answer was another nod. He went deeper into me as I whimpered. His right hand cupped the heavy weight of my breast, and I shamelessly arched into it.

Lust licked at my skin. When he quickened his pace just a fraction, I sucked in a breath of air. "Shit."

"You'll come again."

"Always giving orders," I murmured, all my focus on the spot where we became one.

"It wasn't an order, Rose, just pointing out the obvious."

He buried his face in my neck and pinched my nipple, his thrusts uncompromising. I released something between a gasp and a groan.

God, the strength of him holding me—it was just as powerful as his thrusts. I loosened my hold on his wrist and splayed my hand on top of his, silently telling him I wanted more pressure.

"I'll bruise you," he whispered.

"I want you to," I whispered back, turning my head and pressing my forehead against his hot throat.

"Why?"

"I want everything from you, Jack, everything and more. I want you to leave a mark on me." It was nothing more than a breathy statement that had a double meaning as I realized I was seconds away from another orgasm.

"Open your mouth," he ordered, moving his head back.

I lifted my head and let him invade my mouth in a blazing kiss at the same moment his thrusts became exquisitely demanding. The taste of him, of his hunger rushed over me as I started coming again. He moved his right hand down my body, and the feel of his skin against my sensitive areas caused me to tremble in his arms as he jackhammered into me. He did nothing but cover my pussy with his hand, the heel of it pressing hard on my clit.

Through the fog that had filled my brain, I felt him go impossibly deeper as I whimpered into his mouth, my body shaking in the aftermath. The little grunts of pleasure escaping from him made my toes curl. He thrust deeply two more times then stilled inside me. I groaned softly as my inner muscles quivered around his length. I was lost in his hunger, his hunger for me.

He gave me a few more lazy, luxuriating thrusts that caressed me from the inside as both his hands rested on top of my thighs. I had a feeling he didn't want to let go, which was just fine with me. I never wanted him to let go of me either.

"Is this real?" I asked, out of breath as he started to pull out.

He stilled behind me. "What do you mean?"

"I'm not dreaming this, am I?" I moved my hands up and down his forearms, my head still resting on his broad shoulder.

Rolling my head, I looked up at him through dazed and probably half-lost eyes.

He smiled the sweetest, sexiest smile and kissed my lips. "This—we—are as real as it gets." His hands moved and he wrapped them around me in a tight grip, his forearms holding up the weight of my breasts. After a long squeeze, which I loved, he whispered into my ear. "I need to get rid of the condom, baby. Let go of me."

I dropped my hands and held back a small whimper when he pulled out. However, I couldn't stop the trembling in my body when his palm moved on the curve of my ass.

"Lie down—you're shaking."

I did so happily.

When he came back, I was hiding under the covers, my head resting on the pillow, my hands tucked under my cheek. I tracked his every move and secretly high-fived myself when I noticed he was still naked. His cock was impressive even when it wasn't doing things to me.

He lay down, facing me.

"Hi," I whispered.

He took a deep breath and then released it. "Hello, Rose." His lips met mine and I smiled through our short-lived kiss. "What's the smile for?" he asked, his lips moving against mine as our noses bumped.

"I'd share my door with you any day, Jack Hawthorne."

His brows dipped together. "What are you talking about?"

"If you've never seen *Titanic*, I can't be married to you," I said seriously.

Unfortunately, the confusion didn't clear from his eyes, but a smile did touch his lips. "I think it's a little late for that."

"You haven't seen it. Jack and Rose...the Titanic..."

"I know the movie, but I don't think I've seen it."

"If I was confident I could walk out of this room, I'd force you to watch it right now, but since that's not happening, clear your schedule—we're watching it tomorrow."

His hand brushed my hair away from my face. "Okay. How are you feeling?"

Now I let my own lips curve up. "For a minute there, my brain tingled."

His expression turned serious, his body going taut. "Are you feeling okay? Was it too much?"

I lifted my hand and smoothed out his frown. "I'm fine, but there was definitely a tingle up there." Leaning forward, I kissed him. Closing my eyes, my heart in my throat, I whispered against his lips, "It was the best sex of my life, Jack."

"Good."

I drew back and looked into his eyes, which were hiding in the dark shadows of my room. "That's it? You better say something more."

His eyebrows rose. "You want to hear that you're my best too?"

"Yes, and more. Please."

Then he laughed, and if the sounds he made when he was coming were the sexiest I'd ever heard, the sound of him laughing in bed with me was the sweetest. He sobered quickly, but it didn't stop me from hearing the smile and amusement in his voice. "You're the best I've ever had too, Rose."

I waited. So did he.

"More," I said. "And make it more believable."

One eyebrow quirked up then his hand sneaked behind me and he pulled me to himself until we were skin to skin again. His semi-hard cock pressed against my stomach and he looked into my eyes, no hint of a smile left on his face.

I was already breathless, dammit!

"You're the only woman I want to go to sleep holding on to

and wake up next to, Rose Hawthorne. I will never leave you. I will never forget you."

Heat rushed across my skin, my heartbeat loud in my ears. I cleared my throat. "Not too bad. I guess it's a good thing you're not that bad in bed."

I will never leave you.

That statement—it stole the breath from my lungs. The obvious claim would've easily scared a different woman, but I soaked in every raw word and let them fill me. I'd never belonged to anyone, not like that, not like what Jack was offering me.

"Sex?" I quipped. "Again? You know, just so we can see if the first time was a fluke?"

His answer was whispered against my lips with a smile as his eyes held my vulnerable stare. "Yes, baby. Again."

THE NEXT DAY, I looked exactly like someone who had gotten herself some. It was smiles galore in the coffee shop and I was walking on clouds. Owen didn't mind making sure I knew what he thought of me when I kept smiling to myself right across from him on the other side of the kitchen island.

When I saw Jack's face flash on my phone's screen right before we were about to open, my morning reached a high.

"Hi."

"My Rose." There was that hint of a smile I loved seeing on his lips in his voice when he spoke. "How are you feeling?"

"Perfect," I whispered, moving to a corner as I looked out at the busy, busy New York streets. We had had sex again, Jack and I, once more after the first time, and then again in the morning, which brought our total up to three. It wasn't a bad number when you thought about it, and knowing the first time hadn't been a fluke was just the icing on the cake. I had all kinds of bruises to show for it, but I especially loved the ones on my hipbones and the sides of my stomach. When I closed my eyes, I could still feel his fingers digging into my skin. "How are *you* feeling?"

His answer was soft and gentle, so opposite of him. "Perfect."

I looked down at my shoes and grinned. "We have good sex."

"That we do."

"Did you want to say something?"

"I can't just call my wife because I want to?"

"You can, and you should, too. Whenever she crosses your mind, you should call her or text her. I think she likes talking to you."

"You think so?"

"Yeah, I definitely think so."

"Tell me more. What else does she like?"

I looked over my shoulder to make sure Sally was still busy stacking the sandwiches and couldn't hear me. "She likes when you whisper into her ear." My own voice had dropped into a rough whisper as my body shuddered just thinking about the night before and that morning.

I listened to Jack clear his throat and mutter something to someone who was apparently in his office with him. I waited until he came back to me.

"Sorry. I had a junior associate with me. I'm alone now."

I nodded, forgetting he couldn't see me. "What are you doing?"

"I'm getting ready for a meeting."

"And we're about to open."

"I see."

"I think I missed you," I admitted in a low voice. It had been only hours since I'd stolen one last kiss when he joined Raymond and me on our little morning commute. He'd said he wanted to be at the office early to go over some things, and I'd said he didn't want to let go of me. He had kissed me then, right in front of my coffee shop. *So what?* he had said once he'd left me all breathless and hungry again.

"You think?" he asked, sounding amused.

"I know."

"Would you like to have lunch with me then?"

"Rose?" I looked up and to the side to see Sally grinning at me. "Should I unlock the door?"

"Yes, yes. Sorry, I'll come help in a second."

She waved a hand at me. "I got it." Then, with an even bigger smile, she unlocked the door and welcomed our first two customers of the day. I hadn't even noticed they were waiting outside in the cold.

Basically squeezing myself into the corner, I focused my attention back on Jack. "If you missed me so much that you couldn't continue on with your day without seeing me during your lunch, I would consider that option...but since you haven't mi—"

"You'll always call me out, won't you?"

"I think that's a given."

"Good. Well, if you don't go out to lunch with me, my entire day will be ruined because I won't be able to think about anything but you, you and your taste."

I blushed. He definitely knew my taste.

"Fine. I'll have lunch with you. I'll have to cancel all my other plans, but only because you insisted so much."

As I smiled down at my shoes, there was a heavy silence from the other end of the line.

"Jack?"

"I'll make you happy, Rose. I promise."

Words got stuck in my throat for a short moment. "I'll make you happy too, Jack."

Before he could respond, I heard an unexpected and unwelcome voice behind me.

"Rose?"

My smile dropped before I even set eyes on him. *Joshua.* His hair was slicked back, which made him look like a total douchebag, and he was wearing a suit—nothing as good as Jack's suits, but still a black suit. He looked like a perfect fit for someone as rich as Jodi was. When *we* had been together, he hadn't been like this—no slick hair, no suits. It was as if he had molded himself into a different person, or maybe my cousin had molded him into a different person. Either way, it wasn't my business.

"Jack," I said, still holding the phone to my ear. "I...uh, we just opened. I should go. I'll text you when we slow down a bit."

After a quick goodbye, I hung up the phone.

"What are you doing here, Joshua? *Again.*"

"I'd like to talk to you, if you have a few minutes."

I frowned at him. We had nothing to talk about. I glanced over his shoulder, annoyed that he was almost blocking my way of escape. "We just opened." I repeated the words I'd said to Jack. "I don't have time to talk—I need to work."

He smiled, a small intimate expression that only made me more annoyed because he was messing with my happy morning. He didn't belong there. "I don't mind waiting."

Because we were starting to fill with customers, I couldn't make a scene and straight up kick him out. So, I shrugged and, turning my shoulders so I wouldn't get too close, walked past him.

I made him wait for over an hour, hoping he'd get bored and leave on his own. I couldn't remember a single time he had waited for me even for an extra fifteen minutes, but now it seemed he had all the time in the world. What bugged me the most was the fact that he hadn't even ordered one simple coffee as he occupied a table I could have offered to actual paying customers.

That was why I made my way toward him when the morning rush started to slow down, that and the fact that he was making me feel extremely uncomfortable with the way he was trying to catch my eye.

I figured I didn't need to sit down to say what I needed to say, so I stood next to his seat and, trying to be as quiet as possible, I rushed straight into it.

"I'm not sure how to say this any other way, but I don't want you to come here again. I don't want to see or talk to you."

"I thought we were going to talk."

Was he even listening to me?

"And I thought you'd take a hint and leave before that happened."

"Rose, I think you'll want to hear what—"

"I don't. I don't want to hear it, and I don't want to see you. I have no idea what—"

"I came to tell you a thing or two about your husband."

My short nails bit into my palms as I tried to maintain a smiling face for the customers around us. "Leave."

He shifted in his seat, scooting forward. "I met him while we were still in love. You and I... He paid me to break up with you, Rose. He was too insistent, he wouldn't let me turn him down. I was afraid of what he'd do to me. If I had known he would force you to marry him and play with you like this, I would have—"

With every word coming out of his mouth, I felt my body sway more. The world started to spin around me. My knees weakened, and I had to take the seat across from Joshua.

Once he was done speaking, there was no happiness left inside of me.

He paid me to break up with you.

CHAPTER TWENTY-FIVE

JACK

After we had wrapped up a long meeting with an old client who was considering selling his company, I was still in the meeting room with Samantha and Fred trying to figure out the details when Cynthia walked in after a quick knock. I should've guessed it from the look on her face. I should've guessed my time was up and everything was about to come crashing down on me.

Rose walked in on the heels of my assistant before I could finish my thoughts, and there was nothing but heartbreak written all over her face. Something was really wrong. Was she feeling sick again? My mind ran with that possibility.

"I'm sorry to interrupt like this," Rose started with a quiet sadness in her voice, her eyes on me. No one else in the room mattered. It was just us. "Can we talk?"

I jerked my head up and stood. "Please excuse me." Fred and Samantha's voices were nothing but a murmur in the background.

I counted every single step I took toward her—Rose, my wife. It took twelve steps in total. If I could have slowed time, I would have. I'd never turn it back, though. I'd never change any second of what we had together. Before I could reach her side, she turned around and walked out of the meeting room, pausing just outside the door.

Clenching my jaw, I moved to put my hand on the small of her back, out of habit and need.

Clearing her throat, she took a step away from me. She wasn't here for our lunch. It killed me, seeing her like that, and that was when I knew why she'd come. Knowing I was responsible for it, knowing I'd done that to her—it broke something inside of me.

My hand fell to my side, fingers forming a fist. I pushed both my hands in my pockets as she watched me so I wouldn't feel the urge to reach out to her. "My office?" I asked into the loud silence between us.

She nodded and walked ahead of me as I followed.

Finally we made it to my office, and instead of taking a seat, she grabbed her elbows and stood right in the middle of the room. Before I could turn around and close the door for some sense of privacy, Cynthia appeared in the doorway. Letting out a knowing breath, she looked at me and then to Rose.

"Can I get you anything, Mrs. Hawthorne?"

I wished I could've taken my eyes off of her, because maybe then I would've missed her flinch. She shook her head and her lips tipped up just for a second. "No. Thank you, Cynthia."

The door closed and we were finally alone.

Her eyes met mine as I moved to stand in front of her. "You're not here for lunch."

"No."

I braced myself. "I'm listening."

There was that loud silence again as a few seconds passed and her shoulders drooped in defeat, her expression changing, crumpling in front of my eyes.

"Tell me it's a lie, Jack. Tell me it's a lie so I can breathe again." Untangling her arms, she placed a fist on her heart as if trying to ease her pain.

I gritted my teeth, my hands clenching in my pockets. "You're gonna have to be more specific."

She dropped her hand from her chest and tipped her chin up, her eyes already shining with unshed tears. "Tell me you didn't pay Joshua to break up with me. Tell me—" Her voice broke, causing physical pain in the middle of my chest. "Tell me you didn't lie to me about *everything*."

I sighed, trying to keep it together, trying to keep it locked in.

"I can't tell you that, Rose," I admitted, my voice coming out harsher than I'd intended.

She stared at me as if she was staring at a stranger and her first tear fell down, marking a line down her cheek.

Then the second one came.

Then the third.

The fourth.

She didn't make a single sound. Other than blinking her eyes as her tears kept falling, she didn't move even an inch.

"Did you have fun?"

"Excuse me?"

Her voice got stronger as she raised her voice. "I asked if you had fun."

"What are you talking about?"

"Did you have fun playing your games?"

"You don't know what you're—"

She dabbed at her tears with the back of her hand, her spine straight. That was good. I could handle her gearing up to hurt me —God knew I deserved it.

"You're right, I don't know. I don't know anything. You paid my fiancé to break up with me." The next thing I knew, she was pushing at my chest with both hands. She was shaking, and I rocked back a step as she asked, "Who the hell do you think you are?"

When she hit me a second time, I grabbed her arms right above her elbows before she repeated it a third time. If I'd thought it would help her, I'd have let her hit me countless times, but it wasn't going to change what I had done.

"Calm down."

"Calm down?" She was crying in earnest, trying to get out of my hold, trying to escape my touch. "You've been lying to me from the first moment we met. You ruined *everything*."

I tightened my grip on her arms, pulling her body closer to mine when her breathing started to get all choppy. "I saved you from him," I forced out through gritted teeth. "I'm assuming he came back to your coffee shop since that's what he threatened me with when I told him I was done paying him."

"Saved me? You saved me?" Her breath hitched, but she stopped struggling in my arms. "Let me go, Jack."

"So you can leave without listening to me? No."

"Oh, I'm not going anywhere before I hear an explanation. I want you to let me go because I don't want you to touch me ever again."

Her eyes burned into mine. I'd never forget the pain, the hurt, the anger, the hate I saw in them. Knowing I had to listen, knowing she was right, I let her go and she backed away from me, rubbing her arms where I had held them.

"Are you okay?" I managed to ask, thinking I had held her more tightly than I'd realized.

"Oh, never better." She put more distance between us. She was standing only a few steps away and I could still smell her perfume, yet she might as well have been miles away. "You can stop pretending to care about me. Go on, Jack—tell me more lies. Tell me what you did. I'm listening."

My jaw tightened. I deserved that, but it didn't mean it hurt any less. "I have no idea what he told you, Rose, but he lied."

"Right. Right, because you would never do something like that."

"No. I lied to you, too. I'm not saying otherwise. I lied from the very beginning."

"How noble of you to admit that now after I learn everything."

My patience snapped. "What do you think you know? Did he explain how he was only with you because of your uncle's money? How he only got close to you because he thought you had a better relationship with them? If he did then please, my apologies. You should go back to him."

She glared at me, her eyes boring into mine. "*You* offered him money to break up with me. What gives you the right?"

"That's the only thing I agree with you on. I had no right, but I did it anyway. He is nothing but a con man, Rose. I was trying to help you."

"Who asked for your help? I didn't even know you. Before the day you brought me into your office, I didn't even know you. He broke up with me days—*weeks* before that."

"I told you I met you before."

"And I told you I don't remember!" she yelled back. I supposed we had both lost our patience. I didn't care if the entire firm came to listen; all I cared about was that Rose was still there. As pissed off as she was, she was still listening. Maybe she wasn't hearing everything I was saying, but she was listening, and for that moment, it was enough.

"Doesn't change the fact that I remember. I met you at that party, briefly. I understand why you wouldn't remember—you saw no one but him."

The son of a bitch who had been planning to break her heart, information I had only learned later.

And I was just another bastard with a different name who had done the same, who had accepted the fact that this day would eventually come from before we even said *I do.*

She bit her lip as if trying to keep her pain inside, her eyes shimmering with more tears. "Tell me what you did, Jack. Tell me exactly what you did."

"I couldn't get you out of my mind after I met you. I was interested, but when I learned he was your boyfriend, I backed off, thought maybe in the future if things didn't work I could reintrodu—it doesn't matter what I thought. Sometime later Gary mentioned you had gotten engaged and that he had signed a contract with you. It was added into the will like every other contract, but he'd added a stipulation. When I read it, I found it to be odd that he wasn't just giving the place to you, so I had Joshua investigated. I was only curious."

"Why?" she cried out, lifting her arms high at her sides and then dropping them. "Why would you do something like that?"

"Because I wanted to learn more about him. I wanted to know how serious you two were. Take your pick." I waited for her to ask me what I had learned, but she didn't even blink. "I used the investigator we have here. He found out that he never went to Harvard. He had stolen from three other women. It had started with small amounts, but he'd escalated over time. No one pressed charges because they were ashamed, and one of them was afraid of her husband finding out about the affair. Those three women he found out about in just a week. I didn't have the investigator look further into him because your uncle had passed away. We knew what he was and there was no time to do much of anything. I knew why he was with you."

"Why wouldn't you just tell me? Why?"

"Would you believe me? I was a stranger. And there was no time to do much of anything. Before he could learn about the will, I paid him to go away."

Rose took a shaky breath and backed away until her legs hit the couch and she sat down. Her head bent, eyes closed, she was pressing her fingers to her temple.

I approached her. "Are you okay? Are you feeling dizzy?"

"Stop it," she ordered in a broken voice, looking up at me with red and swollen but dry eyes. "Stop acting like you care."

"I don't care?" I asked, my voice mocking. "You think I don't care and that's why I paid him to leave you alone? That's why I married you? Because I don't care?"

"Do you think caring for someone is forcing them to marry you?"

My body locked. "I didn't force you to do anything, Rose."

"But you didn't leave me any choice, did you, Jack? Everything was just so perfectly set up for you to play your game. You're no better than him."

I crouched in front of her, my hands itching to touch her, to make sure she was okay.

"You know that isn't true," I whispered, her words slicing my heart deeper than I'd expected. "Tell me you know that isn't true. He didn't know he'd get the property when I paid him to break up with you. He took the money without question, Rose. He told me he wasn't going to marry you anyway, that he was just trying to make the best of the situation and see if he could get something from Gary by getting more serious with you. Are you even hearing what I'm saying? When your uncle passed away and he heard about the stipulation in the will, he came back to ask for more money. I paid him more than once, more than twice. When he realized I'd cheated him out of the property, he came back to ask for more money. He only came to you now because I told him we were done after he showed up at your place the last time. I didn't think he'd do it. I thought I scared him off. He wasn't with you because he loved you. I'm not like him."

She looked into my eyes for a breathless moment. "You lied to me, Jack. Your lies are hurting me more right now. What did you want from me? Don't give me that crap about you needing someone to attend dinners with. Was it really the property you were after? Just like him? And don't even think about telling me this is nothing but a business transaction between two people. Don't lie to me anymore."

It was you. I didn't know it then, but it was just you that I wanted.

"Nothing. I wanted nothing from you. I was trying to help."

"You wanted to help a stranger. Am I this year's charity case?"

I ground my teeth and stood up. She rose as well, standing only inches away. My hands wanted to cradle her face like I'd done so many times, but I didn't have the right to touch her anymore.

"You changed me. You worked on it. You tricked me into loving you—you showed me this guy, this guy I could trust and love and not be afraid to be myself around. You showed me that I could have family that I could trust. You *gave* me an illusion. All your help with the coffee shop...and then when I was sick—you were right there, but you were acting, playing with me. It was all a lie, Jack. You were nothing but a lie, and you'll never know how much it hurts me to know that. I wanted something real with you. You knew what Joshua had done to me, but what did you do? You went ahead and did the exact same thing, just with a different game."

A few tears escaped her eyes, rolling over her skin before she quickly wiped them away in anger. I did nothing but watch, my pulse racing and my blood roaring in my veins, helpless.

"I hope you got what you wanted out of this. I hope it was worth it."

"I risked losing you to have a shot at you, Rose. I'd do it again in a heartbeat."

She shook her head and, her shoulder brushing mine, walked away. Stuffing my hands in my pockets, I turned around to watch her leave me.

She stopped with her hand on the door, her head hanging.

"Say something, Jack. Apologize. Something. Please say something."

Her words were a whisper that sliced me open. I took a step forward but then stopped. Now that she knew some things, I wouldn't lie to her about the rest. I wouldn't say something I knew she wouldn't believe.

"I paid twice the amount of the property's worth to Bryan after he showed up at your coffee shop before the opening." Her head snapped back, her expression horrified. "He didn't like the fact that we pulled the rug from under him. He was going to contest the will, he called me countless times, threatened me with you. It wasn't that he didn't believe the marriage, I think he did after you moved in with me—especially after he saw us together at the coffee shop and then later at the event—he just didn't want you to have the place. I paid him after that night at the charity event. That's why he let it go and I told him not to show his face to you again. He was going to be a problem, so we reached an agreement. I paid him off."

"How could he believe what we had is real? Why wouldn't Joshua tell him you paid him?"

Had. Past tense.

"I believe he is playing your cousin, he couldn't admit to what he is. He wouldn't tell."

"Why didn't you buy the damn place if you could before you married me, Jack? Why not rent the place to me if all you wanted was to get close to me?"

"Would you have accepted the offer? You'd never agree to pay low rent. That's not you. It doesn't even matter, I still tried to do it, but like I told you that first day, Bryan was adamant about not selling. You were going to lose everything and lose out on the coffee shop. I thought if I jumped straight to marriage you'd think I was in it for the property, for other things. You wouldn't even consider that I was in it for you. And you didn't. You didn't even like me."

For a second she appeared to be at a loss for words, so I pushed forward.

"I won't apologize for something I'm not sorry for. I'm not happy with how things went down, but I wasn't going to do anything after marrying you. I wasn't supposed to come close, and I tried my best to stay away. I did my best, Rose, trust me, but the more time I spent around you, the more I got to know you...I couldn't stay away. When I realized I didn't want to stay away, *couldn't* stay away, I decided I would try to be what you'd want, what you deserve. Try to win your heart. I'm not lying when I say all I wanted to do was help you when I offered to get married. At the end of two years, we were going to get a divorce and you'd never see me again. That was the plan, but somewhere along the way, I fell for you, and because of that, I'm not sorry. I'd do it again. I wouldn't take back a single moment I had with you."

She turned to look at me, and from the look on her face, I knew she'd already left me. "I will never forgive you for this," she said.

"I know," I whispered. "I love you anyway."

Her posture stiffened even further and she squared her shoulders as if trying to shield herself from my words. She must've known I was falling for her. I knew she was falling for me, so she must have known. It couldn't have been just me. I knew that.

"Love me?" Her lips curved up, but it wasn't the smile I loved so much. "You don't love me, Jack. I don't think you're capable of loving anyone."

I would never know if it was the last words I would hear from her that did me in or if it was watching her leave me. When she was out of sight, I walked to my desk, picked up a glass paper-weight and threw it against the wall.

I STAYED at the office until midnight working my ass off. I finished proposals and called clients, doing everything I didn't need to do to pass time and not go home, but there was nowhere to hide. I'd known what I was doing from the very beginning. I'd knowingly decided against telling Rose what I had done.

I had paid Joshua three more times, and he had still gone to her.

Truth be told, the reason I was avoiding going home was because I knew she wouldn't be there anymore, and I wasn't willing to have that truth slap me in the face. Rose had acted exactly like I'd expected her to. I'd earned her parting remark. Even I hadn't thought I was capable of loving anyone like I loved her before it had happened. Why would she believe me now?

At a quarter past twelve, I got in my car.

"Sir, are we heading home?"

"You can call me just Jack, Raymond. You call my wife by her name, and I don't see a reason why you can't call me by my name."

His eyes met mine in the rearview mirror and he nodded. "Home? Or somewhere else first?"

"To the apartment, please."

I looked outside, my gaze on the empty streets. It was quieter than usual as traffic lights let us pass one by one. A few minutes into the drive, Raymond broke the silence between us.

"She wanted to walk."

My thoughts scattered all at once. "Excuse me?"

"Rose. It had just started snowing so I offered to take her home, but she said she wanted to walk."

I imagined she did.

The rest of the car ride was quiet up until he pulled up in front of our building—*my* building. He stopped the engine and we sat there for a long moment. I wasn't sure why I thought sitting in the car and prolonging the pain I was feeling in my chest was a good idea when I knew what I'd find up there, but there was still a small part of me that was hoping.

"Okay," I said out loud and ran a hand over my face. "Okay then. Good night, Raymond."

"Would you like me to wait here?"

My brows drew together. "For what?"

"Just in case you'd like to go somewhere else. Maybe Around the Corner?"

Our eyes met and it dawned on me that he already knew. Of course he did. They'd spent mornings together for months. Of course she'd tell him what was going on after she was done with me.

"No. No, I don't think that's necessary. Have a good night."

I exited the car, his response falling on deaf ears.

I walked into the building and watched as our trusty doorman stood up to greet me. I was tempted to walk past with just a nod to acknowledge his presence, but it didn't feel right anymore.

"Hello, Steve. How are you?"

"Very good, sir. Thank you. How was your evening?"

I huffed. "Not the best night, I'm afraid." He raised an eyebrow, waiting for me to go on, but I decided to change the subject instead to avoid going upstairs. "Looks like a quiet night tonight."

"Yes, sir. It's freezing outside so everyone seems to be staying in."

"Yes. It must be the snow?"

"I believe so."

"Your daughter...it was Bella, right?"

He nodded.

"How is she doing at the new school? Everything all right?"

"Yes, sir. She is...happier. Thank you for asking."

"Good. I'm glad to hear that." I couldn't think of anything else to say so I nodded back, rapped my knuckles on his desk, and headed toward the elevators.

Unlocking the door, I forced myself to walk in and drown in the silence. I checked the kitchen first because sometimes she baked or cooked. The hand cream she used was gone from the living room, the one that smelled of pears. I walked up the stairs and into her bedroom, which had become ours. The bathroom was empty, the closet...everything looked dull and wrong. In just a few short hours she had managed to completely erase herself from my life. If I hadn't found the ring I had given her on the bedside table, the one on my side of the bed, I would have been inclined to believe I had dreamed her up. I picked up the ring and put it in my pocket.

I walked back downstairs and poured myself some whiskey. After I had swallowed down my third glass, I traced my steps back to her room and stepped out onto the terrace. The snow had started to come down harder. I didn't notice it much, not with the way I was feeling. I leaned my arms on the railing and looked over Central Park. I wasn't sure how long I stood there like an idiot, but the next thing I knew I was walking out of our apartment and catching a cab.

If Raymond had felt it necessary to mention her coffee shop, there was a good chance he had already checked and knew she was still there. The cabbie dropped me off a few stores down from her place and I walked till I was standing right in front of the big window next to the front door, right under the wreath I had put up as she smiled at me with happy eyes. I stood there on the empty, cold, wet sidewalk, on my own save for a few loud people walking by every now and then, and I could see a hint of light coming from the kitchen.

It ripped my black heart into pieces to know she was going to spend the night alone and far away from me, and in her coffee shop of all places, but I'd known from the moment I stepped out of the apartment that I was going to stand there until Owen showed up early in the morning and she wasn't alone anymore. Leaning my back against the side of the building, I tipped my head back and welcomed the soft bite of cold the snow left on my face.

I deserved far worse, and she deserved far better.

But...I was head over heels in love with this woman, more than I could've ever thought possible when I'd first come up with the most ridiculous 'business deal' I could ever conceive of. She had my heart in her hands. She was the only one for me; it was as simple as that. I could be without Rose. I could spend a lifetime without ever talking to her again and I would live—miserably, but I would live, as long as I knew she was happier. Life always moved on whether you chose to move along with it or stay put and let it happen all around you, but I didn't want to do it without her.

That was my choice. I didn't want to spend the rest of my life without her, just looking at her from a distance. I needed and wanted to be right next to her, holding her hand, whispering how much I loved her into her skin until my love became a part of her, a necessity she couldn't do without.

I wanted to be her air, her heart. I wanted everything I didn't deserve to have.

But was that the best thing for her?

Was I the best thing?

Unfortunately, I knew I wasn't, but that didn't change the fact that I would try to be.

CHAPTER TWENTY-SIX

ROSE

It was around two AM when I carefully ventured out of the kitchen so I could get a book from the library. I was still thinking if I could just stop my mind for a minute, maybe I could fall asleep and forget about everything that had happened in the last fifteen or so hours. At first, I was just peeking out from the doorway to the kitchen to make sure there was no one outside on the streets that would notice me. It only took me a few seconds to notice him.

Jack Hawthorne.

He was leaning against the lamp pole that was right on the corner, arms crossed against his chest. I glanced around to see if Raymond was waiting for him nearby, but I didn't see any familiar faces or cars; he appeared to be alone. Confused, angry, excited, and a little surprised, my heart leaping out of my chest in no time, I didn't know what to do for a second as my emotions waged a war in my heart. I kept looking at him, not sure what I should do.

Acknowledge his presence?

Go out there and demand to know what he was doing there?

No answer he could give me would change anything, though.

He was staring down at his shoes, and even though I was mad at him like nothing else, I still thought he looked just perfect in the moonlight. When he moved his head and noticed me standing in the doorway, my breath froze in my chest. We stared at each other, neither one of us taking a step forward. It was then I realized he wouldn't come. He wouldn't press and try to explain or apologize. No, Jack Hawthorne would do none of those things. He had been telling the absolute truth when he'd said he wasn't sorry for what he'd done.

I swallowed down my emotions, not even sure what I was supposed to feel anymore, and that little voice that was screaming at me to go outside to face him came unstuck. Avoiding glancing at him and ignoring his eyes following me, I quickly moved to the library. I couldn't grab a random book and disappear from sight; I didn't even know what I was supposed to do with a book, let alone trying to pick one. I fought back tears because there was no reason whatsoever for me to cry. It was over and done with.

It was okay, but I knew I wouldn't be. I let the tears fall and just picked a damn book that was within reach then, as calmly as I could manage, walked back into the kitchen. As soon as I was out of his sight, I leaned back against the wall and wiped at my tears.

I was still very much pissed off and hurt. It was a tossup between the two of us as to who I was angrier with—him or myself. My heart was broken, replaced with a constant ache. I was such a damn fool for thinking he had been honest with me every step of the way. I'd thought he was too serious not to be. My words, my last words to him echoed back in my head, along with the surprised and hurt look on his face when I'd spoken them. I knew I'd screwed it up at the end there, but I had wanted to hurt him. I'd wanted him to hurt just like I was because misery always loves company.

I chanced another peek and saw he was still standing in the same spot. He hadn't moved an inch. It should've felt stalkerish, him standing outside, wearing a black coat as he leaned against the lamp pole, but it didn't. It hurt my heart even more to see him standing there alone in the snow.

He wasn't happy.

I wasn't happy.

I wished we could've been unhappy together, under the same roof, but I couldn't do it. I couldn't look at his face and ignore that he had lied to me so monumentally. What if I had hated him, hated everything about him?

Marriage for one, please! Coming right up!

But then...

But then...that's when things started to get tricky. As much as I hated to admit it, if he wasn't lying now and what he had said about Joshua was true, it looked like he *had* saved me from him. He *had* given me my dream, and on a silver platter. Not a coffee shop, but a family. Someone I could lean on. He had done all of that just for the chance of a shot with me, for me. He was in love with me, and that knowledge threatened to pull the rug out from beneath my feet.

He was in love with me.

Then again, I already knew that. I'd seen it in his beautiful blue eyes, day after day. I knew the exact moment, that first time I'd seen it, seen the possibility of us: in that dark hospital room when he had crawled in bed with me. That was the first night I'd thought, *You know what, Rose, maybe he actually likes you. Despite all his prickliness and, at times, arrogance, despite all the scowling looks, maybe he really cares about you.*

Feeling dizzy, I slid down the wall and let my head rest against it. I didn't know how many minutes passed, but when I felt okay enough to move again, I glanced around the corner, making sure I wasn't visible to him just in case he was still standing there.

He was.

We had ended as we begun.

I watched him from the safety of the kitchen's doorway, the book I'd picked forgotten on the floor beside me. I must have fallen asleep sometime after four AM and jumped up in a panic when Owen walked through the door with a confused look on his face.

"What the hell are you doing on the floor?"

My mouth was dry, my eyes burning, and my voice came out all scratchy when I tried to speak. "Good morning to you too, sunshine. Just getting some shut-eye, as you can see."

"Right, because that's what you do on the floor. What was Jack doing outside?"

After a few attempts at getting up, I gave up and got on my knees so I could hold on to the edge of the island and pull myself up. "What are you talking about?"

Owen offered me his hand and helped me.

"He was right outside, half frozen from the looks of him. He said good morning and then left. Is this your version of spicing up your marriage, or did you guys have a fight or something?"

I pushed my hair away from my face. "Or something," I mumbled.

As Owen walked past me, shaking his head, I carefully looked out from the doorway, my eyes searching for him. When I couldn't find what I was looking for, I fully stepped out of the kitchen and walked through the tables until I was standing right in front of the window, looking outside.

Just like Owen had said, he was gone.

THE NEXT NIGHT, I stayed at Sally's place, swapping the comfort of the coffee shop's kitchen island and the lined-up chairs for a couch. I spent hours with my phone in my hand as I debated texting him. Eventually I fell asleep with my phone on my chest and never messaged him. I thought I slept for about three hours in total, and he kept me company in my dreams the rest of the time, which was even worse than not getting any sleep because when I woke up, I lost him all over again.

Sally had seen the two suitcases I owned stacked in the little office room in the back and had already guessed that something was seriously wrong. Since I thought I'd lose my ever-loving mind if I didn't tell at least one person what was going on, I told her everything. I rushed through admitting our whole marriage was nothing but a business deal and that we'd been wrong to assume otherwise. Then I'd caught her up on the rest of it.

She was as appalled as I had been the first time I'd heard everything from him, but then she decided she found the whole thing romantic.

"So what's going to happen now? Has he called you?"

"It's over," I repeated, probably for the hundredth time. "He has no reason to call me."

I left out the fact that I'd waited for him to do exactly that the night before.

"What about this place? What will happen to the coffee shop?"

"I don't know," I mumbled.

I truly didn't know.

The lunch rush started, and we didn't have time to do anything but work our asses off the rest of the day. It was around six PM when she approached me with a weird look on her face.

"Uh, Rose, did you say Jack waited for you that first night outside?"

"Yeah. Why?"

"I think he started his shift again."

Trying my best to look like I was busy in the kitchen while Owen was out in the front—me actually doing nothing useful at all, of course—I decided to keep my hands occupied and started checking cupboards, because trying to look for nothing in order to look like you weren't interested in what the other person was saying was always a fun idea. "What are you talking about?"

She waited until she had my full attention, and my heart had started beating too quickly to ignore her until she gave it up on her own.

"I'm talking about him leaning against his car and just standing there, right now."

I didn't have a single word to say to that other than rushing to the doorway and trying to spot him.

"Are you going to talk to him?" Sally asked, coming to stand next to me—out in the open, like a normal person. Owen glanced at us and then, after seeing us craning our necks, shook his head and kept chatting with a customer, talking about the times the coffee shop was the least busy.

"No."

"Have a heart, woman. It doesn't look like he'll budge."

"It'll be a long and cold night for him then." I pressed my lips together to hide my ridiculously pleased smile.

"Oh, come on. Can I at least take him some coffee? It's freezing out there."

"It's his coffee shop. He paid for it, after all. If he wants to come in, I can't stop him, but I'm not going to roll out the red carpet either. I don't care if you take him coffee or not."

"Rose—"

"I love him, Sally," I admitted, cutting off whatever she was about to say. "I love him, but I'm not ready to act like what he did didn't hurt me or that it wasn't wrong. I need him to understand what he did. I need him to take the time to think it through, and if that means he wants to come and wait outside or something, he is free to do whatever he wants."

"So it's not over. It's over for now, but it's not over."

I thought her words over as I watched Jack talking to someone on his phone. He didn't see me watching him, taking in my fill, but his eyes were definitely on the coffee shop.

"I miss him," I conceded into the silence.

Sally pushed her arm through mine and rested her head on my shoulder. "Owen?"

He looked at us over his shoulder.

"I need you to start being romantic now," Sally ordered, and my lips tipped up. She still hadn't given up on him, and I thought Owen secretly enjoyed her attention.

I cleared my throat before they started their usual back and forth. "If you happen to or decide to take coffee to Jack, don't forget Raymond. Jack likes my—*the* lemon bars, and Raymond likes the triple chocolate brownies."

Sally snorted. "Right. I give it a week before you cave."

I gave her a murderous look. "Keep dreaming."

An hour later, I wasn't sure if I was more annoyed with myself because my eye kept wandering over to where Jack was standing, or if I was just annoyed with him for breaking my focus at work. I decided to head to Sally's place so I could cook us dinner as a thank you for letting me stay with her.

The second I stepped outside, my heart started pounding in my chest. Jack straightened up the moment he saw me. I stood just a few feet away from him as we studied each other. If he had walked forward and said something, I wasn't sure what I would've done. Maybe, like Sally had said, I would have caved, but he didn't. So, I did...sort of, still leaving a healthy amount of space between us, enough for four people to easily walk through, actually.

"What are you doing here, Jack?" I asked, raising my voice just a little.

"Wanted to see you."

I opened my arms at my sides. "Now you did. Goodbye."

He was about to take a step forward when a group of girls walked between us, successfully blocking him.

"How are you feeling?" he asked when it was just us again.

"Oh, perfect. Just perfect. Having the best time of my life."

"I meant your head, your nose. Are you still getting dizzy? Headaches? You look tired."

I tilted my head to the side, narrowing my eyes. "Thank you. As you know, it's my default to look bad. You look like hell yourself."

His jaw clenched, a muscle ticking visibly. "You need to take better care of yourself," he forced out, his eyes blazing, as if he had any right to be angry with me.

"No." My eyes still on him, I shook my head. "Don't do that. You don't get to act like you're worried about me, Jack." I looked to the left and then the right. "There is no one around who knows us, so you can stop the pretending."

We studied each other in silence. I wasn't sure if this would be the last time I'd ever see him. He could just wake up the next day and say, *The hell with it, she isn't*—or, even worse—*she wasn't worth the trouble anyway. I had my fun with the business deal marriage. Now it's time to move on.* The thought alone scared the bejesus out of me, but I wasn't ready to ignore everything and act like he hadn't hurt me either. Therein lay our problem.

"Go home, Jack," I said quietly. "You have no reason to be here."

In the great scheme of things, we were nothing more than two people who had passed each other while walking through their lives. Couples broke up every day, and we were not special in that regard either. You cried yourself to sleep then woke up and went to work. When you repeated the cycle enough times, one day you woke up and suddenly it didn't matter all that much. New people walked alongside you and eventually you forgot the ones you left behind.

When he didn't deny what I'd said, I let out a long breath, looked at his eyes for a moment longer to remember, and finally turned to leave.

"I don't have a home to go back to anymore, Rose."

I stopped, but didn't look at him.

"You're my home," he finished.

My eyes filling with tears, I walked away.

And he let me.

So we ended as we'd begun, nothing but two complete strangers.

Closer to midnight, after Sally had gone to bed and I was getting ready to start another sleepless night, I opened the curtains and the window so I could breathe in the cold air. Someone was walking across the street and for a moment I thought it was Jack, but then he walked under the light and I realized it was just a stranger.

For a moment I was shocked, why would it hurt not to see him? Why would I be disappointed?

During the week, he came to the coffee shop around closing time twice. He leaned against his car, then when Ray left he leaned against the lamp pole. Every time he showed up he made it harder to remember why I was so angry at him. He paced and waited. When I came out with Sally but didn't stop to talk to him, he left.

Then he disappeared for several days.

It was the eighth day of our break up and we were getting ready to close when he showed up again. All three of us were in the front. Owen and I were clearing out the dishes on the counter and taking them back into the kitchen, and Sally was stacking up clean coffee mugs and the to-go cups next to the espresso machine. We only had two customers in the shop, and both of them were regulars working on their laptops.

The bell rang, and I looked up to see someone bundled up in her coat and scarf walk in and head straight toward one of the customers, so I got back to work.

Sally was the first one to notice Jack.

"Rose."

I looked at her over my shoulder.

"Yes?"

"He's here," she whispered urgently, and I looked around in confusion until my eyes landed on him. My pulse picked up and my heart started to get all excited, but something was wrong. I couldn't tell what he was thinking from his facial expression, because if there was one thing Jack Hawthorne was good at, it was hiding his emotions. Dread and excitement over seeing him settled over me anyway as my heart betrayed me.

He stood on the other side of the counter and I did nothing but stare at him, my heart pounding in my ears.

I heard Sally clear her throat. "Hi, Jack."

He didn't take his eyes off me when he answered. "Hello, Sally. You're good, I hope."

"Yes. Great."

Then it was back to silence again.

Feeling my chest tighten, I swallowed and wiped my hands on my jeans, managing to look away from his eyes.

I saw his hand tighten around a stack of papers he was holding, creating a tube.

"Uh, Owen did you take the—" I started in a low, rough voice, but Jack cut me off before I could finish my sentence.

"If I could talk to you in private, Rose?"

I looked back up at him, trying my best not to show that I had forgotten how to breathe like a normal person in the last minute or so. I cleared my throat and nodded.

"Kitchen?"

I nodded again and watched as he moved around the counter and walked straight back there. Sally bumped her shoulder into mine and smiled when I gave her a startled look.

"You miss him. Be nice. I think you've made him suffer long enough. You suffered enough as well."

I didn't respond, just turned to Owen. "I'll, uh, I'll be back in a minute. If you could just—"

"I have plenty of things to do out here. Go make up or whatever so we can breathe easy again."

I hit him on the shoulder as I walked past him into the kitchen. I only had enough time to take a deep breath before I was standing across from Jack again, this time with the island between us. I took in his dark grey suit, crisp white shirt, and black tie. He was made to wear suits and break my heart.

I reached for a kitchen towel just to have something in my hands and looked away. While I was busy trying to find the right words to apologize for what I had said at his office, Jack spoke up.

"You can't even look at me, can you?"

Startled by his words, I met his gaze. Was that what he thought?

"Jack, I—"

"It doesn't matter now," he continued. "I came to give you this in person." He unrolled the file in his hands and put it on the island, right next to the triple chocolate brownies, then pushed it my way.

My eyes still on him, I reached for it.

"What is this?" My voice came out like a whisper.

When he didn't answer, I looked down and turned the first page.

Shocked by what I was reading, my eyes flew up to his.

"Divorce papers," he said calmly.

I was anything but calm. My mind in overdrive, my eyes tried to follow the words and sentences, but it was all a jumbled mess in front of me.

"You want a divorce?" I croaked out, the papers slightly trembling. I tightened my grip to hide it from his eyes.

"Yes. It's the right thing...for you."

My brows drew together and some heat started to come back to my limbs. I forced myself to drop the papers on the island and take a step back as if they would come alive and bite my fingers off.

This time I met his gaze straight on, the dread and excitement turning into anger. "For me. How about you? What do you get out of it?"

He tilted his head to the side, his eyes slightly narrowing in a calculating manner. "It's the right thing for me too."

A little dazed, I nodded. Barely able to speak through the tightness in my throat, I said, "I see." Impressive word choices, I know.

I was so out of it that I didn't even notice him taking out a pen from his suit jacket and offering it to me.

I stared at him as if he had sprouted another head.

"You want me to sign it...now."

It wasn't a question, but he treated it as such.

"Yes. I'd like to get it done right now."

"You'd like to get it done right now," I echoed.

"Preferably."

That word—that one annoying word pushed me over the edge of worry and guilt into anger.

Preferably.

I decided right then and there that it was the most ridiculous and annoying word in the world. I didn't touch the pen. I didn't pick up the papers.

I crossed my arms against my chest. "The right thing to do would've been to be honest with me from the beginning."

Cool as a cucumber, he pushed his hands into the pockets of his pants as red-hot fury licked over my skin.

"You're right, which is why I'd like you to sign the papers."

"No."

His brows drew together as he looked at me from across the space. "No?"

"No." I was very good at being stubborn. I was like a cow—if I didn't want to be moved, you couldn't move me, no matter who or what came.

"Rose—"

"No."

He gritted his teeth. "Why?"

I shrugged, feigning nonchalance. "I don't think I feel like signing anything today. Maybe some other time."

"Rose, it needs to be today."

"Really?" I asked, making a thinking face and then grimacing. "Ah, I'm so sorry. I'm busy today. Maybe some other time."

He looked truly taken back. "Why are you doing this? I thought this was what you wanted."

No wonder I had thought him to be a cement block in the beginning—not only did he not show his emotions, he didn't understand them even when they slapped him in the face.

Something wet slid down my cheek and, appalled at myself for crying, I wiped at it angrily with the back of my hand. That's when Jack's face changed and his entire body tensed. He lost the frown, the anger, the disbelief and hid behind his mask again.

I wiped off another wayward tear and lifted my chin high.

He shook his head then rubbed the bridge of his nose. Next thing I knew, he was moving toward me. I did my best to breathe in and out normally and stayed put. Even when he was standing right next to me, his chest almost resting against my shoulder, I didn't move. I stopped breathing too.

"Rose," he started in a low voice, his head bent closer to mine.

I stopped trying to clear the tears away. They were only angry tears, and maybe stress, nothing more, and the same reasons applied for the trembling, too.

When I felt his lips against my temple, I closed my eyes. "You're breaking my heart, baby, trying to hold on to something that should've never been. Sign the divorce papers, Rose. Please."

"I won't," I whispered.

"Why?" he asked again.

"I won't."

I felt the gentle touch of his fingertips as he gripped my chin and turned my head. I opened my eyes and looked straight into the dark blue eyes of the man I had irrevocably fallen in love with.

I wanted to say so much to him.

"Do it. I'll send someone to pick up the signed papers."

He held on to my chin and seemed to map out my face in his mind as his eyes touched every inch. Then his hand slipped forward, cupping the side of my cheek.

My eyes closed on their own as he pressed a kiss to my forehead then the next second he was gone. I was too scared to open my eyes, to face the reality of the hell that had been my life for the last week.

He could send his entire firm to my door if he wanted to. I was not going to sign those damn papers.

"Rose? It didn't go well, did it?"

I took a few deep breaths and opened my eyes, feeling more determined than ever.

Sally was standing right where Jack had stood just moments earlier. I picked up the papers, holding them out for her to take. "He wants a divorce."

She seemed to choke up before she took the file from my hand. "But, he said...how would—did you sign them?"

I shook my head. "Nope."

"Are you going to?"

"Nope."

That evening when we closed the coffee shop, no matter how hard I looked, I couldn't find Jack anywhere, and I took his absence as an invitation.

CHAPTER TWENTY-SEVEN

JACK

She hadn't signed the papers.

I knew that because the guy I'd sent to pick them up had returned empty-handed. So, I headed out to face her myself—again—and when I found her, this time I wouldn't walk away until I got a damn signature. The divorce had to happen, and it had to happen soon.

But before I could deal with Rose, I needed to make a quick stop.

I knocked on his door and hoped he'd be inside.

He opened after a few seconds and looked shocked to see me.

"How do you know where I live?" Joshua Landon asked with a furious expression on his face.

I smiled at him and blocked the door with my foot before he could shut it in my face and shouldered my way in.

"You couldn't stay away from her, could you? Your greed will cost you, Joshua."

"Listen to me you—"

I wasn't there to have a nice long chat. I had better things to do so instead of wasting my time I grabbed him by his shirt before he could back away and ignoring his loud protests punched him straight in the face.

At least that managed to shut him up. He staggered and one hand gripping his nose, the other holding onto the wall behind him he barely managed to stay upright.

"You fucking son of a bitch," he growled.

"This is your last warning. If I ever see you break her heart again, or hear about it, I'll kill you."

Before I could make good on my words, I turned around and forced myself to walk away.

After my quick visit to Joshua I went straight to Madison Avenue, because I knew she'd still be at the coffee shop, working at four PM, but she wasn't where she was supposed to be. Next, I tried the address Sally gave me, where she'd been staying this whole time. She wasn't there either.

The apartment was on the first floor of an old building where anyone walking past could easily see inside and just as easily break in if they had a mind to do so. She would be the first thing they'd see, sleeping on the couch, right in front of the door, which made me impossibly angry. I already thought of myself as a damn stalker, why hadn't I waited here at night? I would've officially earned that title at least.

Somewhere between worried and slightly pissed off, I doubled back to the coffee shop. When I walked in, both Owen and Sally snapped to attention.

Then they gave me more lies.

"She hasn't come back since you left."

"If we knew where she was we'd tell you."

"Oh, I hope she's okay—she didn't look okay when she left."

It didn't matter how terse I was with them, they didn't budge. Since I didn't want to scare off their customers, I couldn't very well demand an answer either. Good for Rose since it seemed like she'd made good employee choices, but not so good for me, unfortunately.

I even walked through goddamn Central Park just in case she thought hiding there in the freezing cold would be a good idea. It wouldn't surprise me in the least. I couldn't go to her other friends, at least not until I could have our investigator dig up their addresses for me, but I knew it wouldn't come to that. She barely saw them anyway. No matter where she was hiding, she'd come back to her precious coffee shop in the morning, and if that meant I had to wait outside or in a car until she showed up before the sun was even up, so be it. As long as she showed up, I didn't care what I had to do. I was going to get a goddamn signature on that paper.

With no other options, I had Raymond drive me back to the apartment.

"Good evening, Steve. Everything all right?"

He smiled at me. "Good evening, sir. Yes, it's a good night. How was your day?"

"Just perfect," I muttered under my breath.

"Excuse me, sir?"

Trying to snap out of my bad mood, I shook my head. "Nothing. How's your girl?"

His smile got bigger. "She is very well. Thank you for asking."

"Of course." Rubbing my neck, I sighed. "I'm gonna head up then."

"Everything okay?"

I was about to start talking about Rose and tell him how frustrated and angry and worried I was, but I stopped myself. In just months, she had turned me into this. "Have a good night, Steve."

"You, too."

Right. Nodding a few times, I took the elevator up and walked into the apartment. The second I closed the door, I realized my mistake.

She was smart. I'd forgotten that somehow. She was unlike anyone I'd been with. Of course she'd be where I least expected her to be. Of course she'd hide in plain sight.

Ten points to her.

I closed my eyes, took a deep breath, and released it.

Relieved that I'd finally found her, I followed the soft clinking noises to the kitchen and noticed the TV was playing on mute. I took my time turning it off to calm myself down.

I crossed my arms and leaned against the kitchen doorframe. Quite a few apples were lined up on the kitchen counter next to where she was working on some dough. So she was baking an apple pie in my apartment when she was supposed to be anywhere but in my apartment.

"What are you doing here?"

I watched as her shoulders tightened and she straightened her spine. Before turning around, she went to the sink and washed her hands, taking her sweet time doing so. I stayed quiet. When I thought she would turn around, she picked up an apple and started washing them one by one. I counted four apples so far, and with each passing second, her frame stood more frigid.

Then she turned off the water, picked up a kitchen towel, and finally faced me as she dried her hands.

"Baking."

I nodded.

"What are you doing baking in my apartment? Did you come here to hand-deliver the papers yourself and then randomly started baking?"

Her chin rose, just slightly, her eyes sparkling with something that resembled anger. It made her look more lethal than she already was to me.

"How was your day...husband?"

I straightened against the doorframe.

"Tell me you signed the papers."

Her head tilted to the side and she dropped the kitchen towel on the counter, her stance mirroring mine as she crossed her arms.

"I didn't." There went her chin, up a little more.

I studied her, a million thoughts running through my mind. "What's happening here?"

She uncrossed her arms and held on to the edge of the kitchen counter. She was wearing her favorite black jeans that hugged every inch of her curves and a chunky sweater that fell off of one of her shoulders. Half of her hair was up in a messy bun on top of her head, the rest tumbling down her bare shoulder.

"Are you seeing someone?"

My brows snapped together. "What?"

"Are you seeing someone? Is that why you want a divorce?"

I came out of my stupor and took a few steps toward her. Her body stiffened, but she didn't lose her stance.

"What the hell is happening here?" I repeated.

"I took vows."

That was what she came back with, and my brows drew in tighter.

"Fake vows," I countered, my voice coming out harsher than I had intended. I caught her flinch but didn't know how to react. I had no idea what the hell was happening or what she thought she was doing. As far as I knew, she was ruining everything.

"I wouldn't say so. They were pretty real for me. We said *I do* in front of the officiant. We signed the papers, and I have the proof. That's as real as it gets."

I stopped when we were toe to toe and stared down at her. My eyes flicked down to her hands and I noticed how tightly she was gripping the marble.

"Where are you going with this exactly?"

"I'm not going anywhere. That's the point."

"I see. So what you're saying is that you're refusing to sign the divorce papers?"

"Exactly." She squared her shoulders, unknowingly pushing her breasts toward me. My eyes dropped from her gaze only for a moment. I took a step back.

"And I'm moving back in." She let go of the counter and opened her arms. "Tada—I'm home! I answered your questions. You didn't answer mine."

Confused about what was happening, I stared at her. "Are you sure you're feeling okay?"

"Are you seeing someone? Is it someone from work? Samantha, maybe?"

"You *have* lost your mind then."

Her hands went back to grip the edge. "You're avoiding the question. Are you cheating on me, Jack?"

I took back the space I'd created between us and put my hands on the counter behind her, trapping her between my arms. I bent down until her face was only inches away from mine and I could look into her beautiful, beautiful eyes.

"What are you doing, Rose? Don't make me ask again."

She didn't bristle at my stern words. Instead her face gentled, her eyes staring right back into mine. "I'm trying to have a fight."

I waited for her to go on.

"You never make anything easy, do you?" She sighed. "I happen to think a little fighting is healthy in a marriage. First of all, it's never good to hold things in, so you have to keep the lines of communication open if you want to last. Which you're not very good at, but you'll start working on it. I'm sure."

"Explain why you're not signing the papers," I insisted.

She started to bite her lower lip, presumably trying to find the right words. I waited patiently. Her response was important.

"Because I don't want to get a divorce."

"It wasn't a real marriage. I lied to you. I tricked you into it.

You didn't have to marry me—I could've bought the property and rented it to you."

"I would've never accepted it. You knew it, you said so yourself. Why did you do it?"

"I already answered that question the day you came to my office."

"To have a shot with me. You never apologized."

"And I won't now either. I told you I wouldn't take the time I spent with you back."

"Yet you want a divorce."

I nodded. Moving just an inch closer, my eyes fell to her lips, which were starting to turn red with all her biting. "I do."

"Why?" she asked.

"You said it yourself—you think I'm seeing someone else."

She shook her head, her eyes dropping to my mouth and then coming back to my eyes. Her chest had started to rise and fall faster. She shook her head, a very small movement. Her shoulders were slightly trembling as well.

"I don't think you'd have the time, what with stalking me and all that."

The things she said to me... My lips twitched, drawing the attention of her gaze.

"A lot of work piled up at the office because of you."

"I can imagine. Rough life, stalker life."

"Tell me why you're not signing the papers, Rose."

"If I do, will you tell me why you want to get a divorce after going through the trouble of tricking me into a marriage?" she countered.

I nodded, my eyes set intently on hers.

"Okay then." She straightened a little and I gave her just enough space to do so. "It's going to be cheesy, but don't blame me. You asked."

"I think I can handle it. Go ahead."

"I...I didn't have the best childhood, obviously. I lived in a house. Not a home. I had people who were related to me, but I didn't have family. I didn't have anyone I could lean on. I didn't have anyone who would take care of me if I needed it. I had myself. I did everything myself. For a really long time, it was just me against the world. Then I grew up and I had other people to hold hands with, but they weren't the right ones. I knew they wouldn't stick so I never let myself become vulnerable. I never let anyone take care of me. Until you. You, big idiot. Until you gave everything that I've longed for since I was nine. You gave me a family. My own. The two of us against everything and everyone. You broke every wall I had up and then—uh, you know what? Never mind. I love you. There. Happy? I don't like you at the moment, but I liked you before—very much so. So, yes, I love you. I didn't want you in the beginning. I barely liked you. You're not my type at all. You're arrogant at times, though not all the time. Actually, who am I kidding? You are, though I don't think you even realize you're being arrogant. You're prickly. You don't notice people. You got better at that, but you didn't even know your own doorman's name when I first came here."

"I talk to him every day," I said.

"Now you do, but you didn't before. Then there is the fact that you're rich. I know this is my own hang-up. This is not on you, but I usually don't like rich people. You are rude. You were rude—same thing, in my opinion. You're surly. Frowny. You already know I used to count your smiles. You never smiled! Never. That's a big thing for me. I like smiling, laughing. I like people to smile at me, laugh with me."

Now that she had gained steam, her voice was slowly rising. I arched an eyebrow, but she didn't notice because she was only meeting my eyes every now and then. She was busy thinking, her breathing hard, her forehead all creased as she was rattling off all the reasons she didn't like me.

"Now I smile," I said before she could keep going. She met my eyes for a brief moment.

"Don't interrupt."

This time I didn't hide my smile. "I apologize. Go on, please."

"You don't smile. You didn't talk in the beginning, let alone smile! What kind of person doesn't talk? You helped every day at the coffee shop, showed up every night to pick me up, yet you barely talked. If you wanted to have a shot with me, you were doing a piss-poor job of it."

"I told you I was trying to stay away so you could—"

"I said, don't interrupt. You never compliment me. It's always, *You look tired, you look this, you look that*."

"You're the most beautiful woman I've ever met. You're usually tired, but beautiful despite that."

She slapped me on my chest then left her hand exactly where it was with her palm right on my heart.

"See! You can't even compliment me to save your life. You frown too much."

She stopped, seemed to be thinking some more.

"You already said that. What else you got?" I asked.

"I'm thinking."

I reached up and tucked a piece of hair behind her ear, my fingertips lingering on the skin of her neck and shoulders.

"You're the most precious thing in the world to me, Rose."

She shivered.

"You're all those things. You did all those things," she whispered.

"I can change for you. I did change for you."

"I shouldn't want you. I shouldn't want *us*."

"You shouldn't, but do so anyway."

She put her other hand on my chest as well, holding on to the lapels of my jacket. "You did change, and I love you despite all the things I don't like about you. I probably love you more because of them. I don't know. I love it when you frown at me for no damn reason. I find it so amusing. I've lost my mind. I enjoy making you frown."

"I usually do have a good reason."

"Yeah, you keep thinking like that. You can be sweet some-times—so sweet, and thoughtful. Around the Corner wouldn't be my reality if it weren't for all your help before the opening—and I didn't even like you back then."

"I think I got that you didn't like me."

"You bring me flowers every Monday, just so I won't use the fake plastic ones. You get me beautiful, real roses and then you act all uncomfortable about it. I love flowers. You know I love flowers."

"I know. I'll always bring them to you." This time, I reached up to catch the tear that fell from her eye. "Tell me. What else?"

"I will. I don't want the florist to bring them—you need to bring them on your own."

"Done. What else?"

"I love that you talk to Steve now. I love that you join in when Raymond and I are talking instead of sulking on your own."

"I don't sulk."

"You do, but it's okay because I find that amusing as well." She patted my tie, sliding her hand up and down a few times. Then her fingers gripped my shirt. "And when I was sick, you held my ankle. Do you even realize how stupid that sounds? But somehow it's the sweetest and most romantic thing anyone ever did for me. You didn't leave me alone for one second. I don't think I could've gone through all that on my own. You were always right next to me, every step of the way, and you made me love you. So, now I can't go back, and it's no else's but your fault. I'm not going to divorce you."

"Okay." I held her head in between my hands and kissed her forehead.

"Okay?"

"You made a good argument."

"Don't make fun of me, Jack. I'm not in the mood."

"I wouldn't dare."

It seemed like she didn't know what to say exactly, so I took over. "You don't remember meeting me, but I remember it, Rose. You barely even looked at me when Gary introduced us. Then we went up to your uncle's office and I didn't even think about it, about you. The meeting ended and when I came down and saw you with that damn puppy in the kitchen, laughing, dancing, I couldn't look away from you. I couldn't move from where I was standing. Then Joshua came. The way you hugged him, the way you looked at him, the way you smiled at him—it was different from all the other smiles you'd given everyone else who greeted you, and I was jealous. For a second there, I wished it was me you were looking at like that...like he was the most important person in your life. Yet he was more interested in other people. I didn't care for him. He wouldn't be the guy I would picture by your side." I caressed her hair and kissed her forehead again. I didn't know how not to, not when she was in my arms like this.

"You would picture yourself by my side, I guess. Then what happened?" she asked, looking into my eyes with curiosity.

"No. If I could let you go, I would want you to have someone better than me. Then I didn't do anything. I was interested, sure, and if you hadn't had a boyfriend, I would have taken a chance, but you had him, so I didn't think much about it. You aren't my type anyway."

"Your compliments, I do live for them. You go for the cold, arrogant, and beautiful ones, right? Like Samantha."

"Something like that, but for a moment there, I could picture you with me. I wanted a shot like I'd never wanted one with anyone else. Then Gary told me about the contract, it went into the will, and you know the rest. The more I learned about Joshua, the more I couldn't just sit and do nothing, so I did something. I didn't hesitate to call him and offer him money if he left you alone, but I hesitated when we were getting married because I knew I was screwing things up and taking things a step too far. I felt nothing but guilt those first few weeks."

"Did you have anything to do with him being with Jodi?"

"No. I swear to you. I learned about them the same night you did. When he learned I had married you and I'd cost him the property, he contacted me again to ask for money and threatened me with telling you everything. I paid him, time after time. The night after the charity event, the night he saw us together—do you remember? I told you I was going to the office, but he had texted me that night so I went to meet him. By then I knew I was falling for you, and I didn't want him to ruin whatever chances we had. That last time we met, I told him I wouldn't pay anymore because of that look he put on your face the day he showed up, and if he pushed his luck, I said I'd let Jodi know who he really was. He shrugged and said there were plenty of Jodi's, but only one Rose for me."

"Don't lie to me, Jack. You didn't love me. You weren't even nice to me in the beginning. I'm not someone who believes you can fall in love with someone without knowing them. Don't feed me bullshit."

I brushed her bangs out of her eyes. "Will you shut up? I wasn't in love when we first got married or even the first time I saw you. I'm not saying it was love. It was just interest, maybe a crush, but the more I got to know you, the more I couldn't not fall for you. If I hadn't known you had bought all the equipment to open your place, that you had spent your money, if there had been no contract, I'd have still paid Joshua to protect you from him, but after that, I'd have approached you like a normal guy. I'd have gotten to know you, asked you out, nothing more."

"Why were you so mean to me? You barely spoke, and don't

think I forgot what you said to me after the wedding. You told me it was a mistake, I was a mistake and said we shouldn't have done it."

I smiled, but there was no humor in it. "That was my guilt. I didn't know what to do with you, and I knew in the end, when you learned about what I did, it was going to kill whatever chance we had or didn't have for good. I didn't know how to get over it. Trust me, it was an unexpected reaction. If anything was going to happen it had to come from you. I wasn't going to let you accuse me of forcing love even though I'd manufactured the marriage part. So, I decided to just let it be and let you have the coffee shop while maintaining a healthy distance. I didn't want to help you set the place up. I didn't want to be around you so much. I even considered telling you everything. That was why I kept asking you to go out to dinner with me, but I couldn't do it. I was gonna wait for the right time. Then you got sick and I didn't care what would happen, whether you knew what I'd done or not. I didn't give a fuck about the guilt, and you were warming up to me, so..."

"You love me now," she whispered.

I cupped her head and rested my forehead against hers. "You are the love of my goddamn life," I whispered back, my voice raw and hoarse. "Somewhere in between all the pretending, I completely fell for you, and I can't even think of my life without you in it."

She cupped my cheeks in return. "You want to divorce me, Jack."

I pressed my body against hers until I heard a little gasp and her back was resting against the counter. "Yes. I want to so I can start fresh and show you that I can be what you need. I want to start over, do it right this time, ask you out like a normal person."

She seemed to think it over as I held my breath and waited. "I don't want to. I don't want to start over. I don't want to divorce you. I want to keep going."

"Okay. Then we won't."

"But you have to promise me, Jack. You have to promise me that you'll never keep anything from me. I need to trust you. It doesn't matter how much I love you, I can't do this if I don't trust you. You have to give me all the information and let me make the decision when it's something that concerns me."

"I promise you. I promise you I'll do everything to earn your trust again."

"Then we won't get a divorce." She cracked a small smile. "You think I'm beautiful."

I smiled back. "The most beautiful woman I've ever seen."

"You're a lucky man, then."

"I'm the luckiest bastard."

She nodded enthusiastically. "That you definitely are. There is nothing else I need to know, right? I want us to be okay, but there are no more surprises, right?"

"Have you read the divorce papers?"

Her stubborn little chin went up again. "No. I tore them up."

My smile in place, I shook my head. "I gave the coffee shop to you. You were going to get it in the divorce. I never wanted it anyway."

Her body stilled, her hands dropping from my face.

"Is it too late to change my mind about divorcing you?"

"I'm afraid so."

She sighed. "Oh well. I'll keep you, you keep the coffee shop —I think it's a pretty good deal."

"I'd have to agree."

We stared into each other's eyes. "What now?" she whispered.

"It's Monday, so I need to cook you pasta. We have traditions."

I got a small smile. "I do love couple traditions. That was the deal."

"Your heart always has a home with me, Rose. No matter what, never forget that."

"And yours will always have a home with me. Certain people are meant for each other and you were meant for me, Jack. And I was meant for you."

"Yes, I'm yours. Only yours."

Something changed in her eyes. "How do you feel about sex?"

My lips quirked. "In general, I approve of it."

"But how about right now, specifically?"

Under her heavy gaze, I thought about it for a moment—for a very short moment—then leaned in to whisper in her ear. "I definitely approve of sex if and only *if* I'm the one who is burying himself deep inside you, Rose Hawthorne."

When I leaned back to look into her eyes, I realized she was already flushed.

CHAPTER TWENTY-EIGHT

JACK

"You want me to fuck you?"

"I mean it's not a necessity, but maybe to seal every—"

My gaze shifted back to her lips and I couldn't help myself anymore.

We crashed into each other, and the moment our lips touched, she let out a long groan and slid her arms around my neck. I grabbed her hips and pulled her forward until my painfully hard erection was squeezed between our bodies.

In response, she arched her back and smiled against my lips.

"Happy?"

Her eyes closed and, still smiling, she nodded. "This is a good marriage."

"Anything you want, it's yours," I whispered then chased her mouth and tongue again. She tangled her fingers in my hair and let me taste her however I wanted. Letting go of her hips, I reached to the hem of her sweater and had to force myself to stop kissing her. Breathless, she let me, so, keeping my eyes on hers, I slowly peeled off her sweater and dropped it on the floor.

"It's you I want," she whispered. "Only you."

Her gaze was intent on me as I looked down and let my eyes roam over her perfect breasts and flawless skin. She had a small birthmark right beneath her left shoulder toward her breast. I had missed it the first time I touched her like this. Not again. I'd learn every inch of her body until I could picture it perfectly when I closed my eyes. I touched her neck with my fingertips and let them slide down toward her heavy breasts. When I reached her lilac bra, I gripped the thin lace cups and pulled them down.

"Look at you," I whispered.

Rose was breathing heavily, her nipples rising and falling, causing me to lose my mind. I glanced at her face and saw her eyes burning with anticipation. I let out a deep breath, feeling sheer relief now that she was truly mine. There were no lies, nothing standing between us.

I rested my forehead against hers so I could breathe for a moment. She cupped my cheek with her palm, letting me have that moment.

"I missed you," I said hoarsely.

"I missed you," she echoed.

I kissed her cheek then moved lower and brushed a hot kiss against the side of her throat. "You're mine."

She didn't respond, but her body shivered at my words and her throat moved as she swallowed. I kept moving lower, tasting her skin with my lips until I reached her nipple. I closed my mouth over it and sucked, hard.

Her body stiffened and she gripped my shoulders at the same time she let out a groan. My hands gripping her waist, I moved to the other one, sucking and pulling.

Then her fingers touched my stubbled jaw and she eased my face away. "You love me. You really love me," she gasped out, breathless. It was a quiet question.

"I love you, Rose," I repeated in a firm voice, my fingers tweaking and pulling her nipples.

She bit her lip. "I love you too, Jack. I just wanted to hear it again."

"Any time." Still looking into her eyes, I reached behind her and undid her bra. Gently, I slid the straps off of her shoulders, holding her gaze the entire time. Then it was her turn and she was undoing my tie and letting it drop on the floor. Her fingers worked on the buttons of my shirt, every action painfully slow. It felt like it took her ages to finish when I just wanted to ravish her, but we'd have all the time in the world to do that.

"You're mine, too," she said. "You're only mine."

"We belong to each other, no one else, till we take our last breath."

"Yes."

The declaration ringing in my ears, I had to force myself to stay still as she put her palms on my chest and brushed the shirt off, the feel of her fingertips burning my skin anywhere she touched.

My self-control vanished when she gently pulled me in for another kiss and let her hand roam down my chest, straight toward my cock. My hands started working on her jeans, unbuttoning, pushing, and pulling as my lips took over our kiss and deepened it.

Her hand reached the bulbous head of my cock in the confines of my pants and she stilled. I gripped her chin, kissed her harder. She palmed my length and let her hand slowly slide down then back up again. She was my undoing.

I only managed to withstand it for a few torturous drags then I pulled her off the counter in one move, swallowing her shriek and laughter with my mouth. I quickly got rid of her jeans and underwear then, grabbing her waist, I planted her naked ass back up there. Her eyes were still laughing when I glanced up from her body, which was all mine now.

"Kiss me, Jack. Kiss me." Obeying her order, I roughly

grabbed her cheeks with one hand, tilted her head, and pushed my tongue into her mouth. I could barely stand still as she insisted on taking off my pants with her hands, brushing mine off whenever I tried to help.

As soon as she pushed it down, my cock bobbed up and down, my balls heavy.

"I want you inside me," she gasped, breaking our kiss. "Now, Jack. Now."

"Nothing else in the world is more important than you."

I was being rougher than I would want to be with her if I had my head on straight, but if the grip of her fingers on my skin was any indication, she was right there with me. I spread her thighs open, pulled her to the edge of the counter, and guided my cock into her center, pushing in with one hard stroke.

Gripping my shoulder with one hand, she hugged me to herself with the other, her forehead resting against my shoulder.

"You okay?" I asked, having trouble staying still when her muscles flexed around my cock.

She nodded against my shoulder. "You don't have to be gentle with me. I won't break, Jack."

"Is that what you want?"

"Yes."

I held her ass in my hands and gently pulled out, letting her feel every thick, hard inch. I thrust back in, grunting against her skin as she tried to catch her breath. She was so wet for me, incredibly tight and wet and all mine. Grabbing her calves, I wrapped them around my hips. Her chest was plastered against mine, her nipples hard against my skin. I pulled her hips closer, forcing her to have every inch of me inside her. I wasn't willing to have even a millimeter separating us.

Licking her neck and earning a soft moan, I started to fuck her, hard and deep—harder than our first time. She held on to my shoulders, her nails marking my skin, her skin burning against mine.

"Jack," she cried out, and her voice, the thickness, the *sex* in her voice pushed me over an invisible edge.

My hands trembling with what I felt for her, I tugged her face away from my neck and caught her lips. I had my cock inside her, my tongue inside her, my hand working her nipples. She shuddered in my arms as my thrusts quickened, pushing her over the edge.

"Jack!"

"Let it go, Rose," I ordered when she gasped yet again. "I want you to come all over my cock." Her muscles tightened around me, and I slowed my pounding as her inner muscles worked. "That's it, baby," I whispered, nudging her into another kiss as she moaned and stiffened. I wanted everything she was willing to give me—her orgasms, her moans, her skin, her mouth. Everything she was willing to give, I wanted for my own.

When she stopped coming, I gave her mouth a break so she could catch her breath and gulp in air as I stilled deep inside her.

I kneaded her breasts with my hands, forcing myself to be gentle, but she covered my hand with her own and squeezed harder, which did nothing to help my self-control.

She tilted my head up. "Don't hold yourself back. Fuck me."

I snapped. "Put your hands on the counter. Arch your back."

She did as I said and I pulled her hips right to the edge. With her hands back, I had all the access to her tits I could want.

I eased my cock out then pushed back in, my eyes down as I stared at where we were connected. My cock was covered in her juices.

Bending my head, I covered her nipple with my mouth and really started fucking her. The deeper I went in, the louder her moans got and the more she screamed my name. I stole another orgasm from her right before I lost the battle and mine hit me.

Breathing hard and still gripping both her thighs from the bottom, I let my head rest on her shoulder, somehow finding the energy to keep fucking her slowly. I wasn't in a hurry to slip out of her heat, especially since I was still hard even after coming inside her.

"No condom." I forced the words when I could speak again.

Her body tightened. "What?" she managed to croak out.

"We forgot the condom. We're not using them anymore."

"Is that so?" she asked, her voice amused, then her hands started to roam my back, causing my dick to twitch inside her.

Splaying my hand on the small of her back, I gave her a hard thrust, getting as deep as I could. Her breath hitched, her fingers biting into my skin.

"Fuck," I muttered, the sensation of her heat and wetness around my cock pushing me closer to madness. "It's been a long time since I haven't used... I'm clean, baby."

"I'm on the pill, and I'm clean, too."

"I don't want to stop yet," I forced out through gritted teeth right before grazing the skin where her shoulder met her neck. All her shudders were egging me on.

She tightened her muscles around me, provoking a groan on my part.

"Take me to the couch," she whispered into my ear.

I pushed my hands under her ass and she tightened her legs around me. I took in a deep breath, letting her light and fresh flowery smell surround me. The fact that I managed to walk and carry her into the living room after coming as hard as I had was a miracle. I squeezed her ass cheeks in my hands because I couldn't help myself.

"Have you gained weight? I like these in my hands."

She laughed and hit my shoulder.

My strength gone, I dropped onto the couch, causing Rose to

slip off my cock. Some of my cum dripped out of her in a rush, sliding down her thighs and over my balls.

She groaned, holding my face in her palms as I kept palming her ass. I wouldn't go to sleep before I bent her over on the bed or anywhere she wanted.

"We're gonna mess up your couch," she said against my lips, her tongue sneaking into my mouth.

"I'll buy a new one."

I kissed her and pushed my tongue into her mouth as she tilted her head to allow me to go deeper.

I held my cock near the base and broke our kiss. "We're gonna do it nice and slow."

She gave me a small smile. "What if I don't want to do it nice and slow?"

"You want me to fuck you? You're not sore?"

"I want to be sore."

She held on to my shoulders and slowly lowered herself onto my thick length. I couldn't take my eyes away as her pussy sucked me in. She was so hot and soaked. She rose on my cock, dropping down with a heavy moan, taking more and more of me with each drop.

"How are you still so hard?" she asked in a hoarse voice, her tits bouncing up and down as she kept moving on me. "And why do I want you to keep going?"

"I have no idea," I answered as I gripped her waist, lifting her as I thrust up.

"Mmmm, I love this."

I looked into her eyes. "How much is too much for you? Every night? I have to be honest, baby, I'm not sure I'm gonna be able to keep my hands off of you."

She lifted herself up by grasping the back of the couch, and I pulled her back down on me, giving her every single inch. She rolled her hips and groaned.

"Every day sounds perfect to me. I don't want you to hold back any part of you, and from where I'm standing, we have months to make up for. I'm still angry at you, don't forget that, but yes, we better do it every day."

"Yes." She looked so beautiful lazily rising and falling on my cock. Her eyes were dilated, her cheeks flushed, lips red and swollen, panting in need. I could already see a small mark on her neck where I had gone a bit too far.

"Now fuck me, Jack."

"Come here, baby."

She came eagerly, and I gripped her waist tighter as she gave me her mouth and let me kiss her as hard as I wanted. I thrust up and she moaned against my lips. I did it again, harder, and swallowed up a groan. She broke our kiss on a gasp with the third thrust.

"How does that feel?"

Her eyes closed. "Thick."

"Good. You're so good at taking me, Rose."

The only response I got was her whimper as I fucked her from underneath just like she had asked.

"I'm falling apart, Jack."

I knew she was close when she started moaning my name and lost her grip on the back of the couch. I increased my pace and she came all over me for the third time that night, nothing but my name falling from her beautiful lips. I buried myself deep inside her as she twitched and shook against me, coming long and hard.

We didn't move for a long time as we caught our breath. My hands roamed on her back as she trembled ever so slightly. When I could move, I cradled her in my arms and, without a word, took her up to the bathroom and put her straight under the hot water. As it plastered her hair all over her face, I pushed it all back. I couldn't take my eyes and hands off of her. She watched my every move as I washed her hair and then every inch of her body. She returned the favor in silence, her hands moving across my chest as she bit her lip. When I had her attention, I kissed her softly, licking her lips and then playing with her tongue. She rose up on her toes and wrapped her arms around me as I hugged her waist and crushed her to myself.

I took pleasure in drying her off with a big towel and helping her get dressed in one of my white button-up shirts. We walked down the stairs hand in hand then she sat on the island as I cooked dinner while she chattered endlessly. I cooked her pasta because it was Monday and we had traditions in our marriage.

Our marriage.

I still couldn't believe she had forgiven me without making me work for it more.

I kissed her a thousand times as she talked on and on. She wasn't wearing anything but my shirt, and I wasn't wearing anything but my black slacks.

"I'm so in love with you, Rose Hawthorne," I said against her lips as she laughed at something I'd just said. "You're the best part of my life."

Her laughter died as she tilted her head and looked into my eyes. She smiled a beautiful smile. "And you are mine, Jack Hawthorne. All mine."

CHAPTER TWENTY-NINE

EPILOGUE

I t had been a whole month since I'd moved back home and accepted the fact that I was officially in love with my husband. I couldn't remember a happier month. As if I had conjured him up, Jack walked into the coffee shop, and just at the sight of him, my heart picked up speed. It was as if the bell rang a little differently when he was the one walking through. It was as if it knew. *This is the man you're in love with, look here*, it said. His face set, not a smile in sight, he was talking on his phone, one arm filled with my roses as he continued toward the cash register. He frowned when someone walked in front of him to get to my little bookcase without an apology. He glared at my customer and, shaking his head, continued with his phone call as I watched him with the biggest grin on my face.

After a few seconds, when he was done with whoever was on the other end of the line, he put away his phone and finally, *finally* looked up. I was still grinning when his searching gaze found me standing in the doorway watching him. He maintained eye contact the entire time as he ignored everyone else around and made his way toward me. I straightened up off the doorframe and, as soon as he was within touching distance, rose up on my tippy toes, grabbed his suit jacket, and threw my arms around his neck.

"I love that frown on your face."

My little grin turned into a big smile when I felt his lips curve up against my neck then he skillfully pressed a lingering kiss to the exact spot. Jack Hawthorne was the first man to short-circuit my brain with a simple smile against my skin and what looked like an innocent kiss.

The coffee shop was somewhat empty, the morning rush having ended only half an hour earlier, and almost all the customers we had currently were regulars, many of them on their tablets or laptops and a few favorites of mine lost in their reads.

Untangling my arms from his neck, I ran my hand down his shoulder and fixed his tie. Just the simple act of being able to do that hit me almost every single time. I had a husband, and a real one at that.

"Hi," I whispered.

"Hello, my Rose." He leaned down and kissed my cheek.

Closing my eyes, I hummed. "These tactics won't help you."

"We'll see," he murmured, tucking away a long piece of my bangs behind my ear.

"Hi, Jack!" Sally yelled from just a few steps away, waving with one hand while the other worked the espresso machine.

I heard Owen mutter something from the kitchen as his head poked out from the doorway behind me. "Sally? Did you say something?"

My perky and sweet employee didn't even look away from the espresso machine. "No."

"Oh, hey Jack," Owen said distractedly when he noticed my husband standing next to me. As they greeted each other—Jack had finally started using his name—I rescued the roses from Jack's grip, gently touching the white and beige petals with my fingertips.

"If you're going to the back, I'll stay in front with Sally," Owen offered.

I glanced at her and watched as she laughed and gave the to-go cup and the little pastry bag to the girl waiting for her order. "It's pretty slow. I'm good up here on my own."

I looked back at Owen and saw his mouth tighten. "Then I'll get to my work."

Sally welcomed the last customer waiting in line.

"We need more lemon muffins up here," I said quietly before he could disappear to the back, and before I got a response from Owen, I felt Jack's hand lace with mine. My toes curled from all the happiness. Owen gave me a quick nod, shot Sally a pointed look, and walked away.

"What am I missing?" Jack asked.

I sighed. "You're missing young love—passion, tension."

"Young love? As opposed to our old love?"

I grinned up at him. "You're thirty-one years old and I'm twenty-six, so you're pretty much an old dude for me. People usually find the age gap thing really sexy, especially if the guy looks anywhere near as good as you do."

He sighed and shook his head, which made me smile even more. "Okay, Mrs. Hawthorne, are you ready for our ten-thirty meeting? I have meetings back to back today so I'd like to get this done as quickly as possible."

"Yeah, you keep thinking that. It'll last as long as it needs to last. This was your idea anyway, so don't even try to be rude about it."

"I'm not being rude. I didn't think you'd take it this seriously."

"You never think you're being rude, but you are, and marriage is a serious business, Mr. Hawthorne." Making sure I had my serious face on, I took a step back from my husband and held up the flowers. "I'm going to leave these in the kitchen—"

Now done with the last of the customers, Sally joined us. "Want me to take those for you, Rose?" she asked, already reaching for my roses.

I turned my body, just slightly, nothing too obvious. "Oh, that's okay. I'll just get them back there and handle them myself after Jack leaves." To say I was a little territorial about my weekly roses was putting it lightly. "Jack? Why don't you pick a seat and I'll be right there in a second then we'll start our meeting."

He shook his head as if I was a lost cause. "Right. I'll go do that."

"Would you like a coffee, Mr. Hawthorne?" I asked, kissing him on the cheek.

"Yes, I would love one, Mrs. Hawthorne."

As he turned around and left, Sally snorted next to me. "I'm not sure if coffee is an innuendo for sex or you were just talking about real coffee."

"Unfortunately that was about real coffee." As I went into the kitchen and placed the roses next to the sink, Sally followed me.

"What's with the diplomacy?" When I gave her a confused look, she explained. "Mr. Hawthorne, Mrs. Hawthorne..."

I laughed. "Oh, he wants to work on our five-year-marriage plan so we're gonna have a meeting about that."

Sally looked at me for a long moment then nodded. "Makes sense."

"I thought so too."

Owen walked out of the stock room with a box full of our to-go cups in his arms, and Sally quickly walked back out.

I leaned back against the counter and eyed Owen. "What did you do now?"

He rolled his eyes. "What makes you think I did something? I didn't do shit. She'll be back to normal in an hour, don't worry."

Since I believed he was right, because Sally was the last person on earth to hold a grudge against Owen, I let it go and left him alone. Grabbing a plate on my way out, I picked up the last two lemon muffins and started on Jack's coffee.

He had chosen the table nearest to the window and was following my every move over the newspaper he had in his hands. Feeling heat rush to my cheeks under his gaze, I hurried and took my seat across from him as he folded the paper and placed it on the table.

"They're dating now," I explained, answering his earlier question just in case I hadn't been clear before.

"I gathered that much. I'm not sure that's a great idea. When something goes wrong, it'll affect your business."

"I love it when you're being positive. And I know, but so far it hasn't affected their work, and they promised."

He gave me an exasperated look as if I was a fool for taking their word for it.

"Plus, it's not like I would fire them for being in love. It's fun listening to them bicker. Owen is a lot like you, actually, so it's extra fun because of that. Suddenly I'm surrounded by grumpy men."

"I'm not grumpy, Rose. I'm serious."

Laughing, I got up, leaned over the table, and quickly kissed his lips before taking my seat again. "And I love you just like that." He was wearing my favorite navy blue suit. "Using everything you have in your arsenal for the negotiations, I see," I commented lightly right before sipping from my tea.

Jack's brows drew together in confusion. "What?"

"Your suit—you know that's my favorite one."

His eyes sparkled with mischief. "And you wore the dress I

told you I'd prefer if you only wore when I was standing next to you, holding your hand."

I feigned shock and glanced down at my dress. "This old thing?" It truly was a pretty basic black wrap dress with long sleeves, but I knew he liked it for some reason. He couldn't keep his hands off of me whenever I wore it.

He arched one perfect eyebrow that basically said *I know your game* and leaned back in his seat.

"Would you like to start?"

I pushed the muffins in front of him. Lemon week was just for him, tart and sweet, just like someone I knew. "Would you like to taste these? I baked them."

"You can't trick me with pastries, Rose. I'll take them with me when I leave."

I smiled. "I would never, Mr. Hawthorne. I'm appalled that you'd even think I'd do something like that. Please go on then. I was just trying to be nice to my husband."

"Right. So, tell me, what kind of marriage do you want for the next five years?"

"Only five? I get the boot after that?"

"I thought it would be healthier to sit down every five years and plan for the next five years."

God, it was a struggle not to get up and pull him to the back. He looked so devastatingly handsome and serious that I was having trouble keeping a straight face.

"How do you know I won't divorce you in the next five years?

"You're not going to divorce me," he said, dismissing the idea.

"Says who?"

"I do. If you didn't divorce me after everything that happened, you're not gonna get rid of me for something small and stupid I'll most likely end up doing at some point."

"I'll divorce you in a heartbeat if you cheat on me."

"Since that's not a possibility, let's talk about our five-year plans."

"No to leaving socks around the house. As small as that sounds, it'd drive me crazy, and that's how the beginning of the end starts. No clothes on the floor, and no chewing your food with your mouth open."

"Can you take this more seriously?"

I frowned at him. "I am," I stressed.

"Have you ever seen me leave my socks around? My clothes?"

"No. I'm just telling you so you won't start."

"Can we get back to the plan?"

"Are you not listening to me? Those things are part of the plan. You can't cheat, you can't *start* leaving your socks or clothes around, and you can't chew your food with your mouth open. The sound drives me insane."

"Those are your relationship plans for the next five years?"

"We're just getting started. Also, why does it have to be just my plans? You tell me what you want for the next five years, too."

"I just need you to stay with me, so that means I need to learn what you want."

"I'm flattered, but no. That's not how a marriage works. I'm pretty easygoing. I want love and loyalty, and for you to talk to me."

"Rose, you're going to have to be more specific. I told you, you have a million things to say about our marriage all the time. Start with one of them. Tell me about the marriage you wanted to have."

"Fine." I nodded carefully. "I want a date night every week. If we're swamped with work, we can do it at home, but I need those few hours of just you and me without anything else getting in the way.

"Okay. I can do that."

"Aren't you supposed to take notes?" I asked, reaching for my tea again.

He tapped a finger to his head, his lips smiling.

"Okay. We'll see. Your turn."

"I want you to come over for lunch."

"To the office?"

"Yes."

"For sex? Are we allowed to have office sex?"

He let out a big breath. "Rose."

I made a face. "What? It's a legit question."

Obviously, he didn't think so from the way he shook his head at me.

He was in the process of drinking his coffee, but he stopped and put the mug back down on the table.

I smiled. So he was thinking about it, too.

"Maybe not in the office since it's all glass, but I'll take care of it."

I was sure he would find a way. I laughed. "Doing it at the office isn't essential, but I'd love to come over for lunch. Can I ask why?"

"I like spending time with you, and I like the idea of you coming to my office to have lunch. I like it when people see me with you."

I dragged my seat a little closer to him, my heart happy.

"Done. My turn: I want spooning. If every night isn't possible, I want it most nights."

"This isn't something you need to mention, Rose."

"I'm sure there will be nights where hugging me in bed will be the last thing on your mind, especially after a long and draining day of work, so I'm just putting it out there. If we start to have those kinds of nights too much, you need to make an effort not to make it a permanent thing. Even if we argue—and I know I told you this before, but it bears repeating—I want to be the kind of couple who wipes the slate clean when they go to bed. Your turn."

This time it was him bringing his chair right next to mine. He reached for my hand and kissed the back of it. Instead of letting it go after, he held it against his thigh, our fingers locked.

"I want you to tell me when I'm doing something wrong," he started, his voice low, his piercing blue eyes on mine. "I want you to let me know when I'm acting distant or distracted, because I can already assure you that it's not you. It can't be you. It'll never be you."

I nodded. "I'll tell you. I want to grow old with you."

He cupped my cheek and rested his forehead against mine. "Yes." His voice had been low and it was just one simple word, but the emotion I could see in his eyes, the emotion I could *feel* behind the word—I knew it was a promise he intended to keep.

"Remind me why we didn't do these negotiations at home?" I asked with a sigh when we had to separate.

"Your idea."

"Okay. Fine. What else do you want from me?"

"Everything you're willing to give me."

I cleared my throat and his hand tightened around mine. "We're not going to lie to each other. No matter how hard the truth is, we're not going to do it. Promise me."

"I won't risk losing you. We will not lie to each other," he agreed easily.

"We are going to make a conscious effort to work on our marriage no matter what's going on in our lives. We will keep working on it, always. I want to make you happy, and you have to talk to me."

"You won't ever find someone who'll try as hard as I will to make you happy. Every time you need to get an MRI, I'll always come in with you. I will always make sure you know I'm there. I will watch every movie you want me to watch, no matter how cheesy or how horrible—"

I raised my hand and stopped him before he could go on with his sentence. "Wait a minute, if you're telling me you think *Titanic* or *You've Got Mail* was cheesy, we have a problem."

"Just listen. I'll always let you steal my French fries whenever you finish the ones on your own plate. I'll always let you have a bite of my dessert. I'll cook for you when you're sick and when you're too hungry to do anything but glower. I'll feed you from my own plate and kiss you after each bite. I'll make sacrifices for you just like I know you'll make sacrifices for me along the way. I'll never be rude to the people you love and care about. I'll never take your smile for granted, and I'll make you smile every day, even on the days when you're the most annoyed with me. I'll talk for hours, telling you everything you want to know about me, about anything, if that's what you want from me."

"Jack," I whispered, my hands trembling. "Jack, I know your heart. You don't need to speak all the time. Even your quiet I love."

He leaned forward and gently pressed a kiss on my lips then kept talking.

"I will kiss you every time you start to worry about your health and get lost in your own fears. I will kiss you every morning, every night and whenever I can in between. I will always text you back whenever you text me, even if I'm only one room away from you. But on the days I want to hear your voice, I'll call you back instead of texting you. I'll always help you when you ask for it. I'll help you even when you don't ask for my help because I'll always be there. I'll eat and drink whatever you put in front of me simply because your hands cooked it, baked it, or made it. I'll try to learn to understand when you want me to make love to you but are too embarrassed to ask for it. I'll work hard to make you happy, to make this the marriage you always wanted to have, and I will never—I promise you, Rose, I will never make you feel unloved. I will never take you for granted. You will always have someone to lean on whenever you need it. I'll always be there even when you don't need me to be, but more importantly..."

He reached out and brushed a tear off of my cheek before lifting my hand up and kissing it again. When had I even started crying?

"I will always love you." he continued before I could catch my breath. "Even when you're annoyed with me, even when I do something you don't like and you have no idea why you decided to keep me, I will always love you."

"You don't talk. For days and weeks, I do everything to make you talk, and then you go and do this to me." I got up from my seat, my eyes never leaving his beautiful blues, and I sat down on his lap sideways. I cupped his face with my hands and just stared at him.

This man I had fallen for, eyes wide open.

This man who was nothing like what I had wanted for myself.

This fierce man who was the only one for me.

My family.

"You make my heart go pitty-pat. Did you know that?

"Hmmm. I do?"

I leaned down and kissed his lips once, slowly, sweetly.

One of my hands resting on his neck, I spoke my next words into his ear. "I am in love with you, madly, desperately, irrevocably." Biting my lip, I caressed his cheek and moved my eyes over every beautiful inch of his face, memorizing the look in his eyes, the shape of his lips. "I will make you happy too, Jack

Hawthorne," I whispered, and I rested my forehead against his as we looked into each other's eyes. "I will do everything to make you happy for the rest of our days. I will never let you go. I will never give up on you, on us."

THE END.

ACKNOWLEDGMENTS

Marriage For One is one of those books that wrote itself, at least the first draft. But that doesn't mean it was the easiest book. No, this one, Jack and Rose challenged me the most. And I'm hoping I didn't make a complete mess of it.

Jack is not like any other character I wrote before and it took some time and help to make sure I was being fair to him. As scared as I am about this release, I love these two. I love their love story, their dry humor, the grumpiness, the smiles, the laugher, the ankle holding...all of it. But this is also the book I'm most scared of. I don't want to fail Jack and Rose. I realize this isn't for everyone, but I want it to be, really badly. I want them to steal a piece of your hearts. I really hope I didn't disappoint you.

Shelly...as always there is nothing I could say that would be enough. There are no words for all the help you've given me with this one—*especially* with this one. I've bugged you endlessly about this book (I probably bug you endlessly with every book, but I know I've been over the top this time around). I can still hear myself repeating the same things over and over again in a voice message about what a failure I am or will be. And you always have the right words for me. Always. Maybe that's why I always keep running to you when I'm freaking out. I'm forever grateful to have your friendship. Forever grateful that I can trust you with everything. Jack and Rose, they wouldn't be out in the world right now if it weren't for you, so thank you from the bottom of my heart. Thank you for cheering me. Love you. Thank you so much for reading my little big book.

Beth...what would I do if I didn't have your friendship? Your comments with this one...they helped me so much. So much. And the fact that you don't enjoy reading long books, but read mine in no time? I love you for that. For helping me. For sending me voice messages with your beautiful voice and beautiful accent and helping me even more—with the blurb, the cover, the teasers. Just like I just told Shelly, I would've messed up Jack and Rose's story too much if I hadn't had you to help me work things out. I'm hoping one day I can help you as much as you help me. I'm lucky to call you a friend and lucky that you're not tired of me yet. I promise I'll keep the next book shorter, but thank you for reading the entire thing.

Erin...here we are again. I'm so glad that you're not tired of me yet. Especially after this one because I know how annoying I've been. We finished another one, and I'm both excited and scared. As always, it helps to know you have my back. I promise I'll try not to freak out this much on the new one. And thank you so much for reading Jack and Rose's story even though you have a million better things to do.

Elena (aka The beautiful thebibliotheque)...you've read this book so fast and so beautifully. And then you gave me life. I'm not even kidding. You already know how much I was freaking out when you started reading it so you know how much it meant to me that you actually loved it (that's if you haven't lied to spare my feelings of course). Loved Jack. Thank you for not making me beg to read my book. Thank you for making me smile so big when I was sure I'd failed in telling Jack and Rose's story. Thank you for the beautiful photo. And last but not least, thank you for talking Jack and Rose with me for days! You made me feel excited about them all over again. I might beg you again, with the next one. Just saying...

Saffron...thank you for reading thirteen chapters of this book even when you were dealing with something so insane. You know how much it helped me with Jack. I really appreciate the support, you know how insecure this book made me so thank you for listening.

The sweetest agent... Hannah, you're the absolute best. You were there for me when I needed a friend the most. You read this whole thing in just a few days and not only once, but twice. I'm forever grateful for the help and the comments. I hope I won't disappoint you. And just to repeat it, thank you so much for your lovely compliments. I wouldn't want to work with anyone but you.

Christina and Yasmin...you two are the first early readers and actually Yasmin is reading it as I'm typing this. Just in case you didn't get it from my messages, I don't like the fact that you're hoarding your notes. I don't know if you guys will love Jack and Rose, but I'm hoping so hard that you will. Thank you so much for being so enthusiastic about it. Every message I get from you guys put the biggest smile on my face. I really really hope you love it.

Caitlin Nelson and Ellie McLove - thank you so much for making my book better and more readable.

Emily A. Lawrence - thank you so so much for editing my synopsis at the very last minute. I can't wait for the next one!

Nina—please don't get sick of me anytime soon!

And thank you to all the incredible bloggers and instagrammers who gave me a shot. I know Jack and Rose's story is longer than most books out there, but thank you for reading and helping me get the word out. ALL of you are amazing, I couldn't do what you guys do. I hope you enjoyed my big little book.

And my lovely readers, I want you to fall for Jack and Rose so much. I hope I won't disappoint you and I hope you'll meet me on my next book. Thank you so much for loving my characters as much as I do. You're everything.